To Murder a Marquis

A Regency Time Slip Mystery

BOOK ONE

ARABELLA SHERATON

Distributed by Bublish, Inc.
75 Port City Landing, Suite 110,
Mount Pleasant, SC 29464,
www.bublish.com

ISBN (print): 978-1-64704-896-9
ISBN (e-book): 978-1-64704-897-6

Editor: Nancy Bell
Cover Design: AM Design Studios
Interior Book Design: Sonia Killik, TB Books
Printed in the United States of America

Praise For Arabella Sheraton's
To Murder a Marquis

A delightful time-travel adventure that transports the reader to the captivating world of Regency England. Author Arabella Sheraton weaves an enthralling tale of mystery, romance, and self-discovery as modern-day historian Jane Carstairs finds herself unexpectedly swept back in time to the year 1815. The vivid historical details bring the Regency setting to life, allowing readers to fully immerse themselves in this milieu of grand estates and old-fashioned courtship rituals. The gripping suspense and clever twists kept me turning the pages, eager to uncover the truth alongside Jane. At the heart of the story is the magnetic romantic connection that develops between Jane and the dashing marquis. The chemistry between the pair is palpable, and the author skilfully crafts a swoon-worthy romance that blossoms amidst the peril and uncertainty of Jane's circumstances. The passionate encounters and heartfelt emotions make for an utterly captivating love story, with a lovely twist at the end that had me sighing with contentment!

—Wendy Leighton-Porter, author of the *Shadows of the Past series*

To Murder a Marquis takes you back in time and has all the trappings of a romantic novel with intrigue, deception, and mystery adeptly woven into it. Nineteenth-century England had its charm, and the author captures it vividly, pulling readers into its web. Stories that revolve around time travel have their distinctness and uniqueness that readers find fascinating, and this book does just that. The author excels in her narration and her characters are always memorable. Arabella Sheraton manages to portray characters with conviction so that they stand out. Her writing style is evocative and descriptive and takes the reader into the story. There's an ease with which the plot progresses. If you are a fan of Regency novels or if you haven't read one before, I would recommend *To Murder a Marquis* and other Regency titles by Arabella Sheraton.

—Mamta Madhavan, poet, dreamer, author of *Connecting the Dots (Poems)*, and travel writer

I was enchanted with *To Murder a Marquis* from the very first page when accidental time traveller Amelia Carstairs opens her eyes to discover she is in an entirely different century. Add a badly wounded marquis and a gorgeous, sexy voice muttering, "Cousin Amelia. Thank you," and I was hooked. Author Arabella Sherton gives us a highly romantic, page-turning tale with the added treat of a suspenseful mystery, which I found quite entertaining. I loved the characters, the dialogue, and the historical accuracy of that period. Of course, I wanted the main characters to fall in love. But then I became anxious to see whether Amelia would choose to remain in the past or return to her own time. The prose is well-written and the plot artfully crafted, making this a book I highly recommend.

—K.T. McGivens, author of the *Katie Porter Mysteries Series*

Arabella Sheraton's *To Murder a Marquis* enchanted me from the first page with Jane's time slip into the vivid, atmospheric scenery of the 19th century. It is a riveting blend of mystery, time travel fantasy, and clean romance in an enchanting Regency setting. The storyline exceeded my expectations. I marvelled at Jane's awesome erudition and knowledge of English history, the witty intrigue, the suspense, and the rigid

Regency etiquette Jane had to endure. But most of all, I liked Jane's brilliant, thought-provoking humour as she viewed life in the Regency period through her 21st-century lens. As I look forward to the sequel, I highly recommend this remarkable novel to Regency romance, time travel, and mystery fans.

—Olga Markova, author, book reviewer, dog rescuer, and nature traveller

I have always been a fan of Regency romances with their inherent elegance, manners, and pomposity, so this was a logical choice for me to read. What makes *To Murder a Marquis* stand out from the genre is the innovative concept of a time slip to propel Jane into the nineteenth century. Author Arabella Sheraton has created a masterfully crafted situation where Regency elegance and feminine propriety meet twenty-first-century permissiveness and feminine power. All the characters in this Regency melodrama are beautifully designed and explored, with typically overdrawn peculiarities. From the foppish and seemingly inconsequential cousin Sidney to the charming, yet wickedly cunning Dowager Duchess, the characters leap off the pages.

This author's attention to detail and descriptive writing place you firmly in the time and fully invested in Jane's dilemma, especially once she realizes her true feelings for her historical, distant relation. The romance is delightful and typically Regency period without being cloying or sickly saccharine. I particularly enjoyed the way that Jane's thoughts about her predicament and her innermost feelings were constantly conveyed to the reader, almost like a narrator's aside to the camera in a movie. I look forward with bated breath to reading more exciting adventures in time with Jane Carstairs and more mystery from this talented author. Given that this story encompasses two of the genres I enjoy immensely, I cannot recommend this read highly enough. I loved it.

—Grant Leishman, author of *The Second Coming Trilogy*

Sheraton seamlessly transports readers back to the Regency era, bringing the period to life with rich, immersive details and offering a great balance of gripping suspense, vivid historical imagery, and passionate romance. The author's clever blend of time travel, mystery, and romance creates a unique and engaging narrative that throws us right into the action. I found the internal logic of how Jane's time travel dilemmas present and resolve themselves to be really convincing and logical in context with the story world. As a dramatist myself, I have to say my favorite segment of the story was the developments around the production of Romeo and Juliet, which was all very suitably scandalous and amusing. The suspenseful plot, full of twists and turns, maintains a thrilling pace throughout, but there's always time for a breather where the romance and relationship elements of the plot have space to deepen before the next shift of the action takes over. Sheraton has a seemingly effortless ability to craft complex, relatable characters with realistic attitudes for the period, and this allows us to connect deeply with the modern heroine as Jane's journey through an unfamiliar world teaches us as much as it teaches her. Overall, I would highly recommend *To Murder A Marquis* as a captivating adventure through time that fans of Regency romances and modern crossover dramas are sure to adore.

—K.C. Finn, author of *The Mind's Eye*

Arabella Sheraton's *To Murder a Marquis* combines mystery with the elusive web of time. The use of descriptive narrative and effective dialogue leads the reader along as the main character unravels her confusion. The author has a solid understanding of history, particularly the Regency period, the main setting of this story. Her fascination with time travel is obvious as she weaves this effectively into the plot. The element of romance adds a bit of flavour as the story develops. This is a powerful tale of courage and believing, not just in oneself, but also in the simple fact that anything is possible, both past and future, as well as the present which quickly becomes the past as we live it. Breathtakingly spellbinding – I loved it!

—Emily-Jane Hills-Orford, author of *Beauty in the Beast*

A fascinating time-travel adventure where Regency-era elegance meets modern-day mystery. What will captivate readers is its seamless blend of historical romance and time-travel mystery, enriched by vibrant character development and an engaging plot. The story's opening scene sets a tone of both humor and intrigue, drawing readers in. As Jane delves deeper into the mystery, her modern sensibilities clash with Regency society constraints, creating both tension and charm. The evolving dynamic between Jane and the marquis, coupled with the suspense of a potential murder, ensures that readers are not only engaged by the whodunit but also by the evolving romance. Arabella Sheraton's detailed portrayal of the period and her clever plot twists make *To Murder a Marquis* a compelling start to a series that promises to delight fans of historical fiction and time-travel adventures alike.

—Demetria Head, *Readers' Favorite* book reviewer

DEDICATION

In memory of my mother Wendy who loved romance.

"Time is the most undefinable yet paradoxical of things; the past is gone, the future is not come, and the present becomes the past even while we attempt to define it, and, like the flash of lightning, at once exists and expires."

Charles Caleb Colton (1777-1832) English cleric.

"Time travel used to be thought of as just science fiction, but Einstein's general theory of relativity allows for the possibility that we could warp space-time so much that you could go off in a rocket and return before you set out."

Stephen Hawking (1942-2018) English theoretical physicist, cosmologist, and author.

"Time is not a line but a dimension, like the dimensions of space. If you can bend space, you can bend time also, and if you knew enough and could move faster than light you could travel backward in time and exist in two places at once."

Margaret Atwood (1939-) Canadian novelist, poet, literary critic, essayist, teacher, environmental activist, and inventor.

CONTENTS

Chapter One

Furious barking woke me from a very nice dream in which my ex-fiancé Allan Hunter was on his knees, begging me to stay, and I had just flung his ring back in his face in a most satisfying manner. The fact he'd dumped me for a full-breasted bistro waitress called Tawnee—that's right, with a double "e"—who clearly said all the right adoring things, had the intelligence of a single-celled organism, and was a tigress in the bedroom was something I chose to ignore.

The dog wouldn't stop barking. I opened my eyes, and there he was, a beautiful russet-coloured retriever, barking like mad, but with his tail wagging. Still slightly dazed, I shook my head. What the hell was I doing lying under a tree? I was supposed to be in the library at Chelston Hall, helping Dad, who was in hospital in London with bronchitis, collate the archives of the Hadley family. I could almost hear him say, "Jane Carstairs, what on earth are you doing there when you should be working?"

The dog was still barking. I'm not afraid of dogs so I raised myself on one elbow. "Here, boy. What's the matter?"

I held out one hand for him to come over and have a sniff as an introduction. The dog took a few steps forward, then ran back to his original spot, and barked once. Clearly, a clever canine. He was telling me something. But what? I struggled to sit up. For some reason, my clothes were constricting; something like a straitjacket encircled my chest. Instead of my casual T-shirt, jeans, and sneakers, I wore an ankle-length flowing dress, and short lace-up boots, along with a tight, short, long-sleeved jacket. I was in period costume straight out of *Pride and Prejudice*. Not funny! Someone had obviously pranked me but managing to undress and get me into this suffocating costume was beyond a joke. Plus, how did I get from sitting in a chair in the library to lying under a tree?

Back to the dog again, which now seemed very agitated. He ran back and forth a bit and whined. By pulling my dress and copious amounts of petticoat up to my knees, tearing something at the jacket shoulder in the process, I managed to stand. The dog ran off through the trees as if on a mission. Maybe someone was hurt, and the mutt was looking for help? Dogs can be so clever that way. Running in the narrow skirt was impossible so I hitched the skirt as high as I could and chased after the dog.

Ten minutes later I arrived, panting, at the scene of a bloody accident. Bloody is no exaggeration. A man, also dressed in period costume—riding gear—lay on his back, his arms flung out. He was either asleep, or unconscious, or ... I didn't even want to consider the last option. The dog stood next to him, its tail wagging. It looked at me, whining as if to say, "Help him." I knelt and took a closer look. Robert William Edward Hadley, the Marquis of Coleston, lay before me. An arrow protruded from the top of his left shoulder, a massive amount of blood soaked the front of his fawn-coloured coat, and he looked very dead.

For a nano-second, I thought it was an extension of the clothing prank played on me. But, looking closer, that ashen colour and horrible stillness told me it was real. To say I was drenched in the cold sweat of fear is an understatement. An icy wave of terror rushed through my whole body. My head was spinning, and I felt faint, bile surged into my throat, and if my legs had obeyed me, I'd be running away. Long slow heartbeats hammered against my already constricted ribcage, and it was hard to breathe. My legs became very wobbly as well. It's lucky I was already kneeling on the ground because I might just have fallen over.

Although I'd never met the marquis, I knew it was him because I'd seen his portrait hanging in the imposing entrance hall when I'd arrived. He was overseeing the genealogy project while his parents, the current Duke and Duchess of Chelston, were off on a Norwegian fjords cruise. It was just a brief glimpse because his nondescript, but extremely bossy, secretary had hustled me into the library with a terse greeting, the advice that I'd "better get onto things straight away," and that she'd send in some lunch and get my bags taken up to my room before she disappeared.

Brief glimpse it was all right, but unforgettable because the marquis is a dead ringer for actor Richard Armitage when he played John Thornton in BBC's *North and South* period drama. But of course, it wasn't the actor, it was the marquis. The weird thing was him wearing a costume right out of the Regency period. The fancy visitors' brochure Dad showed me had a few photos of what looked like a Regency ball. There must be an event, or a Regency convention, at Chelston Hall. One of those dress-up affairs where everyone tries to be Miss Elizabeth Bennet and Mr. Darcy? But the arrow? Plainly, something went terribly, horribly wrong somehow.

The dog barked once, questioningly. I tore my horrified gaze from the marquis and said slowly and clearly, "Go! Go for help!" Pointing in what I hoped was the right direction, I caught a glimpse of the red-bricked splendour of Chelston Hall through the trees. The layout of the park seemed slightly different from the brochure. More trees now, maybe? But then I'm not a country girl and I hadn't had time to visit the grounds. The bossy secretary, a Miss Worth, I think, had worn the kind of expression that said I was there to work; it brooked no argument. The dog barked again and raced off as if he understood the order. I hoped so.

Rustling noises in some bushes nearby made me turn in that direction. Someone was running away, his body hunched over in a furtive manner. That must be the culprit in this re-enactment gone very wrong scenario. If it was an accident, then why didn't he come forward to help, unless he had something to hide? I couldn't chase whoever it was; the wounded man needed my help. My heart sank. So much blood! I vaguely remembered reading that the average person has around ten pints of blood in their body. How much had he lost already? I had to stop further blood loss, but it was easier said than done.

This is the part one always sees in the movies, but no one ever thinks they'll need to do. The arrow was lodged high in his shoulder. Thinking back to biology classes, the words "trapezius muscle" came to mind. Somehow a few snippets of first aid information from my Girl Guide days swam to the surface of my befuddled brain, although from what I remember it was more about bee stings, broken wrists, and sprained ankles. Should I try to remove the arrow? Would I do more damage by leaving it in? Pulling it out could cause more bleeding. Maybe erring on the side of caution was best.

It wasn't the same as a gunshot wound where one could bandage the guy up and leave the bullet for a surgeon to remove. But I couldn't just leave the whole arrow sticking out of him like a skewer. Besides, it might take ages for the paramedics to arrive and Chelston was such a small village—which I'd noticed as I drove through—that the nearest ambulance might have to come from a bigger town, one with a hospital, like Guildford which was quite close.

Still kneeling, and praying he wasn't dead, I shuffled closer to his left side, heaved him up a bit to support him on my thighs, and broke the wooden shaft off, leaving about three inches sticking out. Oddly, it wasn't that difficult, which surprised even me. It was quite a primitive-looking arrow; an amateurish, even flimsy, homemade effort that maybe someone would use to shoot a rabbit or game bird at close range. That was good news for the victim. Then I rolled him forward and to the right side, so I could get my hand behind his shoulder, and feel if the arrowhead had gone through. When I withdrew my hand there was no blood; what a relief. Hopefully the wound was shallow, despite the blood. Padding the wound with something for bandages was next.

He groaned as I laid him gently down again. He was alive, thank heavens. It must have felt like being kicked in the chest by a horse. A few inches down and the arrow, flimsy or not, could have inflicted more damage. As I unbuttoned his coat and waistcoat, even more blood welled up, spreading across his already sodden shirt front. I carefully eased the broken shaft through the rent in the coat and waistcoat fabric. Time to apply pressure and lots of bandages. Happily, I was wearing most of them. Again, just like in the movies, I hiked the dress up, grabbed the petticoat at the bottom, and ripped it. The cotton tore in long strips which was fortunate. I could have used his cravat, but I didn't want to cause him any more discomfort. It would have to be the petticoat. His shirt had a V-shaped neckline, so I tore it open from there. It was just like the one Colin Firth wore in the iconic scene at the lake from *Pride and Prejudice*. Sigh. Back to my patient.

I wadded a very thick pad of petticoat fabric to staunch the blood, being careful to arrange it around the remainder of the shaft to stabilise it, and then tightly wrapped the rest of the fabric around his chest to keep the pad secure. Winding the petticoat strip behind his back and over his chest was a mission. I pulled the coat and waistcoat closed, poked the shaft through the holes in the fabric, and buttoned up both garments. These were quite tight fitting and added extra compression. My hands shook. I wasn't up to this kind of drama.

Please let the paramedics come quickly.

The marquis opened his eyes, stared at me, and said, "Cousin Amelia. Thank you."

What a gorgeous, sexy voice; low and melodious. He took my hand, holding it quite tightly, closed his eyes, and let his head flop to one side. Hopefully he'd just fainted, which wasn't surprising. Why on earth had he called me Cousin Amelia? He seemed to recognise me. But I'd never met the marquis before so how did he know who I was? Vague recollections flitted through my brain, already too stuffed with fright and confusion to make head or tail of what was happening. My second name is Amelia. Jane Amelia Carstairs, family names from yesteryear. I hadn't paid much attention to my ancestors but evidently Mom and Dad had.

Another memory surfaced. In a tenuous link with Chelston Hall, we were actually related to the Hadley family. Dad had said something about how we were sort of related to the landed gentry in a "cousin several times removed" kind of way. That's why he'd been asked to sort out their family papers and find any twigs and branches that might have fallen off the family tree. An Amelia Jane Carstairs had married into the family back in 18-something. Dad had leaped gleefully upon this prize like a puppy onto a juicy bone, but I wasn't impressed. In my opinion, the only thing the landed gentry did well was live in extravagant and luxurious style while moaning and wailing about how they never had any money.

My patient looked less pallid. Staunching the blood flow had helped. His breathing also seemed more regular. With my other hand, I gently touched his forehead. Cold and clammy, but there was nothing more I could do until help came. It was amazingly quiet in this woodland. The wind soughed in the branches; birds sang; an idyllic scene but for the possibly dying man in front of me. I sat back on my heels, not wanting to leave him alone. He still held my hand, and I was reluctant to pull it away. Maybe he was clinging to it as he hung onto life. Maybe the dog never made it back to Chelston Hall and was off chasing a rabbit somewhere. A few moments longer and then I'd run for help.

I had a little time to think, so I did—hard. What did I know about this family? Apart from, no doubt, the usual charitable works, they didn't really feature in the headlines or society magazines. I only knew what Dad told me about them, and from my brief glance at the visitors' brochure. However, one scandalous snippet popped up. In the early 1800s, several assassination attempts were made on the heir to the title. This particular guy, who'd not married yet and thus had no heirs, somehow survived. Had he died, the next in line would have been his half-brother, with the same father but a different mother. The perpetrator was never caught, but since the rightful heir inherited his father's title, got married and had kids, the succession was assured and here we all were today.

A thought struck me like a thunderbolt. Was someone

trying to take this re-enactment a step further? The present marquis was single, that much I knew. Although the duke and duchess were still alive, who would become the heir upon their son's untimely demise? Dad hadn't mentioned any siblings, but I'm sure there would be a male cousin or two waiting in the wings to inherit. If only I'd paid more attention when Dad had nattered on about the Hadley family. I'd only been at Chelston Hall a few hours and already it looked as if I might be embroiled in an attempted assassination. Who had attempted to murder the marquis? Who would even want to murder him and why? The sounds of barking and men's voices floated through the trees. Help at last!

Chapter Two

T hings simply got weirder and weirder. Several men came running towards me, headed by the dog, leaping around and still barking its head off. A chubby, red-faced man, balding, with mutton-chop whiskers, around sixtyish plus, skidded to a halt. Instantly the word "Pickwickian" sprang to mind. He had the air of a doctor, being dressed in black, and clutching a bulky bag, rather like a portmanteau. It was surprising someone had realised so quickly there was a medical emergency, but kudos to them. I prised my hand from the marquis's grip and got out of the doctor's way. He knelt next to the wounded man and began examining him.

"Miss Carstairs," he panted. "Good thinking to send Russet back to the house for help. It's lucky I was in attendance this morning."

I gave him a hesitant smile. He knew my name so, clearly, I was supposed to be there. If this was a re-enactment, then he was playing the part of the family doctor, but meanwhile he'd be on hand if any participants really got sick. Russet was the dog, of course, which now lay next to his master, nose pressed against his right side.

The doctor looked up and said sharply, "Johnson, Peters, stop gaping like idiots. Run and inform the family there's been an accident. Get a door to carry His Grace back to the house."

The men, dressed like footmen in powdered wigs and blue and gold fancy livery, dashed off. Meanwhile the doctor opened his bag, revealing a glimpse of some antiquated-looking instruments, which struck me as odd. Even in a re-enactment one expects the doctor to have modern instruments in his bag. Hopefully, he wasn't going to whip out a jam jar filled with leeches. He fussed about, checking the bandages, peering at the shaft remnant, and tut-tutting under his breath. He held the marquis's wrist in one hand while looking at an old-fashioned pocket watch, which he held in the other. Talk about taking period detail to the nth degree.

"An excellent job in an emergency, Miss Carstairs. His pulse is strong. I couldn't have done better myself under the circumstances. I don't want to undo your fine handiwork out here. I'll clean and dress this wound properly once we get him back to the Hall."

His smile was reassuring because his grey eyes sort of twinkled in the way the doctor's eyes do when kids are a bit nervous about getting an injection. I nodded. It was on the tip of my tongue to ask whether we shouldn't be calling for an ambulance and whisking the marquis off to a hospital with all the benefits of modern medicine and science. Participants in re-enactments took it all quite seriously. I'd heard of mobile phones and laptops being banned, and even confiscated if discovered. But wasn't this playing with a man's life? However, he seemed to be satisfied that all was well.

The marquis groaned, and the doctor instantly said, "Now lie quietly if you can. It's Doctor Potts here. You're going to recover very soon. We'll have you back at the Hall in no time at all."

The marquis mumbled under his breath something that

sounded like a name. The doctor leaned closer with a puzzled expression. Then he stared at me.

"Where's Tempest, His Grace's horse?"

Horse? Of course he must have been on a horse, dressed as he was for riding. I shook my head.

"I'm sorry, I didn't see a horse. The dog, I mean Russet, was barking and I followed him to find the ... er ... His Grace lying here with an arrow in his shoulder."

Actually, calling a marquis His Grace was completely wrong. That's reserved for dukes. For a marquis he should have said His Lordship. So, the doc had slipped up with his terminology. This was understandable. It wasn't every day one was in a re-enactment and must deal with a real medical emergency. There was no point in pressing this detail of etiquette, given the circumstances.

The doctor's expression was incredulous as he gazed first at me in horror and then took a closer look at the marquis's shoulder.

"Miss Carstairs," he spluttered. Dropping his voice to a loud whisper, he said, "An arrow wound? I thought His Grace had been tossed by the horse, that he'd fallen to the ground, hitting a broken branch which pierced his shoulder, and that's how he came to be hurt."

"No, Doctor ... er ... Potts," I replied. "It's definitely an *arrow* wound. I broke off most of the shaft before bandaging him up as best I could with my petticoat."

Doctor Potts looked as if he might faint. He gasped and loosened his neck cloth. "Good God! What an extraordinary thing for a well-bred young lady to do."

This conversation was taking a very bizarre turn, but it seemed the right moment to pursue the matter of the suspicious figure running away. His eyes widened and he bit his lower lip as I related the whole incident.

"Here it is," I said, fumbling around for the broken shaft.

The doctor took the shaft, examined it carefully, and then stowed it in his bag. He fixed me with an anxious stare. "Now, not a word to anyone," he implored. "We don't want to worry the family until we have all the facts of the matter."

"Don't you think we should report it to the—" I hesitated. Should I continue in this whole Regency speak kind of way? He seemed to be really into it. "To a … magistrate?" I continued smoothly.

I was sure they had magistrates back then, although my recollection of there being any kind of organised police force was hazy at best. I thought of mentioning Bow Street Runners but didn't get the chance.

He blanched. "What? And cause a scandal? Not at all. The family is quite capable of bringing the scoundrel to justice. And no doubt it was a poacher … a horrible accident that caused the man to flee."

My mouth almost dropped open. He was mad. Any sane person would be on the phone to the local police in an instant, demanding the matter be referred to Scotland Yard at once, what with the victim being a peer. I was about to say this— attention to Regency detail be damned—when Johnson and Peters arrived, carrying a door between them. Trailing behind were a few more liveried footmen. They laid the door on the ground and very gently lifted the wounded man onto it. He groaned once and then, mercifully, fainted again.

This sorry cavalcade trudged slowly back to the house with the dog leaping up to try to reach his master, and Doctor Potts cautioning the men to avoid bumping his patient any more than was necessary. I prayed we'd get back to Chelston Hall and find someone sane there who would take charge.

Chapter Three

By the time we got to the main entrance of Chelston Hall, pandemonium reigned—literally. The front door was wide open, and loud female shrieks punctuated the raised male voices. Generally, the sounds of the madness that takes over when there's been an accident, and nobody quite knows what to do. No one was visible in the doorway, so most likely it was the family in another room. The footmen must have blurted out the details when they reached the house. News travels fast, bad news even faster.

To give him his due, Doctor Potts ignored the racket and guided the footmen carrying their precious burden through the Hall, up the grand staircase, and possibly to a bedroom on the next floor. The dog ran after them. No one took any notice of me. The noises were intriguing, so I followed them to what one would call the drawing room in a stately home. When I'd arrived at Chelston Hall that morning, Miss Worth hustled me to the left, into the library. The voices were coming from the right. I'd guessed correctly.

As I paused on the threshold, the scene before me could only be described as chaos in the raw. An older woman, very smartly dressed in Regency costume, lay on a crimson velvet-covered chaise longue, while another woman waved a small bottle under her nose. She had the kind of hatchet face, mousy hair scraped back in a tight bun, and plain dress of an upper-class servant. An extremely pretty young woman with blonde ringlets was crying and wringing her hands. An old man, sitting in the most antiquated of wheelchairs, was yelling at a dark-haired young man, who was yelling back.

I coughed. Somehow, they heard me through the din, and the effect was electrifying. Given that the whole arrow incident was so shocking, I'd expected everyone to drop their Regency personas. That didn't happen. The young man, who wore the same style riding gear as the marquis, bounded over to me and grabbed both my hands, pulling me into the centre of the room.

"Cousin Amelia! What's happened to Robert?"

He knew me, but I didn't know him. Somehow in this re-enactment scenario I'd forgotten everyone's names, or was it really a re-enactment? It was like one of those recurring dreams where you've learned the wrong lines and end up on stage in another play. Maybe the organisers decided to give me a role as a distant cousin to the family because of the tenuous link we had with them. Yes, that must be it, because the marquis had also called me Cousin Amelia. My brain wasn't working with its usual sharpness. Was this a scene we were supposed to act out? If so, everyone was taking their parts incredibly seriously. It was stellar method acting. Lee Strasberg would be so proud.

"I ... er ... I'm not sure. There's been an ... er ... accident," I stammered. Should I tell them he'd been shot with an arrow in what appeared to be a potential case of attempted murder? Best not. Let Doctor Potts handle that.

"I knew he shouldn't have gone riding in the woods," moaned the older woman. Her mousy companion patted her hand and waved the bottle under her nose again. "How many times have I warned Robert about those poachers, stopping at nothing to conceal their wicked activities?"

"Now, now, madam," the companion murmured. "Please don't agitate yourself."

The blonde girl was quietly sniffing into a handkerchief. The young man went over to her and patted her shoulder awkwardly.

"Don't cry, Clementine," he said. "I'm sure Robert will be fine."

Clementine ignored him and looked up at me with huge, dewy blue eyes. Tears sparkled like diamonds on the ends of her long, dark eyelashes. I've always thought that was such a ridiculous phrase. Not so in this case. She was so pretty that it would be tempting to toss her down a deep ravine to give other females a chance. She had the kind of porcelain loveliness that turned men's brains to mush and women's good natures to nastiness. She was so dainty and gorgeous that I immediately felt like the Hulk, and I'm actually quite slim.

"Oh, Miss Carstairs," she said, "how shocking for you to have found His Grace thrown from his horse and hurt."

Definitely not a good time to mention an arrow and lots of blood. There might be fainting as well as screaming. Strangely, my own legs felt a bit wobbly again and when I raised one hand to push back my hair, now straggling around my face, it was shaking. The old man made the best suggestion I'd heard since this fiasco began.

"Rupert," he barked. "Get Miss Carstairs a glass of brandy right away. She looks as if she might fall down."

The young man promptly went over to a long sideboard, grabbed a cut glass decanter, and poured far too much brandy into a glass. He thrust it into my hands, at the same time steering me to a large wing-back armchair that looked unbelievably welcoming. I fell into its soft comfort and sipped the brandy. It's not my favourite drink. I'm more of an Irish whisky with lots of ice and water gal, but alcohol is alcohol, and shock is shock. Incredibly, my teeth were chattering.

"Drink up," ordered the old man. "You'll feel better in a minute."

I needed no encouragement and although the brandy burned a long fiery trail to my stomach, it had the right effect. Now I know why people drink. Alcohol does make you feel better. Really, it does and very quickly too. When Doctor Potts appeared in the doorway, a babble of questions erupted but one raised hand silenced them. He went over to the older woman and held her wrist, taking her pulse. She seemed to enjoy the attention because she closed her eyes while her companion gently chafed her other hand and murmured vaguely comforting nothings.

Clearly, this was the matriarch of Chelston Hall. So, no cruising the Norwegian fjords then? After her snooty letter ordering me to come down to help sort out their family papers when Dad ended up in hospital, I wouldn't have tipped her for involvement in this kind of thing, but maybe they needed the money. A lot of these grand families with their stately homes are land-rich but cash-poor, and Regency re-enactments and Jane Austen festivals are wildly popular. Even the idea of the marquis himself participating was surprising but, given his good looks, he'd be a real drawcard for female Austenites. I could just imagine it; they'd riot! They'd be flinging their corsets and other unmentionables at him.

"Is my brother badly injured?" Rupert asked. "I was supposed to go riding with him. I should have been there to help him."

"No, my love," quavered his mother. "I would hate to lose two sons."

Now I could see the family resemblance in his dark hair, blue eyes, and strong nose. Rupert was well built and good looking in a sulky kind of way. Not as handsome as the marquis, of course, but still, he had promise. I pegged him at being about eighteen or nineteen, maybe twenty.

"His Grace has sustained an injury," said Doctor Potts, "just a flesh wound, I'm happy to announce. I've attended to it, and his valet is caring for him now. There's no need for you to agitate yourself."

"Oh, Doctor," breathed the matriarch. "You're such a pillar of strength."

"Don't thank me," he announced cheerfully. "Miss Carstairs saved His Grace's life by stabilising the arrow, staunching the wound, and bandaging his shoulder. A sterling job."

The word "arrow" had the fatal effect I'd suspected it would. The matriarch shrieked and fainted, Clementine burst into fresh sobbing, and the doctor reached for a bell pull which summoned a butler and a housekeeper, judging by their costumes. This whole scenario was so weird, verging on the ridiculous. They should have fired the script writers because the dialogue was terrible. The actors, on the other hand, were very convincing. Maybe they'd been told to improvise, no matter what happened. Had they even guessed the marquis was truly injured? Did they think it was all part of the performance? Which ones were actors and which ones were family members? Maybe there were more guests in the house.

Suddenly, I was so tired that I could have lain down on the floor and fallen asleep. Shivers ran down my body and I felt strangely very, very cold. The doctor took me by one hand, helped me out of the armchair, and walked me to the door.

"Miss Carstairs, you look dreadfully fatigued. Mrs Barlow will take care of you now, my dear," he said kindly. "I will deal with the family."

The housekeeper guided me up the staircase and into a room that I assumed was my bedroom. Not the attic room for a distant cousin, I must say; in fact, far from it. This room was decorated charmingly in shades of blue with touches of gilt. It was furnished with a single canopied four-poster bed, a writing desk and chair, a long cheval mirror, a chest of drawers, an upright wardrobe, and a dressing table. Various small ornamental tables loaded with knick-knacks occupied a couple of corners. The room was like an extremely expensive antiques shop. Think Sotheby's. I had friends in London who'd chew their arms off to get a whiff of these items. A young woman kitted out as a maid was waiting for us.

"Maisie will help you change your dress," Mrs Barlow said. She looked just like a BBC period drama housekeeper should. Her skirts made crisp "starched" sounds as she moved. "I'm sure you'll be wanting a hot bath to get over your shocking ordeal. Doctor Potts advised a nice long soak to help you feel better, so I've made all the arrangements."

Doctor Potts was a sensible man. He must have organised this after tending to his patient. Mrs Barlow rustled off and it was just Maisie and me. I can't imagine having anyone to help me dress and undress but, hey, shocking event or not, this bunch was sticking to their roles like glue, and hers was to give me a hand. Judging by the amount of clothing I was wearing, I was going to need help. Maisie bobbed a curtsey. She was a plain girl, about sixteen, with fair hair stuffed into a maid's cap. But she had a lovely smile and clearly a keen willingness to be useful. I was so tired that nothing mattered.

A bath sounded wonderful, although just the thought of having to get out of this stupid costume was exhausting. Maisie moved aside a painted screen to reveal a bath in front of the fireplace, one of those copper bathtubs seen in period dramas. It was a slipper bath, with one end higher than the other. Steam was rising so someone had taken the trouble to fill it. By now, I couldn't believe everyone was clinging so firmly to the Regency scenario, come hell or high water. But my brain wasn't working all that well.

The cheval mirror revealed the total fright I presented after racing through the woods and doing my Florence Nightingale stunt. Talk about being dragged through a bush backwards—several bushes and thorn bushes at that. Grass stains and large splashes of blood on the skirt of my dress where I must have wiped my hands, my hair hanging in wild clumps, one sleeve of my little jacket half torn off at the shoulder ... I needed that bath.

Maisie knew all the buttons, ribbons, and hooks and eyes to undo, and she did so with swift fingers. Honestly, I had more clothes on than I've ever worn at one time: the short olive jacket—which I remembered was called a Spencer jacket; then the dress—pale yellow, or it was once upon a time—which had some buttons behind; then a waist petticoat which I'd destroyed anyway making bandages; followed by the straitjacket which was a kind of corset, and under that, a chemise. The corset had a narrow piece of wood down the front, possibly for support. No wonder I felt uncomfortable. I later learned it was called a "busk."

Oh, I almost forgot the long, knitted stockings tied with ribbon garters above the knee, and the short lace-up leather boots, by far the most comfortable item of the lot. The *pièce de résistance* of course was the underpants; everything one imagines them to be. Long flapping pantalettes attached to a waist band. Very sexy. Someone had gone to a lot of trouble to dress me in true Regency style. The mind boggles as to who it could be since I knew no one I'd met so far, although everyone knew me. I say the mind boggles, but mine had expired and was possibly lying quivering at the bottom of my skull.

Once the overwhelming number of clothes was stacked neatly in a pile on the bed, Maisie whisked me into a dressing gown, pinned up my straggling hair, and led me to the bath, which was the best bath I've had in I don't know how long. Usually I have an on the run quick shower which is not at all the same as a long, luxurious soak. That feeling of easing oneself into a bubble bath, letting the heat of the water permeate every inch. It wasn't quite a bubble bath, but there was a pleasant scent to the water, and it did all the right things to the kinks in my muscles. It's not every day a girl rescues a handsome marquis from a near-death experience, even though everyone seemed quite mad and determined to stick to a ridiculous script.

Maisie murmured something about cleaning and mending my dress and jacket, both of which to me seemed better off in the rubbish bin, and about lovely hot soup. Mmm, lovely hot soup did sound rather nice. The water was wonderful and, after cleaning up with a sponge, soap, and a nail brush to get the disgusting dried blood from under my nails, I soaked a bit longer and almost fell asleep. But my mind started working as my thoughts wandered with unexpected, horrible, crystal clarity back over the events of the day, starting from when I'd arrived at Chelston Hall.

The place was different; the same but somehow different. Casting what was left of my mind back to this morning, I had the feeling the entrance hall wasn't exactly as when I'd arrived.

Wasn't there a reception desk with brochures and times of the daily tours of the house and gardens? The magnificent modern portrait of the marquis had also been replaced by an older one, like two hundred years older, judging by the dress. The re-enactment, maybe? Everything had to look right for the period. That made sense but something still niggled. It's easy to change a few pictures and move a desk. What had they done with the parking area for guests and my car?

I sat up, grabbed the big linen bath sheet Maisie had so helpfully placed nearby on a free-standing wooden towel rail, and climbed out of the bath. The idea of putting on all those ridiculous undergarments was too much. My own clothes and underwear must be around somewhere. I dried off, put on the dressing gown, and found a pair of slippers next to the bed. Not mine, of course, but they fitted.

A search of the chest of drawers revealed loads more chemises and pantalettes, along with scarves, shawls, dainty lace-edged handkerchiefs, and the like. The wardrobe only contained period dresses. What had happened to my luggage that Miss Worth said would be taken to my room—this room, I assumed? Could one opt out of these events? There must be tons of guests who find that playing dress-up isn't for them. They need their iPads and Smartphones too badly.

Talking of phones, my mobile was nowhere to be seen. Nor was my laptop, my handbag—wait, obviously those were still in the library. My heart slowed down from dementedly pounding like a drum to a more normal rhythm. The best thing was to firmly and clearly explain to the matriarch that as much as I loved the idea of being Amelia in this scenario, I had been hired to work, not to play-act. Another thought scurried across my mind. Possibly a guest had opted out and I had unwittingly been co-opted in their place. I would get dressed in my own clothing, sneak back down to the library, and wait for a chance to confront the woman when she'd recovered from the shock of her son being injured. That part was horribly real. The doctor sounded pretty confident he'd recover so it was all just what Lemony Snicket would call "A Series of Unfortunate Events." Very unfortunate.

I sat on the bed, waiting for Maisie. The fact of having a plan made me feel calmer and more confident. Trust me to get involved with a bunch of nut cases. Dad was desperate to find a closer link to them, but I couldn't wait to get as far away as possible. This was the very last time I'd let myself get roped into something against my better judgement. The landed gentry were all a bit cracked, in my opinion, possibly from a lot of interbreeding when they should have at least allowed in some sturdy peasant stock every hundred years or so. If only I'd listened to my little voice when it hinted that taking on the Hadley genealogy project was not a good idea, in fact it was a Very Bad Idea.

But I couldn't let Dad down while he was ill, and he really, really wanted the job. For all his liberal talk, Dad is a die-hard royalist and he'd jumped at the chance to meet them. I'm sure they're deadly boring as relatives but I didn't say anything, not wanting to spoil Dad's fun. He'd had little to no pleasure since Mom died ten years ago and had retreated into his books and papers and dredging up people's family trees to keep busy. It's amazing how many people want to know who their ancestors are. Now Dad was having the time of his life fiddling around with the Hadley genealogy—possibly hoping to prove we were more closely related than he'd initially thought—until he got sick, of course.

The doorknob turned, and Maisie appeared with a tray. The soup smelled so delicious that my stomach rumbled. She made a little dining place for me at the desk, pushing aside several books and papers. Maisie had done a great job of rustling up a meal at short notice. A small glass of red wine, a few slices of crusty bread with butter, and real soup with chunky veggies and meaty bits. Definitely not instant soup. Yum! My stomach rumbled even louder.

While I wolfed down the food, Maisie bustled about, tidying up what to me looked like an incredibly tidy room compared to my flat. I guessed some poor actor posing as a footman would have to empty the bath and stow it away somewhere. It's amazing how hot food and a glass of excellent wine can perk one up after a truly rotten day. It was all just one misunderstanding after another, something that could be cleared up in a jiffy.

"Maisie," I said, settling comfortably on the end of the bed. I hated leaving my supper dishes like that on the desk. I almost offered to take them down to wherever the kitchen was, but she really seemed to be into this role so who was I to deny her job satisfaction.

"Yes, miss," she replied, carefully folding the towel.

Her country accent was so perfect that she could easily get a part in the next BBC production of yet another period drama. Maybe she should be thinking beyond re-enactments and consider more serious roles.

"Where are my things?"

Her face was a picture of confusion as she stared blankly at me. "Yer things?"

"Yes, my stuff."

She blinked, and her face crumpled a bit. "Are ye sayin' somethin's gorn missin'?"

Uh, oh, she thought I was accusing her of stealing. Maybe she'd get fired from the set.

"No, no," I said hastily in what I hoped was a reassuring tone. "I just mean my things, not these things." I waved in the direction of the chest of drawers and the wardrobe.

Her eyes widened, and her expression now clearly showed she thought I was bonkers.

"But these *are* yer things, miss," she said in the gentle, patient tones of a parent explaining to a fretful child that the toy they want is sleeping now and can't come out to play.

I didn't want to ask. I couldn't bear to face what was growing from a seed of suspicion into a monstrous and impossible reality. There was no lamp by the bedside with a visible electrical cord. There was no light fitting hanging from the ceiling. Not even David Copperfield could have magicked away a whole parking area. That horribly familiar, stomach-churning, cold sweat breaking out sensation came over me again.

I feigned a yawn. "My goodness, Maisie, I think today has been so dreadful that I'm not sure where my thoughts are."

Her confused and cautious expression cleared as she gave me a hesitant smile. I must have sounded more normal. Then I asked the one dreadful question that would solve all my problems and put me in the right century. The question upon which everything hinged.

"What date is it today?"

She beamed. "Why, it's Tuesday, 25 April 1815, miss."

That's when I fainted. It's lucky I was sitting on the bed at the time.

Chapter Four

The smell of one hundred percent cat pee jerked me back to reality. Do not be fooled; forget historical romances where the heroine sniffs genteelly at her smelling salts. Fictional smelling salts are not like real smelling salts. These smell like ammonia, and horrifically so. They should actually be called bad smelling salts. One whiff and the sniffer leaps into action. I didn't quite leap, but I sat up. Two anxious faces peered at me: Doctor Potts and Maisie.

He held up three fingers. "How many fingers am I holding up, Miss Carstairs?"

"Did I upset ye in some way, miss," Maisie bleated on the verge of tears. "I'm ever so sorry if I did."

"Three fingers," I replied, "and of course you didn't upset me, Maisie."

The doctor looked relieved. "It's the shock of today's events," he announced.

He and Maisie exchanged conspiratorial glances. Shock explained many aberrations. Today had been particularly shocking, so anything weird I said and did could easily be explained away.

"Early to bed and a few drops of something to soothe the nerves."

He poured some liquid from a small bottle into a glass of water. I hesitated, eyeing the glass. It had to be laudanum, that much I knew, and wasn't laudanum made from opium? Visions of the worst of the worst drug effects swam before my eyes. The last thing I wanted was to be stuck two hundred years in the past with a drug habit if, in fact, we were two hundred years in the past. I still wasn't totally convinced at that point.

He chuckled. "A very weak solution, Miss Carstairs. I don't advocate taking laudanum all the time, only in cases of shock, like this."

As I'd noticed before, he was a sensible man. The problem was that he had no idea of what had really shocked me, and if I said anything about being an unwilling visitor from the future, I might end up in a loony bin for the rest of my natural life. A horrible thought.

"Now why don't you have an early night and things will look very much better in the morning."

Maisie nodded hard in agreement.

"What's the time?" I asked. It felt as if years had passed in a single day, although in my case, maybe two centuries had flown by.

He fished his pocket watch from his waistcoat and examined it. "It's after six, Miss Carstairs, and although you'll perhaps consider it far too early to go to bed, as a doctor I advise rest as the best medicine."

He held out the glass. "Drink this and have a good night's sleep. I'll tell the family you've decided to turn in."

Since drug addiction didn't seem to be my immediate fate, I obeyed. He was right. Maybe after a good night's rest I'd be mentally more capable of assessing what had happened and if I truly was back in 1815.

Maisie got busy making a small fire and although I

protested, she insisted.

"It'll get colder later on, miss, and it's so nice to go to sleep in a cosy, warm room."

Her tone was wistful, as if implying hers was not a cosy, warm room. I had some idea of how servants lived way back then, and it wasn't a happy fate. She drew the curtains at the window, helped me into a nightdress, I guess mine by default, and tucked the bed covers around me. I wasn't at all tired by now, thanks to the stinky smelling salts, but blow me down if I didn't close my eyes and fall into an incredibly deep and restful sleep.

When I woke up, the room was quite dark but for the remains of the fire glowing. Being back two hundred years— again, if I actually was—could be so annoying. No lamp on the side table, no light switch, of course, but there was a candle. No handy box of matches, although I'm sure they hadn't been invented yet. But thank goodness we were long past the stage of rubbing two sticks together. The candle and a few long twists of paper were my only tools. Paper, coals ... aha! Lighting the candle, I felt like Prometheus. I was wide awake, so it was a good time to assess my situation. Was I really back two hundred years in time?

The fact that both the marquis and his brother had called me Amelia meant of course that Amelia Carstairs must be our relative that Dad had dredged up. She'd married into the Hadley family in 18-something. The guy she'd married just had to be the one who had survived the attempts on his life. The one I'd saved! The pieces of the puzzle fitted perfectly. Calling me cousin was confusing, but if this wasn't a re-enactment and I hadn't been given a part, maybe it was a courtesy title, like when you're a child and you call your parents' friends aunt and uncle, meanwhile they aren't related to you. That was minor. What was major was that I had somehow taken Amelia's place, but had she taken mine? Was the historical Amelia Carstairs maybe floating around somewhere in the twilight zone while I unwillingly usurped her place?

Nature hates vacuums, so if I was here, where was she? Was she sitting in the library at Chelston Hall in 2015, as confused as I was here in 1815, and for that matter, why was I even here? Since the marquis who'd survived the assassination attempts was undoubtedly the one who ultimately married my ancestor Amelia Jane Carstairs, I still had a question. Surely, if I had just saved the marquis in the woods, the 1815 Amelia could have done as good a job? History had happened. Dad and I existed in 2015 so he had to have already been saved.

How does one even go back two hundred years? There was no time machine as per H.G. Wells, no worm holes and quantum technology machine as in Michael Crichton's *Time Line*. Parallel universes as in *Back to the Future*? A *Doctor Who*-style TARDIS? A single timeline as in *Terminator* that one could double back on? A portal or time displacement as in *Outlander*? What about *The Time Traveller's Wife*? I had no genetic predisposition, well, none that I knew of, for time travel, especially if it involved arriving naked at one's destination. Luckily for me, I had ended up here fully clothed. That part worried me. Shouldn't I have arrived in modern clothing? Did that mean I was now Amelia and had left my real self behind? And was Amelia now me and inhabiting my life? Where was she? Back in Chelston Hall in 2015, which would create a huge problem, or was she in my flat, confused as all hell and wondering what the television was?

Weren't there rules? I mean real rules as in physics, not movie and literary rules which script writers and authors make up as they go along. Lest it be thought I get all my science from science fiction, that's not strictly true. I did attend a few lectures when Allan went through a phase of investigating the intriguing topic of time travel and if it was possible. Something I remembered from one of Allan's friend's lectures on physics was that you can't change things; you can't go back in time and kill your grandfather, for example, or else you'd mess up your own chance of being born. Contrary to popular fiction, you can't take things from the modern world back in time— like a hand grenade or a mobile phone—because they hadn't been invented yet.

History couldn't be changed but maybe one could change *how* it happened. The marquis was meant to be saved, no matter who saved him. The important thing was that he was saved, otherwise none of us would be here, including me and Dad. Was it a "time slip?" Allan's friend had been rather dismissive of this phenomenon, but it's the one that made the most sense to me. He'd said in a very pretentious tone, "A time slip is when a person slips into another time period and is either left stranded to cope as best they can or is returned to their own time period in an equally mysterious manner. It's an unpredictable and uncontrolled process."

I remembered this particularly because the example he used, a famous one, really appealed to me. In what is known as the Moberly-Jourdain incident, two women visiting Versailles in 1901 found themselves in the eighteenth century. After a short time, they found themselves back again in 1901. Of course, the story was dismissed as a hoax because one of the women said she'd seen Marie-Antoinette, but I don't know. Maybe that's what had happened to me. Stranded. A lovely thought, I'm sure. I could sell my story to *Hello!* or *OK! Magazine*.

One thing became very clear as I huddled in my ancestor's

robe on the bed; I already knew the future. I knew the marquis would survive, but his attempted murderer did not know he did. Whoever it was would try again. Dad said the marquis survived several assassination attempts. He hadn't mentioned how many were considered "several." Two, three, four? It was up to me to save him, it appeared. How could I do it without getting in the way of actual history? Maybe I'd been brought back because I knew something from living in 2015 that could help, something the killer didn't know. Maybe watching all those *Midsomer Murder* episodes had honed my sleuthing skills. Where were Hercule Poirot and Miss Jane Marple now when I needed them?

Undoubtedly, no matter how many times the killer tried, I would save the marquis as in shades of *Groundhog Day*, a ghastly thought, but after that? How would I get back? Would the time slip gateway or portal, for want of a better description, open again? Or, horrors, would I be modern me trapped in a world with no antibiotics, no roll-on deodorant, no internet, no mobile phones, no my own dad—although I'm sure ancestor Amelia's dad is a nice guy—and no one to help me. What about Amelia? How would people react to her, thinking she was me, and that I'd clearly gone mad because I'd suddenly forgotten how the modern world worked?

Another thing struck me. What was ancestor Amelia doing here anyway? Her clothes and belongings were of good quality, so she wasn't deprived. She had a nicely furnished room, so she clearly was an esteemed guest and not just someone to be relegated to the attic room. Everyone so far treated me, masquerading as Amelia, with some respect. There was a reason for her being here, and maybe her marrying the marquis ultimately was all bound up with him being rescued. Was that somehow linked to me in the future taking Dad's place in the library? If the past couldn't be changed, were our futures predicted or ordained, and could we change them?

This was all so confusing. I had to find out once and for all if this was truly 1815, or a joke version in 2015 with excellent actors propping up the scenario. Unfortunately, the sinking feeling in my stomach was pointing me in the direction of it really being 1815. I needed concrete, incontestable proof. What would my two best friends do?

Zoe, my gorgeous, sexy, dress designer friend, would jump into the role of Amelia Carstairs and act the part, flinging caution to the wind and enjoying being here, without a care of how to get back to 2015. She would totally love the costumes, down to the very last chemise and garter, and would flirt outrageously with all the handsome men and no doubt end up being labelled as a forward hussy. My best male friend, Bryan, also a research assistant, would tell me to examine the facts at hand, given the available information. Bryan was looking after Harold and Maude, my two goldfish, while I was at Chelston Hall. I had some reservations though. Bryan might end up becoming their new owner if I didn't get back.

Where would I find facts? Books! Back to the library. That would tell me if this was an elaborate hoax or a dreadful reality. I put on Amelia's slippers, grabbed the candlestick, and slunk out of the room. The corridor was empty. Although I didn't know my way around, logically going down the grand staircase and getting back to the entrance hall was the next thing. Muddling along in the dark wasn't easy. When movie makers shoot a period drama, and everyone is using candles, yet the audience can see the scene clearly, it's not the candles but loads of strong special lighting. One lone candle in a huge, dark stately home is not much help.

Somehow, I managed to get down the stairs without falling

over and breaking my neck. A few stubbed toes later, and nearly knocking over an inconveniently placed suit of armour, I was in the library. Luckily, there was a candelabra on a centre table which, once lit, improved the lighting enormously. Holding the candelabra high—now I really did feel as if I were in a period drama—the candle glow fell on the endless rows of old leather-bound books on the shelves. But all stately homes had zillions of books like these in their libraries, with curly gold writing on the spines, looking suitably antique. I needed more up to date proof.

Although the desk was the same one I'd seen in the library when I'd first arrived, now it contained not a single modern element from the twentieth or twenty-first centuries. No desk lamp, no computer, no telephone, no mobile phone, no stapler, no paper punch, not even a typewriter. No sign of my handbag and laptop, although who would I call and email?

A silver ink well set and some quill pens lay on the desk, next to a few sheets of writing paper. I put down the candelabra and started rummaging. The drawers had the usual assortment of junk one finds in desk drawers, but antique junk, not modern junk. More balls of string, papers, a pen knife or two, a tattered almanac, a few sticks of sealing wax and some old pencils, rather than desk diaries, day planners, and calculators.

The clincher was in a pile of newspapers. *The Times*, *The London Chronicle*, even a publication called *The Gentleman's Magazine*, probably the Regency equivalent of *GQ*, and an assortment of leaflets advertising old-style farming equipment and seeds. The dates were all March or April 1815. If this was a hoax, it was elaborate to the point of scary madness. It couldn't be a hoax. Now all of me was convinced. This was the horrible reality I'd dreaded. I was apparently stuck in 1815 and my only hope might be to save the marquis and pray that once my job was done, I could go home.

A faint scratching sound came from outside the door, which was ajar. I froze. The killer? This time to get me? The hunched-over person scurrying through the bushes in the woods had seen me, although I hadn't seen their face. I gripped the candelabra firmly, my only available weapon, determined to put up one hell of a fight, despite quaking inside.

"Who's there?" To my annoyance, my voice wobbled.

The door creaked open in that horrible, eerie way one just knows means the killer is outside, holding the biggest knife in the history of murder. Russet pattered towards me. I sank into a chair, letting out the breath I was holding, and put my weapon on the desk. I stroked his ears and gave him a few pats. But he wasn't interested in being petted. He gently took a corner of my dressing gown in his mouth and pulled. He wanted to go somewhere. Honestly, this dog was smarter than Lassie. If only he could speak, he'd have told me everything and I could solve the mystery of the attempted murder and go home.

I blew out the candles on the candelabra and put it back on the centre table because it wouldn't do to signal to all and sundry that someone had been snooping around in the library. Holding my pathetic single candlestick high, I said to Wonder Dog, "Lead the way, boy." Russet didn't have to show me where to go once we reached the bottom of the stairs. To my horror, I smelled smoke.

Oh my god, please don't say the house is on fire. It's 1815 and I'm sure the fire brigade hasn't been invented yet!

The dog bounded up the stairs with me behind him. He knew where he was going and, although I didn't, I kept close on his heels as we barged into a bedroom. Even though the room was in semi-darkness, the remains of a fire illuminated the shocking scenario. There in a huge four-poster bed, all hung with magnificent burgundy and gold brocade curtains, was the marquis, asleep or still unconscious, with flames licking the hem of the curtains at the foot of the bed. The room was filling with thick, choking smoke. My eyes began watering, and my throat closed up. No time to lose and with my Girl Guide instincts kicking in and the adrenaline pumping, I swung into action, extinguishing, and flinging my pathetic candle aside.

First things first, I had to get the curtains away from the bed. I pulled like a maniac and Russet, bless his doggy cotton socks, got the fabric between his teeth, and pulled with me. We tore down probably a few thousand pounds' worth of antique brocade fabric, modern-day prices, and I hauled it over to the corner of the room. Bundling the curtains into a pile smothered any remaining fire. The fabric was so thick that it didn't burn very well but had created a lot of smoke. Next, I grabbed a jug of water from the bedside table. Jug is an understatement; this was a pitcher and darn heavy. I needed to put out the stray tongues of flame inching up the bedclothes.

Suddenly someone took the pitcher from me and emptied the contents onto the flames. "Miss Carstairs, help me get His Grace out of the room."

The man knew me, but I didn't know him. A neat, smallish, dapper guy, also in a dressing gown and slippers, faced me and gave a little bow. He had to be a manservant, a valet maybe. I was right.

"We met when you arrived, Miss Carstairs. Parker, His Grace's valet, at your service. Now we must hurry before he suffers damage to his lungs."

"Where are we taking him?"

Parker darted across the room and opened a door. "This is the dressing room and he'll be quite safe and comfortable here for the moment. It appears the fire is out."

Parker flung the bedroom windows wide open, letting in the cool night air and dispersing the smoke. Together we hauled the marquis out of bed and dragged him as gently as possible into the next room, where there was a smaller and thankfully much lower bed, more like a day bed for the occasional nap in between one's noble duties of running an estate and bossing the peasants around.

He was no light weight being at least six feet and well built. Try dragging a dead weight off a bed and across a room to another bed, and then lifting him. I'm fit, but this was beyond hefting a few dumbbells and doing the super circuit at the gym. Every muscle in my arms, legs, and back screamed in silent agony. Somehow, we managed before I collapsed in a heap on the floor. Russet took up his sentry position at the foot of the day bed. During this frantic rescue mission, the marquis was still unconscious, only groaning feebly a few times as if he were in pain. At least he was alive.

Once we'd made the marquis comfortable, and Parker had checked his bandages, he said, "It would be advisable for you to return to your room, Miss Carstairs, and let me tidy up."

I got up and peered back into the main bedroom. Could it have been an unfortunate accident, even by Lemony Snicket's standards? Had a stray lump of coal fallen from the fireplace onto the carpet, rolled into the centre of the room, and the flame somehow travelled a bit further to the bed curtains? A big stretch of even Lemony's imagination.

Parker answered my unspoken question. "No, Miss Carstairs. No piece of coal could have made its way across the carpet without burning the material."

I stooped to check. The incredibly expensive-looking carpet was untouched between the fireplace, where coals glowed in the grate, and the bed. Not a scorch mark, not a burn.

"Someone did this deliberately," I said flatly.

He gave a delicate shrug. "I don't think the intention was to burn the house down, just to cause enough smoke so that His Grace would asphyxiate."

Although I didn't know this man from a bar of soap, he was the marquis's valet, and no doubt was fiercely loyal. I had to trust someone at some stage. The doctor and the dowager had instantly thought of a poacher in the first incident. To have another attempt on the marquis's life so soon after that was just far too much of a coincidence for me.

And for Parker as well. "In His Grace's weakened state, he would not have been able to get out of bed and save himself."

That sentence spoke volumes.

"Goodnight, Miss Carstairs. I'll put everything to rights and perhaps you should not say anything if someone mentions it tomorrow."

"I'll put on my very best surprised look," I assured him.

He chuckled. As I went to the door, he said, "Pardon me for asking, but how did you know his lordship's bed curtains were on fire?"

I laughed. "I was in the library ... er ... looking for something to read and Russet came to find me. How did you know?"

"I'm a very light sleeper and my room is not far from this one. I heard sounds of heaving and panting and ... er ... some thudding. I came to investigate."

"All very fortunate then."

"Yes, all very fortunate," he said dryly. "Let's hope we circumvent any more unhappy incidents." He pointed to my hands. "You should put some cold water on those burns right away, so they don't blister."

He picked up my candle from where I didn't remember

throwing it aside, relit it from the glowing coals, and handed it to me. I said goodnight and somehow managed to find my own room. I bathed my now stinging hands in a jug of water on the side table. The burns weren't so bad, just red marks really, and the water cooled them down. I could always say I'd dropped my candle if anyone asked. I got into bed, now resigned to my fate of solving the mystery of the assassin's identity and hopefully preventing any further murderous attempts on the marquis's life.

But what move would the assassin make next?

Chapter Five

Wednesday, 26 April 1815

Maisie heralded the next morning by creeping into my room at what must have been the crack of dawn. It hadn't all been a bad dream. I wasn't back in my untidy, but oh so beloved, flat. I was still here in 1815, for better or worse.

I blinked at her. "Maisie? Is anything wrong?"

She bobbed a curtsey. "No, miss. Nothin's wrong, but ye did ask me yesterday morning to remind ye where the water closet is situated."

Since obviously I hadn't asked her, it must have been ancestor Amelia, although I don't blame her. In my mind, a chamber pot, which I was sure resided under everyone's bed, was all right for a quick pee, but not for serious business. The water closet. My heart sank yet again. Isn't it amazing how in historical novels and movies one never reads about or sees the hero or heroine engaged in basic ablutions, unless they're having a sexy bubble bath together. They never go to the loo or have to brush their teeth. I now desperately needed the loo. Maisie was dressed and ready to start the day's work. I shuffled into my slippers and dressing gown, hoping not to bump into anyone on the way to wherever the water closet was located. My entire body ached as if I'd been run over by a herd of stampeding elephants. It's not every day one saves a member of the nobility from death by fire and drags him to safety.

"His Grace has ever so many modern ideas," Maisie confided in an admiring whisper as we crept along the passage, hung with portraits of stern lords and ladies, and obscure landscapes in gilt frames, and then down a narrow back staircase which seemed to lead into the rear end of the building.

"He said we have to move with the times and puttin' in the water closet was the first thing. He's talkin' about puttin' in water pipes next. Imagine that. No more buckets." She grinned at me. "They say there's piped water already in the fancy houses in London."

Thinking back to the pamphlets in the library advertising agricultural equipment, I guess that was cutting edge technology for the time, although the images were reminiscent of farm implements from *Game of Thrones*. What would a "modern" toilet be like in 1815? Sounds of pots clanging and dishes clattering, along with a few screeched comments, indicated that the household servants were up much earlier than the grand folk, getting ready to serve the rich and privileged. I was now one of those rich and privileged, it seemed.

Maisie opened a door into a very small room, literally a closet, where the toilet, for want of a better word, reposed. It had a wooden seat and there was a small pile of neatly cut squares of newspaper on a shelf. Newsprint is not like double ply, trust me. Pitying my ancestor, I shuddered, did what I had to do, and pulled on a lever, which resulted in loud clanking and then whooshing sounds.

Back in my room, now with a vague layout of the place in my head, it was time to do the morning ablutions and get dressed. Maisie disappeared for a few minutes, came back with a huge pitcher of steaming water and a basin, pointed out a very charming marble-topped washstand I hadn't noticed before, arranged the screen so I could wash my relevant bits in privacy, and said she'd lay out my dress if I wanted to go down to breakfast.

"You'll have to show me where to go, although you must think me very forgetful, not knowing my way around."

"Oh, no, miss," she chirped. "Ye've only been here since late Monday and ye did say it's been ten years since ye were last here. His Grace's made a few alterations since he got back from the war two years ago. I'm sure ye'll find lots of things are different."

Ten years? That's a long time. If Amelia and I were the same age, then she was fourteen when, for some reason, she and her family stopped visiting. War two years ago? Robert must have been involved in the Peninsula War which ended in the French defeat at the Battle of Vitoria on 21 June 1813, in Portugal. I know my battles. It seemed a bit much to pump Maisie for more information without arousing suspicion. Hopefully, the rest of the family would drop helpful snippets.

One thing I now knew was that ancestor Amelia had only been at Chelston Hall since Monday, 24 April. Late, Maisie said—maybe in the evening after travelling from somewhere? I had "arrived" on the morning of Tuesday, 25 April, been involved in the bow and arrow debacle, slept the night after helping with the fire incident, and it was now Wednesday, 26 April. Had she spoken with Robert when she'd arrived? Had they exchanged letters over that ten-year period? Not that this information was going to do me much good, but as any prisoner will attest, it's useful to know the time, the day, and the date to keep sane. Considering that I might be trapped here for a while, one thing I would definitely need was my sanity.

Teeth! How was I going to clean my teeth? For a desperately mad moment I thought I'd have to cut and chew a twig for dental hygiene, but there was a perfectly respectable wooden toothbrush on the washstand, next to the basin and jug I'd been using, along with a dainty porcelain container which bore the label *Oriental Tooth Powder*. Intrigued, I examined the contents which looked a bit like bicarb. Needs must and all that. It wasn't too bad, although the toothbrush bristles were a bit stiffer than I'm used to.

No deodorant, alas, but further digging around in Amelia's toiletries revealed a small box of what looked like talcum powder, with a powder puff of sorts. I've used talc before when I've run out of deo and it does work, providing one isn't going to play a strenuous game of tennis or go to the gym for a hectic workout. A quick dab under each arm did the trick and thank heavens I'd waxed all that needed to be done before my ill-fated journey to Chelston Hall. As for moisturiser, I rubbed a blob or two of *Bloom of Ninon* cream into my skin. It smelled quite nice, like roses. No cosmetics like blush and mascara, but then Amelia and I shared another habit; we didn't use anything. I did on special occasions back in 2015, which seemed ever increasingly like light years away.

Getting dressed was quicker than getting undressed, or maybe I was just more into the swing of things. Maisie had picked out a very pretty dress in a pale blue pinstripe, with long sleeves, a scooped neck, and a blue ribbon threaded under the bust line. The fabric might have been muslin because it was quite fine. Ancestor Amelia had more or less my taste in that

I'm not a frilly person. I sat obediently while Maisie brushed my hair with a beautiful and probably hideously valuable silver-backed hairbrush. She tweaked and twisted and fiddled while putting my hair up. Then she led me to the mirror for approval.

I stared and leaned closer. Was it really me? I'm not unattractive, far from it, but I've never really thought of myself as a beauty, more of being "interesting" as far as looks go, with a slim figure, shoulder-length dark hair, and green eyes. Allan always said it was my mind that entranced him, but one glance at Tawnee's DDs bursting out of a tight, fake leopard print top proved him the liar. It was me, only different, staring back from the mirror. My skin was more glowing, my cheeks faintly touched with pink, and my hair was now in a very fetching "up style" involving charming ringlets. Even my eyes looked greener than usual. Was this how Amelia looked?

"Oh, miss," Maisie breathed in an adoring way. "Ye look like a real picture."

I wasn't sure about the real picture bit, but I looked the part and that was what counted. The fact that Amelia's stuff was unpacked and in drawers and the wardrobe meant that she and Maisie had already met and done all that between Monday evening and Tuesday morning. They had also done the whole loo thing yesterday morning on Tuesday. I was going to drive myself mad trying to connect these little threads to keep some kind of continuity going between Amelia being herself yesterday morning, going into the woods for a walk, and then me coming back in her place.

"I was so caught up in my own thoughts yesterday, Maisie," I said, "but thank you so much for helping me. I could never have managed without you."

Maisie's cheeks turned bright red, and she did a sort of

curtsey bob. She nearly fell over her feet.

"It's such an honour to help. I nearly fell flat on me back when Mrs Barlow told me that His Grace himself had said she must appoint someone competent to be yer lady's maid while yer here, since ye hadn't one of yer own."

"Really? That's very kind of him," I said.

Everyone kept calling the marquis His Grace, and since this was 1815 and not a re-enactment error, clearly, he'd been elevated up the social ladder. His father must have died and that meant he was now the duke, and the older woman was indeed the dowager duchess. If only I'd paid more attention to Dad when he tossed out facts about the peerage. I should know this kind of detail, but I was having a hard time keeping it together being Amelia. Interestingly, Amelia was important enough for Robert to think ahead about her comfort. This sounded very promising for their romance. Amelia didn't have her own lady's maid so possibly the family wasn't that well off for her to afford one. Her clothes and belongings were quality, but perhaps a personal servant was beyond the budget.

"Oh yes," Maisie said, letting the cat and all its kittens right out of the bag in her naiveté. "The dowager was none too pleased about everythin', and especially when he said this partic'lar room was to be spring cleaned and made to look perfect since it's the very room ye stayed in when ye visited before."

Aha, the old bat! She would've had Amelia in the attic room in a trice, that much was clear.

"I noticed right away how lovely the room looked," I said. "I'm sorry I forgot to say how it brought back such pleasant memories." There I was lying through my teeth again, but I assumed Amelia had had pleasant times, since she was visiting again.

Maisie did her bob curtsey. "I'm ever so pleased yer pleased, miss."

She rummaged in yet another little box on the dressing table and laid out a small pair of gold earrings and a chain with a blue enamel locket. "Don't forget yer jewellery."

I wasn't wearing jewellery yesterday so maybe Amelia had left it off because she was going for a walk in the woods and was afraid something might get lost. I put on the earrings and opened the locket to find a dark-haired woman's miniature portrait. It must be Amelia's mother. I clasped it around my neck. For better or for worse, I had to play this role to perfection. I couldn't let Amelia down.

Breakfast, the meal of the day the experts say one should never miss. Maisie draped a very nice shawl matching my dress over my shoulders and pointed me in the direction of the breakfast parlour. It wasn't as grand as the drawing room, but still sumptuous by my standards. An antique sideboard groaned under the weight of various silver salvers, while two of the footmen from yesterday were on standby to pour tea and unfold napkins. And this was just breakfast?

Doctor Potts was hunched over his plate, shovelling bacon and eggs into his mouth. Clementine, looking enchanting of course in a pale pink frilled number, sat with a rather mournful expression while crumbling a bread roll and gazing into her teacup. There was no sign of the old gent in the wheelchair, or of the dowager. Rupert scowled into his cup of whatever he was drinking and then, after mumbling, "Morning," stomped out of the room.

The butler drew back my chair and, once I was seated, poured me a cup of tea. Again, Amelia and I were similar. Two boiled eggs, which I prayed were not too runny, and two triangles of buttered toast awaited my approval. It was all perfect. Just how I like it, and evidently just how Amelia liked it as well. She must have made her breakfast preferences clear yesterday morning.

Doctor Potts finished his breakfast and slurped the last of his tea. "I expect you're keen to see how the patient does this morning, Miss Carstairs?"

I was, and I wasn't. Basically, I was an imposter and sooner or later someone would find me out. Up until now no one had, but it was inevitable. The truth would surely come out. I could only play the "ten years away" scenario so far. I knew nothing about Amelia in 1815. How was I to find out more?

Staring at him, I must have looked desperate because he said in that hearty doctor voice, "Now then, nothing to be worried about. I've already checked on my patient and he's coming along nicely. Slept like a log, he said."

For want of anything to say, I crunched on a piece of toast. Not a word about a fire, potential asphyxiation, and hadn't anyone noticed the very fancy bed curtains had disappeared? No doubt Parker had spirited the burned ones away, but I'm not sure his valeting skills extended to whipping up a new set overnight. I swallowed and took another bite to avoid having to answer.

"You and Miss Eccles might want to take a turn around the garden for a while and then pay His Grace a visit at, let's say, eleven o'clock?" Without waiting for an answer, he pushed back his chair and stood. "Excellent. I'll see you ladies later."

My breakfast companion looked like a Miss Eccles. Clementine Eccles. The name suited her to a tee. Another time perhaps I would have laughed and thought it was a made-up name for sure, but not today. Today was another century. I smiled at the downcast Clementine who looked as if something was bothering her.

"Shall we take a walk after breakfast, Miss Eccles?"

Her shrug was noncommittal. I was almost tempted to can the idea, but it flashed into my mind that while I knew nothing about Amelia, other people would know a whole lot more. Miss Eccles could prove to be useful.

"I'll see you in a few minutes then."

My smile felt brittle and false, but she didn't seem to notice. Her problems were bigger than anything else, that much was evident. I was hungry and made short work of my eggs and toast. I finished eating and then nipped upstairs to wash my hands and grab one of Amelia's many hankies. I had a feeling we'd need one. Back downstairs and heading in the direction of a garden walk, easily found by following a gravel path, I soon discovered the dismal Clementine perched on a small stone plinth.

She looked up as I approached, then jumped down, grabbed me by one hand, and led me further into a pretty rose garden. There was a discreet kind of bower with a stone bench that hardly looked comfortable, but Clementine sank onto it, let go of my hand, and burst into sobs.

"Miss Carstairs, I apologise for my impolite behaviour at breakfast yesterday and even again today. I haven't been feeling quite myself."

Not having met her yesterday and having no idea how impolite she could have been, I was in no position to judge. I didn't even think she'd been rude this morning, just preoccupied.

Patting her hand, I said soothingly, "Think nothing of it, Miss Eccles. We all have bad days."

She sniffed and dabbed at her eyes with the tiniest, most ridiculous handkerchief, all lace and no substance, so I fished Amelia's much more serviceable one from my sleeve and handed it over. Clementine took it gratefully.

"You are so kind to me, Miss Carstairs. And on such short acquaintance."

This was too much like being in a play, so I said, "Please do call me Amelia. I feel we are friends already."

Her face lit up. Poor girl. She must have a real weight on her mind. Although, apart from trying to decide what fluffy confection or bonnet to wear, which admirer to smile at, and how to arrange a bunch of flowers, it was hard to imagine what her problems were. She was drop dead gorgeous with probably every titled suitor from one end of London to the Isle of Wight after her. Her clothes looked expensive, so poverty wasn't an issue, and she was young. What was there to worry about?

Maybe she was distressed about the accident. A young and sensitive girl might feel that way. It was a shocking incident to happen as a guest somewhere and not really knowing the people. However, I couldn't have been more wrong. It wasn't at all about her host; it was all about Clementine. In fact, Robert's injury was pretty much an afterthought which couldn't get into her brain because there was no room for it. But I was being unkind. She couldn't help being gorgeous and as thick as a plank.

"My life is over, Miss Car—I mean Amelia, well and truly over."

More sobbing. More hand patting. I waited. It was pleasant sitting there. The roses smelled wonderful, and the sun peeking through the clouds was nice and warm.

"I never wanted to come here, but Mama insisted," she burst out. "I've been sent here like an unwanted parcel."

A more unlikely parcel if ever I'd seen one. There must be a reason.

"I thought you'd come to visit the family."

She gave a contemptuous little snort, like a kitten sneezing. "Ha! That was Mama's idea. Last year I had my coming out during the Season and Mama decided I was setting my sights too low on a mere viscount or Honourable."

I put on my Most Interested Expression which must have spoken volumes because Clementine continued, "Even though I received some very attractive offers, Mama said no one less than a duke would do. She made me turn them all down because *she'd* set her sights on the duke."

"What duke?"

She looked at me, puzzled. "His Grace, of course, your cousin. That duke. And I'm so sorry he's had such a terrible accident."

I made a show of tapping my forehead. "Of course. My cousin."

My cousin? Dad would be utterly beside himself with excitement. Clementine had just filled in an important piece of the puzzle. Although we were related to Amelia, I didn't know she was related to the Hadley family even before the marriage. That explained why people called me Cousin Amelia. Not part of a re-enactment, sadly, but a real-life relationship. How Dad would have loved this! He's the expert on the nobility, not me. He's also an expert on how one addressed members of the peerage, their wives, their mothers, their children, and the spouses of their children. He'd be over the moon when I told him—if, in fact, I ever got back.

Happily for me, Clementine's curiosity about the new guest and her tendency towards grasshopper thoughts were to my advantage.

"I can understand," she said, "that it must be difficult having been away so long after your father went down to

Plymouth to take up a living there. The dowager told me a little about you before your arrival."

What on earth kind of a living would a man take up in Plymouth? Apart from fishing, maybe.

She stared expectantly at me. "I mean, is the parish very pleasant? Or is it dull residing there? I'm sure there's no entertainment or society of any note."

A living! Amelia's dad was a vicar. Never having been to Plymouth, I had to lie, hoping that back in 1815 it had had some appeal, although what kind of fun would be available was anyone's guess.

"Oh, very amiable, very pleasant people," I hastened to assure her. "And I'm always busy helping Papa with his ... er ... pastoral work."

I assumed I'd be doing that. Ministering unto the poor, helping with the sermons, arranging the flowers in the church kind of stuff. Clementine was proving to be most useful with Amelia's bio, although I confess, I'd become a bit side-tracked with wanting to know why her life could possibly be over before it had barely begun.

"Was the journey very uncomfortable?" she asked. "I've only travelled a long distance in a coach once and it was shockingly bumpy. I thought my teeth would fall out from being rattled around so much. I'm certain the inns must be positively dreadful. One is also never sure about the sheets when one has to travel a long way."

No doubt Amelia had had to travel by whatever passed for public transport and, from what little I knew about it, the distance of around 190 plus miles meant a journey of a few days. I cast my mind back to the occasional lurid historical romances I'd read. As well as some very entertaining Georgette Heyer novels a friend had lent me, plus of course, my collection of Jane Austen novels which focused on this period. Unfortunately, neither popular fiction authors nor Miss Austen described all the gory daily details. The emphasis was on when the hero was about to rescue the heroine from the villain's unwelcome embrace in the former cases, and Miss Austen's succinct observations on human nature and relationships in the latter. But there was no harm in erring on the side of probability.

"Oh yes, very bumpy, but fortunately the inns were quite comfortable and clean."

She looked pensive. "It must have been hard for you growing up so close to the family, what with your father and His Grace's father being second cousins once removed, and then going to live in Plymouth."

She made it sound as if we'd had to live in a yurt in Outer Mongolia, herd yaks, and drink tea with butter and salt in it. Although, I'd read that yurts were very cosy inside once one shut out the howling winds from the steppes of Central Asia. I felt for Amelia and her dad. So, she and Robert must be second cousins twice removed. Or would they be third cousins? No matter! No chance of any inbreeding there with such a suitably healthy genetic divide. My knowledge of how family trees work is hazy at best, and I've only ever understood first cousins. But one thing remained; tenuous though the link might be, Amelia and Robert were related enough for him to call her Cousin Amelia. That sounded promising. I could rightfully call him Cousin Robert.

Hopefully, my expression was suitably downcast. "Very hard indeed. It was a great wrench to leave. But we made a new and happy life there."

"Until your dearest mother died, and then having such a petulant aunt as your father's sister Harriet made it so difficult for you to return to visit. Well, that's what Her Grace said."

The dowager must be a terrible gossip to tell all and sundry about Amelia, although, to be fair, Clementine was just being curious about a guest. At this stage, any information was welcome. I'd take anything I could get. All details gratefully accepted.

"Yes, Aunt Harriet has been very petulant indeed."

Clementine nodded. "My father also has a sister, my Aunt Sarah, and he always has to rush to her side because she has a spasm or something which I'm sure is all made up. Mama gets very annoyed. It must have been so infuriating that just when you and your father had decided to visit, his sister needed him at the very last minute."

Aha! So that's why Amelia was here without her dad. Her annoying Aunt Harriet, a natural and enthusiastic hypochondriac it seemed, had decided to play ill and he'd stayed behind while Amelia came to visit. She would logically have told the family the reason she'd arrived without her father. Maybe she'd even written before leaving Plymouth. That could also be the reason the dowager knew so much and was able to tell Clementine.

I steered the conversation back to her predicament. "We were talking about why you're so downcast, Miss Eccles."

She looked at me with those large, limpid blue eyes. "Please, if I am so privileged to call you Amelia, you must call me Clementine. I feel that even on such brief acquaintance, it's almost as if we've been friends forever."

"Of course, Clementine."

Best friends forever.

She gave a little sigh. "Not content with chasing away any interested suitors, Mama took it into her head that I must agree with her, set my sights on His Grace, and forego anyone else. As if I have no choice in the matter!"

"But did you meet anyone else with whom you could … er … form an attachment?" I asked, falling quite comfortably into Regency speak.

She bristled. "No, although it certainly wasn't from a lack of offers. I must say I was very much in demand. I hardly had a moment to myself with so many balls, parties, routs, breakfasts, and picnics. I was inundated with flowers and gifts, and invitations to all manner of amusing entertainments."

She sighed, as if remembering something unpleasant. "But so many of the titled gentlemen were positively ancient, at least forty or more in some cases. And what with wretched fortune hunters haunting one's every footstep, it wasn't a completely happy experience."

At her age Clementine considered anyone over forty to have one foot in the grave and the other on a banana peel. Poor old Allan, at forty nearly in his dotage by Regency standards.

"But that's not the point," she said with a little huff.

I raised my eyebrows to show just how interested I was in her opinion.

"The point is that I want to choose my own husband at my own leisure, and not because he's rich or titled or has a big estate in the countryside."

"But do you want to get married?"

She gave me what can only be termed a patronising smile, although in her naiveté, I'm sure she didn't mean it that way.

"Naturally I want to get married, everyone does, but not to someone as old as His Grace. I mean he's thirty! He's a whole twelve years older than me."

She made him sound like Rip Van Winkle, and here was I, an aged and spinsterish twenty-four.

Clementine put one hand to her mouth. "Oops! I don't

want to be insulting, Amelia, but Grandmama says I'm far too young to become attached to anyone without seeing something of life."

Sensible woman, this Grandmama.

"What do your parents say about this?" I asked since her parents' opinion would obviously come first.

It was a bit worrying to meet a rival for Robert's hand, albeit a reluctant one, since history said he had to marry Amelia. They still needed to fall in love somehow. I didn't want to have to push Clementine into a lake and hold her down to make sure this happened. Clementine's very ambitious mama might take steps to make sure she won Robert's affection.

She sighed again. Clementine's sighs were eloquent and soulful. "Mama has the most dreadful attitude towards Grandmama, her own mother."

I shifted closer and assumed my other Very Interested Expression, which consisted of widening my eyes and saying, "Oh?"

"Yes," she continued, "you see my Grandpapa, whom I never met because he passed on before I was born, made a lot of money in trade, in cotton, and ... oh, useful things like that. He left Grandmama an absolute fortune and so Mama had only the best upbringing, education, everything a young lady could want."

She hesitated.

"But?" I prompted her.

"It was sad that Mama didn't want Grandmama to launch my coming out, so a close friend of Grandmama's did the honours. Lady Strathclyde is one of Grandmama's oldest and dearest friends. In fact, she has many friends with titles, and no one is at all bothered about her having been married to a man in trade."

The one amazing thing about having money is that it opens all the doors that might have remained closed to anyone without it.

"Your grandmother sounds like a wonderful, caring person."

Clementine perked up. "Yes, she is, and she says I don't need to be bullied into marrying just anyone, even if he has a whole string of titles, because I'm an heiress and can make my own way in the world. Grandmama wants to take me abroad to interesting places and see the sights."

"Would you like to go?" I asked, although who wouldn't.

"I would love to go." This came out in a small wistful voice.

"What does your father say?" seemed the next natural question.

The corners of her mouth turned down. "Oh, Papa is very weak. He's bullied so mercilessly by Mama. He isn't titled or anything. He's only an Honourable, but Mama was no beauty when she was younger, and, despite Grandmama's money, she didn't have many offers."

"But you love your father?"

This time she cried again, sniffing into Amelia's hanky. "I love them both, but Papa says I should just be a good girl and visit Chelston Hall to please Mama. Mama says I must try to capture His Grace's interest and make a good match to please them. I'm afraid I was very rude to both of them as I took my leave."

The burning question.

"Has His Grace ever indicated a … er … romantic interest in you?"

The fateful answer.

"Oh no," she chirped, quite cheerfully in fact. "He's been so polite and charming, as he was when we met in London.

Even when Mama practically forced an invitation out of the dowager, he still maintained such an amiable demeanour. I'm happy to say he's not interested in me at all. I'm sure he thinks of me as someone just out of the schoolroom. He spoke to me the way any gentleman would speak kindly to a niece or young female family member."

She put on a thoughtful expression with another little frown. "He's very eligible and handsome, of course, and I think that's why Mama wanted to secure his interest in me. But he hasn't paid any other ladies particular attention, from what I've heard."

She leaned closer, widened her eyes, and said in a mysterious tone, "I think his heart beats only for one, for a lost love, although no one I spoke to seems to know who it is."

Phew! Clementine and Robert both seemed to be safe from each other, thanks to politeness and mutual disinterest. The enigmatic lost love was a bit alarming though. Could it be Amelia? Maybe they'd formed a bond while growing up together. Had they written to each other?

"Are you interested in Rupert, perhaps?" I asked. "Seeing as His Grace is a little too old for you."

Clementine's derisive snort was eloquent. "Lord Rupert is such a boor. You can't imagine how difficult it is trying to have a genteel conversation with him. He doesn't know how to speak to a young lady properly, even though I know he went to the best schools and had excellent tutors."

"Really?" Clementine was a fount of information on the family.

"Yes, it's like having a tooth drawn trying to be polite and well-mannered when he throws himself around in a room like a bull trying to jump over a fence. And he is so very clumsy. The other evening at dinner he trod on my skirt and the flounce tore. When he bent down to see what he'd done, he managed to spill his coffee on Doctor Potts' coat tails. I can't imagine what he is like at a ball. He'd probably tread all over a lady's feet."

That sounded like Rupert, from what little I'd seen of him.

"And he makes no effort to be amiable and good tempered, which is correct behaviour even when one might be down in the dumps. A well-bred person must show their good breeding by always being polite and affable. That's why I'm so mortified I was hardly as polite as I could have been to you when we first met."

I patted her shoulder. "Think nothing of it. I've forgotten it already."

The diatribe against poor Rupert continued.

"And I can't believe that someone in his social position would actually be so careless in his dress. I mean, his shirt points are not particularly high and yesterday his collar looked as if it hadn't been starched. I don't think he even has a valet, and all gentlemen of quality should have a valet."

In my situation, having been unceremoniously transported back two hundred years, without any real hope of returning to my own century, the quality or lack thereof of Rupert's shirt points was unimportant. I got the feeling that it was more a case of the lady doth protest too much, to paraphrase Shakespeare, and maybe Clementine didn't like the fact that she actually fancied Rupert just a tiny bit. He was handsome, tall, and well-built. Also, very eligible.

"Lord Rupert knows absolutely nothing of culture. He knows more about *agriculture*, in my opinion," she said with a pout. "All he can talk about is horses, farming, the condition of the fields, and various animals. A lady should always converse on topics of interest, so I asked him if he'd read any of Lord

Byron's poetry." She bristled with indignation. "Do you know he actually said that Lord Byron was a prosy fool, and that poetry was for fops and dandies."

Clementine gave a little huff. "When I said that gentlemen should know how to pen a few verses for a lady's pleasure, Lord Rupert had the gall to say a lady was better off meeting a man who could go out and shoot game or a rabbit for her dinner than muddle about with pen and paper."

She glared at me. "He actually said *bag* a rabbit! The man has utterly no sensibility. When I think of the delightful poems several of my admirers have written, it's clear Lord Rupert has no artistic leanings."

I felt I knew Rupert well already. Not a ladies' man. But I had to intervene on his behalf.

"I must say," I ventured. She looked at me enquiringly. "I'd rather have someone get a rabbit for the pot than sit at an empty table with nothing but poetry to satisfy my appetite. And perhaps his attitude comes from mostly living in the countryside."

Clementine looked away. "I suppose you're right," she said grudgingly. "It's just that the duke is so suave and sophisticated and next to him Lord Rupert comes across as a country bumpkin. He's not even interested in town life and elegant society. He said social events like balls and parties are a waste of time and money."

She folded her arms and frowned, which involved a dainty pout and the tiniest wrinkling of an alabaster smooth brow. "He doesn't even know how to address a young lady. Why, he even called me Clementine yesterday when you came in to tell us what had happened. He should know that he may only address me as Miss Eccles."

From this it sounded as if Rupert carried a torch for

Clementine, would rather die than show it, and had called her by her first name because that's how he thought of her. Her inordinate concern over how unsuitable Rupert was as a prospective husband meant she was more interested in him than she'd like to admit. I didn't say anything like this, of course.

"Perhaps he was so agitated and distressed by the news that he forgot himself. It's clear he cares deeply about his brother."

Clementine gave another thoughtful little wrinkle of her brow. "Yes, he seems very much attached to his brother, which is commendable, but all the same, he should know better. He's just like a rude schoolboy."

"Maybe he's just like a rude schoolboy because you treat him like one," I suggested. "Try treating him like a man and you might see a difference."

She stared at me. "Mama thinks Lord Rupert isn't a good prospect because His Grace is not so old, although of course far too old for me, and when he marries, he'll have his own children. It's not likely Lord Rupert will inherit the title unless something happens to his brother."

Aha! This hit me like the proverbial bolt of lightning. Therein lay the rub, as the bard said. Unless something happened to his brother. Was Rupert the dastardly scoundrel intent on ending Robert's life? He didn't strike me as the villain. His concern for Robert yesterday seemed genuine. Rupert had said "my brother." Maybe they were close, and Rupert looked upon his half-brother as a real brother. Or was he just a very good actor?

Clementine's plaintive voice broke into my ponderings. "I don't know why we're even discussing Lord Rupert when I have a greater problem on my mind. What shall I do about

Mama and Papa? How can I go back home without securing a proposal from the duke?"

"Make them happy," I said. "Your mama just wants to know that you are here being a delightful guest and a credit to the family. As far as the proposal is concerned, you could scarcely force one out of your host. If His Grace isn't interested in you, there's nothing you can do about it."

Clementine gave me a long stare. This time her expression showed she was digesting each point very carefully, perhaps storing these up as ammunition against her ambitious mother later in a showdown.

I patted her hand. "No one could accuse you of not being your most charming self. When it's time to go home, you can return knowing that you've done all that was possible to fulfil your duty as a good daughter. It won't be your fault if His Grace doesn't propose."

I gave an exaggerated eye roll. "You can hardly throw yourself at him. That would be most unseemly and very forward. Very low class."

I thought I should rub that in because it was evident her parents, well, her mother at least, prized social standing very highly.

"Then perhaps your grandmama can suggest a wonderful trip abroad, so no one gossips about how you didn't manage to secure the duke's affections."

Then the final detail against which no ambitious or domineering mother could argue. Actually, I could have kicked myself; I should have thought of this before.

"And, of course, aren't we forgetting something so compelling as to preclude any immediate thoughts of matrimony?"

Clementine stared at me in such confusion that for a

moment I thought I'd overdone the Regency speak.

"Something so compelling? What could that be?" she breathed.

I put on my Absolutely Astounded Expression which involved eyebrow raising, much eye widening, and hands clasped to my bosom in a dramatic pose.

"Why, His Grace is lying upstairs in his bedroom at this very moment with a grievous wound and with Doctor Potts in attendance. I'm afraid he most likely won't be thinking of proposing to anyone for quite a while."

I thought she was going to explode with joy.

"Oh, Amelia," she said, leaning forward and giving me the tiniest squeeze of a girly hug. "You're so clever to think of such a perfect solution. Much cleverer than me. I'm going to write to Mama and Papa today, tell them what has happened, and apologise for my horrible words. I feel so much better already."

I felt like Methuselah, wise beyond my years. The sun had gone behind the clouds and the air felt chilly. I shivered and pulled my shawl closer around my shoulders. One of the footmen approached us and said Doctor Potts sent his compliments and we could visit the patient now. My heart jumped just a little. It was now or never. Would I fail Amelia?

Chapter Six

The footman led the way back to the house and up the stairs to Robert's bedroom. My heart was pounding in the stupidest way. The breathless kind of pounding that constricts your chest and throat. For some silly reason I hoped I was looking my best; well, Amelia's best. Clementine paused on the threshold.

"Would you think me most dreadfully rude if I don't come in right now?" she whispered.

I stared at her, aghast. I'd be alone with a man I knew nothing about, a man who'd known his cousin all her life, if the details were right. A cousin whose place I'd taken.

Aargh!

"No, of course not," I lied. "Is anything wrong?"

She flashed me a radiant smile. "Not at all. It's just that I'm anxious to send my letter to Mama and Papa today. I know I'll feel so much happier once I've done that. I shall also write to Grandmama. I don't want her to be worried about me and thinking Mama has bullied me into being here."

She was so ingenuous that it had to be true.

"I shall see you later at nuncheon," she said, with a little wave of one dainty hand before sailing off in a cloud of pink frills and golden curls.

She pronounced it "noon-shine" and I had no idea what she meant. Maybe a sort of luncheon? Like brunch in Regency times. Clementine disappeared down the passage to, I assumed, her own room. I took a deep breath, composed myself, and entered Robert's bedroom. To my enormous relief, I wouldn't be alone with him. Doctor Potts was fiddling about with some medicine which he was pouring into a glass, and Parker was doing whatever mysterious duties valets do, which involved hovering in the background and looking busy.

Robert lay propped up in bed, wearing a dark blue dressing gown. He looked utterly terrible. His face was as white as a sheet, there were dark circles under his eyes, and he looked gaunt, exhausted, which was unsurprising after what he'd gone through, including my clumsy field hospital surgery. I couldn't help gasping.

He smiled, and my heart went *boing-boing* just a tiny bit. I got a grip on myself, willing my pulse to calm down. No falling in love with this man as myself. He was earmarked for Amelia. No hanky-panky of any kind, although from what I knew about Regency rules, an unmarried woman couldn't even be in the same room as a man without a chaperone. I'm sure it was different if they were related, though, even as distant cousins. Anyway, I had two, actually three, chaperones if you counted Russet, lying next to his beloved master. The dog gently wagged his tail when he saw me.

"Come in, come in, Miss Carstairs," Doctor Potts said in his hearty doctor tone. "His Grace isn't feeling all that up to snuff, but a few minutes will be fine."

He handed Robert the glass. "Drink that now, and let's have no more protests."

Robert swallowed the potion and grimaced. "I'm not sure if this'll kill or cure me."

The doctor ha-ha-ed and started packing away his medicine bag. "Very droll, Your Grace. Very droll indeed."

Robert looked at me and smiled again. "Dear Amelia, come closer."

He'd left off the cousin. Hmm, should I follow suit?

A chair materialised behind me, thanks to Parker. I sat down. Robert didn't look quite so haggard and ill when he smiled. His left arm was in a sling, but he reached out his right hand and took mine.

"Thanks to you, I'm alive," he said. "Now we're even."

Oh no, just what I was hoping wouldn't happen. Childhood memories, incidents from the past, things I couldn't possibly know about. When in doubt, agree. Maybe he'd let slip what it was later on. It sounded as if he'd saved me from some danger during childhood.

"Don't say that," I said, giving him my sweetest smile. "I'm just so relieved you're safe and being cared for." I meant it as well. He had to live for all our sakes. The future was depending on it.

He squeezed my hand feebly. Evidently, he was weaker than I'd thought. He closed his eyes and a flicker of something crossed his face. Was it pain? I hadn't noticed before, but his eyelashes were long, dark, and absolutely wasted on a man. He opened his eyes and stared at me. His gaze was so piercing I felt as if he looked right through me and found me out for the imposter that I was. But his next words dispelled that notion.

"I was so looking forward to seeing you again after all this time, and now here I am, laid up like an invalid. I can barely lift a finger to help myself."

I glanced up at the ever-vigilant valet. "You shouldn't be trying to do anything at all. That's what Parker is here for."

Parker gave a neat little bow. "Of course, miss. I keep

trying to tell His Grace the very same thing."

I gave Robert a mock serious look. "You see? I'm sure everyone will agree with me."

"There's so much to do, so much to arrange," he said feebly, sounding utterly frustrated. "The lower fields—"

The doctor butted in. "And you know very well, Your Grace, that Wallace and Simpkins have everything in hand." He glanced at me. "The estate manager and his assistant, both excellent, hard-working men."

It must have been difficult to smile and put on a brave face when Robert was in as much mental distress as physical pain.

"The sooner you heal, the sooner you can get back to those pressing estate concerns," I said, "and we can catch up on everything."

Did that sound too modern? I'd better watch myself.

The doctor bustled to the door. "I'll look in on you later, Your Grace. No trying to get out of bed again either." He gave me a meaningful stare. "Not too long chatting, Miss Carstairs. My patient needs his rest."

Phew, I could escape soon, although I loved the idea of sitting next to this handsome man, holding hands so romantically. Yet I couldn't avoid the nerve-wracking thought that, sooner or later, he'd be feeling better, and we'd be "catching up" on old times that I knew nothing about. I was going to blow it for Amelia, I just knew it.

"Be honest now," I said. "Were you trying to run away?"

He chuckled and then grimaced. "Anything to get out of this bed. I feel as if the walls are pressing in on me."

He was clearly no couch potato.

"I'll try to think of something to keep you entertained," I said. "In the meantime, you must rest." I stood. "I should go now and let you sleep."

Robert still held my hand, gripping my fingers just a tiny bit tighter. I felt like a teenager not wanting to leave her boyfriend. Just a few minutes longer holding hands, being with each other. I couldn't remember ever feeling that way about Allan.

My heart melted when Robert asked in a wistful tone, "You'll come back later? I mean soon. After dinner tonight?"

What else could I say except, "Of course I will."

Parker escorted me to the door. Suddenly, I noticed something I hadn't seen before, what with my anxiety about coming face to face with the man who thought I was Amelia. The bed curtains had been replaced! The fabric wasn't the same as the ones that had been burned last night, but it was very similar. How had Parker managed this? He stepped out into the passage with me. I glanced back. Robert's eyes were closed now, so maybe he was dozing. I looked at the valet and raised my eyebrows.

"Are you a magician, Parker?"

He gave a little smile, more a twitch of his lips. "Not really. There are many bedrooms in Chelston Hall, and some aren't occupied. It was a simple matter to ... er ... replace the damaged ones with another set of a similar fabric."

I had to laugh. "Very clever, very resourceful of you."

He gave that characteristic little bow like before. "Thank you, Miss Carstairs. I must put His Grace's safety first and no one has remarked upon it."

People are like that. They don't notice things. I was sure I'd said all the wrong things, been as stiff as a board while talking to Robert, but he didn't seem to notice anything different. Maybe he was feeling too dreadful. Maybe Amelia had been away so long that his memories had faded. She'd been fourteen and he twenty when they'd last seen each other.

She'd been just an impressionable teen, and now had grown up. People change. Hopefully he'd think that was it.

I had a vague idea of where my room was, so I headed there. Maisie was taking her new elevated position in the household very seriously because my room was impeccably neat, all the dressing table paraphernalia was tidy, the big bathtub had vanished, and a wooden box sat on the desk.

"Oh, miss," she said, appearing behind me. "I've set out yer portable writing case, and here's fresh ink from His Grace's study." She handed me a small bottle.

A portable writing case? How miraculous!

"Would ye like a cup of tea?"

I nodded, keen to rummage in the writing case and find out if Amelia had letters or something to give me a clue about her past connection with Chelston Hall. But I couldn't dig in too eagerly with Maisie there.

As casually as possible I said, "Yes, that would be lovely, Maisie. I'm quite parched after my walk in the garden with Miss Eccles."

A bit of a lie, but we did walk a little way, as far as the stone bench to be precise, and I did feel like a nice cuppa. Maisie disappeared, and I sat down at the desk. Opening the case revealed nifty compartments for writing paper and letters, a place for pens and an ink bottle, and even a little blob of sealing wax. But the jewel in this crown was a diary. Amelia's diary, and hopefully the repository of all her thoughts and emotions. I was saved. I longed to fling myself on the bed and dive right into it, but there was no flinging myself about in these clothes.

Perching primly on the chair, I held the diary closed in both hands, hesitating. Somehow it felt wrong to read it, as if I were prying into the secret, most intimate thoughts and opinions of a stranger. But was she really a stranger? However, being a distant two-hundred-year later relative hardly gave me the right to peep into her daily life. On the other hand, I was living her daily life right now and I needed to save the man she was going to marry, otherwise we might all be doomed. I needed to know her thoughts. Argument over. My heart thumping a tad, I opened the diary.

It was more of a journal, with the date written at the top of the page. Amelia's handwriting was quite simple, the loopy kind one learned at school before living in the computer age, which destroyed any ability to write anything legibly. As I studied it, the ghastly thought struck me. For as long as I was here in Amelia's place, I'd have to write up her journal. How else was she going to know what had happened? Hopefully, she'd think she'd had a bout of amnesia or some kind of memory loss. Of course, I was assuming now that we'd both get back to our respective time periods. Although it was quite enjoyable playing a cross between Cupid and Miss Marple, the thought of not returning home was rather depressing.

Maisie put a cup of tea down on the desk and slipped out of the room. The tea was just how I liked it, which was clearly just how Amelia liked it. A nice change to have a dainty cup and saucer and not a big thick mug like I had back in the flat. Sipping my tea, I read. It was probably a good idea to go backwards in chronological order, instead of just jumping around, to pick up on the details of the journey which they would be sure to ask me about and, of course, poor Aunt Harriet's ill health. Amelia was an excellent diarist. Her last entry was the night she arrived.

"... and it all seems so strange, yet so familiar being back at Chelston Hall. New faces, and yet some old familiar ones with Higgins bustling around as busily as I remember."

Higgins must be the butler I'd met yesterday. Mental note to make sure he knows I remember him.

"... although, sadly, I hear Mrs Crowdie has passed away and Mrs Barlow has taken her place."

Phew, one less person to worry about in the housekeeper.

"... just a brief hello to Cousin Robert and Cousin Rupert. Given the lateness of the hour of my arrival, I will see them tomorrow after their morning ride."

Aha, that was where I came in. We'd time slipped between her going for a walk and him going for a ride. Wait a minute. Rupert was meant to go riding with his brother. I cast my mind back, trying to recreate the moment when I'd walked into the drawing room. Rupert had been wearing riding gear, but I'd found Robert alone and injured. Rupert had blurted out how he was supposed to go riding with Robert but hadn't said why he didn't go. Had Rupert made an excuse to stay behind on some pretext, then snuck out after his brother and shot him? Yet again, I couldn't ignore his obvious distress when he'd learned about the incident.

I flipped back a page. The journey, she reported, was as bumpy and tedious as Clementine had suggested. I was safe there. There was mention of a chaperone. Of course, Amelia had to have a companion on the journey if she was travelling without her father. No young woman of any social standing would make such a trip without a female chaperone. This happened to be Miss Clutterbuck who played the church organ in the parish.

"... and although Papa and I were extremely grateful for Miss Clutterbuck's offer to accompany me on the journey, since she has a married sister in the area and was delighted to have the opportunity to visit this relative, I cannot imagine how her sister can endure the endless chatter. Miss Clutterbuck

is loquacious to a fault, and very soon I thought my head would burst from her commenting on every passing vehicle on the road, on the poor condition of the roads themselves, her suspicion of the sheets at the inns, and generally her jaundiced views on humanity and its iniquities. I bade her farewell with unrestrained relief."

Her dry wit made me smile. I liked Amelia already. It sounded as if she didn't suffer fools gladly. I turned back a page to find her previous entry was the night before they left. It might not have been convenient to write up her journal while on the road. This entry was telling, albeit a bit scattered, as if Amelia had been trying to convince herself of something. Maybe she was trying to cushion herself against a blow she might feel to have come all this way, only to discover they were both two very different people with two very different life paths ahead of them. But I could only speculate.

"... I can hardly express my own thoughts now that I am faced with meeting Cousin Robert again after so many years apart. I was a child when we came to live in Plymouth, and although he has been a sporadic correspondent, I can forgive his remissness, what with the years of war and the death of his father. He was not obliged to continue writing to a young cousin, anyway, given that once grown he would have heavy responsibilities to fulfil. What horrors he must have endured on the battlefield."

Years of war. The researcher in me jumped on this. I'm a research assistant, but since my dramatic break-up with Allan two months ago, I'd been unemployed. Hence my being able to pitch in and help Dad. Call me weird, but I actually prefer military history. Give me a good stonking battle with blood and guts and drama any day. Putting it all into context, European history was a bit of a mess with the rise of Napoleon and the Revolutionary Wars, which broke out after the French Revolution of 1789. The Napoleonic Wars lasted from about 1803, when Britain declared war on France in May, thus ending the Truce of Amiens, to 1815, when Napoleon was defeated at the Battle of Waterloo on 18 June 1815.

Just a bit of a timeline: Napoleon had been forced to abdicate in 1814, and was exiled on the island of Elba, from where he escaped in March 1815. So, given that this was April 1815, Napoleon was now rampaging around Europe, picking up support, and would be engaged in the Battle of Waterloo in around two months' time. Britain was still at war.

Amelia had said "years" which, to me, was a clear indication that poor Robert had been involved in horrific fighting for a long time. What could he have said to a sheltered young female relative who knew nothing of what soldiers endured in battle? Modern warfare is a lot more at arm's-length, what with drones, guided missiles, and the like. Back then it would truly have been a bloody affair. With modern-day soldiers coming back home suffering from PTSD, and with organisations at hand to help, what did the soldier of the 1800s do when he came back and had no one who could understand his mental state, except for comrades in arms who'd also survived. No wonder Robert hadn't written much. As the eldest son, he'd had to come home after the death of his father to run the estate and fulfil his ducal responsibilities. That was his duty, one he would have understood and accepted as his lot, being the eldest son and next in line of inheritance. Back to the journal.

"... *Did I adore him with a girlish admiration because I had no older brother to be my support? We were so close, so much time spent together. But I could hardly wait for some indication of his sentiments when we seemed to be worlds and years apart. I think he was surprised when I announced my engagement to Cedric Fishwick."*

What? I nearly dropped the journal. Who on earth was Cedric Fishwick? Another suitor? Damn and double damnation!

"... although he wrote a delightful letter of congratulations and even sent a beautiful set of crystal wine glasses. Perhaps his stepmama picked them out for him because I know men are not well versed in such things. Now that Cedric has passed, it would be appropriate to return the gift."

What a relief. Cedric had done the right thing by popping off just in time. Hopefully, no one would ask me how he died.

"... and his letter of condolence about Cedric was very well expressed. Papa was surprised but immensely pleased to receive this recent invitation from Cousin Robert. Papa would so have loved to officiate at His Grace's funeral, but Cousin Robert's stepmama had made her own plans. In his letter, Cousin Robert said it had not been convenient to invite us before, what with so many arrangements to be made regarding the estate and sorting out his father's papers, and the amount of work required to set things in order. But now it was perfectly convenient, things were running smoothly, and he was so looking forward to seeing us both."

He'd been back two years and had been busy sorting out the estate? That sounded like a bit of a stretch. More than likely Robert had felt uncomfortable inviting Amelia while she was engaged to Cedric. Perhaps he couldn't stomach the idea of her with another man. Or maybe it wasn't etiquette to invite a cherished cousin on a visit while she was engaged to someone else? Besides, with the old duke still alive, the stepmother had probably bossed the old boy around anyway and made sure he couldn't invite his longtime friend and cousin to visit. The last thing she'd want would be for Amelia to come back into

Robert's life, because if Robert had a soft spot for her, and if Cedric had already conveniently died, he might have proposed. Bang would go Rupert's chances of inheriting the title once an heir was on the way. It would have been easy for the dowager to make excuses as to why they couldn't entertain. But now Robert was the duke, he could invite whoever he pleased to stay and since Cedric had died, the field was clear for him to press his suit.

But a suspicion nagged at me that there was more to things than met the eye. Was the dowager truly capable of trying to bump Robert off so Rupert could succeed, being the next in line and his father's son? Robert had had the title for two years now. If the dowager was the would-be murderer, why had she waited this long? It was hard to imagine her doing the deed herself, of course not, but hiring someone else might be possible. Was my imagination running away with me? Probably. I could feel my brain painting itself into a corner.

Back to Amelia.

"... I wonder if I have changed so much in ten years, and if Cousin Robert has changed as well. Are we both so much altered? Writing a letter several times a year is not enough to maintain the bonds of youthful affection. I feel a sense of trepidation as to what to expect. Am I expecting too much? Did I ever really love Cedric? I question what I even know about love."

No, of course you didn't love Cedric. You said yes only because someone asked you to marry him. Even Jane Austen said something about how just because a man asks a woman to marry him is not a good enough reason to say yes.

"... It would have been so much easier with dearest Papa by my side. He is so at ease with everyone, I know he would have smoothed away any uncomfortable moments and *had everyone smiling and laughing at his silly jokes and anecdotes."*

Amelia's dad sounded just like mine. Poor old Dad. He was lying in a hospital, feeling as sick as a dog, and probably wondering why I hadn't come to visit him yet. But I had to focus on the here and now. I was here at Chelston Hall and my now was 1815.

I scanned the entry again. Please let her reveal how Robert had saved her. There it was. How convenient.

"... and how often I've wondered what would have happened if Cousin Robert had not been fishing downstream when I fell into the river and was swept away by the current."

He'd saved her from drowning. Good show. If he brought it up again, I'd ask him to tell me how he remembered it happened. It must have been important for them both to remember something that occurred when they were kids. Now just a little bit about the dowager and Rupert would be useful. I read further.

"... The dowager always seemed to me to be a cold, unfeeling woman, although clearly devoted to the duke when he was alive and to Rupert. Such a sweet, happy little boy. He was only ten when we left for Plymouth, but I remember him always being full of mischief and very affectionate towards his older brother. Cousin Robert doted on him too, which I thought was admirable, seeing as his new stepmother would naturally put her own child first."

Rupert was a sweet, happy little boy no more. Ten years later he seemed frustrated and angry about something. Resentment towards Robert? Resentment against his mother, who was possibly clinging to all that she had left? There was no mention of meeting the dowager on the evening Amelia had arrived—it was late, after all—nor at breakfast on the morning of the accident, and I hadn't seen her this morning. Hopefully, I could assume that she usually slept late, had her breakfast in her room and, in fact, apart from the brief encounter when I'd announced Robert's "accident," hadn't seen Amelia for ten years. Even then their acquaintance had been sparse, although she seemed to know a lot about Amelia going to Plymouth. I'd better watch myself.

I flipped back another page or two to scrape up some domestic details, for a start as to why Aunt Harriet was ill, and Amelia's dad had to stay behind. I found it.

"... and even though I told Papa that Aunt Harriet is as fit as a flea, and has nothing wrong with her at all, apart from not taking enough exercise and eating too many rich dishes, he says we should be guided by Doctor Parsloe and err on the side of caution. Aunt Harriet's Spasms seem very feigned to me and always manifest when he is planning to go away or is needed on a special occasion. Papa is so kind to her, but that is just his caring nature, and she is his last living sibling. She says time and again how she did not know what she would do without her younger brother as her mainstay."

Right, so Aunt Harriet is a chronic hypochondriac with too much time on her hands, and Amelia's dad is her younger brother who is chained to her side by feelings of guilt and family love. I flipped back another few pages, but the entries were mostly domestic details relating to the preparations for the journey to Chelston Hall. It seemed as if her emotions had only caught up with her on the eve of departure.

It wasn't as much as I'd hoped for, but it was enough to get by, fly by the seat of my pantalettes, so to speak. Cedric might be an issue, but I could always say in tearful tones, with a few heartrending sobs, that it was too difficult to speak of it. I was as prepared as I'd ever be. A nap seemed like a very good idea, and I wasn't hungry enough for any lunch, oops, I meant nuncheon, so I lay carefully on the bed so as not to crush my dress and went to sleep.

Chapter Seven

Maisie woke me with another cup of tea and the announcement that I'd slept all afternoon and dinner would be served at six, so I should get changed. Changed? Little did she know she was talking to someone who invariably had dinner in front of the television, clad in scruffy pyjamas and an ancient, faded dressing gown. Said repast was more often than not baked beans on toast, or a takeaway from the nearby Yellow Pagoda Chinese restaurant that delivered, or Marks and Spencer microwave macaroni cheese. Yum. The single girl's godsend and answer to not cooking. Allan never liked spending the night at my place, which is understandable, so I used to go to his arty, designer flat. He thought of himself as quite a gourmet cook, always whipping up culinary confections that Jamie Oliver would die to brand as his.

Through my sleep-bleary eyes, it soon became apparent that Maisie had not just ambitions, but truly grandiose career aspirations in the lady's maid/dresser department. My evening attire was already laid out for me. A gorgeous dress in a dark green silky material, and a gauzy overdress, for want of a better word, with a few diamante sequins sewn here and there. Again, not too many frills and furbelows as was Amelia's wont, but still very pretty. A pair of dainty slippers, a bit like ballet shoes, a pair of long gloves in a shade of ivory, and a gossamer evening stole to drape over my arms rounded off my ensemble. It was fortunate or perhaps fated that Amelia and I were exactly the same dress and shoe size.

Maisie beamed. "Will ye be happy wearing this, miss?"

She didn't know that I was the laziest person in the world when it came to choosing outfits and usually ended up wearing jeans, a T-shirt and jacket, with boots. This was like going to the Queen Charlotte's Ball, which is the event of the London season, the debutantes' ball. Since King George III introduced the Queen Charlotte's Ball in 1780 to celebrate his wife's birthday, Clementine must have gone to the one last year; the one she said was full of ancient suitors. It was a weird feeling.

"It's perfect, Maisie, just perfect."

The idea of wearing gloves was a little off-putting. How was one expected to wield cutlery? When in doubt, copy everyone else. I'd wait to see how Clementine handled it. A quick freshen up, thanks to Maisie bringing yet another bucket-sized pitcher of hot water, then shoehorning me into my finery, fixing my hair, and brandishing a pair of evening "ear bobs," which were very pretty pearl and diamond chip drops, and I was ready to battle the family *en masse*. The dress was rather low-cut for my liking and, with the corset pushing up my assets, I had more bust on display than I'd ever enjoyed before. Amazing that in those days one couldn't look at a woman's ankles, but her daring cleavage was fine.

Upon being assured again that I looked like a real picture, I sallied forth, and found my way down the grand staircase just as Higgins sounded the gong to assemble the guests. Clementine, Doctor Potts, three people I'd never seen before, and the Hadley family were clustered in the drawing room. For a brief moment upstairs, while being dressed, I'd had the silly idea that people couldn't possibly go to such sartorial lengths when having their evening meal. How wrong can someone from 2015 be about the customs of 1815? Very wrong.

For a start, Clementine looked utterly ravishing in a pale blue evening dress, even more elaborate than mine, and with loads of dainty little fabric tweaks, silky tassels, and just so much intricate work that one wanted to stand back to admire her like a dressmaker's dummy. No wonder poor Rupert was besotted. He had also made a huge effort with his appearance. He looked sternly handsome in a dark coat, with—believe it or not—cream satin knee breeches and white stockings. His shirt points were very starched, very high, and framed his face so that even Clementine would approve. His neck cloth was suitably complicated and must have taken hours to tie. Amazingly, he didn't look at all silly, just rather attractive in a BBC period drama kind of way.

Doctor Potts didn't fare so well and looked seriously uncomfortable in his getup. The old gent was there in his wheelchair, with a rug draped over his legs. He was nursing what looked like a glass of brandy. I longed for one to get me through this ordeal. Actually, any alcohol would have been welcome, but I had the feeling a clear head was needed to pull this evening off.

Clementine floated towards me and took my hand. "Oh, you do look charming, Amelia. I'm so glad you're here." She dropped her voice to a whisper. "My first dinner was very awkward."

"Rupert!" The dowager's voice boomed across the room. She was sitting on the same chaise longue as before. "Bring Amelia over to me. It's inconceivable that she's been here nearly three days now and I still haven't seen her properly."

She held out one gloved hand in an imperious gesture. One couldn't deny she was still what one would term a handsome woman and must have been striking in her youth, with dark eyes and hair, dressed in an elaborate style, relatively untouched by grey. It was hard to fathom how old she was, but if Rupert was twenty, she must have been in her late forties to early fifties.

Dressed in a navy-blue satin dress, with even more frills and furbelows than Clementine's outfit, she looked very regal, especially loaded down with all that jewellery. The diamonds in her bracelets dazzled, as did the very beautiful tiara on her head. Someone had money. Were they part of the "Hadley Hoard?" Just kidding. All these old families had tons of jewels locked up in their safes. One could starve to death because of no ready cash, but one would never ever, and on pain of death, sell the family jewellery. Rupert winked at me and offered his arm to escort me over the acres of expensive, possibly Aubusson, carpet to where the dowager held court. Remembering the number of times I'd watched BBC period dramas, I made her a little curtsey and took her hand.

"I'm very pleased to see you again, ma'am, after such a long time away."

I was taking a chance with a ma'am and not Your Grace, but Amelia was family, a cousin in a couple of times removed way, and Robert had dropped any formalities. But it was the right thing to say because she gave me a gracious inclination of the head and squeezed the tips of my fingers.

"Very pretty manners, and you've also vastly improved in looks over the years."

She patted the chaise lounge. "Come, sit next to me and tell me everything that has happened to you. I'm very sorry your poor father was unable to accompany you."

Thank heavens for Amelia's diary. At least I had something to say. I parroted the details of Aunt Harriet's spasms which elicited the comment "Ridiculous woman!" from the dowager, Doctor Parsloe's advice, which I made up, and the journey with the garrulous Miss Clutterbuck.

"I can't abide a chatterbox," she announced, and waved in the direction of a couple who were each perched on a tapestry-covered chair, smiling intently, and nodding eagerly at me.

"Let me introduce the vicar and Mrs Wilby. You may remember them. Then again, you were just a child, so you might not remember them. It was so long ago so possibly not."

I made some murmuring noises in agreement of not remembering because it was so long ago. It seemed that time and distance were to be my friends for as long as I was stuck in Amelia's place. They looked like a married couple, closely resembling Jack Spratt and his wife. The vicar was tall and thin, unfolding himself from the chair to bow to me. Neither of them appeared at all insulted that I didn't remember them, although they remembered me, I mean, Amelia. Mrs Wilby looked just like the actress Magda Szubanski who played Mrs Hoggett in *Babe*. She had a round, rosy-cheeked face and a short, stout body encased in pink satin, rather like a pink sausage. Her sandy hair was crimped into tight curls. No tiara for the vicar's wife, but she did have a pretty, feathered ornament perched in her ringlets.

She glowed when she spoke. "Please tell your dear papa that we have kept on the fruit orchards and the vegetable garden just as he left them."

At a loss for words, I smiled and nodded.

"Oh yes, and they continue to yield a fine bounty!" her husband added. With his grey hair, he looked quite a bit older than his wife. "Such a blessing."

My brain went into Amelia overdrive. Her father was a vicar; this guy must be the new vicar who took over the living when Amelia and her dad went to Plymouth. If the parsonage was nearby that would explain how Amelia spent so much time at Chelston Hall when she was younger. I couldn't really ask, though. As Amelia, I'd be expected to know.

"Papa will be very pleased to hear this," I said, "and he's so disappointed he was unable to accompany me."

Well, he would be pleased about the update since he'd left the new vicar and his wife with a thriving orchard and veggie garden. I'd better make a note of it when writing up Amelia's diary later.

They both gave solemn nods.

"The Lord makes His own plans," the vicar said in funereal tones.

I had to agree with that because here I was, chatting and about to have dinner two hundred years in the past, when it should have been Amelia in my stead. I'd be most eager to find out what His plans were in this matter. If only I'd known them in advance, but that's not how the Lord works in strange ways His wonders to perform.

The dowager interrupted our little tête-à-tête, to my huge relief. She tended to do this, as I was yet to learn over the coming days, but in fact it was quite useful. She also often took the liberty of telling someone what they thought or what they should be thinking.

She waved again. "Sidney, come over here and meet Miss Carstairs."

I rose, and my heart sank. What can only be described as an apparition came mincing towards me. Perhaps I exaggerated, but this guy was unbelievable. A fashion victim of the highest order, he made the singer Prince look dowdy.

"Sir Sidney Sidebottom, my nephew," she announced with a fond smile.

What a name. Sir Sidney Sidebottom. Like before, two hundred years into the future I would have chortled at it. It sounded like a character in the pantomime. But I'd learned my lesson. No laughing. Sidney was, well, let's say there's always one lurking at a party or propping up a bar. The guy that specialises in oily charm, cheesy pick-up lines, oozes his way across the dance floor, and who thinks he is truly God's gift to women. So smooth he could slide uphill, as Dad would say. The one that hits on anything with a bra and a pulse and thinks that "No!" is another word for foreplay.

Sidney couldn't have been much older than me, maybe he was twenty-six, with skinny arms and legs, and ginger hair combed into an elaborate style that clearly required much more hair to make it work. His coat was not like the sober hues sported by the other gents in the room; no, his was burgundy satin and his knee breeches were purple. His stockings had funny designs on them, the neck cloth looked as if miles of ruffles were involved, and his waistcoat was a riot of colour. Added to that, he had more rings on his fingers than Liberace, and an abundance of what could only be called trinkets hanging about his person, with fobs and seals attached by ribbons to his waistcoat.

He wasn't good looking, with a long face, pointy nose, and small brown eyes. He had a vaguely ferrety appearance, although I'd hate to insult ferrets, which are very clever creatures and make wonderful loving pets. I could have forgiven him anything, since we can't all have model looks, but when he took my hand and sort of "smooched" it, I was incredibly grateful for those long gloves.

"Charmed, I'm sure," he simpered. Then he had the cheek

to lift his quizzing glass, sort of a mini magnifying glass—one of the trinkets—and stare at me through it.

I gave the little curtsey bob, which I'd now perfected, while suppressing the wild impulse to punch him in the nose. Thank heavens for small mercies; Higgins sounded the dinner gong.

As we filed into the dining room, the dowager took the lead with Rupert giving her his arm, followed by the vicar and his missus. The idea of having Sidney touch my arm, even though I now saw the once despised gloves as haz-mat protection, was unbearable. Before Sidney could suggest it, the old gent zoomed up in his wheelchair at amazing speed. He seemed to get around quite quickly and didn't like having his manservant push him in the chair.

"Miss Carstairs?" he said by way of introduction. "Please allow me to escort you to dinner. I'm Sir Harold Lowestoft, Robert's great-uncle on his mother's side."

He said the last four words so pointedly that of course the dowager heard him.

"Pardon me, Sir Harold," she said in a throwaway tone, with just a brief backward glance over her shoulder. "I'd almost forgotten you were there."

Talk about being rude. The old gent trundled along beside me as we entered the dining room. Sidney was making small talk to Clementine behind us as he escorted her. Several footmen materialised to guide us to our places and draw out the chairs. The dining room was huge; it had to be to accommodate a long table that could easily have seated twenty to thirty people. It was straight out of a stately home brochure—more sideboards loaded with enough silver and crystal to start an antiques emporium, and numerous portraits and assorted paintings on the walls.

The table itself boasted place settings bristling with cutlery and glasses, and endless candelabras and table ornaments. It was quite daunting. What was the tip? Start from outside the place setting and work one's way inside with the silverware, or was it the other way around? Since I wasn't in the habit of hob-nobbing with the upper crust, my knowledge of dining etiquette was sadly lacking when it came to fancy dinners.

There were so few of us compared with the size of the table that we were seated clustered at one end. The dowager sat at the head, with Rupert on her right-hand side, and Clementine on her left. I was seated next to Rupert, with the ghastly Sidney next to me, and Mrs Wilby next to him. On the other side of Clementine sat Doctor Potts, Reverend Wilby, and Sir Harold.

There was a general fluttering of starched linen as napkins were unfolded. Clementine discreetly removed her gloves, as did Mrs Wilby, and they probably stuck them under the napkins. I followed suit. Dinner wasn't as daunting as I'd feared. The soup arrived in a huge tureen, and we began. From observing everyone else, I learned that the rule was to start from the outside and work inwards when it came to silverware. Nobody took any notice of me anyway. Everyone was too busy eating and, apart from a few comments, no one talked very much.

The food was actually delicious, not too rich in terms of sauces and dressings, but tasty. After the soup came fish, which the dowager informed us was caught fresh from the estate's own lake, then meat, which I didn't have, vegetables, which I did have, salad, and an assortment of cheese, fruit, nuts, and a creamy pudding plus a jelly. All throughout, Higgins and the footmen kept everyone's glasses topped up. As per my initial decision, I stuck to water. When impersonating someone it's best to keep a clear head in case any really uncomfortable questions are asked. I didn't know the family, but they knew Amelia and had a history and a relationship with her, details I'd have to learn very quickly if I was going to maintain my charade.

"I'm sure I speak for everyone here when I say what a capital meal," announced Doctor Potts as he set down his wine glass. "Just the way it should be. Fresh, wholesome food, without too many sauces."

Instead of being pleased at this compliment, the dowager put on a sour expression, pursing her lips. Although things looked really elaborate to me, apparently this was how the upper class lived when economising. From her face, one would have thought we'd just dined on crusts of stale bread and mouldy cheese, washed down by dirty river water. Once one has discovered the delights of microwave pot noodles, a dinner party with a real menu takes on a new meaning.

The dowager sighed. "Although Cook will be pleased to hear your praise, it galls me to serve such a simple repast to guests. Ever since his father died, Robert has enforced strict economies, quite out of keeping with the way we are used to living."

Rupert turned on his mother in a flash as he leaped to Robert's defence. He wasn't rude, but his tone was sharp.

"How can you say such a thing, Mama? First, there's no need for us to live like they did in olden times, wasting food and resources in a profligate manner. Second, Father almost plunged us into ruin by making foolish investments and bad decisions regarding the estate. If Robert hadn't come home when he did, Lord knows what might have happened to us."

Since Chelston Hall was flourishing two hundred years later, with guest houses, organic farming, retreats for artists, and parts of the historic stately home open to the paying public, Robert must have done a sterling job in pulling the estate up by its bootstraps. The silence, well, as the old saying goes, one could have cut it with a blunt butter knife. The dowager's stare was positively basilisk, giving the impression that this was not a new argument.

Rupert looked round the table at the open-mouthed guests who must have been shocked at this revelation of family squabbling. They looked appalled, sort of stunned at his outburst.

"My mother forgets that times have changed, and we must move on. My brother has put almost all his own money into improving the estate and the cottages, modernising the farming methods, and investing in his tenants."

That would explain the leaflets in the library advertising farm equipment and seeds.

"Very laudable," said the vicar hastily. "Excellent project. Investing in the future. Ensuring the family tradition continues strong."

Mrs Wilby twittered something incomprehensible in support of her husband's opinion. Clementine continued eating her dessert, pretending nothing had happened, as did Sir Sidney. Doctor Potts looked as if he wished he could swallow his words and Sir Harold just glared at the dowager.

Rupert warmed to his subject. "We're quite self-sufficient here at Chelston Hall. Everything we've eaten this evening was either produced or grown on the estate."

There was a general murmur of approval, everyone sounding a bit embarrassed, though, because it was very clear his mother wasn't too happy. The dowager rose and a footman drew back her chair.

"Ladies," she announced, arranging her evening shawl, "we shall retire to the drawing room and let the gentlemen enjoy their port and cigars."

The other women didn't put their gloves back on but just carried them, so I did the same. Once we ladies were settled in the drawing room, Higgins brought in the tea tray and the old bat poured it into cups, which Higgins then handed round. He was well trained because an imperious wave of one hand dismissed him. If I'd thought the dowager wanted the opportunity to grill me, far from it. She just wasn't interested in anything that didn't concern her welfare or comfort. Amelia was at the bottom of her list of priorities. The woman seemed to be preoccupied, as if she had things on her mind. Was I wrong to suspect her of attempted murder? If not Rupert, and not her, who could it be? Was it just a horrible accident after all? However, the nagging feeling it wasn't just an accident persisted.

Mrs Wilby crept closer to me on the sofa. She was such a sweet harmless thing that I could hardly dislike her. I couldn't place her age; it could have been anything between thirty and forty. She then revealed details of her two darlings, twins Jessica and Edward who, at six years old, sounded like the rudest, naughtiest brats on earth in dire need of a sound slap or two. I made all the right noises and duly admired two miniature portraits she retrieved from her large reticule, a kind of Regency era handbag.

"And has your dear father settled well into the parish?" she asked, as if ten years hadn't gone by.

"Oh yes," I replied enthusiastically. "Papa fitted in right away so very comfortably, and everyone deeply admires and respects him. They hold him in the highest esteem."

Not a lie. Judging from Amelia's diary, they sounded settled in Plymouth.

She nodded, the sandy curls bouncing up and down around her ears. "I'm sure they do. I only met him the once before we moved into the parsonage, but he seemed to me to be a most amiable, respectable man of God."

She looked at me with her head on one side like a bird, especially with those feathers bobbing in her hair ornament. "I felt very bad initially, almost as we were evicting you and your dear papa, but he assured us both it was something he felt strongly moved to do."

I smiled and just stared back, hoping she'd give me the answer.

She gave a little sigh and fiddled with the lace on one sleeve. "As my dear husband says, when the Lord calls one to minister in a certain place, one must obey. And we've been very happy here as well. Living so close to Chelston Hall enables us to walk just a short distance to partake of a fine dinner when Her Grace invites us."

At last, one detail. The parsonage was close enough for Amelia to have been playmates with Rupert at least, since she was only four years older than him. Also close enough to spend time with Robert and close enough to stay overnight as Maisie had implied when she told me the bedroom was the one Amelia had stayed in before. Apart from the Lord calling Amelia's dad to minister in Plymouth, what was the real reason they'd left? Had the dowager made it clear they weren't welcome? Amelia had said in her diary the woman was cold and unfeeling, but so far, she just came across as disinterested and self-centred. It was hard to make her out. Rupert was clearly her darling, but she had a beef with Robert over holding those purse strings so tightly. On the other hand, she'd had hysterics when she heard the news of him being attacked. She had me flummoxed.

"Do you still play the pianoforte, Amelia?" demanded the dowager. "I remember you were always so remiss about practising."

Inner sigh of relief. Thanks to our very own musical Gorgon Medusa at school, a Miss Cuthbertson, I was still quite proficient. Luckily, Amelia also played, or was it the other way around? Did I play because somewhere way back in the past Amelia's musical talents were in my genes?

"Yes, indeed I do still play, ma'am," I replied, wondering madly what pieces I knew by heart from this era. Beethoven, of course, Schubert, Liszt, Haydn. I could follow sheet music quite well although I hadn't played for a while.

"When the gentlemen return, Miss Eccles may favour us with a song, if you will play, Amelia?"

"Of course." Maybe I could just plonk my way through the piece while they all admired the dazzling Clementine.

Clementine seemed very pleased at the idea and immediately went to the pianoforte and began sorting through the sheet music on the top of the instrument. The silence hung heavily for a few minutes until the men returned. It was as if life came back into the room. The dowager had a very dampening effect on people. In the bustle of the men getting their tea and coffee poured, and carrying on their previous conversations, Clementine came over with some music.

"Will you be able to play this, Amelia?"

"I'm sure I can," I said, casting a quick glance over the notes.

It was a simple tune, a song about a soldier bidding his love farewell. Possibly I fluffed a few notes, but that didn't matter. Clementine made a gorgeous picture standing there and singing her heart out, quite simply expressing what the composer had intended. Her voice was very sweet. Rupert stared at her with such longing that it was clear, to me anyway, he was smitten and just tried to hide it. Clementine basked in the applause and went to sit next to the dowager, who patted her hand and said, "Very prettily done, my dear."

There was a bit of a marital scuffle between the vicar and Mrs Wilby, with some hissed whispers as he tried to persuade her to sing and she, blushing furiously, demurred.

"Oh, do sing for us, Mrs Wilby," said the dowager, sounding exasperated, and the matter was settled.

Mrs Wilby had come prepared, despite her protestations. It seemed as if blushful refusals were part of the whole lead-up to her singing. She extricated some music from that capacious reticule, clearly the forerunner of Mary Poppins' carpet bag, and handed it to me. It was a bit religious, something about seraphim and glory, but why not?

Mrs Wilby sang like the proverbial angel. I couldn't believe my ears as her incredible voice soared upwards. She would have had Simon Cowell foaming at the mouth to sign her up. I played on, very aware that her singing vastly outstripped my playing. At the end, to even more applause, she modestly refused to perform another song and went to sit next to her husband. Just shows how one can't judge a book by its cover.

The well-trained Higgins must have been waiting for some kind of invisible signal because he and two footmen appeared with a couple of small unfolding tables and packs of cards. I hate card games. I'm utterly useless, but since Scrabble and Monopoly hadn't been invented yet, I'd have to endure the evening. The dowager announced she'd be playing whist and rounded up the vicar and Mrs Wilby as her opponents, and Sidney as her partner. Rupert wasn't interested in playing so he just lounged against the mantelpiece, drinking his coffee, and casting surreptitious glances at Clementine, who studiously ignored him. Doctor Potts and Sir Harold got into a game of something that looked as if they made it up entirely but turned out to be piquet.

Clementine sat next to me on the sofa and, judging by her expression, she wasn't keen on card games either. We sat with our heads together, pretending to be engrossed in conversation. Once everyone was involved in their games, the dowager decided to discuss something I'd wondered about. Before and during dinner, she hadn't mentioned a word about Robert's accident. Now it seemed the time was right. Maybe a couple of glasses of wine at dinner had mellowed her mood.

"How does my stepson?" she called out to Doctor Potts.

He half turned in his chair. "Oh, very well indeed, Your Grace. He is making sterling progress. As I said before, luckily, it's just a flesh wound, which is healing nicely. I swear by basilicum powder to prevent infection. I was more worried about blood loss and him having taken a bad fall and hitting his head. He needs rest. However, I'm happy to say he can possibly get out of bed in a few days."

"A few days?" Rupert burst out. "Robert won't stay quietly in bed. You'll have to tie him to the bedpost."

"He's already tried to get up, but I told him he must rest," said the doctor. "If he doesn't, he'll only delay complete healing."

The dowager gave a lugubrious sigh. "I cannot express how this accident has cut me to the core." She ignored Sir Harold's snort, which sounded very much like one of disbelief. "Robert is like my own son to me. What would we have done if this event had been fatal?"

She fished a small lace-edged hanky from a sleeve and dabbed at her eyes, the picture of stepmotherly grief. Another expressive snort came from Sir Harold, but he kept his head down and scowled at his cards.

"And yet," she continued, "was it an accident? I'm convinced those wicked poachers are back and their efforts to strip the woods of food for their cooking pots have led to this. Who else would be roaming the place with a bow and arrows?"

"They'll have to do a lot of poaching to get anywhere near to stripping the woods, as you so eloquently put it," said Sir Harold.

He and the dowager exchanged dagger stares. If looks could kill .... No love lost there between them.

"Oh, Mama," said Rupert, sounding exasperated. "There are no poachers around and haven't been for ages."

"Well, the villagers then, the workers, the tenant farmers and their families, it could be any of those peasants." She gave a dismissive wave of one hand, relegating the lower classes to their rightful position in society, and turned back to her cards.

"But why would they do something so foolish?" asked the doctor. "Haven't they got permission from His Grace to take rabbits and small game within reason?"

"Exactly!" said Rupert. "No one with a grain of sense would upset a good arrangement."

"Humph," said his mother. "I don't think there's a grain of sense between the lot of them. They're jealous and resentful of their betters, that's what I think."

Sidney piped up and, although I didn't like his slimeball self a single bit, his words did spark the next fateful step that changed absolutely everything.

"I say," he drawled. "If Cousin Robert won't take too kindly to being bedridden, we'll have to think up some kind of amusement to keep him occupied. He's not used to being tied to the sick room. You know how Robert is. He's always doing things, always busy, always up and about. Makes me tired just watching him."

The most fantastic idea struck me. I'd already told Robert I'd think of something to entertain him. Now that the household was in a group, more information was coming out, and people were revealing themselves and their true opinions. Sir Harold and the dowager, on different sides, seemed to despise each other. Doctor Potts knew enough about the family to be aware of Robert's arrangement with his tenants. Sidney was something of an idiot, but he knew his cousin quite well, it seemed. The dowager disapproved of Robert's economising and his leniency towards his tenants.

What would get everyone together and keep them together, so I could do some sleuthing as to who was behind the attempted murder, plus encourage the relationship between Robert and Amelia so that they'd realise they were meant to be together? Maybe even fling Rupert and Clementine together, although that might be misconstrued as meddling. Fate might get annoyed if I messed up her plans for them.

There wasn't much to do to keep people occupied, interested, and together, given that movies, video games, television, the radio, mobile phones and assorted apps, and computers had yet to be invented. People had to make their own fun, so the men would obviously go hunting, riding, and get together to smoke and drink after dinner, with the women being left with the boring stuff like taking walks, sewing, reading, painting, and writing to people.

Of course, there were always dinner parties, and from what I remembered from my Regency reading and BBC Classic Drama viewing, charades and balls, but options were limited when it came to getting everyone together for a very good reason for an extended period. But everyone loved a show, and amateur theatricals would surely have been part of the fun. Even Jane Austen wrote about them in *Mansfield Park*, although that little episode had had dire consequences for one lady's reputation. With the dowager in attendance, however, that would never happen.

"We could do a play!" I announced. "That would cheer him up."

Everyone stared at me, wide eyed and open mouthed.

"What a good idea," said Sidney enthusiastically. "That'll be something novel. I think I saw a play once." He screwed up his face as if trying to remember. "Lots of singing and dancing in it, not so much of talking. Very pretty girls too if I remember correctly. Quite ... er ... scanty costumes."

It was obvious his idea of the theatre stretched only as far as the music hall. Sidney was clearly one of those social butterflies with limited powers of comprehension. But perhaps I was being too hard on him.

"A theatrical performance?" the dowager asked in such tones of disgust one would have thought I'd suggested dancing naked on the town hall steps. She shot her nephew a positively glacial stare. He simply grinned in a sheepish way.

"A play!" Clementine squeaked. Her eyes shone as if she'd just won a prize. "What a wonderful idea. Grandmama took me to a theatrical performance in Drury Lane last year and although I didn't really understand the story, it was so beautiful, and the actors were very good. When the heroine died, I cried and cried."

Definitely some kind of melodrama.

"Oh!" Mrs Wilby gasped. "The theatre!" She clasped her hands together. "I love the theatre. We went to the pantomime at Christmas, and it was remarkably entertaining."

The pantomime wasn't quite what I had in mind, although I didn't yet have anything concrete to offer.

The dowager turned a weird puce colour. She stared at me with her basilisk expression. "Are you suggesting staging a *pantomime*?"

Her tone intimated that this was even lower than a theatrical performance, really scraping the bottom of the entertainment barrel.

"No, of course not," I said, standing my ground, thanks to the enthusiasm of my fellow lesser mortals who were enraptured by the idea of any kind of live amusement.

"'The play's the thing wherein to catch the conscience of the king,' eh," said Sir Harold, sending me a very penetrating look.

"I wasn't thinking of doing *Hamlet*," I said, giving him back as pointed a glance.

The dowager still looked on the verge of having me hanged from the battlements when Doctor Potts intervened.

"A theatrical performance just among ourselves as friends and family would be considered quite respectable," he said smoothly. "Mrs Siddons is renowned for her thespian skill, and she too is considered very respectable. Very popular she was, although she's now retired."

The dowager hesitated. Technically she couldn't actually refuse permission, but with Robert in his sick bed and Rupert being underage for making any decisions, she could say no.

The doc clinched it with a huge dollop of flattery. "And naturally Your Grace's inestimable grasp of elegance, literature, culture, and the arts would make it a most worthy endeavour. A dramaturgical evening."

Was "dramaturgical" even a word? No matter, it had the right effect.

A tinge of pink appeared on her pale cheeks and the faintest of simpering smiles stretched her lips. The doc's bedside manner worked very well indeed!

"And what shall the play be about?" asked Mrs Wilby. She was so excited that her spouse began to look vaguely worried. He leaned over and tried to mutter to her, but she just pushed him aside.

"Shakespeare, of course," announced the dowager. "The only respectable pieces I am prepared to tolerate beneath this roof."

Since the bard tackled the worst as well as the best of human nature, it looked as if Her Grace hadn't actually read any of his plays. Clementine didn't quite pull a face, but her expression said it all.

"I was hoping for something more ... er ... romantic and exciting," she said.

I glanced at Rupert, who'd offered neither a yea nor a nay to the whole idea.

He shrugged as if he didn't care. "I'd never have thought of Robert liking a theatrical performance, but anything to occupy his mind."

"Perhaps *A Midsummer Night's Dream*?" Mrs Wilby suggested. She clasped her hands to her bosom this time. "With Oberon the fairy king and Titania the fairy queen!"

"Hardly suitable for this lot," said Sir Harold brusquely. "I have a feeling no one would want to play the part of a rude mechanical called Bottom."

The old man was certainly well read. Clementine giggled and Rupert gave a shout of laughter. His mother glared and Sidney looked anxious.

"I say, most definitely not," he said. "I don't think anyone would want to play a rude mechanical, whatever that is, called Bottom."

"Please stop saying that word!" said the dowager. She laid

one hand on her bosom. "It's not a word for polite company."

My plan seemed to be disintegrating, but then Sir Harold gave me the perfect opening.

"So, what is it to be?" barked Sir Harold. "Not *Coriolanus* or *King Lear*, I gather."

"*Romeo and Juliet* would be a good choice," I said, with as innocent an air as I could muster. "There are a few interesting character parts besides Romeo and Juliet, and there's action, a bit of sword fighting, the feud between the Montagues and the Capulets. It could be very exciting."

I remembered this play particularly because we'd done it as an amateur theatrical for the university drama society in first year. I didn't have a starring role although I wasn't quite the level of a rude mechanical. We'd had a great director though, a real hunk who'd somehow managed to extract very worthy performances out of us.

The dowager stared at me. "And who do you anticipate playing the main characters?"

"Rupert must play Romeo, of course, and Miss Eccles must play Juliet. They're perfect for those parts."

The dowager appeared to be torn, although no doubt pleased by the idea of her darling boy playing the lead. One hand fluttered to her lips as she considered this novel idea. "Well, I'm not sure … a romance … is it fitting, I wonder?"

Clementine flew over to the dowager's chair and sank to the floor in a susurration of pale blue satin. She was the perfect actress already. She glowed, she shone, and she played the part unwittingly.

"Oh, ma'am, it's a splendid idea. Such a charming play, it'll be so beautiful."

Since a few people end up dead in this piece, including the star-crossed lovers, her ignorance was a clear indication she hadn't read much Shakespeare either.

"You're not thinking of staging the whole play?" asked Doctor Potts.

"No, of course not," I said. "It would be far too long. I thought we could just choose the best scenes and have a narrator explain to the audience in between the scenes what has transpired to lead events to each point."

I added, "It'll be quite an educational exercise as well."

"Plus, it'll just be us," said Clementine, clasping the dowager's hand. "So please say yes."

But it's funny how word of mouth spreads. It wasn't going to be just us at all, not by a long shot.

Chapter Eight

The dowager mused on this idea for a few moments while we all waited in anticipation; some of us breathless, others not.

"Well," she said, "I think a small, select, discreet family gathering to put on a mild entertainment for the benefit of my stepson might be acceptable."

Clementine was in raptures. "Oh, ma'am," she breathed. "You are so good, so kind, so wonderful to say yes!" She looked around at us in delighted amazement.

"Will there be parts for us all?" asked Mrs Wilby, her expression a mixture of anxiety and anticipation.

Before I could answer, the vicar tried to intervene. He patted her arm in a condescending manner. If he were my husband, I would have slapped his hand away.

"Oh no, my dear, I don't think it would be fitting," he murmured. "Your position in the church, in the parish, in the—"

But the worm had turned. Irrevocably.

"You just don't want me to enjoy myself in this ... this ... venture," she snapped with the kind of wifely bitterness that does not bode well for when a couple goes home.

"My dear, I assure you—" he tried to expostulate, but she

mowed him down like a ten-ton truck.

"All I ask is that you do not stand in the way of my participating in a cultural event that would give me great pleasure." Her glare verged on dragonish while her feathered hair ornament waggled ominously.

"Of course not, my dear, but is there a part for you?"

It was a sensible question. He then looked at me, pleadingly. Since everyone else was staring quite gob-smacked at this interlude, it was clear Mrs Wilby had been the proverbial country mouse until the fateful mention of a performance. Something had snapped inside.

"I used to sing," she said, tossing her head defiantly. "In fact, I sang many times before I was married. My parents hired an Italian-trained opera singer to teach me. She said I was gifted, and it was a shame to waste my voice."

And here I was thinking she was nothing special. Again, it just shows never to judge by appearances.

Clementine came to the rescue in her radiant breathless way. "Really? And you have such a beautiful voice. You sing like an angel. Where did you sing?"

Mrs Wilby blushed. "Only at private functions, family gatherings, parties, that sort of thing, but I was very much in demand." She then glared even harder at her spouse. "Once we moved here, there was no opportunity, except singing in church on a Sunday."

The corners of her mouth turned down. The situation was as clear as day. Reverend Wilby didn't say anything. He just squirmed. It looked as if his wife had given up her talents for the sake of what was expected of a vicar's spouse.

Time for me to smooth some ruffled feathers. "I ... er ... don't know if this part will appeal, but we would need someone to play Juliet's nurse."

Mrs Wilby looked at me, her eyes wide with hope, joy etched on her face.

"It's a very respectable role," I added hastily for her husband's benefit, "and very important in the plot. Although there's no singing."

Mrs Wilby's face fell; she looked crushed. I couldn't ignore that disappointment. I also felt we shouldn't ignore her incredible voice.

"But we could put in a lovely, appropriate song at the end," I added.

Mrs Wilby smiled beatifically.

"Of course, you must play that part then, my dear," interjected the vicar. "If you feel confident—"

She stared at him, her eyes narrowed, daring him to take that one fatal step further into marital oblivion.

"Confident that you will ... enjoy the part," he added hastily. "That's what I meant to say."

Mrs Wilby gave a deep, satisfied sigh. "Thank you, Miss Carstairs," she said. "I'm truly grateful. I've so longed for some avenue to express my creative talents. I shall look for an appropriate song."

"Now that's finally settled," said the dowager with a slight edge of sarcasm. "I'm sure we need other characters."

She glanced at me; her eyebrows raised.

"Yes, we need Mercutio, Romeo's friend, and then we need Tybalt, Juliet's cousin," I said, madly wondering if we could pull this off with such a tiny cast.

"I say," Sidney announced. "I could play one of the male parts. Either of those would do very well for me."

"You'd need to be able to wield a sword because both get killed in a sword fight," I said.

Rupert burst out laughing. "Not Sidney! He's afraid of his

own shadow. He's been like that all his life."

Sidney went red, either from embarrassment or anger. "I am *not* afraid of my own shadow. Don't talk utter nonsense about me, Rupert. I'm not like you, always leaping about and doing dangerous feats. I'm just not an aggressive fellow. I don't like swords, or knives, or any kind of weapons. Nor blood. I positively hate the sight of blood. It makes me feel quite queasy."

That was very useful to know. So, it hadn't been Sidney who'd shot the near-fatal arrow at Robert, although he might have paid someone to do it for him.

Rupert gave a derisive snort. "Of course, you do."

The dowager pinched her lips together. Not a good sign.

"It seems, Miss Carstairs, that your idea for entertainment is having a very divisive effect on this gathering." Her tone was acid as she looked down her nose at me.

"Not at all," I said gamely. "In fact, I have the perfect role for Sir Sidney, a very essential one."

He perked up. "Really? What is it?"

"As I mentioned before, the play is long and there are too many characters for us to fill those parts, so the narrator will explain what has happened in between."

He stared at me hopefully. "And is this an important role?"

"Oh yes," I said. "It's very important. The narrator will keep the story intact for the audience, and he'll explain the whys and the wherefores of everything."

"That sounds wonderful, Sidney," said the dowager to her pet. "And of course, you'll easily be able to learn the words."

His eyes widened. "I-I think so. It depends on how many words there'll be to learn."

The dowager announced in a smug tone, "Sidney always recited his poems from school so beautifully. He'll be perfect for the role. I have complete faith in his talents."

"Who else do we need?" asked Clementine.

"We need a Friar Laurence, also an important role," I said, looking at Doctor Potts. "If you would be so kind, sir?"

He chuckled. "I'm sure I fit the part already. Of course, anything to help."

Sir Harold spoke up. "There's nothing for an old man in a chair, I suppose?"

"But there is," I replied, pleased I'd already thought of this. "We'll need someone to prompt lines, make sure that everything is fine backstage, see that any props don't go missing, that sort of thing."

He looked delighted. "It would be my pleasure."

"And who will direct this venture?" asked the dowager. Her tone was faintly sarcastic.

With one accord, everyone looked at me.

"Miss Carstairs, of course," said Clementine, giving me a little round of applause. "After all it was her excellent notion." She glanced at Sidney. "Not forgetting Sir Sidney's original clever idea of an amusement, though."

If Sidney could have preened himself, he would have done. He reddened and mumbled his thanks.

"And what experience do you have, Amelia, to perform this task?" asked the dowager in her familiar cross-examining style.

Lies, lies, lies again. It was shocking how easily they tripped off my tongue. It was even more shocking how easily I thought of them, making up Amelia's false backstory as we went along.

"We have a small ladies' group in the parish where we get together and exchange views on books, read aloud passages, sometimes have poetry recitals, that sort of thing."

The nearest I've ever got to a book club was having my

monthly meet-up with old varsity friends where we drank loads of cheap wine, ate pizza, moaned about our boyfriends, and sometimes talked about books. More like Bridget Jones and her buddies than Oprah's book club. As for directing a play myself, the nearest I'd ever come to the director's chair was doing *The Pirates of Penzance* at school where I played the pirate king as well. But this would hardly be the Royal Shakespeare Company level, so how difficult could it be? I just had to make sure everyone knew their lines and didn't bump into the furniture.

My blatant untruth met with the dragon's approval.

"Well, that's all settled then, apart from the two characters that have to be killed off," said the dowager.

"How about Johnson and Peters?" said Rupert.

The dowager frowned. "The footmen?" Again, she sounded as if we were dragging the sewers for the scum of society to participate.

Rupert shrugged. "Why not? They are available, tall, well built, and if there's sword fighting involved, I'm sure they'll be keen to learn."

"Humph," said his mother. "The servants will get ideas above their station. We can't have that happening."

"No, they won't," he said irritably. "We'll need them anyway to change scenery, run about, and do things. It'll be fine. I'll take charge of them."

The dowager could hardly back down now that permission had been given, so she subsided.

"Won't we need extra copies of the play?" asked Clementine.

"There must be a copy of Shakespeare's collected works in the library," said Rupert. "It's the kind of thing Father would have."

"I have a copy," volunteered Sir Harold.

"I'm sure we must have a copy in the library at home," Mrs Wilby said to her husband, who murmured something about perhaps that might be so.

She smiled at me. "Your dear papa left so many books behind and I'm sure there's a copy somewhere among all those volumes. He said he didn't need to take all his books although I did press him to remove his favourites."

"We'll need a copy for everyone, including one for me, and remembering Sir Harold already has his own, so that's ... eight, let's say nine for good measure," I said.

"I'll send a note over to Lady Hamilton who lives on the next estate. Her husband has a huge library. They must have a copy," the dowager said very graciously. "I also have a number of very literary minded friends who would be delighted, I'm sure, to lend their copies for a good cause."

"What about costumes?" asked Clementine. "What will we wear?"

Sidney, ever fashion conscious, butted in. "I say, as the narrator I should wear black, something sombre to create a suitable atmosphere. I have the perfect opera cloak to wear. Black with a red silk lining."

Clementine frowned. "Yes, but you must make your character the picture of elegance, Sir Sidney, and not wear so many fobs and seals. You want to impress the audience with your eloquence and delivery of your lines. All that stuff—" she waved at his array of ornaments "—will be too distracting."

He looked crushed. "Oh, do you think so?"

"Definitely," Clementine said innocently. "In my opinion, it's a gentleman's bearing and presentation that should impress. I'm sure you can do it."

Rupert added, "There are a few boxes of old costumes and things we used to dig in when Robert and I were younger and played dressing-up games. They're in the attic. We were knights of the realm and Amelia was the damsel in distress who had to be rescued from a fire-breathing dragon."

He smiled at me. "You must remember that, don't you, Amelia?"

My heart sank. Just when I thought I was safe about Robert saving Amelia from drowning. The dowager rescued me unexpectedly.

"Rupert, if by that you mean the day you and Robert made a tent out of the very precious brocade I'd set aside for curtaining!"

He laughed. "Mama, you told us very specifically to go and play upstairs in the attic because it was raining, and we were being a nuisance."

She sighed, but the memory must have sparked some pleasure because then she smiled. "The things you remember. Anyway, I'm sure we all have enough to think about. I'll write a little note for Lady Hamilton, Rupert, and you can take it over tomorrow and refresh Amelia's memory of the place."

With that, the dinner party broke up. Rupert obligingly wheeled Sir Harold out to where his brawny manservant was waiting to carry him upstairs. Mrs Wilby said breathless goodbyes mingled with thanks for including her, although her husband still looked a bit glum about the idea. Clementine danced off to her room, the dowager sailed off to her quarters, and I was left with Doctor Potts.

He crooked his arm for me to slip my hand through, which I did.

"I'm sure you'll want to say good night to His Grace, and I must have a final look at my patient before I leave, so, shall we?"

He escorted me upstairs and we proceeded to Robert's

room where an unbelievable sight greeted us. Robert lay on the floor, groaning, while Parker tried valiantly to lift him which, as I knew from the night of the fire, is a two-person job. The dog bounding about didn't help either. Doctor Potts leaped to help the valet and together they managed to heave Robert back into bed. Russet jumped onto the bed and lay close to Robert. His face was white and sweat beaded his forehead. He must have been in such pain. While the doctor checked Robert's bandages, Parker wiped his brow with a cloth.

"I'm not a child, damnation. I can help myself," he fumed, pushing the valet's hand away although it was clear he didn't have the strength to even stand.

He looked up and saw me there. "Amelia, I thought you weren't coming!"

"I hope you didn't attempt to get out of bed to fetch me," I said, trying to inject a light tone into my voice. "And I did promise I'd come to say good night."

"There now, Your Grace, safe and sound back in bed," said Doctor Potts in his cajoling doctor to patient voice. "You won't mend if you keep trying to get up too soon. As well as the flesh wound in your shoulder and blood loss, you took a nasty fall and have sustained a lot of bruising. Not to mention you were unconscious for a good few hours yesterday. The body needs rest to heal properly."

Robert had a mutinous look that did not bode well for the doctor's orders. This was Amelia's moment. I sat on the bed next to Robert, reached over and stroked Russet's head as if this abnormal scenario was the most natural thing in the world.

"And at dinner we all came up with a wonderful idea to amuse you while you're recuperating."

"Now, Miss Carstairs, actually it was your idea," said the

doctor while he took Robert's pulse. He looked very doctorly.

Robert smiled; he seemed calmer now. "Plotting, eh? And what might that idea be?"

"We're going to put on a theatrical production. One of Shakespeare's plays."

Robert frowned. "My stepmother would never allow anything like that," he said bluntly.

"Actually, Her Grace proved to be quite enthusiastic once we'd persuaded her that it would be the height of elegance and style to do such a thing," said the doctor dryly.

"Aha! Flattered her into saying yes, did you?" Robert laughed, flinching as he did so.

I smiled. "She could hardly say no with everyone being so eager to help entertain you."

"And what's the play to be?" he asked.

"*Romeo and Juliet.* It's the best one for the cast members available. Rupert is to play Romeo and Miss Eccles is to play Juliet."

He looked flabbergasted. "My stepmother said yes to that?"

I nodded. "I think it's hard to refuse when your beautiful young female guest is offered the part of the leading lady, and your handsome son is offered the part of the leading man."

Robert still looked incredulous. "And Rupert agreed? That's really not his idea of enjoyment."

"He said yes. Anything to keep you amused while recuperating," I said lightly. "Mrs Wilby is to play the Nurse, and Doctor Potts is to play Friar Laurence."

I looked around for the doctor, but he had discreetly absented himself. Parker had also disappeared, but a few sounds like the opening and closing of drawers in the dressing room were evidence he was being the chaperone, albeit an absent one.

"Even Sir Sidney is to play a part."

Robert rolled his eyes and snorted. "Sidney? Thankfully not my cousin by blood. An annoying fellow, albeit generally harmless. Nothing but a fribble."

"I gather you mean his ... er ... penchant for fashion?"

He chuckled with a slight wince. "If you will be so kind. And what part could Sidney possibly play? He's a complete featherhead if ever there was one. I doubt he can remember one line of an entire play."

"No, it's not the whole play of course, just a few scenes. Sir Sidney is to be the narrator and I'll write his lines so that he can tell the audience what's going on between scenes."

I smiled. "However, I think we'll have to talk him out of wearing his black opera cloak with a red silk lining. And even Sir Harold has a part. He is to be stage manager and prompt."

He reached for my hand and clasped it. "And have you cast a magical spell on the whole company to get them to do your bidding?"

On any other occasion I would have died of joy to have this absolute hunk holding my hand and gazing soulfully into my eyes, but Amelia, I had to remember Amelia. I was doing this for her. Yanking my hand away would give him the impression she wasn't interested, but I'd have to keep things within reason.

"Everyone is very keen and tomorrow we're going to search various libraries and get copies."

He frowned. "And what am I to do while everyone is rehearsing and learning their lines?"

"If you promise to obey the doctor's orders," I said, "I'm sure Doctor Potts will allow you to get up by tomorrow afternoon and sit quietly somewhere and observe. And I'll need your help anyway."

He raised his eyebrows. "In my state?"

"We need to find a suitable room to put on this performance, and then some clever person has to work out how we go from one setting to another without breaking the magicality of the piece."

He looked thoughtful. "Hmm, the ballroom would be best because there's a small ante room off one end where the actors could dress and use for entrances. The estate carpenters could knock up a stage, and with a few essentials one could create the ambiance for different settings."

I squeezed his hand. "See? You're very useful to this project, and it's all for your benefit too."

Maybe I shouldn't have done that. He looked at me with such warmth that I almost pulled my hand from his. Coupled with that was the fact that I was suddenly having trouble breathing. His gaze had a way of sending delicious thrills up and down my body in a way that I hadn't felt for a very long time.

"You truly have cast a magical spell. And Romeo and Juliet themselves? How will they fare?"

"As I said, Rupert is happy to go along with my scheme to entertain you, so he doesn't mind learning some lines. Miss Eccles is in transports of delight. This is the most exciting thing that's happened to her. I don't think she was enjoying her visit here before this."

"Poor Miss Eccles," he said, shaking his head. "She has a dreadfully managing mother determined to marry her off to the highest bidder. I hope she hasn't formed a *tendre* for me, although I knew well in advance what her mother was up to by sending her here for a visit."

"Oh, don't worry. You're perfectly safe. Miss Eccles confided to me that although you are a true gentleman and ever so pleasant and amiable, she has no romantic interest in you at all and thinks you're far too old for her."

He tried not to laugh. "I shall appear suitably crushed by her rejection, but that's a relief. I can bravely bear the burden."

I couldn't help blurting out my next words. "It's a pity so many young women feel pressured into marrying men they don't love, just to please their parents, or because they need financial security."

He gripped my hand hard. "But you don't feel like that, do you? After all, there's no need for you to feel you have to ... er ... marry someone for security."

He obviously meant Cedric Fishwick.

"You're safe here. You're with family," he said softly.

Now that was really stretching it, given that Amelia's father and his father were second cousins once removed. Did I say so to him? Of course not. Amelia and Robert had to fall in love and get married.

"And I feel so secure knowing this," I said demurely.

He raised my hand to his lips and held it there. I could have drowned in his gaze. My heart gave a little *pitter patter* which meant it was time to go. I rose, gently sliding my fingers out of his grasp.

"I'll say good night now, Robert. Tomorrow we'll have lots to do getting this play arranged."

"Until tomorrow," he said. "A question before you go."

I raised one eyebrow. "And that is?"

He smiled. "Isn't *A Midsummer Night's Dream* usually more popular?"

Wagging one finger cheekily at him, I said, "But as Sir Harold pointed out, no one would want to play the part of a character called Bottom, who is a rude mechanical to boot."

He laughed and winced with pain at the same time.

"Doesn't anyone know that *Romeo and Juliet* is a sad play? The main characters die tragically."

"But they die tragically of *love*, and that's what counts."

As I closed the door gently behind me, I could still hear him chuckling.

Maisie was waiting for me back in my room, yawning and looking sleepy.

"Maisie!" I said, half crossly. "Why are you still up? You should be in bed."

Her shocked expression spoke volumes. "But it's my job to help ye undress and put ye to bed, miss."

This was the way things were done, and since I could hardly wrestle my way out of my evening finery on my own, I said nothing. Once undressed and in my nightgown, I sent her off to bed. I was dying to jump into bed, but there was Amelia's diary to write up. Slipping in a bit about feeling more for Robert than before was easy. He aroused sensations in me that I hadn't felt for so long, like a delicious, breathless, heart-pounding giddiness. Since I didn't know him as a person, it must have been infatuation, but it was wonderfully romantic. I was writing down my own feelings as well and assuming Amelia would feel the same way in meeting Robert after ten years apart. Besides, someone had to get the romance ball rolling. How would she react once this was all over, and we were both back in our respective time periods? Would we even get back there? There was no way of knowing except to cling to what I did know about the future: it was where I belonged.

Chapter Nine

Thursday, 27 April 1815

The next morning, after ablutions and breakfast, Rupert informed me he had a note from his mother for Lady Hamilton and the gig was waiting. It turned out that Doctor Potts was with the dowager. Clementine had commandeered the sole copy of Shakespeare's collected works from the library. Sidney was researching fabrics and costumes with the help of a book called *Costumes Through the Ages*, also found in the library. Sir Harold, who had his own copy, was busy reading the play as well in his room. There was nothing for me to do but accompany Rupert since we all needed our own copies. It was doubtful that Lady Hamilton's husband had several copies lurking in his library, but this was an excellent opportunity to spy out how things lay with Rupert.

I also reminded myself that my primary mission here in 1815 was not to put on a play, but to prevent another attempt on Robert's life. In a quick mental review, Robert was on very good terms with his tenant farmers, so it was unlikely to be them; after all, why destroy a good relationship with a kind and fair landlord. Last night, Sidney had demonstrated that he was hardly the epitome of a hardened killer, given his abhorrence of blood. He'd blanched at the idea of a pretend sword fight in a play, so he definitely was not up to wielding a bow and arrow in real life. He also wouldn't want to damage his expensive clothes by skulking in the bushes. Him paying an assassin to do the dirty work also seemed to be beyond his dilettante frame of mind.

Rupert had mostly convinced me he wasn't the culprit by his devotion to his brother. Was it the dowager? So far, she was being very co-operative about this play for Robert's amusement, even seemingly against what she would normally do, which was to say no. Would Doctor Potts kill for her? From what I could see, he was a jolly Friar Tuck type and, besides, what would he gain? He was more the Hippocratic Oath doctor one expects, not a Machiavellian figure by any stretch of the imagination.

There wasn't much time for introspection because the gig, despite its cute name, was very uncomfortable. It was a two-wheeled vehicle pulled by a single horse called Dolly. Even with the cushion Rupert offered, it felt like being in an old car with no shock absorbers. My ancient Mini was more comfortable. Rupert didn't seem to notice as we clip-clopped along at Dolly's distinctly sedate pace, so I grinned and bore it. To my huge relief, he stopped every now and then to point out things that Robert had built, improved upon, or renovated.

Today I felt almost overdressed, with a shawl draped over my shoulders, short gloves—a new experience for me—and the Hated Bonnet. It was quite hard to look around wearing the stupid bonnet that Maisie had picked out for me. It was very pretty, made of straw with silk flowers around the brim, and ribbons that tied under my chin, but think horse blinkers. To look at anything, I had to stare in one direction; this style of bonnet did not allow for peripheral vision. She'd tried to push a parasol into my hand, but I put my foot down and said no.

"As I said last night, my father let things go rather badly," he confided, "so by the time he died the estate was in a parlous condition."

"What about the estate managers?" I asked. "Doctor Potts mentioned them last night."

Rupert nodded. "Excellent men who know their jobs, but my father wouldn't listen to them. I think he was losing his mind as he got older. He would make foolish decisions and do erratic things. He put money into investment schemes that fell apart. Robert had a huge task on his hands when our father died. It was quite a shock when the full extent of the debts and mismanagement was revealed."

"But he's succeeded?"

"Only just," he said. "Robert sank all his money from his mother's inheritance into refurbishing the place, reviving pastures that had fallen into disuse, and lots of other things. My mother has forgotten that without Robert watching the purse strings, there wouldn't be anything left."

His expression turned grim. "That's why I get annoyed when my mother criticises his decisions. He's done all this for the sake of the family, the estate, and the future."

Naturally, I couldn't tell him that Robert had done a fantastic job because two hundred years later the place was still going and, if the brochure was anything to go by, was doing well.

"And I'm sure he's created a solid foundation for future heirs," I said.

Then he asked the kind of question I didn't want to answer ... because of course I didn't have an answer, not a truthful one anyway.

"Have I changed since we last met?" he asked. "Have I

changed in the past ten years?"

It seemed as if there was a reason he had changed from the cheerful little boy Amelia remembered, and he just wanted to tell someone.

"Well," I began, just repeating what Amelia had already said in her diary, "you were only a young boy, but I always thought you were such a happy child. What has changed you?"

"I have no freedom," he burst out passionately. "My father wouldn't hear of me joining the army and going off to fight like Robert. He said if we both died, who would inherit, and someone must inherit the title and the estate so that the direct line continues. And even when Father died, and Robert came back, my mother wouldn't let me join the militia. I'd be based in England with very little likelihood of actually fighting in the war and seeing any action, but I'd be doing something, anything better than kicking my heels here."

His expression was a mixture of sad and sulky. "With Napoleon back in France, war is inevitable again. And here I am, forced to cower behind my mother's skirts. I can't do anything yet without her saying yes."

With Napoleon busy raising an army in France, I could see how galling it was for Rupert to be denied something as exciting as the threat of foreign invasion. Well, exciting to someone who'd never actually been in the thick of battle. He just wanted his freedom to make his own choices.

"That's sensible," I ventured.

"Sensible? But what about me? What about what I want? I don't want the title and the burden of keeping up this place. Robert was born to it. It's his. I've been learning to manage the estate for when I have a place of my own, but that's not yet. Not for a long time. This is now."

It was a plaintive cry from the heart for a life of his own.

"What does Robert say?"

He sighed and flapped the reins. "What can he say? He's my half-brother, and although he's the head of the family, he cannot countermand my mother's wishes for me, even if he didn't agree with her, which he does. I couldn't believe that Robert sided with Mama, saying he wouldn't condone any young man being sent off to become cannon fodder."

"If you had the chance to do anything you like, what would you do?" I asked.

"Travel," he said promptly. "Visit Europe, India, the Americas. Just to see a different life. Just to go somewhere new and interesting. I feel trapped here."

"And would you want to come back?"

He laughed. "Of course, I would." He made a sweeping gesture with one arm. "This is my home, but I want to see what's out there first."

Poor Rupert, he was just like any other young man desperate to spread his wings. He and Clementine, interestingly, wanted to do the same things.

He drew the reins as we arrived at Hamilton House. Although not as grand as Chelston Hall, it was still quite a pile. A groom hurried up to us and, once we'd alighted, he led Dolly off to the stables, no doubt for some horsey nosh. An ancient looking butler answered the door and bowed us into the drawing room. Lady Hamilton appeared, with two teenage girls in tow.

"My dear Lord Rupert," she twittered as she glided towards us in a flurry of gauzy trailing scarves. "How absolutely lovely to see you. And how is your dear mother?'

Lady Hamilton looked rather like a bird of paradise. She was a fading blonde, maybe late thirties to early forties, but still pretty. Her slightly chubby teenage daughters closely resembled their mother, although both had quite a few freckles. I remembered that was considered a huge no-no in Regency days.

"Mama is very well, thank you. I'd like to introduce my cousin, Miss Amelia Carstairs," he said, bowing to her. "And this letter is from my mother."

I did the little curtsey bob and said how pleased I was to meet her. The two girls, introduced as Caroline and Henrietta, also bobbed their curtsies, staring wide-eyed at Rupert who ignored them. Teenage girls, handsome young lord ... adoration was inevitable.

"Do sit, please," Lady Hamilton said as she pointed to the sofa. "Smithers will bring tea directly."

Smithers tottered off. Tea might be a long time coming judging by his pace. Rupert did not sit but made his way to the fireplace and leaned against the mantelpiece. This seemed to be his favoured spot. I took off my bonnet and laid it next to me. Perhaps I could leave it behind by accident on purpose, although Maisie would be annoyed. She took an almost jealous pride in Amelia's wardrobe. I had no idea how Amelia's dresses were cleaned, or how her undies were washed. All I knew was that Maisie took the laundry away and it then reappeared beautifully washed and pressed. I felt a bit guilty but who was I to cheat her out of a job and her lofty career ambitions?

Having sashayed her way to a large chair, Lady Hamilton unfolded the letter, read through it, and cried out, "A play? How wonderful. Girls, listen to this. Her Grace is putting on a small production of *Romeo and Juliet*, with the help of Miss Carstairs, just something informal and discreet for the family and friends."

Lady Hamilton didn't mention Robert's accident so maybe the dowager wanted to play down that as the reason for even agreeing to it.

She looked at her offspring, who'd squashed themselves into a love seat, and cooed, "And what do you think? She's asking if we have any copies of Shakespeare in the library and we are invited to attend the performance."

Lady Hamilton was a master in the art of hand flapping to convey her thoughts and emotions. She favoured us with a display of clasping her hands to her bosom and rolling her eyes heavenwards. "Her Grace is so cultured, so *distinguée* in her tastes. What a treat for us all."

Henrietta, who looked a bit older than her sister, burst out, "Have you filled all the parts already? Is there possibly a tiny part for me?"

"You!" exclaimed her sister in disgust. "What about a part for me?"

Lady Hamilton cast an imploring glance at me. "Would it be possible to find two very small places in the play where my girls could take part? They so love the theatre and cultural activities."

As I said, so much for it just being us.

She added, "I think we have a volume of Shakespeare's collected works in the library. My husband is very literary minded. He's always reading something, always with his nose in a book."

"*Romeo and Juliet* is by far the most wonderful, romantic play," Henrietta gushed. "Please say yes and we can be in it, or me at least."

Caroline scowled and elbowed her sister. "Why you? Why not me?"

"Because I'm older than you," Henrietta retorted, pulling an ugly face at her rival.

"Girls," Lady Hamilton said feebly. "Don't argue, not in

front of the guests, please."

They both ignored her, intent on winning the battle of the glares. Smithers interrupted this sibling rivalry by reappearing with a huge tray laden with a big teapot and crockery. He placed it on a low table, bowed to her ladyship, and tottered out again. Lady Hamilton began pouring the tea, all the while regaling us with an account of an exceptional performance of *The Merry Wives of Windsor*, unfortunately ruined for her by the man in the next box's persistent snoring.

"And would you believe it, Miss Carstairs?" she said, holding out a cup and saucer for me to take. "His wife never did a thing to stop the noise. She could have nudged him at least to wake him up."

I put on my Very Interested Expression and murmured something about how inconsiderate people could be, especially at the theatre. Our hostess poured tea for Rupert, the girls, and herself. Henrietta and Caroline made short work of the biscuits and small pastries that Smithers had thoughtfully provided. Lady Hamilton gazed fondly upon her clearly over-indulged offspring gobbling down the goodies, and then turned that big-eyed spaniel look on me.

"So, what do you think, my dear Miss Carstairs? Just a tiny part for my two angels?"

Their mouths full, the two angels stared at me with bulging cheeks, also optimistically wide-eyed.

"Certainly not speaking parts," Rupert said brusquely, saving me the trouble of dashing their hopes. "Those are all taken. This is just a small selection of scenes to convey the idea of the story."

"And what part do you play, Lord Rupert?" asked the doting mama.

Another indication that the exact details of the play were

unknown to her ladyship.

"Romeo," he said bluntly.

Two muffled squeals escaped from the girls, who then chewed madly to be the first one to speak.

Henrietta won. "Oh, Lord Rupert," she breathed in tones of awe and hero worship. "I think you'll make the most wonderful Romeo."

"So that means you'll die!" Caroline announced triumphantly. "Our governess read the play to us, and she cried at the end because just about everyone dies."

"You haven't an ounce of romance," Henrietta retorted, giving her sister a scathing glance. "It's a love story, stupid, and so of course the hero and heroine have to do something dramatic like die."

Rupert glanced at me. His expression spoke volumes, but he said nothing, just finished his tea.

"Girls!" said Lady Hamilton sharply. "Now that you've eaten all the refreshments that were meant for our guests, please go into the library and find your papa's copy of the collected works of Shakespeare."

They sat, looking at her with mutinous expressions. Of course, leaving the drawing room meant they wouldn't hear any gossip the adults might exchange.

She gave them a warning frown. "Or there will be no parts for anyone."

With one accord, they leaped up and stampeded out of the room. The sounds of squabbling and a few thuds—maybe books falling off the library shelves—wafted back to us.

Lady Hamilton tittered and said archly, "The joys of having children, always something happening."

Rupert came over to me and held out his hand, which I took as I stood. Message delivered, tea drunk, clearly the visit was at an end. Ignoring the hated headgear, I went over to the door, but my crafty efforts were foiled.

"Miss Carstairs, your beautiful bonnet!"

I turned as Lady Hamilton floated towards me, holding it.

"Thank you so much," I said, suppressing the urge to rip it to shreds on the spot. "Goodness me, in the flurry of locating these copies of the play, my mind is quite elsewhere." Somehow, I managed to get it on straight and tie the ribbons.

Lady Hamilton dimpled. "I'm the same way. So much to think about, so much on my mind, sometimes I even wonder what day of the week it is."

She glided closer and whispered while giving me the full Maternal Pleading Look, "Any small part for my two darlings would be wonderful."

I hesitated, unwilling to make promises I couldn't keep. "There is a ball scene where Romeo first sees Juliet. Perhaps they could be part of the guests?"

This meant that I had to magic up several more guests to make it feasible. No doubt there would be more of the dowager's friends with stage-struck offspring. The girls appeared in the doorway, both trying to pull the volume out of each other's grasp.

"Girls!" Lady Hamilton cried, clapping her hands. "Miss Carstairs has promised that you may both be guests in the ball scene."

That stopped all the squabbling. Henrietta relinquished her death grip on the book, which Caroline then handed to me with the meekest expression.

"There are no speaking parts, you'll just be dancing," I added, hoping they could dance.

Lady Hamilton favoured me with the indulgent smile of a besotted parent. "You'll find nothing to complain about there,

Miss Carstairs. My two angels dance beautifully. His lordship has spent enough on a dancing master to make sure they do us proud."

Both girls looked too young to have come out and had their debut, as Clementine had, but their mother was determined to make sure her girls had a role. Her next words confirmed my suspicions.

"Of course, neither Henrietta nor Caroline is out yet, but I don't think there'll be anything amiss in letting them take part as guests in a scene."

She looked a bit worried as she spoke. My reply was reassuring, even though I was hardly an expert on social niceties or the rules of the Regency era.

"This is just an informal occasion between friends and family so hardly anything to excite comment."

She laid both hands on my arm. "My sentiments exactly." Then she glared at her daughters. "Of course, this means there must be excellent behaviour from both of you to warrant being part of this exciting event."

Silenced by this Damoclean threat, they just nodded, staring at us with big eyes.

"We'll visit very shortly to get details of the costumes required," she added. "Perhaps tomorrow?"

"I look forward to it," I said with a curtsey bob.

Rupert put a firm hand under my arm and steered me down the front steps. The gig was already waiting, with Dolly still chewing the last of her refreshments from the stables. How did the groom know when to bring the gig? Maybe there was some kind of unspoken timing arrangement, with a visit lasting no more than twenty minutes.

"Goodbye!" the Hamilton females chorused from the front door as they all waved madly at us.

I turned to wave and then allowed Rupert to hand me up into the gig. The groom held Dolly's reins as Rupert got in beside me.

"Thank God!" he said. "I couldn't have borne that demented chatter for another moment. Bird-witted, the lot of them!"

"It's all right for you," I replied, almost crossly. "No one expects a man to make small talk or elegant conversation. You can get away with saying two words."

I glanced at him. He was laughing silently.

"The joys of having children!" He snorted. "No daughter of mine would ever behave in such a tomboyish way."

"And now we're stuck with them," I said mournfully. "What on earth am I going to do with them?"

"You mentioned there's a ball scene," he said. "To have a ball scene you'll need a few more dancers, not just those two silly girls."

"With a few more dancers it could work, but to find them is the problem."

He chuckled. When I managed to manoeuvre my line of vision to glance at him, he was sniggering in a most annoying way.

"What's so funny?"

He gave another snort. "You'll see. We'll have half the county pestering us to let their dear, darling, prodigiously talented So-and-So be part of the production."

It definitely wasn't going to be just us at all.

As we entered the house, the dowager called out from the drawing room, "Rupert, Amelia, come in here."

Her voice carried so no need for a footman to convey her commands.

Rupert gave an eloquent sigh. "I wonder who we must

meet now?"

The dowager was draped on her usual chaise lounge while her guests occupied the sofa and several chairs. The remains of tea and cake littered a low table.

"Come over here, my dear," she said, beckoning to me. "I'd like to introduce a dear friend, Mrs Beasley, her daughter Tiffany, and a ... er ... young relative of theirs, Tiffany's cousin Anne."

Although she didn't have a title, Mrs Beasley must have been socially connected for the dowager to consider her important enough to have over for tea. She was an attractive woman around forty, with a bit of a beaky nose but otherwise very well dressed. We all did the graceful bowing, shaking hands number, while Tiffany and Anne did sweet little curtseys. Anne had something wrong with one leg, making her stand awkwardly. Tiffany was one of those confident, very pretty teenagers with flawless skin, good figure, large blue eyes, and masses of dark auburn ringlets. She had "mean girl" written all over her. The poor cousin, who turned out to be just that, was thin and pale, with brown hair and eyes, and not dressed quite as well as her glorious cousin. They were both about fourteen.

"Her Grace has told us all about the play and we're so very excited to have a significant cultural event in the area," said Mrs Beasley as she sank back onto the sofa. She patted the place next to her to indicate I should sit beside her, which I did. Rupert, let off the hook as always, helped himself to tea and what was left of the cake.

Eyeing me with that conspiratorial look so prevalent among managing mothers, she said, "I always encourage any artistic project that offers an opportunity for young people to express themselves. I do hope you'll have a part for my Tiffany."

She glanced at Anne, who'd shrunk back into a chair. "Do sit up, Anne! Your posture will never improve if you loll like that."

"I told Lady Hamilton already. No speaking parts," Rupert said in his usual abrupt tone. He tossed back the dregs of his tea and banged the cup down on the tray. The dowager flinched at the clatter of china and frowned.

"Only some dancing in a ball scene. Her two girls will be dancing."

The knowledge that Lady Hamilton's darlings were already in the thespian fold must have shocked Mrs Beasley to the core. Her eyes widened and her mouth almost dropped open, but with sterling self-control, she maintained her composure. However, one could almost see the machinations of her mind; how to make sure her daughter got a part or die trying. Her jaw clenched.

"Lady Hamilton's two daughters are dancing?" she said, not quite grinding her teeth.

"That's right," Rupert said carelessly. He bowed over his mother's hand. "I'm off, Mama. Got some estate duties to attend to in Robert's absence."

His mother gave him a fond lingering look as he stalked out. "What a godsend to have a good son to help while Robert is indisposed," she said in such loving tones one would never think they quarrelled.

Mrs Beasley rolled her eyes and did some bosom clasping, something I'd noticed was a favourite gesture among women.

"Oh! What a terrible experience," she squeaked. "How awful for you, Your Grace. Such a dreadful accident right on one's very own doorstep."

Not how awful it must have been for Robert being shot at, but for his stepmother who, in my opinion, didn't give a rat's arse about Robert.

"Yes," sighed said stepmother. "It's the least I can do to try to distract him from his pain and suffering while he recuperates. A delightful entertainment will be sure to raise his spirits."

"So, will there be dancing parts, Miss Carstairs?" asked Tiffany. "I mean, for me at least." She cast a contemptuous glance at her cousin. "Not Anne, of course. She's a cripple."

Mrs Beasley, doting mother that she might be, was no slouch in the etiquette department. "Tiffany!" she said in a voice of thunder that had Tiffany turning bright red. "You will apologise to your cousin right this minute."

Tiffany was a consummate actress. In fact, if Clementine hadn't got the part already, I might have been tempted to cast Tiffany as Juliet. She dropped down next to Anne's chair, took her hand, and very prettily begged her forgiveness. Anne, clearly uncomfortable with the attention, mumbled something and withdrew her hand from Tiffany's grasp. What an act. I saw through Tiffany as plainly as glass.

"I do apologise for Tiffany," said Mrs Beasley in a low voice. "She has been indulged a little. Her father dotes on her. High spirits, you know."

I did know, and it wasn't high spirits; it was just plain old spite.

"I'm sure Amelia can find a dancing part for Tiffany," said the dowager. "But what to do about Anne? We wouldn't want to leave anyone out."

The dowager was also aware of etiquette. No child or young relative of any friend could be left out. The pecking order in the hierarchy must be maintained and the dowager was going to dispense largesse, come what may.

I smiled at Anne, definitely relegated to the status of poor cousin, and asked, "Do you have good handwriting, Anne?"

"Why yes, she does," said Mrs Beasley clearly used to answering for Anne. She perked up instantly. "Anne has a very pretty hand. Very neat writing. Her governesses have praised her for it. Why do you ask?"

My Afflicted Expression involved brow wrinkling and a rueful little smile. "What a task I have undertaken in putting on this play," I said. "I'll need an assistant. Someone who can take notes, so I don't forget the important details."

Anne smiled, her aunt beamed, and the dowager said, "That's settled then. Tiffany will dance, which she does beautifully, Anne will assist Amelia, and I am sure she will do this most efficiently."

Order was preserved in the kingdom.

Tiffany, who was scowling at Anne getting attention, brightened as she went back to her seat. "I won't let you down, Miss Carstairs," she said in an annoying simpering tone.

"Now, Amelia," the dowager said. "If there is to be a ball scene with several young dancers, we can't have only girls. They must have partners. I will ponder thereon. I have several friends with suitable young male offspring who can dance."

Obviously, she wanted to help, or rather interfere, but since I was two hundred years out of my depth, I wasn't going to complain. The Beasleys took their leave, promising to return the following day to start rehearsing. So now I had the Hamilton girls and the Beasleys to manage. Plus, I had to cut the bard's famous love story into bite-sized pieces for public consumption by an audience who had very likely never read a single play, let alone seen one. And I almost forgot, I had to find Robert's would-be assassin before he or she struck again. I made my way back to my room, exhausted by the mere thought of it all. I had Caroline, Henrietta, and Tiffany as dancers, no boys to partner them, no idea of music and stage settings, no idea how to start hacking the play, and no idea how to catch a killer.

Dinner that evening was a very different affair from the stilted atmosphere of the previous night. The same guests as before, minus the vicar, but what a change in their attitudes. Chatter was animated in between mouthfuls as they wolfed down Cook's excellent meal, and lively to the point of being loud. Rupert and Sir Harold were involved in an intense discussion with Doctor Potts about, I learned later, how to create the best lighting effects since they agreed with Robert that the ballroom was the perfect place to stage the play. Creating lighting for a Shakespearean production using only candle power might be an insurmountable task that only MacGyver could crack. Maria Wilby, Sidney, and Clementine were arguing about costumes and if one should go for current dress or Renaissance. I had no one to talk to but the dowager, who seemed inclined to be chatty.

She picked at her food, and then said, "So you have us all in a twitter, Amelia, all delightfully embroiled in this stage play fantasy of yours."

It was hard to fathom her mood. Was she annoyed at not being the centre of attention? Surely, she was pleased at her beloved Rupert playing the leading role and Robert being entertained during his convalescence. Her next words echoed my thoughts, but I still didn't trust her. A gleam in those dark eyes made me shiver.

She put down her fork and gazed at me. "Of course, I am

eternally grateful that Rupert has snapped out of his doldrums and seems to have regained his usual lovely temperament. He was so pettish and almost cantankerous before. Now he has an activity to occupy his mind."

She sighed and picked up her fork again, toying with her food. "And Robert has something delightful to look forward to in an entertainment. But what will we do when you are no longer here, my dear? I wonder how we will amuse ourselves then?"

The cold shiver down my spine turned into a subzero chill. She was already contemplating Amelia's departure. Her impassive gaze was disconcerting, to say the least.

She continued in her signature slightly hectoring tone, "You needn't worry about finding more dancers to fill out the troupe. I have communicated with several friends who would be very pleased for their talented offspring to participate. The young people will be here tomorrow with their chaperones."

An imperious wave of one hand dismissed my mumbled thanks.

"Higgins will supervise moving the pianoforte and a worktable and chairs into the ballroom where I assume the young dancers will practise?"

Her eyes widened in a Lady Catherine de Bourgh way, and I hastily assured her yes, of course, exactly the place to practise the dancing of which I had no knowledge. By her next statement, she must have been psychic.

"The local dancing master will be here on the morrow to assist." Her lips pursed as she considered the fellow mentally. "Mr Roach taught Rupert to dance, and I assume he taught Robert as well. He's very competent and has instructed the youngsters of the very best families. You will find them all to be most capable. How else are young people to meet members of the opposite sex if they cannot dance?"

That made complete sense. With the degree of vigilance young women were subjected to by chaperones and watchful mamas, the only private place where a young man could converse with the girl of his dreams was on the dance floor.

Her gimlet gaze fell upon me again. "You do have some idea of what you'd like them to do, I presume?"

I had absolutely no idea, of course, except the word "minuet" kept circling in my brain but that was the 1600s. *Romeo and Juliet* was set in the 1300s, the Italian Renaissance. Would anyone notice a minuet?

"I hope being part of the production won't interfere with the young people's ... er ... tutoring?"

The dowager favoured me with a smug, satisfied expression. "Of course not. This is a golden opportunity, as I suggested to my dear friends, for their children to benefit from an enlightening and rewarding educational and cultural experience. Their tutors and governesses will take the opportunity to instruct them on Shakespeare, Renaissance Italy, the customs, costumes, and dances of the era. You'll see."

She spoke as if the whole thing had been her idea from start to finish. I was floored and speechless. Luckily, Clementine drew the dowager's attention away with a burning question about the costumes that required her expert opinion. Thankfully, dinner was over quickly, and the men must have smoked those cigars at top speed because they were soon back in the drawing room. Interestingly, Rupert and Clementine sat together with a copy of the play, no doubt talking about their parts. Doctor Potts and Sir Harold had put a card table to good use by making sketches on some spare pieces of paper. Sidney, ever the dutiful nephew, was playing piquet with the dowager. I sat with Maria Wilby who turned out to be a blessing, musically I should say. Her frizzy curls dancing with yet another feathered ornament waving back and forth, she clutched my hand as she took some sheet music from her reticule.

"My dear Miss Carstairs, oh, may I call you Amelia?" she said. "And you must call me Maria from now on."

"Of course, Maria." I patted her hand in solidarity. First names were a big step forward in socialising. We were almost besties by Regency standards.

"I've been doing some research," she said in tones of triumph. "And I have come up with the perfect song for the end, when the two lovers are lying dead for all to see."

"That's wonderful, Maria," I replied. "How clever you are."

She blushed. "Not at all. However, I do know my music and this piece is just right."

She waved it under my nose and from a brief glimpse it did seem suitable.

"Of course, this song should be accompanied by a lute, if one were aiming for period authenticity, but we'll make do with the village musicians."

"Are there any?"

"Oh, yes," she said with supreme confidence. "There are some excellent local players. Flute, violin, and I think one gentleman plays the cello. Then we have the pianoforte here. Perhaps one other instrument to make the performance interesting." She added knowingly, "And with there being a dancing troupe, we must certainly have suitable music. You can rest assured, my dear Amelia, that is my area of skill. Music!"

I smiled warmly, albeit I didn't feel that confident. This was going to end up being a musical if I wasn't careful. She stared at me, unflinchingly. It seemed that, like it or not, music was to be involved and so was Maria Wilby.

"People love music and what would a theatrical performance be without music? We'll need to distract the audience between scenes as well, so they don't notice any scenery changes," she said firmly.

Scenery? Musicians? Dancers? This was growing out of all proportion. What had I got myself into?

"If you like," she said hesitantly, her expression hopeful. "I would be more than happy to manage everything to do with the music and songs."

She flapped the music sheet for emphasis. "To relieve you of yet another burden," she added. "You'll be so busy with writing Sir Sidney's part and directing the performers."

I gave in as gracefully as I could. Maria was determined to sing and to include ambient music. The dowager was determined to have her friends' offspring be a dancing troupe. What next?

Chapter Ten

Friday, 28 April 1815

Although I was downstairs bright and early for breakfast, I was not bright and early enough. Clementine and Rupert were already poring over the play, pencils in hand, marking their lines together.

She looked up as I entered. "Amelia, I hope you don't mind but Lord Rupert and I have been looking over the scenes where Juliet and Romeo converse, just acquainting ourselves with the lines."

"Not at all," I said. Higgins poured my tea, and I buttered my toast.

"The prodigiously talented So-and-Sos are waiting for you in the ballroom," said Rupert, frowning over a page.

I stared at him. "The who?"

He gave one of his annoying chuckles. "I told you so. My mother has rounded up the rest of the dancing troupe for the ball scene, the local boys and girls of families of her acquaintance. I'm sure she mentioned it to you last night. It's not the kind of thing she'd forget. They're in the ballroom and the dancing master is on his way. Before you see them, my brother has been asking for you."

My heart gave a joyful jump and then sank, deflated. I hadn't seen Robert last night. I'd been too busy writing up Amelia's diary and perusing the play to get a grip on Sidney's lines, which all had to be written fresh. At least I had something to talk about though; the progress of the play. I gobbled my breakfast and went upstairs. Russet and Parker greeted me at Robert's door. Parker looked worried.

"Good morning, Miss Carstairs," he said. "His Grace did not pass a comfortable night, just to let you know in advance."

"I'll try to cheer him up," I said, although I felt doubtful.

Robert was pale and heavy-eyed, but he smiled as I entered the room. He reached for my hand when I sat next to him on the bed. Russet jumped up on the other side, tail waving happily.

"How goes the invalid this morning?" My tone was cheerful, but not too cheerful. Sometimes patients get annoyed by what they feel is patronising.

"Better for seeing you," he said, squeezing my fingers. Was that tingling sensation actually electricity running up my arm or was it my imagination?

Be still my beating heart!

"I have plenty of updates for you on the progress of your entertainment. It seems the entire county is agog with the projected festivities and eager to be part of it, no matter how small or insignificant."

I then regaled him with comical versions of our meetings with the Hamiltons and then the Beasleys. While he was chuckling at my thwarted efforts to ditch The Hated Bonnet, I finished off with, "And I believe a group of young ladies and gentlemen from Verona is waiting downstairs to complete the troupe of dancers for the play."

He smiled. "I know. The prodigiously talented So-and-

Sos. Rupert already told me."

In just a few minutes of our conversation he looked more animated. Parker hovered solicitously in the background.

Robert sighed in a mock lugubrious fashion. "Having forced me to eat a very healthy breakfast, Parker is now going to help me dress and come downstairs for—"

I stared at him in horror. "Downstairs? What for? You should rest, recuperate."

He shook his head. "I feel like a caged animal. I need to get up, move about. Besides, someone must design the stage for the performance."

Before I could protest, I saw Parker's expression. He rolled his eyes.

"I have to agree with His Grace, Miss Carstairs. He is working himself into such a frenzy lying in bed that I think if he takes it slowly, he'll get better quicker."

"The estate carpenter is coming with his crew so having him design the stage under my instructions will keep me occupied and not thinking about my injury," said Robert. "I'll be in the library with them and out of your way. Now you'd better go and meet the young ladies and gentlemen of Verona."

Somehow, I managed to wend my way to the ballroom, an enormous and imposing rectangular room with tall windows down both sides and mirrors in between the windows. Two large sets of French doors led out onto a balustraded narrow patio on one side, with steps down to a beautifully laid out rose garden. No doubt this was to give the guests a chance to cool off after whirling around the dance floor. Three massive chandeliers, swathed in protective mutton cloth, graced the room. These would be magnificent when fully lit. It must have been an incredible sight as the setting for a full-scale ball, with women in beautiful satin gowns and sparkling jewels, and men in their formal evening attire. In one corner stood the pianoforte, and next to it a worktable with chairs, as the dowager had promised. The juggernaut of theatrical production was moving inexorably forward.

A number of people were awaiting my arrival. Clustered together in a small group were five boys, more like mid-teens, freshly scrubbed and pink-cheeked, and with hair slicked back and wearing their Sunday best. Those stiff collars must have been so uncomfortable. They weren't alone. Caroline and Henrietta Hamilton, Tiffany Beasley, and two other girls made up the girls. Anne stood slightly apart. Maria hurried forward, clasping her hands in glee.

"My dear Amelia, so exciting! Our first day of this creative endeavour has begun."

She turned to draw forward three plain young women, thirty-ish, who could only have been the girls' governesses and one young man, a tutor, who flushed profusely and seemed dumbstruck in the presence of this many females. The introductions were so rapid fire I'd already forgotten their names by the time she finished.

"Now," Maria said, "let's meet our young dancers." She introduced cousins Walter and Charles de Montfort, freckle-faced and gangling with sandy blond hair. They looked like naughty scamps and turned out to be just that. Then came Rowland and Gerald Keene, good-looking, dark-haired brothers. Then a very handsome boy, Peter Wardell, a bit older than the others, maybe sixteen, with golden hair. Luckily, the boys were all more or less the same height, so no one stood out as a scrawny wimp.

"Girls!" cried Maria. The girls all stepped forward. Anne came to my side, armed with a large notebook and a pencil. Maria introduced blonde-haired, blue-eyed sisters Cambria and Ardelle Collingwood. I would never remember all their names.

Maria was a mind reader. "You'll never remember their names, so we have devised name labels."

She clapped and this was the signal for the governesses and tutor to fuss about with pins and labels that had been made in advance. If I'd had any doubts about boys thinking dancing and being in a play was sissy, I was wrong. Yes, they sniggered and poked each other in the sides and eyeballed the girls, but they were all as keen as mustard. I had to remind myself that this was two hundred years in the past. Teens were different back then. Maybe the lack of digital technology? Nothing else to do and this was a welcome distraction from the schoolroom.

"Now, my dear Amelia," said Maria confidingly, "the moment you think I am overstepping the mark and intruding upon your position, you must just say so."

Maria Wilby was a woman transformed. She glowed, she effused, she sparkled. Even if I had wanted to say so, I couldn't have rained on her parade. She was in her element. It would have been criminal to spoil it for her. Perhaps she had given up more than people imagined when she married Reverend Wilby.

"The dancing master, Mr Theophilus Roach, and his daughter will be here shortly. She plays for him. Celeste is a very talented pianist."

A footman appeared at the entrance to the ballroom.

"Aha!" she said happily, "I think they have just arrived."

Mr Roach was elderly and cadaverously thin, with beady, watchful eyes, and a beaky nose. He wore clothes somewhat of yesteryear with knee breeches, stockings, and buckled shoes. No modern, new-fangled pantaloons for this dancing master. Celeste was a quietly pretty woman, fortyish, modestly dressed, with pale skin, and light brown hair tucked under a lace cap. She had an armful of sheet music with her.

The youngsters all knew Mr Roach well because they bowed and curtseyed most gracefully. He cast an expert eye over the gaggle and said, "Of course you all brought your dancing shoes?"

The governesses nodded and rummaged in their capacious reticules to indicate yes. The tutor whipped out a portmanteau he'd been hiding somewhere with the young men's shoes.

"Well, then," said the dancing master. He clapped. "Get ready, ladies and gentlemen, for some good warm-up exercises. Ladies, remove the excess finery. You know the rules. No scarves, shawls, gloves, or extra paraphernalia. Gentlemen, get rid of those coats. We want to breathe and stretch. Breathe and stretch."

The youngsters scurried to obey, assisted by their chaperones. Mr Roach beckoned me to the piano where Maria introduced us formally. He nodded and tutted as he sifted through the music sheets, pulling out some pages and setting them aside.

"Well, Miss Carstairs, *Romeo and Juliet*, eh? Her Grace has been kind enough to explain the nature of the entertainment. Very ambitious." He looked at me and there was not a hint of the geriatric in those sharp grey eyes. "Not the whole play, I gather. Just selected scenes?"

"Yes," I said. I quickly outlined my intention: a narrator, scenes involving Romeo and Juliet, especially the ball scene where he sees her, the fight sequences, and several character interactions, with the dancers used where appropriate. He nodded all through my garbled explanation as if agreeing with me.

"I think this will work very well, Miss Carstairs, and no

doubt once the actors start rehearsing, we can seamlessly include the dance sequences. Being familiar with the play, I have given it some thought."

Phew! What a relief.

He continued, "And I think, depending of course on the seating arrangements, we should have a centre aisle where the dancers can perform a procession dance to open the play, with elements of perhaps the pavane, some formal courtliness to hint to the audience this is something special."

Pavane? Urk!

He then performed a few dance steps and twirled around. "Once the dancers are up on the stage—you will have a stage, I gather?"

"Yes, His Grace wants one built for the performance."

"Good, good, as I was saying, once the dancers are up on stage, we can then use them for whatever scenes you wish to include. We'll discuss this in greater depth once you have an outline of the events for me. This morning we'll work on an opening dance to create a grand impression."

He strode towards the youngsters, who all appeared eager to get dancing. Anne looked at me hesitantly. I beckoned to her. No time like the present to start working on the star-crossed lovers' speeches and Sidney's narration. Maria hurried along next to us as we exited the ballroom, accompanied by the tinkling of the pianoforte.

"I have several more copies of the play, Amelia," she gasped as she scurried to keep up. "Mr Wilby and I found two copies in your Papa's old library, and de Montforts, the Beasleys, Mrs Wardell, and the Collingwoods have all sent theirs, so we have enough copies, I think."

She dug in her reticule, a very large knitted one today, and handed me two copies. "For you and Anne."

Although I anticipated having Anne and myself write out everyone's lines, hopefully everyone would read the play first.

She stared intently at me as if reading my mind. "I'll share these with everyone involved, shall I? And impress upon them the importance of reading the play in its entirety. For context."

"Thank you, Maria. I'm sure Sir Harold has made short work of it and Miss Eccles and Lord Rupert have been reading the parts where they both appear. However, I'm not sure Sir Sidney will cope with reading the whole play."

"But he's willing to try and that's what counts," she said quietly.

"Perhaps you could ask everyone to convene in the drawing room later today, around three?"

"Consider it done," she said and bustled off.

I glanced down at my youthful helper. "Come, Anne. It's time to set you to work being an assistant."

A touch of pink stained her pale cheeks. "I won't let you down, Miss Carstairs."

Since Robert was in the library with the carpenter, and the dowager was in the drawing room, possibly with the parents of the dancers judging by the sounds of laughter and conversation, Anne and I repaired to a small parlour, which very conveniently had a round table and chairs, where we set up camp. By great good fortune, Anne had read the play several times for pleasure. It was mortifying that I had to rely on so youthful an expert but there was no looking a gift horse in the mouth.

Anne produced a pencil for me. We worked out and wrote down a timeline to include mostly interaction between Romeo and Juliet, and then with Nurse and Friar Laurence. Tybalt, Juliet's cousin, and Mercutio, Romeo's friend, were included just in their fight scenes. I wasn't sure if Johnson and Peters, the footmen, could cope with more than a few basic lines, let alone read the whole play. Luckily both men were tall, well-built, and no doubt Rupert could get them to wield a rapier with a few days' practice. Hopefully the armoury had a few rapiers knocking about. An armoury had been mentioned in the Chelston Hall brochure. Anne was a quick little worker and between us we wrote down a timeline for each person involved and one each for us. The hours flew by, but thank goodness, Maisie remembered food. She opened the parlour door, and a footman placed a large tray with a sumptuous spread on the table for us. Anne's eyes gleamed. My stomach growled.

"Maisie, you are a godsend!" Then I remembered the dancers. Those kids must be starving. Maisie must have read my mind.

"Don't worry. Cook sent a lovely nuncheon for everyone, sayin' since the young people are growin', they'll as like be hungry with all the dancin' about." She gave us a conspiratorial wink. "Mr Roach is very partic'lar. No pies and stodgy stuff. He sent word t' kitchen that Cook must only prepare plain bread and butter, cheese, cold meats, and fruit. And lemonade."

She leaned in closer. "They're sittin' outside now under the trees to get some fresh air while they eat. Havin' lots of fun, just like young people should."

Anne and I got up to peer through the window and there were the dancers, sitting on blankets which the house staff must have supplied, laughing, eating, drinking, and apparently having the time of their lives. Mr Roach's word was eccentric, but it was law, that was clear. Once we'd eaten and put in another hour's work, I hurried back to the ballroom with Anne in tow, hoping to catch Mr Roach. I was just in time. Celeste was busy packing up the music scores.

He rubbed his hands together, looking very pleased. "Ah,

Miss Carstairs. We had a most successful morning. Achieved a lot." He looked at the sheaf of papers in my hand. "Is that a timeline of events? A copy for me?"

I handed him a page. "Yes, albeit a very truncated version of the play. You'll see where I've underlined the action and indicated where we could have the dancers perform either an actual dance or just be a group looking on."

He glanced over our work, nodding. "Yes, yes, very good. I'll work around this. Naturally it's all very exciting for the performers. Young people never have a chance to be in a concert in front of an audience, but they'll do very well indeed. I've appointed Peter to lead the young men and Tiffany to lead the young ladies. They'll partner in the other dances as well."

Celeste gave a discreet cough and waved.

Mr Roach swung round to stare at her and then back to stare at me. "Ah, yes, my daughter has just reminded me. Scenery. What are you doing about the backdrop?"

Oh no, one more thing to think about!

"Well," I said, thinking on my feet, "perhaps we could aim for a generic backdrop that'll fit in no matter what the scene. Why do you ask? Is this important for the dancers?"

He shook his head. "No, but I was thinking that if we have the young people here dancing in the morning, they can help with the scenery painting in the afternoon."

The man was a genius. "That's a wonderful idea. I'm truly grateful for your suggestion."

He nodded. "They can all either draw or paint so let's keep 'em busy while they're here. They can bring smocks to wear over their clothes." He fixed me with a beady gaze. "No ideas on costumes yet?"

"Not yet," I said guiltily. "It's on my list of things to do."

He bowed. "Good day to you, Miss Carstairs, Miss Anne.

Until tomorrow."

Once they'd left, I said to Anne, "Why don't you join the others? I have lots to do and you can find out how your friends enjoyed their first day of rehearsals."

"Thank you, Miss Carstairs. I'll see you tomorrow." She gave a little bob and went off.

There was a hubbub of conversation when I went back to the drawing room. Tea was being served with Higgins handing out cups and saucers, and a footman hovering with cake plates and dainty forks. Even after that sumptuous nuncheon, I was sure I could fit in a slice of whatever was going in the cake department. Sir Harold and Sidney had their heads together over a copy of the play, with Sidney's morose expression testimony to his worries about his thespian skills. Doctor Potts and Maria were no doubt discussing their parts, while the dowager, Clementine, and Rupert sat on a long sofa, with what looked like the costume book. The dowager looked up as I entered.

"Ah, Amelia," she said in such affable tones that I thought I was hearing things. "Just in time for tea." She waved imperiously at Higgins. "A cup for Miss Carstairs and a slice of cake."

Laden with refreshments, I sank into a nearby armchair and stuffed the sheaf of papers down the side. The armchair was so comfortable. The tea was delicious and so was the cake. I polished off my tea and cake asap since it looked very much as if a dowager discussion was in store for me. Higgins and the footman discreetly vanished once we were all served.

The dowager announced, "We're just discussing the costuming of the performers."

"I very much look forward to your opinion," I said.

She narrowed her eyes at me, as if suspicious of sarcasm, but then gave a dismissive wave of one hand. "After some thought about modern or Renaissance dress, it's my opinion we should have an adapted version of the Renaissance style."

I kept quiet but put on my Very Interested Expression which thus far was guaranteed to elicit more conversation. It did. Her explanation made complete sense though. She might be lots of unpleasant things, but she was no fool.

"While it pains me to say this of some of my very best friends," she said, with a bit of hand clasping to the bosom. "I find that loving mothers tend to want their own child to shine, perhaps to the detriment of others. This will not do in an ensemble performance."

Of course, every parent would want their child dressed to outdo the others. I can imagine Mrs Beasley going full-on Sweet Sixteen with Tiffany's outfit. Cloth-of-gold and the like, no doubt, festooned with jewels. I nodded sagely.

"So," she continued, "if they are all dressed the same, adhering to a costume from the past, we will have no rivalry, no disappointed parents, and no problems."

Clementine flipped over a few pages and held up the book. "See, Amelia? Her Grace has most fortuitously picked out the best possible design for the young ladies and gentlemen." She tapped the images. "So clever."

The dowager bestowed a genteel smug smile upon her as Clementine handed me the book. Old bat she might be, but the dowager had an eye. The dress depicted was a flattering low-cut square neckline with a slightly nipped-in waist and a long billowing skirt. Silver ribbons created a crisscross effect on the bodice. The long sleeves were tight to the elbow, caught with a silver ribbon, and then flared out to the wrist in a trumpet style. A simple, but eye-catching design. The male costume was also simple: a long-sleeved, V-necked tunic to mid-thigh with hose.

"Her Grace suggested we have one colour for the girls and one for the boys so it's not too confusing, like a *corps de ballet*, and then a different colour for me and Lord Rupert," said Clementine.

Rupert jumped up from his place on the sofa. "I don't care what I wear, as long as I remember my lines."

Clementine looked up at him, laughing. "No doubt you will, Lord Rupert. We'll rehearse until you can recite the lines in your sleep."

He chuckled, looking down at her with a gleam in his eyes that only a young man in love could produce. The dowager glanced from one to the other. Ever watchful, she must have already sussed out that Rupert was in love with Clementine. They'd spent some time together reading their lines and Clementine certainly hadn't looked displeased at the prospect of spending a huge amount of time with someone she'd first described as a clumsy boor. How things had changed between them. How much further would things go as the fateful moment of the stage performance drew ever closer? There was supposed to be a kiss. Dare I keep in the fateful kiss? Would the county erupt in shock and horror?

"I say," Sidney called out in a plaintive voice from across the room. "That's what I'm afraid will happen to me. I'll stand there and just forget everything."

The dowager frowned. "Sir Harold will make sure you don't forget anything." Her tone brooked no argument. Sir Harold nodded and muttered something to Sidney.

Clementine gave him one of her sparkly, mock exasperated expressions. "No, you won't, Sir Sidney. You have Sir Harold to tutor you and once you stand there in your elegant costume with your wonderful opera cloak, the audience will be entranced."

"No ... er ... jewels?" he ventured with a hopeful expression.

"You won't need them," she said. "I can just imagine you appearing on stage, all dressed in black, your opera cloak closed, then you fling your arms back to reveal the blood-red lining." She sighed. "So dramatic." Then she thought again. "Maybe one striking medallion to hang in the middle of your chest, but nothing more. You don't want to distract the audience from your performance."

That girl could sell ice in winter!

Sidney brightened up. "I say, that sounds splendid."

The book was passed around so everyone could see the costumes. Doctor Potts and Maria pronounced themselves satisfied with the standard friar's and nurse's clothing of the period. Before I could bring up the small matter of material and dressmakers, the dowager had more to say on the costumes.

"I have made enquiries," she announced, "and it appears that the de Montforts are very eager to sponsor the costumes and the making thereof." She frowned and then raised her eyebrows, staring at us. Instantly on cue there was a low murmur of the obligatory "How kind, yes indeed, very kind, how thoughtful" remarks. She smiled and looked gratified.

"I shall convey everyone's thanks. Lady de Montfort has also undertaken for her own personal dressmaker and several seamstresses to make the costumes once we have settled on colours." She looked at Rupert and Clementine. "And what colours are to be chosen for the Montague and Capulet families?"

"I like blue," said Clementine firmly. "Blue is my favourite colour. I look my best in blue because my eyes are blue. I think a royal blue for Juliet."

"It's immaterial to me," said Rupert carelessly.

"How about green for Romeo?" Clementine suggested. "A lovely forest green will offset the blue."

Everyone agreed those were ideal choices for the young lovers and after a bit of squabbling, the general consensus for the dancers was that the girls would wear burgundy dresses with silver trimming and the boys would wear mustard tunics with black hose. Tybalt and Mercutio would be dressed in black because the footmen might be needed for behind the scenes. They would each have a detachable short cloak in the Capulet and Montague colours that they could remove. To avoid more parental competition among the young ladies, there would be no elaborate hairstyles. Each female dancer would wear her hair loose and drawn back simply from her face with a silver ribbon. It was all going swimmingly. But there was still the matter of fixing a date, invitations, and of course refreshments for the guests who, according to the dowager, seemed to be multiplying at an alarming rate. However, she didn't look at all displeased at the idea of the guest list expanding. In fact, she appeared delighted.

"How will we accommodate everyone?" she said with a patently fake doleful sigh. "It's so very hard to say no since some of them are my oldest and dearest friends. And once word got around, so many people are greatly interested in attending."

Naturally, this would elevate the family socially to monumental levels of success, that was clear.

"I think we should invite everyone," said Clementine, clasping her hands with the enthusiasm of someone who has never had to organise any kind of get-together or event, or pay for it.

The dowager pursed her lips. "The seating will be a problem."

"Let them bring their own chairs," said Rupert, busy helping himself to the last piece of cake. "The guests can send their chairs over the day before with a footman or two to help set up. But no fancy chairs. Just plain simple chairs that don't take up too much space. They can pin a name label on the seat to indicate the owner."

"Very good idea," said Doctor Potts. "But mind you, they can't be picking and choosing to put their chairs in the best place for viewing. It should be first come, first served."

The dowager nodded slowly and sipped her tea.

"They can send their carriages and servants the day after to take them back," said Rupert. "That way we won't be put out having to find seating for everyone."

He gave his mother a stern look. "Mama, I think you should put on the invitations a reminder that the ladies are not to wear very high hair styles. No one wants to be peering over nodding ostrich plumes and other frills and furbelows."

Maria, prone to feathered aigrettes, went bright red and raised one hand to her hair to smooth it down.

The dowager gave a loud sigh. "Rupert, you have quite embarrassed poor Mrs Wilby, but it is a very good point. Maria, by your expression I feel sure you have a question?"

Still blushing, Maria tentatively asked, "Will you be offering refreshments, ma'am?"

The dowager put her cup down. "I have been considering it. It would hardly be good form to send everyone away right after the performance. People will want to mingle and chat, congratulate the performers and dancers, and mention how much they enjoyed the play."

Sidney offered his tuppence worth. "I say, Aunt, we could set up tables in the garden and guests could stroll around and partake of a finger supper. Nothing too elaborate. Savouries, tarts, small cakes, and the like. And champagne! Lots of it!"

There was a murmur of appreciation and it also sounded like the answer about what to do with the guests after the show. One could hardly boot them out with a hearty, "The show's over, so goodbye, folks!"

Clementine said excitedly, "We should have programs printed so everyone who participates can be mentioned and thanked."

The genie was out of the bottle and the play was now assuming the enormous proportions of a Royal Shakespeare Company performance. I thought the dowager would say something about the expense of it all but evidently the thought of her sky-rocketing social standing far outweighed any costs, and maybe one of her cronies would sponsor the programs.

"And now, Amelia," said the dowager, turning her Gorgon gaze upon me once more. "How far are you with the outline of events and who is doing what? And when will the play be ready for performance? We need a date to inform our interested guests."

This was the moment to hand out the timeline of character appearances and events. Everyone snatched up their page, scanning it eagerly.

"I thought we could be ready by next Saturday," I said. "Romeo, Juliet, Nurse, and Friar Laurence can work with their copies of the play for now. I'll go through the lines with everyone to show which sections we'll use. Mr Roach assures me the dancers will be ready and it's a simple matter of fitting them in between the acts."

"Don't forget me," said Sidney wistfully. "I need my lines if I'm to learn and memorize them by next Saturday."

Making a rash promise, I said, "I'll have your lines tomorrow and a copy for Sir Harold to help you rehearse."

Sidney subsided into his seat, still looking morose.

The dowager nodded. "Yes," she said slowly. "I think next Saturday will be suitable. Lady de Montfort assures me her dressmaker is quick. Mr Roach is an excellent teacher, and the dancers will no doubt be ready." She turned to Maria. "And the music, Maria?"

Flustered, Maria bustled up to the dowager and sank onto the sofa in the space Rupert had vacated. "Oh, Your Grace, no need to worry about the music. I've been consulting with Mr Roach and his charming daughter, Celeste, and we've chosen music for the dancers as well as for my songs."

The dowager raised an eyebrow. "Songs? Plural?"

Maria blushed. "Just two, if that's not a problem. I was only going to sing at the end, but Miss Roach and I thought perhaps if there's a space between, maybe a scene change, I'll have something to fill in the gap, so to speak."

The dowager stared. Maria blanched. Then the dowager gave her a brilliant smile. "Of course, very sensible thinking. A spare song, just in case. A very good idea."

Maria gave a relieved sigh and then looked round at us, possibly also still holding our breaths, and beamed. The dowager had a very unnerving effect on people. We all let out a collective sigh.

"Since no one has asked about the fight scenes," said Rupert pettishly, "I'd like to tell everyone that my old fencing master is coming tomorrow to help out. So, he should get a mention as well in the program."

The dowager promptly said, "My dearest boy, of course I

did not forget. I knew you'd have it in hand."

"And he's bringing the foils we need," Rupert continued. "The ones in the armoury are quite old."

"But are you sure you want to include this dangerous element," said the dowager with an expression of motherly concern. She shook her head. "Perhaps we should cut those parts out."

Rupert paced the room, looking annoyed. "Mama, the whole point of making the play exciting is having a sword fight. Who wants to watch a boring play with only a couple of silly lovers mooning over each other and then dying in the end?"

The silence in the room could only be described as deathly. Talk about playing with fire. Clementine was aghast. Actually, that was an understatement. She was outraged. She jumped up instantly, her cheeks pink, her fists clenched, and her eyes sparkling with a martial light.

"Well! A fine thing this is, Lord Rupert. You seem to have changed your mind very quickly about the play. All the time we've spent on the lines and talking about the characters meant nothing to you."

We were riveted, staring at the couple as, like a vengeful Valkyrie, Clementine advanced on Rupert, who backed away making ineffectual bleating noises.

"Is this what you really think of all the efforts we're putting into the entertainment for His Grace, who is recuperating upstairs from what could have been a mortal wound? A *boring* play?"

Clementine didn't wait for an answer and Rupert was so gob-smacked he wasn't capable of giving her one. Then she turned on her heel, gave the dowager a perfunctory curtsey, and swept out of the room, making a very grand, applause-worthy exit. She had the makings of a diva.

"Thank you, Rupert. Very well done in your dealings with sensitive young women," said the dowager dryly, and I had to agree with her. "You've only managed to upset the leading lady, without whom the play cannot go on. I suggest you go after Miss Eccles and make your apologies."

Rupert looked around the room helplessly, finding only our mortified stares, which were no help at all.

"Damn! Damn and blast!" he swore and stomped out.

One could have heard a pin drop except for the fact that the room was carpeted most luxuriously. Maria was the first to break the silence.

"Oh dear," she twittered. Her expression was totally downcast. "Is this the end of the play." She blinked as her eyes filled with tears, her dreams of performing in front of a real live audience dissipating before her eyes.

The dowager patted her hand. "What?" she said reassuringly. "And give up the chance of being the centre of attention in a beautiful costume? No young lady is going to toss aside the opportunity of playing Juliet, even if it's only a private performance in a country house. Of course not. A mere *contretemps*."

She motioned for Sidney to yank on the bell pull. This was the signal for Higgins and his henchmen to clear away the tea things and for everyone to vacate the drawing room and go about their own business.

The dowager raised one hand as I stood up. "Amelia, one moment. Robert has asked most particularly if you will dine with him in his chambers this evening." She smiled. "A wonderful opportunity to tell him about the progress of the play and to share reminiscences of your past time spent here."

Before I could say anything, she rose and swept

majestically from the room, tossing over her shoulder a reminder that perhaps one should not mention Clementine and Rupert's little *contretemps*, as she put it.

Dinner with Robert. Did I really want to reminisce about a past of which I knew nothing?

If I'd had any ideas about flinging on some old day dress for a private dinner with Robert, Maisie soon set me right. I hadn't seen much of her with all the play activity, but she was busy behind the scenes, keeping my room spick and span, making sure my clothing was laundered, and of course waking me up with a much-needed morning cup of tea. The news had travelled fast and when I got to my room, Maisie had already laid out a charming gown of dark lilac, with matching slippers, gloves, and a fetching gauzy scarf to drape over my arms.

"We're only dining in his room," I said, "so is this all necessary?"

Her expression of utter horror made me want to take back the words instantly. Her eyes boggled and her mouth fell open. This was sacrilege of the highest order, and it was her duty as an aspiring lady's maid, hopefully future dresser, to set the record straight and educate me in the process.

"It's dinner with His Grace," she said in reverential tones. "It's a special occasion." She looked at me meaningfully. "Just ye and him." Her expression was reproachful. "Cook's bin slavin' away all afternoon preparin' sum'pin' really special."

I couldn't argue with that. If Cook had put in the extra effort, we'd better eat it and enjoy it. Maisie bustled around a bit more, then said I should have a bit of a lie-down, so I'd be fresh as a daisy for the dinner date. She didn't actually say the word "date," but it was implied. By the sound of it, everyone below stairs was rooting for Amelia and Robert to get together. I wasn't tired until I lay down to rest my eyes, as Dad would say. When Maisie crept back in with a large jug of hot water, I'd slept for two hours, and it was six o'clock. Maisie was an excellent dresser, and it didn't take long to shoehorn me into the gown, redo my hair, dab some perfume behind my ears, and of course, not forgetting the "earbobs" and the scarf. Maisie then solemnly escorted me along the passage to Robert's room, where Parker was waiting. He bowed formally and murmured, "Please enter, Miss Carstairs."

It was hard to believe how nervous I felt, like a teenager on a date with a guy she really fancied. My stomach was filled with dementedly fluttering butterflies and I was breathless. The room glowed with candles. A round table was placed in front of the fireplace with plates and silverware, and a dainty crystal vase with red roses. Robert rose from an armchair. He looked very much better and had dispensed with the sling. When he took my hand and raised it to his lips, an electric thrill ran up my arm. Did he feel anything, or was it just me? Luckily, Russet with his tail wagging gently was waiting for a pat on the head, which was perfect for covering up any awkwardness on my part.

"You look utterly charming," he said. He gestured at his velvet dressing gown with frogging. "I apologise that Parker has reduced me to this casual attire, which is completely inappropriate for dining in company. He says I can't wear any tight coats for a while in case I strain my shoulder. I fear he has hidden all my clothes." He glanced down at his feet, encased in monogrammed velvet slippers. "And all my shoes."

"I was forced to dress up," I said, relaxing. "Maisie had my outfit all ready and waiting and she is not to be trifled with."

Parker herded us to the table and drew out a chair for me, and then for Robert. Smiling, Robert surveyed the dining arrangement.

"Isn't this cosy," he said. "This is, I believe, a folding table, which makes it very easy to get it in and out of the room."

Discreet tinkling sounds came from the dressing room before Parker emerged with a decanter, from which he poured wine into two glasses.

"Dinner is going to be very much like a picnic," Robert said with a rueful look. "Parker tells me he can manage, and I must admit I'm not inclined to have anything too formal."

A soft tap at the door heralded the arrival of dinner. Parker managed very well on his own, hissing commands to whoever waited outside for the plates. The dinner itself was simple. A plain soup followed by fish, vegetables, salad, fruit, and cheese. Dessert was an elegant trifle served in crystal bowls. It was enough for me, and, by the looks of it, Robert as well.

"Is this to your satisfaction, my dear," he asked. He frowned. "I'm not given to large banquets but Cook assured me she would provide something delicious."

Of course, I could hardly break down and confess about the Yellow Pagoda takeaway being on speed dial. I broke my vow of not having any wine, hoping that Robert would do all the talking, or most of it anyway. As I relaxed, so did he, and since the conversation mostly revolved around the play and the antics of the performers, I felt on safe ground. He briefly referred to his injury as, according to Doctor Potts, being a mere flesh wound and an accident. This threw me for a bit. Did he really think it was a poaching incident gone wrong or maybe he didn't want to worry me? He didn't seem to want to discuss the matter in any great detail. There was one wobbly moment when he spoke about his horse, Tempest.

"Perhaps you could wander down to the stables when you have some time and take a look at Tempest, to see if he is well," he said. "My groom assures me he came to no harm and found his way back home with no trouble at all." His amused expression told me something else was coming. "I hope Dolly nipping you all those years ago hasn't entirely put you off the stables?"

Robert's remark implied Amelia didn't ride or didn't like riding, but I wasn't going to press this point. I'd escaped thus far in my pretence. No good in pushing my luck. Luckily, Dolly had behaved beautifully when taking us along to the Hamiltons and I was able to say so with a clear conscience. One more tidbit of information. Dolly had nipped Amelia. Clever me. I was able to turn this into something funny.

"I was very tempted to hand over a flowered bonnet that Maisie forced me to wear on that excursion," I said. "I might still do so since Dolly seems to be very partial to anything that looks edible."

Robert looked tired and when Parker appeared with what Doctor Potts said was "a strengthening cordial," he didn't make a fuss about drinking it. It was also a good excuse for me to say goodnight. He raised my hand to his lips, then held it against his chest.

"Good night, my dear Amelia. What a wonderful evening. I wish we could dine together every night."

To say I tore myself away was an understatement.

When I got back to my room at around ten, Maisie was waiting to help me undress. She looked as if she was going to explode with suppressed excitement. She burst out with the news that everyone was "all in a bother" about the argument between Clementine and Rupert. Apparently, below stairs was of the opinion that the play hung in the balance, and it would all be Rupert's fault for being such a clod, and not being sensitive to a lady's finer sensibilities. Further scandalous news was that Sir Harold had dined in his room, pleading that he was going over the play in peace and quiet. Maria had declined to dine at the Hall on the excuse that her husband and her children were feeling neglected. Clementine had asked for a tray in her room "on account of her havin' a mortal bad headache."

The dowager had dined just with Rupert and Sir Sidney for company and what a frosty occasion it had turned out to be. According to Higgins, the dowager subjected Rupert to a litany of his blunders in dealing with the fairer sex and a list of all the things he should do to mend relations between himself and his co-performer. It was imperative that poor, dear Robert not be disappointed by the total failure of this one attempt that the dowager was making to cheer him up. Rupert had scowled his way through dinner while Sidney had beaten a hasty retreat as soon as he could. This state of affairs did not augur well for the performance.

Chapter Eleven

Saturday, 29 April 1815

The wheels of theatrical production keep turning, even when the small cogs act up. By the time I had risen, performed ablutions, submitted to Maisie's fashion choices, breakfasted alone without my fellow thespians of the previous day, and wandered off to the ballroom clutching my pencil, a copy of the play, and a wad of writing paper, the young dancers and the others had arrived. Clad in smocks and sensible shoes, they were clustered together listening to Mr Roach explaining to the estate carpenters what was required in a backdrop. Their chaperones hovered in the background. Surely everyone knew that Juliet had flounced off in a huff the previous night, given the usual grapevine. But no one seemed perturbed, and it looked as if the performance was going on anyway. The dowager must be right. No socially ambitious young woman would turn down a chance like this to be the star of the show.

Mr Roach turned to greet me. "Ah, Miss Carstairs. I was just explaining to Mr Smithers and his workmen what we need for our general backdrop of Verona."

Mr Smithers, the estate carpenter, was thickset, dressed

in workmen's clothing, and ready for whatever task came his way. His team, which I later learned comprised his four sons, all doffed their caps. In an absolutely unintelligible brogue, he described how best to go about creating the backdrop. Everyone else understood him but me. I heard the word "canvas" and that was it. He pointed to one side and there was a huge roll of said canvas. Next to it was a collection of buckets of paint, brushes, and all the accoutrements a team of enthusiastic amateur scene painters would need. Thank heavens no one had asked me to help with size and measurements. The youngsters all looked eager to get sketching and painting. This was something Anne could do as well.

Mr Roach beckoned me over to the worktable where he had laid out several books depicting typical Italian street scenes. "I thought that a generic street scene with houses would be best," he said, pointing to the images. "There won't be time for formal scene changes and of course the audience will afford us the leniency we require in creating this ambiance."

Samuel Taylor Coleridge introduced the concept of the suspension of disbelief in 1817, so we were two years too early, but how else had theatre flourished since ancient times if not for one of Aristotle's principles of theatre wherein the audience accepts fiction as reality. The genius of the human imagination. Coupled with this eager team of would-be artists, Verona would be unforgettable, to this unschooled audience at least.

Mr Roach, like Maria, had the bit between his teeth as he confided to me that he had once been honoured with the task of supervising the scene painting in a production of *Two Gentlemen of Verona* put on at the Astbury Theatre, no less. I'd never heard of this possibly now-defunct theatre, but I nodded and said admiringly, "The Astbury? What an honour indeed. You must have been so proud."

"Yes," he said happily, "so as you can imagine, I have an idea of how best to portray Verona." He stared at me with a now worried expression. "Of course, unless you have other artistic concepts, Miss Carstairs? I'd hate to be considered *encroaching*."

He said the word as if it were some horrific creeping disease. Since my repertoire of artistic concepts was nil and I'd been winging it from the day I arrived, I smiled and assured him that he was doing me an enormous favour by taking on this burden.

He beamed. "Naturally, the young people will have varying degrees of artistic talent but since they all have lessons in sketching and painting, I'm sure the results will be acceptable. We can't expect Bernardo Bellotto or Claude Lorrain." He winked conspiratorially. "And given the universal nature of parents to regard their offspring's efforts with an indulgent eye, all will be well."

Mental note to self to Google Bernardo Bellotto and the other guy when I got back to the twenty-first century, if I ever got back.

Mr Smithers and his helpers rolled out the canvas, telling us again almost unintelligibly, that it was all measured and the budding artists could start their sketches. Once the sketches were done, the carpenters would fix the canvas in place and the youngsters could start painting. To avoid artistic quarrels, Mr Roach divided them into pairs, with Cambria and Ardelle, Caroline and Henrietta, Rowland and Gerald, and Walter and Charles, leaving only Tiffany and Peter aside. They were to work on their leading dance into the ballroom. It didn't seem as if I was needed.

Each group took a book and started sketching with

charcoal. The governesses and the boys' tutor hovered over them, making suggestions. It was the perfect time for me to finalise Sidney's lines. The tinkling of the pianoforte, the chattering of the young artists, and the hammering of the carpenters as they began setting up the stage told me that everyone could manage very well without me. As I turned to go, Anne came up to me, slightly breathless.

"Oh, Miss Carstairs, you don't need me today, do you? Can I work on the scenery with the others?"

"Yes, you can. You've worked so hard already on the script with me."

She looked delighted to be relieved of her secretarial duties and joined Cambria and Ardelle who had waved her over to join them. I returned to the small parlour we had commandeered the day before and attacked Sidney's lines. Oh, for a computer. I had almost forgotten how to write in my own handwriting and had to force myself to copy Amelia's looping style. Doing Sidney's lines wasn't as bad as I had feared. Hopefully, he could manage the opening lines of the original play. *"Two households, both alike in dignity, in fair Verona, where we lay our scene, from ancient grudge break to new mutiny, where civil blood makes civil hands unclean."*

He only needed a couple of lines before each scene, with the epilogue to wrap it all up. I was not forgotten at lunch time, or nuncheon, as Cook sent a footman with a tray. I munched as I worked and managed to get Sidney's lines down in duplicate, as well as the lines for Friar Laurence and the Nurse. I just hoped Sidney could pull off the Prince of Verona's closing lines: *"For never was a story of more woe than this of Juliet and her Romeo."*

Possibly a country audience would not be too judgemental when faced with the poignant vista of the two star-crossed lovers who died for love, performed by a beautiful young woman and a handsome young man.

My hand felt positively crippled from all the writing so come three o'clock I packed it in. Judging by the sounds emanating from the ballroom, the carpenters were still hammering, the pianoforte was still tinkling, and the young artists' chatter was unabated. Nope, I was still not needed. A stroll in the grounds sounded like a good idea. I left my script on the table, went outside, and meandered off in no particular direction, just exploring. It was an unexpectedly mild April day. Anyone who knew English weather would be surprised, but Maisie always sent me out with a shawl, so I never felt chilly. Since I hadn't actually looked carefully at the Chelston Hall brochure and I wasn't Amelia retracing her childhood steps, it was happenstance that took me towards the stables. This was the perfect moment to keep my promise to Robert and look in on Tempest, although my knowledge of horseflesh was scanty to say the least.

A young stable hand polishing a saddle doffed his cap and one of the grooms nodded to me as I wandered inside. The stables stretched a way down with a few horses peering interestedly from over their stalls at the unaccustomed visitor. There was a glossy black mare, a shining chestnut, and a silvery stallion that looked exactly like Gandalf's horse, Shadowfax. From Robert's description last night, that must be Tempest. A magnificent horse indeed. Dolly was chewing diligently at something, and a few other workaday-looking horses peered over their stalls. The place smelled very horsey, like manure, hay, polish, and beeswax. Sunlight fell in long shafts through the windows, capturing scores of dancing motes in the beams. Life in the countryside. Idyllic indeed.

In fact, it was so pleasant there, and despite the dowager

and the would-be assassin, and not forgetting that Robert was meant for Amelia, not me, I felt a bit wistful about leaving. I'd settled quite comfortably into the whole routine of daily life at Chelston Hall, even though I'd only been there since Tuesday morning and had no idea how, when, or if I could leave anyway. Thoughts of my former life and my friends hadn't crossed my mind, and I didn't miss social media and my gadgets one bit. That was strange. I also felt more peaceful, even with the above-mentioned danger looming. My tranquil thoughts were rudely interrupted by the last person I would ever want to be alone with—Sidney.

"I say, Cousin Amelia, good day!" he warbled, looking as dapper as ever and picking his way carefully past scraps of hay and a few piles of manure. "May I speak with you on a very important matter? If you're not too busy."

He must have been really desperate to speak to me, given his horror of anything that would spoil his exquisite attire. The important matter was clearly related to his lines for the play. Was he still worried about having too many? Hardly. He basically had to appear on stage, looking imposing, and say a few lines to introduce each scene.

"Yes, of course you may, Sir Sidney," I said sweetly. "What is it? Is it about your lines? I've completed your script, and you can start working on it with Sir Harold." In a fatal move, I smiled at him.

He scurried right up close to me, his usually pale cheeks flushed, his beady eyes gleaming, looking more ferret-like than usual because he was excited about something.

"No! It's about something far more important. I cannot conceal my emotions any longer. I must speak!"

If this had been Colin Firth with me in a re-enactment of *Pride and Prejudice*, I wouldn't have taken a step back.

I would've leaped into his arms faster than one could say "Regency romance." But this was slimy Sidney and I tried to back-pedal. Sidney moved with lightning speed and, as I retreated, he advanced until I fell backwards over a hay bale and landed on the floor with a bruising thud that knocked the breath out of me. As per usual, there was a ripping sound that heralded the ruin of some part of my clothing. But my focus was on Sidney's behaviour. Some madness gripped his mind since he threw himself on top of me like a starving dog on a bone. I was squashed beneath his surprising weight for one so thin and scrawny and almost suffocated by an overwhelming smell of pomade or cologne or whatever men used back then. His choice of fragrance was unfortunate; a sweet cloying scent.

"Amelia, my love!" he panted. He tried to put his arms around me as I fought him off. Worse, he leaned in to kiss me, making disgusting smacking sounds with those horrible lips. I turned my face away to avoid the suction as his hot breath puffed against my cheek.

"I love you. I adore you, darling Amelia. Be mine. Say you'll be mine!"

I managed to get one hand free and gave him a hard slap across his face. My hand stung and he jerked back a little. "Get off me, you swine!"

Even though I fought like a woman possessed, my fighting back only increased his excitement. Clearly, my first impression of him was right; one of those men for whom no means yes. He wriggled and squirmed on top of me and from the stiff thing poking into my leg, either he had a fire hydrant in his pocket or was just pleased to be so close to me. Strangely enough, I wasn't afraid, just very angry. Instinctively, I brought my knee up and, despite the dress, I managed to get him in the right spot. He yelped and slid sideways. Then all hell broke loose.

"You lecherous bastard! Get off her right now before I kill you!"

A hand reached down and dragged Sidney off me by the scruff of his neck. As I sat up, all I saw was Sidney flying through the air. His eyes were as big and round as saucers as he landed against the nearest stall with a crash. Sidney slid to the ground and lay in a crumpled heap, moaning pathetically. His face red with rage, his chest heaving, his eyes flashing retribution, Rupert stood over Sidney like an avenging angel. I was stunned. So, apparently, was Sidney.

"How dare you bring your disrespectful ways into my home?" Rupert bellowed. "How dare you treat my cousin like some trollop? Like some cheap harlot? You should be horsewhipped for your gross effrontery."

"Ah-ah-ah-ah-ah!" Sidney bleated in terror, trying to scramble backwards but not going anywhere since his back was against the stall. His legs bicycled ineffectually in one spot. "I meant no disrespect. I was overcome by ... er ... my feelings, my emotions."

I glanced at the stable entrance. There, to my horror, was a small rapt audience, transfixed by the unfolding events. Clementine stared with her mouth open, as did the stable boy and the groom I'd seen on the way in. My heart sank. There was no covering the incident up. The local grapevine would spread this shocking scandal fast.

"Feelings? I'll show you what you deserve, you despicable worm!"

Rupert grabbed the nearest weapon leaning against the wall, which happened to be a deadly-looking pitchfork. As he raised it over his head, the combined sounds of our hysterical banshee screams—me, Clementine, and Sidney—must have brought him to his senses. Sidney was as white as a sheet, trembling, whimpering, cowering with his arms over his head for protection.

Rupert came to his senses, thank heavens. He shook his head and tossed the pitchfork aside. The sound of it clattering to the floor made Sidney flinch even more. Rupert came over to me and gently lifted me to my feet, dusting off the hay and whatever else was clinging to my clothes and hair. He picked up my shawl and carefully arranged it around my shoulders.

"Are you all right, cousin?" he asked so gently that it was hard to imagine the raging fury he'd demonstrated just a few moments before.

Actually, I still felt a bit shaky but that was from Rupert's outburst more than having Sidney on top of me, trying to shove his tongue down my throat.

"Yes, I'm fine, thank you," I quavered.

Sidney had scrambled to his feet and with trembling hands was trying to brush straw and manure off his clothes. He looked like an absolute fright with his hair awry, his coat torn, his collar askew, and his neckcloth ruined.

"I say, that was most uncalled for, Rupert," he said, shuddering. "Most ungallant and most uncousinly." Several buttons had popped off his waistcoat. He almost sobbed as he tried to pull the garment closed. "You could have killed me with that vicious attack. I never meant to hurt Cousin Amelia and I humbly beg her forgiveness."

He looked at me with a pleading expression.

Before I could reply, Rupert butted in. "You should pack your bags and leave right away. You don't deserve Cousin Amelia's kindness and the fact that she gave you a part in the play. You're a disgrace to the family." He snorted contemptuously. "You're nothing but a ridiculous creature, always prancing down to the village decked out in some dandified finery. You don't know how much people laugh at you behind your back."

His tone was scathing as he looked Sidney up and down with naked scorn. "In fact, when I tell my mother about this, no doubt she'll forbid you ever to come here again. I'll see to it."

Sidney looked utterly stricken. I glanced at the stable door; to my relief the audience had melted away, no doubt spreading the astonishing news of the fight and Sidney's near demise at his murderous cousin's hands.

"Rupert, that's enough!" I said sharply. For some reason I felt sorry for Sidney. He might be a menace to the parlour maids or the village maidens foolish enough to take him seriously, but not to me. "You won't tell your mother and you won't tell anyone. Promise me, please."

Rupert stared at me, wide-eyed in disbelief and anger. "Not tell Mama? What do you mean? You should join me in casting this vile viper out."

There never was a more unlikely viper. Sidney looked so disheartened. He plopped down onto a hay bale and put his face in his hands, his shoulders heaving. There was nothing else to do but save the day. We needed the play to go on so I could flush out the assassin. All the preparations were a nice cover for my detective work, such as it was. The last thing I wanted was for Rupert to upset the apple cart over Sidney's clumsy attempts to get my attention.

I took Rupert's hand. "I'm very grateful that you saved me, Rupert, but telling your mother will only upset her because she holds Sidney in great affection. Besides, we don't want to spoil the play which we're putting on for Robert's entertainment and to help him feel better." I looked him straight in the eye. "I assume you and Miss Eccles have sorted out your little disagreement?"

Having calmed down, Rupert had the grace to blush. He shuffled his feet and looked away. "I've apologised to Miss Eccles for speaking out of turn and she has accepted it. I was wrong to overlook the pleasure other people will get from the play. We've been rehearsing our lines and that's ... er ... how we came to be near the stables."

I patted his arm. "Wonderful. Now please go and reassure Miss Eccles that all is well. It was a complete misunderstanding. I fell over a hay bale and Sir Sidney attempted to help me up by reaching for my hand and he ... er ... fell over as well. You got the wrong impression. Everyone is on perfectly amiable terms."

Out of the corner of one eye, I saw Sidney brighten. I had just given him a dignified exit from this enormously embarrassing situation.

I turned back to Rupert. "The play must go on, Rupert." I widened my eyes meaningfully, hoping he would get my drift.

He did, although he stared at me with a grim expression. "Hmm. I see. The play must go on and this ruffian is to be allowed to stay. What kind of justice is that?"

"Please, Rupert. Think of Robert and your mother. They don't need to be upset by this silly incident because that's all it is."

He gave me a slightly mocking bow. "As you like, cousin. I will comply with your wishes." He cast a disdainful glance at Sidney before stalking out. "Fribble!" was his parting shot.

Sidney leaped to his feet and then fell on his knees before me. "I beg your forgiveness, dear Miss Carstairs," he babbled. "I am truly, truly sorry. I lost my head."

"Just get up, Sir Sidney," I said abruptly. "Pull yourself together."

"You don't understand what this play means to me," he said pathetically, his voice cracking. "I have nothing in the world. I have no one."

Looking at him, that was hard to believe. He didn't appear to have nothing. He dressed well, he had a valet to care for his expensive clothes and trinkets and see that he looked stylish on every occasion. He lived in London, and he had transport because how else had he arrived. He must have money.

"No," he corrected himself, "I don't mean I have nothing. My parents left me with a neat little house in town and a comfortable independence, but my aunt and Chelston Hall are all I have as a family and a home." He cocked his head as he thought. "I do have a much older aunt, but she lives in Scotland, and I never visit because she lives in a very cold, run-down establishment that's quite ghastly." He shuddered. "Turvey, my valet, won't accompany me there."

He rolled his eyes. "And if Turvey won't go, who would take care of my needs?"

Rupert's resentment of his cousin could spring from envy of Sidney's independence. Sidney might be a fribble, but he had the physical and financial freedom Rupert so desperately wanted. I couldn't help him with that. Rupert had to paddle his own canoe. For now, all I could do was smooth things over and make sure that the show went on.

Sidney gave me a hesitant glance. "So, am I still the narrator? Can I still be in the play? I am truly sorry for my shocking behaviour. It will never happen again. Never ever. You have my word."

He looked and sounded so contrite that I said, "Yes, you're still in the play and no, I will not embarrass myself and you by letting the real story get out. As far as I'm concerned, what happened was exactly what I said to Rupert. I fell over and you fell over trying to help me up."

He gave me a smile brimming with relief. "Oh, thank you, thank you." He frowned. "I say, do you think Rupert would have killed me?"

Rupert's face hideously contorted with rage came to mind. His eyes bulging, his expression of fury, had frightened me. His resentment of so many things had found a weak and pitiful target in Sidney and his pathetic attempt to win me over. In truth, if we had not all screamed at once, Rupert might well have impaled Sidney on those wicked-looking prongs. But of course, I said nothing of the sort. Instead, I laughed carelessly.

"Kill you? Of course not. Rupert was simply being dramatic. He's been practicing his swordsmanship with his fencing master, don't forget. He just got carried away."

Sidney tittered half-heartedly in response, but he didn't sound all that convinced. Dishevelled and dirty, he limped to the stable entrance and then disappeared. I looked down at my filthy dress. Maisie would be horrified.

Maisie being horrified was an understatement but being poised on the path to greater heights in her chosen career, she took this as an occupational challenge. She was more interested in the drama, so the news had spread like wildfire as I suspected.

"Oh, miss," she breathed, all agog with big eyes. "Is it true Sir Sidney tried to force his attentions on ye personage and Lord Rupert came to the rescue and almost kilt his cousin with a pitchfork?"

I wasn't sure just how informal one should be with a lady's

maid, never having had one before, of course, but this was my golden opportunity to quash the rumours once and for all. Hopefully, she would convey the PR version below stairs.

I laughed. "Don't be silly, Maisie. How could Lord Rupert kill anyone? I fell over and Sir Sidney was kindly helping me up and he slipped on some … manure … and he fell over too. The only victim here is my dress, and I'm so sorry about making it dirty."

She stared at me for a long moment and then winked conspiratorially. "Of course. Ye fell over and then Sir Sidney … er … he also fell over." She pressed her lips together trying to suppress her giggles. So much for the PR exercise and covering up the whole shebang.

Dinner proceeded very well without any cold glances between Rupert and Sidney. True to his promise, Rupert behaved quite normally, even addressing a few innocent remarks to Sidney. Still jumpy, Sidney gave him nervous answers and devoted his attention to his plate. But no one seemed to notice anything was amiss. Since Clementine and Rupert were back on speaking terms, it was smiles all round. Everyone now had their lines, so their parts were the topic of dinner table conversation. Then the Gorgon Medusa threw a spanner in the works during an unfortunate lull in the chatter.

The dowager laid down her fork and stared at Rupert. "What's this I hear about you and Sidney having an altercation in the stables. Coming to blows by all accounts. *Brawling* like common stable boys."

Once again, one could have cut the silence with a blunt butter knife. Rupert stared back at his mother and then looked at me. I didn't know what to say. Sidney blanched and stopped in mid-chew, looking like a startled deer caught in the headlights. Clementine froze and looked at me. Sir Harold and Doctor Potts, bless them, just carried on eating, as did Maria, who might not have heard the dowager since she was busy scraping away at her plate.

Rupert gave a careless laugh and flapped his napkin at his mother. "I say, Mama, what's all this? Servants' gossip, I'll warrant."

The dowager pursed her lips and nodded. "I did hear it from Milvers."

"That sly tattletale!" Rupert burst out. "I can't see how you abide having that dreary creature in your employ, Mama. She's just a troublemaker with the servants." He scowled at her. "I think—"

His mother raised one hand to silence him. "Milvers is not paid to be popular, Rupert. She is paid to attend upon me. Occasionally she brings me news of events that I am sure no one else would bother to tell me, events I should know about." Her implication was obvious.

She continued, "So exactly what happened and why does Sidney have a red mark upon his cheek." She turned to Sidney, who let out a muffled yelp.

The dowager frowned at him. "Sidney, please do not make such peculiar noises at the dinner table. It is most unbecoming. I cannot imagine where you got this dreadful habit from. Perhaps your foppish London friends think it is amusing and frivolous, but I don't. They seem to be a very bad influence upon you."

Sidney reddened. "Sorry, Aunt Minerva."

Rupert made a show of sighing in an exasperated way. "This is all a big misunderstanding that's been blown out of proportion. Let Amelia tell you, Mama. She was there. She saw everything." He picked up his wine glass as if this was the end of his involvement.

The dowager raised her eyebrows and looked at me, for once surprised. "What is this, Amelia? How does this involve you?"

Talk about passing the buck. I took a leaf out of Clementine's book and gave a little sigh and rolled my eyes helplessly. "Such a silly accident, ma'am. I took a walk down to the stables, wool-gathering about the play, I must confess. When Sir Sidney approached me to ask about his lines, I turned around too quickly, and I fell backwards over a hay bale."

The dowager's frown deepened. Sidney and Rupert were both nodding eagerly so I pressed on.

"Of course, being chivalrous, Sir Sidney rushed to help me up but, in his haste, he slipped on some manure, as the stalls hadn't been mucked out yet, and he also fell over. That's how he hit his face."

Sidney beamed and gave a happy wriggle in his seat. Rupert looked relieved and tossed off the last of his wine. Sir Harold gave a disgusted snort and Clementine smiled nervously.

"Then Rupert must have heard our commotion because he entered the stables and tried to help us both up." I gave a sorrowful sigh and cast my gaze downwards. "All my fault and all so unnecessary."

"And what about this pitchfork?" the dowager demanded. "I hear Rupert very nearly attacked Sidney with a pitchfork."

Maria and Doctor Potts both jerked their heads up at the word "pitchfork" and gawked at me. Maria's mouth fell open in shock.

I widened my eyes in my best Surprised Look. "Pitchfork? I think there might have been a pitchfork leaning against a stall, this being the stables, and possibly it fell to the ground in all the tumult."

The dowager swung her gaze to Rupert. "So, you didn't

violently attack Sidney with a pitchfork, Rupert?"

"What? Attack my very own cousin with a pitchfork? Where on earth did you hear this ludicrous tale?" Rupert put on an excellent imitation of astonishment.

He laughed and pointed to Sidney. "Ask Sidney, Mama, if I attacked him with a pitchfork. What a preposterous idea! I was trying to help everyone get back on their feet. Is this the thanks I get?" He faked an offended expression. "Next time I won't bother to put myself out for anyone else."

Great acting. Rupert was very convincing. If I hadn't known the truth of the matter, I would have believed him. The dowager wavered, looking intently from one to the other, perhaps hoping to break their unspoken pact of covering up the truth. United in deceit, they held firm, not even glancing at each other this time.

Sidney blanched but seemed confident enough to speak up. "Yes, Aunt Minerva. It's exactly as Cousin Amelia has described. I'm afraid I'm guilty of startling her. It's all my fault her dress got soiled." He flapped both hands in typical Sidney fashion. "And my coat! I can't tell you how dreadful it looks. The state of my coat is quite shocking." He shook his head mournfully. "Poor Turvey was most upset. He was almost in tears. I can't imagine how he'll manage to get the stains out. It's completely ruined. And a good coat is so expensive."

"Yes, all right, Sidney," said the dowager testily. "I see the situation now. Clearly, I have been misinformed and there were no fisticuffs."

Sidney and Rupert both spluttered that there had been absolutely no brawling and that was the end of the debacle. But the incident reminded me of the dowager's personal maid, Milvers. I had quite forgotten about her. She never made an appearance, except for the occasional whiff of mothballs in the corridors. Evidently, she reported back to her mistress all the goings-on in the house. Was she dangerous? The black stare she had given me before should have warned me.

The evening continued without any more bombshells. Sidney stayed clear of his aunt by huddling together with Sir Harold and quietly reading his lines with his mentor. Maria regaled us with the song she had chosen for the end of the play. It was a plaintive melody and perfectly suited for the death scene. She sang unaccompanied because the pianoforte was in the ballroom, but her voice was so exquisite that she didn't need any help. After that, Clementine and Rupert put their heads together on their dialogue while Maria and Doctor Potts discussed their lines with the dowager and asked her opinion on their delivery, something she was always happy to give.

Later that evening I visited Robert who was highly amused by the whole incident, which of course had found its way back to him. He looked much better and was very pleased to see me. We sat in our usual chairs in front of the fire, with Parker discreetly pottering away in the dressing room, making a poor show of chaperoning us, while Russet lay on the hearth rug. Two glasses of wine awaited our delectation. Everything was so cosy and comfortable that it was hard to imagine leaving, although I had no idea of any kind of future. Just being in the present with this wonderful man was enough.

"You could always join us for dinner," I said. "Then you would hear all the news straight from the source."

He sighed and pretended to look contrite. "The one excuse I have to absent myself from my stepmother's company and now you seek to deny me this unexpected respite?" His eyes crinkled at the corners as he smiled.

"Do you dislike her that much?" I blurted out.

He was silent for a few moments. "Let's just say we get on better apart. She made my father happy after a fashion although she bullied him mercilessly and forced him to make decisions he didn't want to make regarding his family."

That sounded as if it was related to Amelia and her father leaving the parish and moving to Plymouth. I didn't want to ask though and he didn't expand on the topic.

He patted my hand. "Besides, the play is meant to be a complete surprise. If I were to join the dinner table, I'd hear what's going on and that would spoil everything. Designing the stage is one thing but consorting with the actors is another."

Then his expression became serious. "I know you've laughed off the incident with Sidney, but if he hurt you in any way—"

"Not at all," I interrupted him. "Apart from him earning Maisie's undying hatred for ruining my dress, there's no harm done. I think he got the fright of his life when Rupert went berserk. Besides, I'm quite capable of taking care of myself."

He chided me gently. "That's not the point. No female under my roof, whatever her social status, should endure any insult or attack on her person." Then he frowned. "I'm not saying Sidney's a danger, but he's a nuisance to females if he thinks he can get away with his primitive form of lovemaking."

Sidney had the romantic finesse of a rhino. It was hard to imagine him winning over any female with his clumsy methods.

"Has he done this before?"

Robert nodded. "My father had to give him a severe talking-to and a warning when several maids complained about his unwanted attentions. Then the innkeeper stormed up to the Hall, swearing death and destruction on Sidney if he ever approached his daughter again. Sidney was so terrified he hid in his room for a week."

I couldn't help giggling. "To be honest, I was surprised at his efforts to ... er ... win me over because I thought he was batting for the other team." As I spoke, I realised the expression was totally wrong for the era. Damn! Luckily Robert thought it was just a quaint figure of speech.

Robert stared at me, puzzled. "Batting for the other team?" he repeated. Then he roared with laughter and grimaced with pain. "My dear Amelia, how you always manage to make me laugh. He is *only* interested in women, I can assure you, but poor Sidney hasn't had any luck capturing the affections of any women because he isn't very manly."

My expression must have spoken volumes because he continued, "By that, I mean he doesn't ride, hunt, play sport, shoot, drive a curricle to an inch, write poetry celebrating a lady's eyes, engage in genteel conversation, and any number of things a young woman would expect a man to do to impress her. He's also not very good at social games like whist and the like."

"But his aunt says he can recite very well," I said. "Maybe the play will give him a chance to shine. Women like a man who can recite poetry, even though he hasn't written it."

Robert smiled, shaking his head. "You're very forgiving, Amelia, but I don't hold out much hope."

"Does he have any ... er ... prospects? Anything to offer a lady?"

Robert nodded. "If you mean does he have any money, he's certainly not penniless. His parents left him comfortably off, providing he is prudent, which he is. His mother, Celia Cole, was the youngest of three sisters. Augusta is the eldest, then came Minerva, my stepmother, and Celia. They all married well despite not having large dowries. The girls' parents weren't nobility but came of respectable stock. They were all very attractive, especially Celia who married a baronet. Augusta found herself an earl, albeit a slightly impoverished one, with an estate in the north of Scotland."

His expression hardened. "Then Minerva, of course, who caught my widowed father's eye and married him within months of their meeting."

He didn't seem to want to expand further on the subject. Just the mention of the dowager had soured the mood.

He looked thoughtful for a moment, then said, "Shall I speak to Rupert about attacking Sidney? I'm concerned that his reaction was so violent."

"No, don't say anything," I said quickly. "Rupert and Sidney banded together when the dowager was grilling them both for the truth. They stuck to the story of how we all fell over. Anyway, they seemed to have buried whatever hatchet was between them by the time dinner was over."

Robert stirred uncomfortably and winced again as he moved his left arm. Parker was there in an instant, but Robert waved him away.

"There shouldn't be any real animosity between them because they grew up together," he said. "Sidney is a few years older than Rupert but he's a little immature so that levels them out. Sidney's parents died when he was quite young and although he went to boarding school during term time, he spent all his holidays here. You and your father had left for Plymouth by then, so I don't think you and he crossed paths at all."

Lying again, I shook my head.

"Chelston Hall was a second home to Sidney, you could say. Minerva is the closest thing he's had to a mother in his life. To give her all due respect, she dotes on Sidney and treats him with as much love as she lavishes on Rupert."

He mused for a moment. "I wonder if Rupert somehow resents that."

This was my chance to push for Rupert's dream. "I don't think so. They squabble more like siblings than rivals. I think Rupert feels he'd like to spread his wings and see the world, not be tied to his mother's apron strings."

He nodded. "Yes, I agree. I know he wanted so desperately to join up to fight and now he thinks with Napoleon on the loose, this is his chance. Of course, Minerva would never let him sign up and she'd rather die than buy him a commission." He sighed. "For once I agree with her. I wouldn't let him be subjected to the carnage I've seen. All the glory stories don't tell the real brutal and horrifying truth."

I couldn't tell him that within a very short space of time Napoleon would be defeated and safely ensconced on the island of St. Helena. Robert suddenly looked tired and when Parker appeared with his medicine, he swallowed it without objecting. As I rose, he caught my hand. His expression was almost pleading.

"Will I see you tomorrow? You will come back to see me, won't you?"

If I could have stayed the night, or in fact stayed forever, I would have.

"Yes, I'll see you tomorrow night with perhaps more amusing antics to relate." My tone was light but given his expression and my deepening feelings, I didn't feel at all light-hearted. That was how the evening ended.

Chapter Twelve

Sunday, 30 April 1815

C hurch was a given on Sundays and the dowager usually expected the household to attend, where no doubt, the Reverend Wilby would be preaching. However, given the impending play, she sent word that those who felt they could not attend would be excused. I didn't expect to see anyone at the breakfast table, but Rupert and Clementine joined me.

"Would you mind hearing our lines after breakfast, Amelia?" Clementine asked with a very pretty smile.

"Of course," I said.

The morning promised mild weather, so we took ourselves off to a part of the garden with a few flower-lined walks and stone benches. With no one else to worry about, we just concentrated on their lines together. I'm no director but they didn't need directing. They put their scripts to one side and opened the scene quite naturally.

The magic began when Rupert took Clementine's hand and said, *"If I profane with my unworthiest hand, this holy shrine, the gentle sin is this: My lips, two blushing pilgrims, ready stand to smooth that rough touch with a tender kiss."*

Gazing up at him Clementine replied, *"Good pilgrim, you do wrong your hand too much, which mannerly devotion shows in this; for saints have hands that pilgrims' hands do touch, and palm to palm is holy palmers' kiss."*

As they continued, they forgot about me. They were so clearly in love it sent a pang through my heart. They were lucky to have found each other. Since Maria wasn't here to play the Nurse in that section, they jumped to the famous balcony scene. Clementine stood on a bench while Rupert pretended to wander about below. He looked up and caught sight of her.

"But soft, what light through yonder window breaks? It is the East, and Juliet is the sun."

I could just imagine the audience in paroxysms of emotion with the handsome Romeo and the beautiful Juliet, playing out this scene. At the end of Romeo's speech, Juliet replies, *"O Romeo, Romeo, wherefore art thou Romeo? Deny thy father and refuse thy name, Or, if thou wilt not, be but sworn my love, And I'll no longer be a Capulet."*

The scene was very moving, and I was transfixed. Somehow, they managed to capture the meaning and emotion Shakespeare had intended. They had no experience in performing but just their own feelings and a fresh approach. I was faced with two love relationships that just seemed to unfold so naturally: Rupert and Clementine who were well suited even though they didn't appear to be at first; and Robert and Amelia.

That was the hardest part for me. I could feel myself falling in love with him and pulling back for Amelia's sake. Yet at the same time, I had to give him hope that Amelia loved him so he would propose, because they had to end up together. The way he looked at me, as Amelia, spoke volumes although his behaviour was impeccable, never overstepping the mark. His expression was so loving, his tone of voice so warm, drawing me in. The occasional touch of my hand, his engaging smile, all told me that Robert and Amelia were heading in the right direction. If I seemed reticent about showing any emotions, Regency era rules would indicate I was being modest, as any young woman would be. Every night I visited his room to regale him with mostly hilarious anecdotes of the play's progress and what was happening in general, chaperoned by the now-invisible Parker and Russet. It was going to be hard when I left but, hopefully, the real Amelia would pick up the threads. I'd been keeping her diary up to speed by writing whenever I could and putting in my growing feelings as hers. It was tearing me in half. Would she love him as I did? Would I ever feel this way about someone else when I got back to my own century?

Clementine snapped me out of my self-indulgent pity party as she sat next to me on the stone bench. "What do you think, Amelia? Are we doing well?"

"I think the bard would be extremely proud to see these parts played so beautifully."

Clementine beamed and applauded.

Rupert reddened. "Naturally, we have no experience," he said gruffly, "but I'm sure the audience will be forgiving of any flaws."

They had no experience except for the best kind; the actual feeling of being in love, even if neither of them recognised it. The rest of the morning was spent very pleasantly as they went through all their scenes together. The bulk of the performance rested on their shoulders since most of the other parts had either been cut out or whittled right down to the bare minimum. Apart from the occasional missed word, they were almost word perfect. We'd have to work on the actions on stage, but the lines were paramount.

"I have a question," said Clementine. Her cheeks turned faintly pink. "In the last scene, Romeo is supposed to kiss Juliet and then she is ... er ... supposed to kiss him." She blushed brighter and glanced at Rupert. "Are we supposed to kiss each other?"

This would be a problem. In Regency times, a single man and an unmarried woman couldn't even be alone in the same room without there being a big social scandal. The audience would go berserk if they actually did kiss.

"No, of course not," I said smoothly. "This is a play so you and Rupert will just pretend to kiss each other."

They both stared blankly at me and then at each other.

"How?" said Rupert.

"When Romeo is leaning over Juliet as she is lying on the bier, he can cup her face in his hands and hide the gesture. When Romeo is lying against the bier, having drunk the poison, then Juliet's hair can fall naturally to create a screen as she leans over him."

They looked at each other again and nodded.

Phew! Hopefully they could pull it off.

"Good day!"

We all turned to see Maria Wilby huffing and puffing her way towards us, waving her script in the air. Her cheeks flushed and her eyes bright, she was eager to join the impromptu rehearsal.

"Are you rehearsing?" she called. "I managed to get away early and I'm so anxious to practice my lines, even though I only have a few."

"Yes!" chorused Clementine and Rupert. Maria had to sit down first to catch her breath, but within minutes she and Clementine were doing their scenes together, while Rupert followed lines for them. I'd included a small part of Nurse's lines to Romeo as well. Friar Laurence had a few lines with Romeo to arrange the marriage. So much had to be cut to keep the performance within one hour and a bit. I could only hope that Sidney managed to remember the lines joining the various scenes.

Dinner was much like the other dinners since we'd started the rehearsals. Conversation revolved around discussing the play and everyone's parts and their progress, but the dowager didn't seem to mind. She presided over the dinner table with her usual watchful eye. Naturally the glory would all be hers and she basked in it already.

"The costume fabric will be here tomorrow," she announced. "Lady de Montfort's dressmaker and her seamstresses will take measurements. After that, the costumes should be ready by Thursday at the latest."

"And the program?" asked Maria, who had stayed to dine after many of her usual blushful protestations.

The dowager nodded. "Ah, yes, some good news there. Since the de Montforts have sponsored the costumes, the Beasleys were determined to contribute in whatever way they can, so they have undertaken to attend to the programs. The local printer is delighted to do the job and assures us that the end product will be worthy of Chelston Hall."

She looked extremely satisfied.

"I say, Aunt," Sidney piped up. "Are you still going to provide refreshments? What do you think of my idea?"

The dowager sipped her wine. "It is an excellent idea,

Sidney, and I have discussed it with Lady Hamilton, who is also eager to participate. Her cook will confer with ours and come up with a variety of delicacies for our guests to enjoy after a wonderful theatrical performance."

After dinner was over, the rest of the evening was filled with more discussions of the play, the likelihood of the costumes being exacts replicas of the pictures in the costume book, the wording of the program, and the response from our audience. It sounded as if all the actors were a tad nervous. Sidney was most concerned about the quality and quantity of the champagne and exactly what refreshments would be provided. He and the dowager spent some time on this interesting subject, with her assuring him that Chelston Hall's cook and Lady Hamilton's cook would no doubt do both households proud.

Yes, I was also nervous. Not just because the actual performance was drawing nearer, but because I was still no closer to finding a suspect in the attempt on Robert's life. Part of me began to think that it actually was just a terrible accident with some poacher taking a chance on a shot that had ended in near tragedy. My usual visit with Robert was cut short because he looked really exhausted. When I scolded him a little about overdoing it, he just gave me a weary smile. Writing up Amelia's diary was cathartic in a way. It gave me an excuse to share my own anxiety about his health, but it was so hard to stay objective. How could I? At this late stage, I was invested heart and soul in his life, in his very survival.

Chapter Thirteen

Monday, 1 May 1815

The ballroom was a hive of activity once the fabrics for the costumes arrived as well as Lady de Montfort's dressmaker and her team of seamstresses. The youngsters must have caught wind of this event via their various adoring parents. Dancing was set aside while they were being measured. Mr Roach and Celeste were there of course, with Celeste tinkling quietly with a piano piece. Being males, the boys horsed around a bit, as was expected, with their tutor trying to maintain order. The fabrics were beautiful. Plain, with no pattern, but the quality of the material was excellent. The blue and green for the houses of Capulet and Montague were deep and rich. The burgundy and mustard combination for the dancers was striking and the silver ribbons excited much interest among the girls. Excellent choices. Lady de Montfort was racking up points there. Nurse's and Friar Laurence's outfits would be dull in comparison, but Maria was so excited that she would have been happy to wear a sack just to be involved. Doctor Potts also arrived for his measurements but since his was simply a basic brown robe, he soon trotted off to attend to the dowager and look in on Robert.

Then we had an almost-fatal setback. One of the seamstresses took Anne to one side and started measuring her. No one had thought about Anne in the grand scheme of things beyond her role as my scribe. To my great shame, neither had I.

Tiffany, who had finished her measurements, did a pirouette, and stared at Anne. "I don't know why you're bothering with Anne," she said in a piercing voice. She gave a contemptuous toss of her head. "I mean she's not going to be doing any dancing with her lame leg. She's only a helper. She doesn't need a costume. It's just a waste of fabric."

The silence was deafening. The governesses gaped at Tiffany in shock and the seamstresses exchanged wide-eyed glances. Lady de Montfort's head dressmaker rolled her eyes and then busied herself with folding fabric. The Hamilton girls' mouths fell open. They elbowed each other in gleeful horror as if they couldn't wait to dash home and reveal all to their mother, who would no doubt revel in the downfall of any rival parent. Tiffany had committed a hideous blunder, a solecism beyond compare. Even I knew that no well-bred young lady would ever say such a thing in company. Anne went white. She looked utterly crushed as a tear trickled down her cheek. Cambria surreptitiously passed her a handkerchief. Everyone had stopped what they were doing, now staring at Tiffany. She reddened and looked defiant.

"What?" she said, looking around at the stunned faces. "It's true, isn't it?"

Tiffany had made the terrible mistake of thinking that her beauty and popularity allowed her to say what she liked without consequences. She also forgot that Anne was a very personable young girl when she came out of her shell, and she'd forged friendships with the others over the past few days. The dancers all liked Anne very much.

But Walter de Montfort, a mischievous, freckle-faced scamp he might be, knew how to behave. He sauntered towards Tiffany, who took a few steps back. Her face was a picture of confusion, as if she'd expected everyone to laugh with her at Anne. I looked at Mr Roach, expecting him to intervene, but he simply folded his arms and watched the scene play out. Since he knew the youngsters well and had taught all of them, he must have had his reasons for hanging back.

"Tiffany, that's a beastly thing to say to Anne," Walter said.

The dancers all murmured their agreement. Tiffany retreated even further until she was quite isolated from the group. She looked panicky.

"In fact," Walter continued, "it's such a beastly thing to say that I think we should call you Tiffany Beastly from now on. How would you like that?" He cocked his head and stared at her. "Tiffany Beastly. It suits you because you're quite beastly."

He turned his back on her and joined the others, who also turned their backs on her and clustered around the devastated Anne. Tiffany resorted to the weapon she no doubt used to bully her indulgent parents: tears. Floods of them. And a tantrum. A full-scale one. Drawing herself up, she sobbed and stamped her foot. No one said a word. Everyone ignored her and Celeste started tinkling again on the piano.

"How dare you speak to me like that, Walter de Montfort, you horrible little freckly *boy*! I refuse to stay here a minute longer and be insulted like this."

Her cheeks flushed with anger, she stormed up to Mr Roach who remained impassive in the face of the brewing tempest.

"I won't be performing in this play any longer, Mr Roach. I refuse to be part of this dance troupe. I'm going home this very minute to complain to my parents. See if you can manage without me since I *am* the best dancer."

Mr Roach frowned. "I'm very sorry you feel this way, Tiffany, but Walter did the gentlemanly thing by defending Anne, whom you grievously insulted. It is most unbecoming behaviour for a young lady to refer to the infirmity of another like that."

Tiffany looked as if she was going to explode. Her face went scarlet, and her body stiffened. She balled her fists at her sides and screeched, "Oh! Oh! Unbecoming? Me? How can you even say that? I'm the one who was insulted by that nasty de Montfort boy, and I won't stay to be insulted any more. You'll be sorry I've gone. Just wait and see! You can't replace me!"

Mr Roach nodded. "No doubt, Tiffany, no doubt, but we'll simply have to manage without you, won't we?" He looked over at the group of dancers and said musingly, "Now, let's see. If I move Cambria up one place to partner with Peter, that should do it nicely."

That was the final straw for the incensed Tiffany. She stomped over to her governess, grabbed her things, and hissed at the woman, who very reluctantly followed her obnoxious young charge. Once they'd left the ballroom, the buzz of activity resumed, with lots of giggles from the dancers who evidently thought this was the biggest joke in the world. I went over to Mr Roach.

"Can we manage without Tiffany?"

He shook his head. "Not really, but there's nothing to worry about. She'll be back soon."

I stared at him, not comprehending. "But she's the best dancer and we need her and Peter to open the play with the pavane."

Was this all for naught? I'd just rescued the play, my detective cover, from Rupert and Sidney's quarrel. Now it seemed doomed once more.

He nodded again. "Yes, and I'm not at all worried. Be patient. All will be well very shortly."

"How do you know? She seemed very determined when she stormed off."

He sighed and gave a wry smile. "I know these children, Miss Carstairs. I have taught all of them to dance. I know the families. I have taught their parents to dance. Mrs Beasley will certainly not let young Tiffany's tears and tantrums upset her good standing in society, both local and farther afield."

He clapped and the dancers jumped to attention. "Come, boys and girls, let's show Miss Carstairs our idea for the end of the play. Peter, just sit to one side for now." He waved to Maria and Celeste. "Ladies?"

Maria readied herself next to the pianoforte, beaming like a lighthouse, while the dancers lined up. Then we were rudely interrupted by the whirling dervish that was Mrs Beasley as she burst through the ballroom doors. When I had first met her, she was very well turned out as befitting her status in polite society. Today she looked positively dishevelled. Her smart bonnet was askew and the feathers on the brim were limp. Her hair looked as if it had been hastily bundled under the bonnet and her Spenser jacket wasn't buttoned properly. Added to that, her face was crimson with outrage. Behind her she dragged Tiffany, who was equally bedraggled. Her face was streaked with tears, and she looked very down in the mouth. Hovering behind mother and daughter was the unfortunate governess who also looked despondent. I braced myself for the inevitable wrath that Mrs Beasley seemed to have borrowed from on high.

Mr Roach was unperturbed as he bowed to the lady. "Ah, Mrs Beasley, welcome to our rehearsal. How can I be of assistance?"

"Mr Roach!" she said. "There has been a most terrible misunderstanding. Quite dreadful." She let go of Tiffany, flapped, and then clasped her hands. "I have utterly no idea how this confusion arose."

Mr Roach raised his bushy eyebrows and fixed her with a steely look. "Misunderstanding?"

Once more, everyone was transfixed. This was better than reality television for me. The young dancers instinctively clustered around Anne again.

"Tiffany had no right to be rude to Anne." She glowered at Tiffany. "Again!" Then she turned back to Mr Roach. "And to walk out of the play like that is not how her father and I have brought her up. She was quite mistaken to behave in such an unseemly fashion."

Mr Roach shrugged. "If Tiffany no longer wants to be part of the play, I won't stand in her way."

"No, no, you don't understand," said Mrs Beasley, sounding frantic. She clutched his arm. "She *must* be in the play. She *will* be in the play." She glared at her daughter so severely that Tiffany nodded and hung her head, all the wind taken out of her sails. "All the expense of the costumes, the time spent on dance rehearsals, Her Grace's kindness in including our family, none of this must go to waste. It would be too shocking. Too shocking for words!"

So, back at the ranch, Mama Bear Beasley was just trying to salvage their ravaged family reputation. Mr Roach was smooth and tactful as he hid a smug smile behind one hand.

"Of course, it was a complete misunderstanding," he said. "I quite understand. Young people, hot tempers, and cross words exchanged. Come along then, Tiffany, and join the others."

Mrs Beasley gave a loud sigh of relief. "Thank you, Mr Roach. You know the children so well. I knew you'd understand." Then she looked at me. "But Anne *must* have a costume as well. I insist upon it."

"Yes, she will," I said. "There's plenty of ways Anne will be helping out in front with the guests." I had no idea what these ways would be but handing out programs to guests was a start.

"Yes, well then, that's settled," said Mrs Beasley with a radiant smile. "Wonderful. I'll say good day. I left the house in such a hurry, and I have so many things to do today."

She sent Tiffany a last parting death stare and the hissed admonition to comport herself as her dear mama and papa had brought her up to behave. Tiffany, now completely trounced, slunk behind her governess. Mrs Beasley sailed off, happy that the family reputation remained intact, and their social standing was preserved. The seamstress attending to Anne quickly finished measuring her and then the ladies packed up the material, their tape measures, and pins, and swished out. No doubt the tale of this drama would spread far and wide as well. Poor Mrs Beasley.

Mr Roach didn't waste any time dwelling on past injuries. "Girls and boys, if you have been measured for your costume then assemble for the last dance of the play."

"The last dance?" I asked. "I thought we were only having the opening pavane and the ball where Romeo sees Juliet."

Mr Roach winked at me. "It's a surprise. Actually, Mrs Wilby's idea and I think it'll work."

Maria rushed up with a worried expression. "Oh, I hope you don't mind, Amelia, but I thought we should have something to round off the dramatic ending as well as give the youngsters a chance to show off their dancing at the end."

She waved some sheet music under my nose. "I've picked out the music and the dancers will be performing in the background after Sir Sidney has said the epilogue." She stared at me with a tentative smile. "What do you think?"

"I say why not?"

Maria gave a big sigh of relief. "I hope Her Grace won't mind me going ahead with this idea. It's a bit more than just a song."

I patted her arm. "Maria, you are the musical director. Mr Roach is the choreographer. You are both in charge of music and dance. Her Grace knows this. Let's see what you have done."

Mr Roach clapped, and the dancers got into position. One of the governesses and the tutor graciously agreed to be the dead bodies of the two lovers to give context. Maria stood behind the "corpses" and Celeste began to play. Maria's voice was superb, the song was an excellent choice, and the dance gave a solemn, almost elegiac element as the dancers slowly walked in a weaving pattern to and fro, without distracting from the main centre stage. It would be the perfect conclusion.

Chapter Fourteen

Tuesday, 2 May; Wednesday, 3 May; Thursday, 4 May 1815

Tuesday and Wednesday flew by with much progress. I could hardly believe it. The performers practised so hard that by the end of Wednesday, everyone was word perfect, even Sidney. I rehearsed with everyone separately and in their particular scenes, but we needed to pull it all together, plus incorporate the dancers as party guests and, in a way, mourners in the last scene. The dancers were brilliant. Even the Hamilton girls, who had cast doubt in my mind on first acquaintance by galumphing into the library, acquitted themselves very well. Once Tiffany had gotten over herself, she and Peter made an exceptional couple. The opening dance was the grand pavane, slow and ceremonial, with a touch of drama, heralding what was to come. The party dance was a galliard, a lively dance with hopping steps, and quite energetic. The youngsters loved it. Mr Roach confided with some excitement that he'd incorporated a touch of the saltarello. This meant nothing to ignorant me, but it looked good. The concluding dance was a slow weaving in and out dance, more as background than anything else, a foil for Maria's moving finale song.

Meanwhile the stage grew into a very passable imitation of the streets of Verona. Robert made a brief discreet appearance, now without his sling, to check that his design worked. Juliet's balcony was very cunningly constructed like a slim tower so Clementine could get up there from behind the painted scenery. Somehow the carpenters had managed to rig up a rope that went from one side of the room to the other, with a black curtain that opened in the middle. It would have to be manually opened and closed but there was no shortage of volunteers. The performers could walk behind the scenery to get to their designated side. Sir Harold, who had a copy of everyone's lines as prompt, would be hidden from view once the curtains opened. The musicians, with Celeste accompanying them, produced a very professional sound. Maria had chosen well.

The only bugbear was the lighting. How could one recreate the changes in day and night with no electricity? We couldn't, so we didn't. Sir Harold took it upon himself to solve this conundrum. The three crystal chandeliers were lowered and cleaned, and then filled to half capacity with candles. The dowager firmly insisted on beeswax, not tallow. On the night, the candles would be lit, and the candelabras raised before the audience came in. The long pier mirrors would help to reflect the light. As Sir Harold said, "It must not be so bright as to dazzle the audience, yet not so dim that they cannot see the performers."

The additional lighting was from standing candelabras which could easily be removed. There was no lack of staff wanting to "man" the lights. Since sunset was around 7.30 p.m., if everyone was seated by seven, natural daylight would be on our side. The dowager had set the arrival time for six-thirty sharp, giving time to get the guests seated. Guests had already started delivering their chairs. The invitations had included the message that latecomers would not be able to enter once the play had started. But given the general air of excitement the project had generated, no doubt people would be there well in advance of curtain up.

The issue of stage makeup raised its head. At first the dowager was dead against it. "No," she said firmly. "Painted faces do not belong in this house."

Once again, that fount of all things acceptable and respectable, Doctor Potts, stepped in.

"Your Grace," he said with exquisite tact, "since time immemorial, since the ancient Greeks who *invented* theatre, players have worn ... ahem ... cosmetics to enhance their features, so the audience are able to see them."

I think he got her at "ancient Greeks" because she raised her eyebrows and listened. He carefully explained that her friends and other guests would not be able to see the performers' expressions and that was unacceptable, not after all the time and expense that had been put into the production. Mollified, she agreed. I had no idea where to get any circa 1815 stage makeup, but somebody knew somebody else who arrived with some interestingly labelled little jars and pots, and we had a practice run. There was a weird kind of white foundation simply called "Paint," rouge for the cheeks, loose powder to take off any shine, and "Lip Salve." "Black Powder" could be mixed with water and used to darken eyebrows and as eye liner. There was enough to do quite a good job and, given my *Pirates of Penzance* days, I volunteered my services and roped in Maisie to help with the dancers' faces. Our first makeup session went swimmingly, everyone looked professional, and the only person who shrugged and said he didn't care was, of course, Rupert. The girls and Clementine looked gorgeous, and

Rupert stared at her for quite a while. Things were developing nicely on that front.

The dowager had adopted the program as her pet project and was very secretive about it until a rough copy arrived on Wednesday for our perusal. The village printer had outdone himself with elaborate writing and many swirls, squirls, and flourishes. It was a single page announcing *The performance of Romeo and Juliet by Wm. Shakespeare, a selection of moving scenes, presented by Her Grace, the Dowager Duchess of Hadley*. This made it appear as if the whole thing was her idea, but never mind. Everyone in the production was listed by name. Maria was listed as the Musical Director and as the Operatically Trained Principal Singer. Maria went bright red and fumbled in her reticule for a handkerchief.

"Oh, Your Grace," she said, sniffing, "such an honour. I don't know what to say. I feel quite overwhelmed."

"Nonsense," said the dowager affably, with an airy wave. "Everyone's talents must be acknowledged. You *are* operatically trained, aren't you?"

She stared at Maria who twittered and squawked in confusion, "Yes, Your Grace, as I said before, Mama and Papa spared no expense to give me the best operatic training."

Already bored with the subject, the dowager turned away. "Don't make a fuss out of nothing then, Maria. The program is correct."

Mr Roach appeared as Dance Choreographer. Given his stint at the Astbury, I felt sure he would be delighted. The de Montforts and the Hamiltons were also mentioned for their kind sponsorship. I was surprised that everyone who had a significant role was acknowledged, down to the names of our rustic musicians and the carpenters. Nonetheless, the dowager was a crafty woman, and this perceived graciousness was not done out of kindness but simply to increase her social standing.

Robert's wry smile and comment confirmed my suspicions.

"I hardly think my stepmother is promoting the skills and talents of others out of the goodness of her heart. She's only too happy that thus far no one in the neighbourhood has been able to top this theatrical production."

He shrugged. "However, just participating has made many people happy and so one must consider the benefits accruing to others in this case."

He sounded rather haughty and lord of the manor, but he was of the nobility and that kind of pomposity came with aristocratic territory. Dad would have loved him to bits. It was a pity they could never meet.

The costumes were ready, as was the stage, so Thursday afternoon was the dry run, the first run-through of the entire play. No one would be wearing their actual costumes, except for the dancers who needed to get used to dancing in their apparel. I'd said the cast should just walk through the lines and action, but everyone ignored me and threw their hearts and souls into the performance. There was no audience although quite a few of the servants felt compelled to execute their tasks by walking past the ballroom's open doors and lingering. But it was good for the actors to know someone was watching them.

The fight scene was suitably dramatic, although severely cut since we had only three players, but with Sidney narrating the linking bits, the audience would get the picture. Who doesn't love a good sword fight? This was the first time anyone had seen the fighting, and it did not disappoint. The performers outdid themselves with much circling warily, then leaping about, ferocious swordplay, and metal scraping on metal as

Mercutio and Tybalt fought, with Romeo trying to intervene. Adding to the excitement was the fact that the players used two rapiers each, which made it all the more thrilling. The action stalled for a few minutes when Rupert complained that Johnson as Tybalt was not aggressive enough towards him. He kept saying, "Pardon me, my lord," after Tybalt calls Romeo "a villain" and "a wretched boy."

"Johnson," Rupert scolded him. "For pity's sake stay in the character of Tybalt. Stop saying 'my lord.' You're making me angry."

"Pardon me, my lord," said the hapless Johnson, hanging his head. "It's not respectful to call you a villain."

Rupert glared at him. "But you're not speaking to me as Lord Rupert. You're speaking to me as Romeo, and you must call me a villain. It's in the play. Do you understand."

Johnson nodded. "I'll try, my lord."

The action wasn't quite Franco Zeffirelli's standard but was pretty impressive. Rupert was transformed. I'd never seen him so energised, so passionate, except for the stable escapade. There was much gasping from the rest of the cast which added to the atmosphere. Clementine kept uttering shocked squeals which I'm sure spurred Rupert on. It was all very masculine, very dramatic, and testosterone driven. Sidney stood on the side, waiting to deliver his lines, shuddering, and closing his eyes every now and then.

The actual play is two and a half hours. I'd squeezed everything into one hour plus with much hacking of lines and scenes. But the whole story hung together well: drama, feuding, tragedy, love, misunderstanding, death, and reconciliation. What's not to like? After the run-through, the cast huddled together, discussing their lines and where they could do better. Sidney scuttled off to Sir Harold for confirmation that he hadn't missed a word.

Sir Harold cast a proud glance in my direction from under those beetling brows. "Well done, my boy!" he said to Sidney. "I'll say one thing. You can recite well."

Somehow Sidney had grasped the meaning of the lines instinctively. I never thought he'd understand but whether he did or not, he conveyed the emotion in a suitably sonorous voice. In fact, Sidney's stage voice was so different from his usual quite high-pitched voice that the cast clustered around him to express their admiration. Sidney was in his element. For once he received genuine admiration for a talent he never knew he had. To my surprise, his head didn't swell and explode with ego. He humbly thanked everyone for their confidence in him and hoped he'd acquit himself well on the night.

Naturally, the excitement of the play had taken the edge off my sleuthing abilities and diverted my focus. Robert had mostly recovered although his shoulder and arm appeared to be stiff. There hadn't been any other attempts made on his life. Surrounded as he was by his vigilant valet, a devoted dog, and a house full of strapping footmen, it would have been nigh impossible for anyone to get near him, one would think.

That night at dinner everyone was filled with excitement, chattering about how well the dry run had gone. Discussions ranged from who had forgotten what, to how superb the sword fighting had been, to how well the dancers had performed. There was much praise for individual performances, praises blushingly received.

"Oh, ma'am," breathed Clementine with a starry-eye gaze guaranteed to melt any Gorgon's stony heart. "I had hoped for a ball but doing this play is far better entertainment than any I've ever enjoyed in London."

A general murmur of agreement followed, and elicited a

simpering smile from the dowager, who presided over the meal with a watchful eye. To start, mushroom soup was served. Not my favourite, so I declined as did Clementine and Sir Harold. Rupert and Sidney gulped down their soup, while Doctor Potts and Maria toyed with a few mouthfuls between talking. The dowager had a large serving, saying how delicious it was and Cook had outdone herself. Then, just when the footmen were hovering behind to remove the dishes, quite literally, all hell broke loose. The dowager gave a strangled gurgling sound, clutched her throat, threw herself back in her chair, and then, leaning to the side, vomited profusely.

"Poison!" she gasped. "The soup is poisoned!"

She collapsed over the arm of her chair, one hand clutching the tablecloth and dragging a portion of it with her. Several wine glasses, soup plates, and cutlery slid off the table, smashing onto the floor. The bitter smell of vomit filled the air as we all stared at her, shocked. This was like being in a stage version of an Agatha Christie murder mystery. The doctor dropped his spoon, as did Maria, and leaped to his feet. Maria spat into her table napkin and then gulped down some water. Shocked, Higgins was rooted to the spot, but the doctor's orders spurred him into action.

"Higgins! Quick! My bag! You two—" he pointed to the two stunned serving footmen "—get jugs of water now!"

Both Sidney and Rupert jumped up, with Rupert knocking his chair aside in his haste to get to his mother and carefully move her back into her chair. Despite her being a horrible old bag, she was his mother, and he was a dutiful son. She lay slumped in the chair, her head to one side, and, given her pallor, I didn't think she was acting. Her breathing was shallow, rattling horribly in her throat. Rupert knelt next to her, clutching her hand, and calling out to her. Sidney hovered behind him, making little squeaking sounds, staring helplessly at his aunt, and wringing his hands.

"Doctor Potts," Rupert wailed in anguish, "do something! Mama is dying."

"Not if I can help it," the doctor said grimly as the footmen rushed back into the dining room with jugs of water, almost knocking over Higgins who also arrived with the doctor's bag.

"What can we do to help?" I asked, with a hideous sinking feeling. The would-be assassin had struck again and this time in the heart of the family home, not outside. But why had they targeted the dowager? There was no time to ponder though because the doctor was barking orders. He soaked a table napkin and instructed Clementine to wipe the dowager's face, which she began doing. Then he poured two large glasses of water and handed one each to Sidney and Rupert.

"Drink this and then go outside and vomit!"

Bewildered, they gulped the water before stampeding out the dining room. The front door banged, and then retching sounds came from the flower beds outside. Clementine shuddered but continued wiping the dowager's face. She opened her eyes briefly and moaned. Maria twittered something about fetching the housekeeper and disappeared. Doctor Potts rummaged in his bag and pulled out a jar of black powder.

"Charcoal powder." He shook a quantity into a glass, poured water onto the powder and mixed it all together with a dessert spoon. "Been used since ancient times to absorb poison. Luckily, I always carry it with me. One never knows when it will come in handy."

Luckily indeed. Clementine and I held the dowager's head up while he carefully tipped the black liquid down her throat. She coughed and sputtered but did not vomit again.

"Good, very good, well done, Your Grace," he said soothingly.

She croaked something unintelligible. The doctor laid a hand on her forehead. "We are all quite well, Your Grace, so you're not to worry. Are you strong enough for us to move you to the drawing room?"

She nodded feebly and under the doctor's direction, Higgins and the footmen carried her carefully to the drawing room and laid her on the chaise lounge. Clementine and I trotted after them, feeling very useless. Higgins shepherded the footmen out of the room while the doctor felt the dowager's pulse. When Maria arrived with Mrs Barlow, Doctor Potts had a whispered discussion with her, with much nodding and shaking of their heads. A whirlwind then arrived in the shape of Milvers, who flung herself, screeching and sobbing, down next to the chaise lounge.

"Oh, my lady, my dear lady," Milvers sobbed, caressing the dowager's hand, and then holding it to her own cheek. To my astonishment, she leaped up and went for me like a tigress, fingers clawing at my face.

"You!" she shrieked. "It's your fault. All this trouble started when you arrived."

Stunned, I didn't make a move to defend myself, but Rupert had come into the room and managed to grab her by one arm, swinging her away from me. Mrs Barlow astounded us all by giving Milvers a ringing slap across the face. Milvers collapsed into a wailing heap.

"Pardon me, Lord Rupert," said Mrs Barlow briskly, "but a good slap is the only way to stop hysterics. I'm sure we're all deeply worried about Her Grace but we're not behaving like lunatics in the asylum."

Rupert was as shocked as if she'd slapped him. He just

nodded. Mrs Barlow then heaved Milvers to her feet.

"Come along with me now, Milvers, and you can have a nice cup of tea to settle your nerves. This is no way to behave in front of Her Grace. Leave it to the doctor. You're no use here to milady. Compose yourself now."

Milvers hiccupped and snuffled into a handkerchief.

"Thank you, Mrs Barlow," said Rupert, looking relieved.

Mrs Barlow nodded. "Not at all, your lordship. Her Grace's bedchamber is ready for when Doctor Potts thinks she can be moved upstairs. I'd be grateful if you could look into the kitchen—"

Whatever she was going to say about the kitchen was lost because the kitchen arrived next in the shape of Cook, plump, red-faced, and wild-eyed as she burst into the room. Her cap was awry, her apron askew, and she was sobbing as she babbled, "Oh, yer lordship, it b'aint me! It b'aint me wot poisoned the soup, I swear! I knows me mushrooms, I do!"

It would have been a comedy of errors, or one of those French farces where everyone arrives on stage at once, but for the telling fact that someone had tried to poison the family and guests by contaminating the soup. The question was who. Could I now cross the dowager off the list of suspects? Would she stoop to poisoning herself to poison Robert? It didn't seem possible. Poison in a tureen of soup wasn't the same as three drops of whatever in someone's drink. Soup was so imprecise, for want of a better word.

Rupert was now the *de facto* head of the household. He rose manfully to the occasion and, with Sidney hovering behind like an agitated shadow, arranged for Sir Harold, who had been abandoned in the dining room, to be escorted back to his quarters. Then for his mother to be carried to her bedroom, Maria to be taken home by carriage, and the footmen, supervised by Higgins, to clean up the smashed crockery and vomit in the dining room. He also asked for Cook to be given smelling salts to settle her shattered nerves. Clementine and I stood back and let Rupert be the hero of the hour. After all, this was 1815 and a woman was not expected to restore order out of the confusion and to make sure peace reigned in the household. In this time of chaos, only a man could bring order to the home. Clementine gazed at Rupert as he gave the orders, clasped her hands under her chin, and gave a wistful little sigh. This was a very good sign for their burgeoning romance.

Robert! The object of two previous attempts. How could I forget about him? A cold chill swept over my body. Had he eaten any soup? I flew up the stairs and met Parker at the door to Robert's bedroom. My face must have said what I was thinking. The servants knew everything, and Parker already knew what had happened in the dining room. News had travelled like lightning.

"No," Parker said gently, "His Grace did not partake of the soup." He pursed his lips. "I myself am not in favour of mushroom soup. It tends to hide a multitude of ... ahem ... never mind."

He bowed me into the room. Robert was sitting up in bed, reading, with the remains of a meal on the small table we had dined at previously. He was dressed in a velvet robe with a light rug over his legs. Russet lay on the bed next to him but bounded off and ran to me. Robert looked up and smiled as I petted Russet. My heart just turned over and kept spinning.

"Amelia! I was just saying to Parker he should investigate what seems to be a terrible commotion downstairs. What a noise. Did something explode in the kitchen? Is the house still intact?"

He looked enquiringly at me. I glanced at Parker who gave the tiniest shake of his head that I doubt Robert even noticed. There was something afoot, something Robert didn't know, but perhaps it was better he didn't know about this potential third attempt on his life.

"Nothing for you to worry about," I said with a smile, lying through my teeth again. I sat down on the end of the bed, with Russet leaping back onto it, and started mock tussling with his paws. "Somehow Cook did something wrong when preparing the soup and the dowager was taken ill."

To give him his due, Robert wasn't spiteful. He sat up straighter, his expression concerned, and threw back the rug. He stood, fumbling for his slippers. "I must see to her. Where is the doctor?"

Parker leaped to stop him. "But Your Grace, there's no need to distress yourself."

Robert gave him a glacial stare. "I would be remiss if I did not investigate further, Parker. This is my house, and she is my stepmother."

Parker bowed his head and murmured something noncommittal. Robert stopped and stared at me. "Does she need me? Is it serious?"

"Doctor Potts very luckily happened to be dining with us," I said calmly. The last thing we needed was for Robert to get involved tonight. "He also had an amazingly effective medication with him, so very fortunate, and she isn't in any danger. He and Mrs Barlow have made her comfortable in her room."

I must have said the right thing because he visibly relaxed, walked over to the small table, and poured a glass of wine. "Come, sit here with me, Amelia, and tell me everything."

I accepted the glass and told him not quite everything while

Parker discreetly cleared the table and absented himself.

"Mushroom soup?" Robert frowned. "I certainly wouldn't recommend mushroom soup at this time of year. Mushrooms are best picked in autumn and winter. What was my stepmother thinking?"

My instincts went on red alert, and I put her back on the suspect list.

"There was no soup served to me tonight, so I'm not sure I've been having the same food as the rest of the household," he said. "Parker has been seeing to my meals." He looked around just as Parker materialised from the dressing room.

"That's right, Your Grace," he said smoothly. "Cook has been preparing special nourishing meals to build up your strength, what with you being an invalid at the moment."

Robert gave a derogatory snort. "Invalid? I take exception to that."

Parker glanced at me. It seemed as if he and the cook had teamed up to keep Robert safe. Parker because he thought someone might try the age-old method of disposing of an enemy. Cook because she no doubt thought Robert must be given special food to boost his recovery after the incident in the woods. It all boiled down to one thing: Robert was getting different meals. I was able to persuade him that the dowager was in good hands, and no one else had suffered any mishap, apart from the smashed crockery and glassware.

"How did the run-through go?" he asked eagerly. "Is the stage suitable?"

Since the stage was his design, of course he wanted to know everything. This was my opportunity to take his mind off the dinner incident and it worked. But a thought struck me. How could we continue with the play when the dowager was ill? Tomorrow was the final dress rehearsal in the evening, with lighting to recreate the exact conditions on the actual performance on Saturday night. Maybe we'd have to cancel.

Robert shook his head. "Not at all. I know my stepmother. The very idea of cancelling the play, losing face in front of all her grand friends, not to mention the village, would be anathema to her. She's extremely proud. Her image and social standing mean everything to her. Ask her tomorrow when you visit her room."

He took my hand. "I'm so pleased the production is proceeding well. You must be delighted."

His smile tugged at my heartstrings. "It's for you, to cheer you up after the accident."

He laughed. "It seems so far away now, even though it happened last Tuesday. Far away and unimportant in light of other, more significant events."

He didn't elaborate but just the way he spoke and his expression told me that deeper feelings had grown between him and Amelia, whatever their emotions had been after so long apart. When I sat with him in the evenings after dinner, he saw Amelia with the weight of their past relationship behind them. I only saw the handsome, charming man who had managed to captivate me in such a short time, despite my holding back. Could he feel the electric thrills when our fingers touched? I felt fourteen again, just like when Billy Thornton held my hand for the first time behind the bike shed at school. Robert continued talking, clasping my hand as if it were the most natural thing in the world. It was so romantic; a man holding my hand, not pressing me for anything more, happy simply to be with me and talk. Sadly, I reminded myself that it was Amelia he was happy to be with, not me. How could it be more? Advice to self: enjoy the moment. So, I did.

Later that night I wrote up Amelia's diary, but leaving out

the greater part of the drama, making it into a minor culinary mishap. It was becoming harder each time I mentioned Robert, which was the most important part of my enforced masquerade. Details of the various antics everyone got up to were funny and part of me hoped Amelia would be amused as much as I was, even the unromantic encounter with slimy Sidney. My emotions threatened to spill over from real life onto the pages, even though I wrote with what I thought was Amelia's level of modest restraint and the conservative attitude of the era. It would be very hard for Amelia to understand how she went from going for a walk and tentative romantic thoughts about Robert to spending evenings with him and holding his hand. Hopefully, love would find a way.

Chapter Fifteen

Friday, 5 May 1815

I hadn't expected to see anyone at breakfast, but Rupert and Clementine were there, chatting animatedly over the remains of their meal.

"Good morning, Amelia," Rupert practically sang out as he saw me. He stood and drew out my chair before the footman could get there. Once I was seated, he sat as well and leaned forward conspiratorially.

"Clementine and I were just discussing if we should try to make stage blood for Mercutio's and Tybalt's deaths."

Clementine also leaned forward, positively glowing with excitement. "And for Juliet as well, when I stab myself."

Up until then, the actors had faked their deaths by sword or knife. Of course, there was no blood, just the gestures and Mercutio's and Tybalt's loud dying groans. Now she wanted there to be stage blood. How Miss Eccles had been seduced by the allure of the stage. Mercutio and Tybalt would be wearing black tunics so no one would see the blood, but I suspected Clementine wanted to make an impact.

"I have no idea how to make stage blood," I said, trying not to disappoint her. "The men are wearing black so no one will see it. There seems to be no point and aren't you afraid of spoiling your costume?"

She gave me a pitying look. "It's not real blood, silly, so it'll just wash out. Just think how impressed the audience will be."

"I know," said Rupert with a brainwave expression. "Let's ask Mr Roach. He has theatrical experience."

They both pushed back their chairs and stood, eager to be off to collar Mr Roach. But despite Robert's assurances that the dowager would want the show to go on, someone had to confirm it.

"Wait! We have no idea if Her Grace would want us to continue with the play now that she is indisposed."

Their expressions of horror spoke volumes. Stagestruck was not the word.

Clementine gasped and looked at Rupert. "Not continue with the play?"

Rupert frowned. "I saw Mama this morning, albeit just for a few moments, and she looks vastly recovered." He shrugged. "The real performance is tomorrow night. I'm sure she'll be perfectly well by then."

I stared at him coldly. Now that the immediate danger was over, it was back to what made him happy.

"You didn't ask her if she wants the performance to continue?"

He reddened and looked uncomfortable. "I didn't even get the chance. I barely said good morning and asked her how she was feeling when that wretched female Milvers hustled me out of the room as if I had no business being there."

I'd made up my mind to confirm with the dowager anyway what we should do. Rupert and Clementine seemed eager to dash off, so I waved them away. We had all agreed to do some tidying-up of scenes and a check list that morning, with the afternoon off so the cast and dancers could rest before the dress rehearsal. This performance had to be perfectly timed to make use of the natural light, in the absence of any proper stage lighting. Maisie pointed me in the direction of the dowager's suite of rooms. She hesitated as if she wanted to ask me something.

"Is something wrong, Maisie?"

She blushed and clasped her hands. "Oh, miss, we all know it's the dress rehearsal tonight and it's ever so important." She stopped and looked at her feet.

"What is it?"

She took a deep breath and gabbled, "D'ye think Her Grace would mind very much if the staff was to watch the rehearsal performance tonight? Be an audience like, to give the actors the feel of people watchin' 'em?"

It was an excellent suggestion since we needed a real audience. "That's a very good question, Maisie. I'm going to confirm with Her Grace that she is well enough for the proper performance to go on tomorrow night, and I'll ask her."

Maisie shivered with suppressed delight. "Oh, thank ye. We'd all be ever so grateful. It looks wonderful from the bits we've seen and the dancin' is sumpin' special." Then her face fell. "But there's just one problem."

I stared at her. "Now what?"

"Can we sit on the chairs in the ballroom, them belongin' to all Her Grace's friends? Maybe they won't like it?"

The chairs had been coming in at top speed with their owners' names discreetly pinned to the backrests. They ranged in grandeur from simple to sumptuous and by now the ballroom was half full. We were anticipating a large audience.

"I'm sure the chairs are the last thing we should be worrying about," I said firmly.

When I knocked gently on the dowager's door, Milvers opened it. She didn't look me in the eye but gestured for me to enter. The room, grandly furnished in the ubiquitous style of ornate furniture, many valuable paintings, and expensive ornaments, was overly warm and smelled of old-fashioned medicine, wintergreen, and lavender. The dowager sat propped up in a huge four-poster bed, wearing a white ruffled nightdress, and looking pale and hollow-eyed. To my surprise, she seemed quite fragile. She beckoned me forward.

"Come in, Amelia, my dear. It's very kind of you to visit. Milvers, bring a chair for Miss Carstairs."

This was so unlike her usual acerbic remarks that she must be unwell. Milvers scurried to get a chair for me. I came closer and sat next to the bed.

"How do you feel, ma'am?"

She gave a faint smile and waved one hand feebly. "What can I say. Middling, I should think. Doctor Potts was here early this morning to examine me, and he says I will be fully recovered by tomorrow night for the performance. He says that, luckily for me, I vomited up most of the poison and his noxious mixture—" she made a face "—also seemed to do the trick."

She looked so deathly white that I had to ask. "Are you sure we should continue with the performance? Perhaps we should cancel."

The dowager was so taken aback by my suggestion that she tried to sit up even further. Milvers, hovering behind me, was there in an instant to help her with another pillow behind her back.

"What?" Her eyes widened, showing the old spark. "Cancel the performance? After all the hard work the actors and dancers have put into it. After all the efforts of everyone concerned. The costumes, the musicians, the program, the expense." She plucked at the bed covers in agitation. "Most certainly not. What would people think?"

"I was just thinking of you, ma'am—" I stammered. The suggestion of throwing in the towel had touched a nerve there.

"Well, don't think of me, Amelia," she said with a touch of her usual caustic self. "Think of the actors and dancers all no doubt waiting for you to tell them that they should go ahead. We must continue regardless." She sighed theatrically. "My condition is nothing to be concerned about." Her voice cracked.

Milvers hurried to hold a glass of water to her lips. She took a few sips, then pushed Milvers' hand away.

"Think how disappointed Robert will be if the very performance designed to cheer him up and entertain him is cancelled just because I am unwell." She stared at me. "No one else was taken ill?"

"I don't think so, ma'am, just you." That fact alone was enough to cause suspicion. In the cold light of day, it was inconceivable that she would poison herself. First Robert, now the dowager ... what on earth was going on? Did I have two would-be assassins to flush out?

She sighed. "What a relief. Thank heavens, Robert escaped the suffering I endured last night with an excruciating fever, headache, and *malaise*. In his weakened state, who knows what might have happened."

She reached out her hand to me and I took it. "Great houses and influential families always have enemies, my dear. We must be ever vigilant. I will be perfectly well by tomorrow night to welcome our guests and open the performance."

She withdrew her hand from mine and lay back on the pillows as if exhausted. "Was there anything else?"

"The staff was wondering if they might attend tonight's dress rehearsal," I said. "It's an excellent opportunity for the actors to have a real audience." I added, "To prepare them for the important audience tomorrow."

"Yes, of course," she said testily. "They can invite their families who live nearby as well. We want a proper audience. It's no good having only a few people sitting there. One needs the right kind of ambiance."

Her magnanimity was overwhelming. Either she was truly still sick, or she wasn't going to give up on her dream of being the last word in anything cultural.

I rose to leave. "Thank you, ma'am."

"One moment." She gestured to Milvers. "Milvers has something to say to you."

Milvers did not look me in the eye. Her chalk-white face was expressionless as she stared past my left ear.

"I am truly sorry for my presumptuous behaviour last night, Miss Carstairs," she mumbled. "It was unacceptable and will never happen again."

The smell of mothballs was quite strong. It was surprising the dowager hadn't noticed or perhaps she was just used to it.

"Think no more of it, Milvers," I said, still stunned by the apology. "It's very understandable that in a distressing situation one's emotions run high."

Milvers said impassively, "Yes, Miss Carstairs. Thank you."

The black stare she turned on me then was quite the opposite. I suppressed a shiver. If looks could kill, I'd be dead and buried already.

"Off you go now," said the dowager. "Make sure that everything is perfect for tomorrow night's performance. The family name depends on it, Amelia, and I am depending on you."

I closed the door behind me, glad to escape the overpoweringly warm atmosphere. Maisie pounced on me.

"Oh, miss, what did she say?"

I patted her shoulder. "Of course, it's quite all right. The dowager says the actors need an audience and the staff can invite their families who live close by. So, let's see if we can fill the ballroom."

Maisie's expression was joyful, then her face fell.

"Now what?"

"Did ye ask if we can sit on the chairs?"

"Maisie, you're starting to annoy me. What else will they sit on, and the rightful owners won't even know anyway."

Beaming, Maisie bobbed a curtsey. "Thank ye, miss."

Watching her disappear around the corner, with a skip in her step, I thought how I would miss her when I got back to 2015. If I ever got back, of course, and how I would get back was anyone's guess. Would I just fall asleep and wake up back in my own era, in the library? I didn't even want to think about it and luckily there was no time to ponder on the question.

Everyone had assembled in the ballroom, waiting for the verdict. No doubt the news had spread like wildfire through the house. Why else would everyone appear so anxious? Maria looked tense while Sidney paced up and down, mumbling to himself. Celeste was tinkling on the piano, with Anne turning the music sheets. The dancers were playing hopscotch, or the Regency version thereof, while Mr Roach paged through some music. Clementine and Rupert were standing together, talking quietly. Sir Harold sat reading a book. Johnson and Peters stood to one side, looking apprehensive. They were all waiting for me, of course, because when I came through the doorway, their faces lit up. Doctor Potts was just behind me.

Maria bustled up right away, her expression almost

tearful. "Amelia, will the play go on? Is Her Grace well enough to attend?"

"Yes, the play must go on," I said loudly. "Her Grace insists upon it."

Celeste did a little ripple up and down on the piano keys, and everyone laughed. Mr Roach clapped to get the dancers into line, the musicians arrived just then, and soon the ballroom was the usual buzzing hive of activity it had been for the past few days. Mr Roach and I conferred and decided we'd work on some sticky patches for the morning, then give everyone the afternoon off to rest before the evening performance. The timing had to be exact to catch the waning of natural light. Sir Harold wheeled himself over to me and confirmed that the footmen who'd volunteered to man the candelabras had been primed, all was ready for the evening, and I wasn't to worry. Mr Roach then confided that he actually did have a recipe for stage blood from his heady days at the Astbury, which he had shared with the star-crossed lovers, and he hoped I didn't mind. It involved flour, water, beetroot juice, and some red paint from the scene painting. Given that the beetroot might stain her dress, Clementine decided to save it until the actual performance. One could only hope that it worked.

The hours flew by and even though Maisie forced me to lie down and take a nap, I didn't sleep. The dress rehearsal had to be an exact replica of the real performance the following night. The players and dancers arrived looking refreshed. Everyone wore their full costumes and Maisie and I did the stage makeup. Sidney had kept his final outfit a secret until tonight. When he did the Big Reveal, we were all gobsmacked. Despite my initial doubts about the garment, his magnificent black satin cloak lined with red swished impressively back and forth as he walked. He wore a black shirt with black pantaloons tucked into half boots that gleamed like mirrors. He had allowed himself only one item of finery: a splendid silver medallion that hung in the middle of his chest and suited the part of his role as quasi-narrator, quasi-Prince of Verona. He'd really taken to the idea of makeup and asked me for a bit more eye liner to "define his eyes." Combined with the white stage makeup and red lip salve, he looked more like Count Dracula than the Prince of Verona, but I said nothing. No doubt the locals, both gentry and peasantry, would be very impressed.

"Oh, Sir Sidney," breathed Clementine, looking ravishing in her costume with full stage makeup. Her eyes sparkled like sapphires, her blonde hair was spun gold, and Rupert looked at her with such yearning that I wondered if I was the only one who could see how smitten he was. "That cloak is just perfect for the role. You look marvellous."

Sidney beamed like a lighthouse. "Yes! I just knew it was right for the part. My valet Turvey was most disparaging when I had it made. He asked me if I was going to a costume party." He twirled and then strode forward, sweeping the cloak back on one side most dramatically. "How rude. And when I think of how good I am to him."

"Now, remember," I said, addressing the performers, "Don't think about anyone else and what they're supposed to be doing. Just concentrate on what you're supposed to be doing."

From the stage side of the curtain, we could hear hushed whispers and a few giggles as the captive audience filed in. Anne, costumed and made up, was out front at the ballroom entrance, practicing her role of greeting people and pointing them to the seats. Sir Harold had taken the lighting project completely in hand and he managed the team of footmen, our lighting technicians, also dressed for the occasion, and anonymity, in black. Watching from the wings, I could keep an eye on the lighting changes, such as they were, as well as entrances and exits. The dancers and Mr Roach were waiting outside the ballroom entrance for everyone to take their seats. At his signal, the musicians, who'd been quietly tuning up with Celeste, would give one long chord to herald the arrival of the dancers and the start of the play.

The heady combination of costumes, full makeup, music, an audience, and the pressure of an actual performance wrought its magic. Somehow, despite their complete lack of experience, everyone did the right thing. There's something about treading the boards and having an audience. In a nutshell, it was a roaring success. The audience couldn't have been better for the players. They oohed, aahed, gasped, wept, and emoted with every scene. Rupert was incomparable and Clementine was entrancing. Every moment they were together was electrifying and they held the audience in the palms of their hands. They were no longer acting; they *were* Romeo and Juliet.

The dancers acquitted themselves extremely well and Maria's voice was in top form. She'd managed to sneak in that extra song besides the finale song. But the star of the performance was Sidney, who was astounding. He rose to the occasion in a commanding manner and did us all proud. Whether he truly understood his lines was hard to tell but he delivered them as if he did and the audience was hushed, captivated, drinking in the tragic story. The conclusion had the audience sniffing, blowing their noses, and crying as Maria sang over the two dead lovers. What a great audience. They were every actor's fantasy, every director's dream.

The ending was carefully structured to give the performers

a curtain call. Two eager helpers drew the curtains closed, and the dancers assembled first for their bows. The curtains opened and, after bowing and curtseying, the dancers peeled off to each side and Friar Laurence and Nurse appeared, followed by Johnson and Peters wearing their Capulet and Montague cloaks. Then it was Sidney's turn, followed by the lovers. The applause was resounding as Rupert and Clementine bowed and curtseyed. Then Rupert indicated to Mr Roach to take his bow. He gestured to the musicians and Celeste to be acknowledged. It was so professional that it was hard to believe we'd pulled it off. But we had. Now all we had to do was repeat the whole thing the following night with no mishaps and no one trying to kill anybody.

Chapter Sixteen

Saturday, 6 May 1815

The cast and musicians assembled at 5.00 p.m. Maisie was on hand to do makeup and hair and the governesses also volunteered their services. I was nervous although I'd filled the day, having spent the morning writing up Amelia's diary and some of the afternoon with Robert, who again assured me he would look astonished and amazed at the performance to come. One could only hope that the audience too would be astonished and amazed. The dowager had kept to her rooms but had sent her orders regarding the "finger supper" Sidney had suggested. The terrace garden below the ballroom was transformed with small tables where the food would be laid out and Chinese style lanterns strung around for lighting after sundown. The gardeners had slogged away, making sure the paths were clear, the hedges trimmed, and every rosebush and shrub looking luxuriant.

Maisie had already picked out my dress from Amelia's array of delightful evening gowns. Tonight's fashion statement was a rose-pink satin underdress with an overdress of gauzy fabric dotted with pink sequins all over it. It must have taken some poor seamstress hours to complete. The gossamer overdress subdued the pink and gave the dress an ethereal quality. Long gloves, of course, a soft pink stole to drape over my arms, and an up-style hairdo completed my ensemble. Since Maisie had wangled me another bath, I did feel fresh as a daisy although guilty about the footmen who'd lugged all those cans of hot water upstairs.

Maisie stepped back as she surveyed me and clasped her hands. "My word," she breathed. "Ye look wonderful, miss."

I tweaked the stole around my arms. "Thanks to you, Maisie."

"His Grace will only have eyes for one person tonight."

I stared at her in surprise. Maisie looked down coyly with something suspiciously like a smug smile. Things were so precisely balanced right now with Robert and Amelia that the last thing I wanted was for below stairs gossip to upset the applecart. But it's true; the servants know everything.

I tried to laugh it off with a careless remark. "Don't be silly, Maisie. His Grace and I are cousins, and we have the utmost respect and affection for each other."

My nonchalance didn't work. She pressed her lips together the way she always did when pretending to agree with me, then said, "Of course, miss. Utmost respect."

Soon the cast was dressed, made up, and assembled behind the stage curtains. Everyone looked nervous, even Mr Roach who flexed his fingers as he spoke quietly to the dancers. Peter and Tiffany were every inch the lead dancers, both good-looking, and they were the best dancers. The girls looked charming, as was to be expected, and the boys had been scrubbed and their hair trimmed as well. This time there was no larking about. Rupert and Clementine stood together, whispering. Rupert smiled down at her as he gently stroked her cheek with one finger. Sidney had a quick consultation with Sir Harold who assured him that of course he had a script at the ready, should Sidney forget his lines, but that he would not. Fretting, Sidney did not seem convinced. Maria looked anxious as she fanned herself madly. Doctor Potts appeared calm, and that was reassuring. Johnson and Peters, impressively handsome and well-built, didn't seem nervous but all they had to do was fling a few insults and do some sword fighting. Everyone knew what to do since they had already done it the previous night, but one couldn't help being a tad agitated that everything would go off smoothly, given the importance of the audience. Celeste and the musicians were already in their places. The faint sounds of them tuning their instruments filtered through the curtains. There's something exciting about hearing that prelude to a concert, although Hadley's motley musical group was hardly the Royal Philharmonic.

Anne was positioned at the entrance to the ballroom with an armful of programmes and a hastily recruited scullery maid to help her hand them out. That fortunate maiden, attired in an extra dancer's costume since we had material left over, had almost fainted with joy at being asked to help and declared that her parents would "scarce know 'er" after this prestigious social elevation. A touch of stage makeup had sealed her joy. From the murmur of voices, it was apparent the audience had begun to arrive. One of the kitchen staff, also awestruck by the appointment to messenger and a costume, was delegated to report to the side entrance leading into the anteroom as to when Higgins would close the ballroom doors once everyone was seated.

Not for the Regency country audience the *ennui* with life and arriving fashionably late for an event. At 6.15 p.m. precisely, the carriages had begun rolling up the driveway and letting out their well-dressed owners. I shouldn't have peeked through a crack in the curtains, but I did. The place was filling up quickly. Thank heavens, no high hairdos but lots of diamonds, pearls, silks, and satins were on display. The *crème de la crème* of local society had arrived and in full evening regalia. Higgins's helpers all had a copy of the seating plan with the owners' names accompanying each seat. A mild fracas broke out when a portly gentleman complained that someone had nicked his seat. The someone replied with, "Do you know who I am, sir?" This remark threatened inevitable insults to someone's parents. Thankfully, Higgins, with a copy of the seating diagram, swooped in to restore peace.

Fingers plucked at my dress. I turned to find everyone staring at me with angst-ridden expressions.

"The ballroom is full!"

"I'm so nervous," whispered one of the Hamilton girls.

"Now, Miss Caroline," said Mr Roach soothingly. "You did a performance last night."

"But that was only a dress rehearsal," she said, frowning. "Not a real performance."

Raising his beetling eyebrows, Mr Roach favoured her with a beady stare. "My dear girl, *every* performance is a *real* performance."

Our Hermes arrived, red-faced and stammering, to whisper that the audience was seated, Mr Higgins was ready to close the doors, and I should come with him because His Grace was ready to walk me to my seat. I gave the performers a reassuring smile and accompanied the dancers and Mr Roach out the side entrance and along a path that led to the front of the house. That way we circumvented the ballroom entirely. Robert was waiting for me in the Hall. He looked so handsome and smelled so deliciously of sandalwood that my heart jumped, and my breath caught in my throat. If only this evening would never end. If only time could stand still for eternity and us with it.

"My dear Amelia," he said quietly, "how beautiful you look tonight."

This was definitely heading in marriage proposal direction.

"Thank you, Robert," I said, trying to sound calm. "May I return the compliment and say how elegant you look as well."

There are some men who can wear Regency evening attire, and some who cannot, and Robert was one who most definitely could. Satin knee breeches and silk stockings might look ridiculous on a lesser man, but Robert was no lesser man. I knew in that wonderful but dreadful fateful moment that I had fallen deliriously in love with him and had to leave him. The agony of this realisation was so intense that for an instant I could hardly breathe. I'd never felt this way before, and it tore me apart inside.

Higgins opened the double doors to the ballroom and Robert escorted me down the center aisle to the front row seats on the right-hand side. Curious guests peered at me most interestedly as I passed. The dowager was already seated on the opposite side of the aisle. Her face was chalk white, but she looked better than the previous morning. Her dress of dark fuchsia with green trimmings was elegant, as one would expect, and she had certainly raided the family store of jewels. Her gloved arms were loaded with bracelets and the tiara on her carefully arranged curls was sumptuous, to say the least. If the family was short of ready money, the dowager was not going to let anyone suspect it. Once the audience was quiet, she signalled to Robert, who went up to her, offering his hand. He led her to the front, and then stepped back, waiting. She was a real diva, smiling warmly and extending her arms wide in a gesture of welcome.

"My dear friends. Welcome to our small intimate gathering of like-minded, culturally inclined patrons of the arts."

A murmur of appreciation swept through the audience. Naturally, everyone wants to be thought of as a culture vulture.

"When I deplored the lack of theatre and the arts in our small community, it came to me that we should not have to wait for it. We should create our own hub of artistic endeavours. Thus, this evening we present a selection of excerpts from William Shakespeare's famous romantic play, *Romeo and Juliet.*"

She clasped her hands to her bosom as she said the play title, then continued, "You may wish to glance at the program given to you and you may recognise some familiar names among the performers and the kind patrons who have made the production possible. We thank them for their wonderful generosity."

A collective rustling ensued as the audience looked at the program and little murmurs of appreciation were heard. The dowager held out one hand and Robert took it to escort her back to her seat. Not a word about whose idea it was, why, and who had basically rewritten the whole thing to make it all fit into an hour and a bit. Half of me was miffed for Amelia's sake and the other half was relieved because I didn't want to draw undue attention to myself.

As he sat down, Robert whispered, "Don't be upset. Everyone knows it was your idea."

I didn't answer because Mr Roach gave the signal to start. The musicians played a long chord, and the play began. A modern audience is quite spoiled in what a theatre or even movie experience offers the viewer. There were no dimmed lights here, no special effects, nothing we'd consider mandatory, given how pampered we've become. No one could pretend the candelabras were proper lighting, but the guests seemed oblivious to these deficiencies. They paid rapt attention as if it were the finest production a top London theatre had to offer. For them, this was superb entertainment indeed.

From the moment the dancers came slowly down the aisle, the audience was transfixed. The curtains opened to allow Sidney to stride downstage and address the audience as if they were the good citizens of Verona. Sidney was the gift that kept on giving. His sonorous stage voice had astounded us at the dress rehearsal and tonight it astounded the audience as well. Those who knew him as Sidney the silly fribble were riveted. His pantaloons clung to his lower half like cling wrap and if anyone had any doubts about Sidney's manliness, these were quicky dispelled. I wondered if Turvey had taken the pantaloons in a tad. Perhaps the combination of eloquence and being well endowed would work some special kind of magic on the right young lady for Sidney.

I glanced at Robert to see if he was enjoying the play. He was looking at me with such a loving expression that took me by surprise. Adoration was clear in his eyes. My heart hammered and a thrilling, dizzying sensation rippled up and down my body. He raised my gloved hand to his lips and kissed it gently before releasing me. I could have died of joy on the spot. I'd never met a man who demonstrated old-fashioned courting manners. How could I? The modern dating pool offered mostly frogs who couldn't understand why one might not want sex on the first date, if there would even be a second date, and had no idea of meaningful or intelligent conversation. I'd spent time in the company of a wonderful, cultured, handsome man for whom my mere presence was enough to arouse deep emotions in him. What more could a woman ask for?

The drama, the emotion, the action, the intensity, everything an audience wants in a production was there in spades. Despite trying to hold onto my director's hat, I soon forgot about it and just enjoyed the play. If anyone fluffed a line, no one noticed. Dressed to the nines and dripping with jewels next to their husbands, the ladies gasped most appreciatively when Romeo appeared. Coupled with a ravishing Juliet, it was an inspired piece of casting. The tall, muscular figures of Mercutio and Tybalt also excited female appreciation, given their tight leggings. If the menfolk weren't interested in the production, the ladies were glued! So many men to adore, all handsome and strapping and so well endowed. When Romeo drank the poison and collapsed against Juliet's bier, audible sobs and sniffs were heard from the entranced audience who by now had totally suspended their disbelief.

However, the most astonishing moment was yet to come. Seeing Romeo dead, our Juliet uttered a piercing and heart-rending scream that jolted everyone. After saying, *"I will kiss thy lips; haply some poison yet doth hang on them to make me die with a restorative,"* she leaned forward and kissed Romeo full on the lips. In the dress rehearsal, Clementine had discreetly tilted her head, so her gorgeous blonde tresses flowed around Rupert's face. One couldn't really see what was going on. Tonight, her action could only be described as shocking. A collective gasp echoed around the ballroom as the audience leaned forward, eyes wide, mouths agape, mesmerised. I was stunned. Would they have to get married now? Just how strict were Regency rules? More was yet to come in the conclusion, or the "blood scene," which took us all by surprise.

"O happy dagger!" Juliet cried out, snatching the dagger from Romeo's belt. *"This is thy sheath, there rust, and let me die."* Somehow Clementine must have poured her concoction into the sheath and when she plunged the blade into her breast, actually just down the front of her dress, an impressive amount of stage blood was visible. Another collective gasp swept around the ballroom, punctuated with a few genteel shrieks. One sensitive damsel sitting in the front row fainted but since no one paid her any attention, she quickly recovered.

The play had sped by so fast that I was quite surprised when the curtains swung closed. After the proper curtain calls and tumultuous applause, the curtains opened once more, and Sidney walked forward. He turned and gestured behind him for Sir Harold's manservant to wheel the old man out in his chair. Sidney bowed to Sir Harold, who looked as if he might burst into tears. His face contorted as if he was suppressing his emotions. Then the curtains swished closed, and the play was finally over. Robert stood up and escorted the dowager to the front again.

She clapped to get the audience's attention and announced, "Dear friends, we hope you have enjoyed our humble theatrical offering tonight. Please move towards the French doors and follow the steps down to the garden terrace. A buffet supper and refreshments are available for your enjoyment."

A murmur of appreciation rose as people stood up to go. Robert stepped forward to give her his arm as the audience surged towards the side doors. He caught my eye and nodded as if to tell me to follow him. The terraced garden was much larger than I'd thought and easily accommodated the guests flocking around the various tables laden with food. Footmen glided in and out of the crowd with trays of drinks. I didn't recognise some of them so the dowager's friends must have lent her a few to help out. The hubbub of excited chatter and happy guests was very satisfying for any hostess worth her salt.

Looking gorgeous, her cheeks flushed, Clementine, still in her Juliet costume, was escorted by a vigilant Rupert. She held court, her laughter tinkling as she recounted some amusing rehearsal anecdote to a group of entranced mostly male admirers, hypnotised by her beauty and charm. The de Montforts and the Beasleys clustered around the dowager, both mamas clutching their darlings. I was pleased to see Anne was being treated with as much affection as Tiffany, who had linked her arm through Anne's, playing the loving cousin perfectly. In fact, all the dancers, still made up and costumed, were enjoying much adulation from their proud parents and friends.

Beaming, Maria was also holding court in a circle of no doubt devoted music aficionados. She wore her Nurse costume as a badge of honour. Reverend Wilby, looking a tad bewildered by the meteoric rise in popularity of his wife and helpmeet, nodded and smiled as she said modestly, "Yes, I am the Musical Director. I have some experience in the music world. My dearest Mama and Papa spared no expense in my singing tuition. Only the finest operatic training." She gave her husband a brief glare before saying, "Of course I will no doubt be singing at some of the best salons in the future. Just selected engagements of course. Only the best families in the county."

As her fans murmured in agreement, the vicar looked

torn between basking in the glow of her reflected glory and considering the temptations attached to the fleshpots of the high society salons of only the best families in the county. I hoped she would get the singing engagements she missed so much.

Sidney's dream of impressing women had come true. He was surrounded by a bevy of adoring women who all appeared eager to hear his account of preparing for the part as someone who appreciated Shakespeare. His tight pantaloons surely helped as well, since any damsel lucky enough to snag him could see in advance what was on offer in the bedroom. He looked as if he had died and gone to heaven. No doubt he would soon have the pick of local beauties to choose from. The play had done so much for the cast that I should have been delighted having achieved only that. Everyone looked happy, relaxed, and part of the world where I didn't belong, although Amelia did. A sense of loneliness and a sudden wave of depression washed over me. For the first time in my life, I knew love and it was not mine to enjoy.

"There you are," said Robert from behind me. "My stepmother is safely engaged with her friends and now I'd like you to meet some of mine."

He crooked his arm, and I put my hand through as if it were the most natural thing in the world. In that moment I felt loved, special, singled out for particular attention, and no doubt others thought the same. People nodded or bowed slightly as Robert carved a path for us through the crowd. He was in his element here, the duke, lord of his manor, even regal in his bearing. He was born to it. How dare I fall in love with him? I wasn't even from his era. Robert led me into a group of animated guests.

"This is my very talented cousin, Miss Amelia Carstairs.

The play could not have happened without her," he said.

A tall, good-looking man with blond hair and a quirky smile took my hand and bowed over it. "Miss Carstairs," he exclaimed. "The architect of this moving theatrical piece. Indeed, you are talented if you could whip such a cast into giving a very creditable performance. I never thought Rupert had it in him but look how well he does as Romeo."

"Jack, you scoundrel," said Robert, laughing. "Miss Carstairs won't be taken in by your flim-flam." He smiled down at me. "My best friend and fellow soldier, Jack Burrows. He has a title, of course, but he hates to use it."

Jack bowed again and he and Robert moved away as several ladies mobbed me most genteelly, asking how I had cut the play down, who had written the narrator's lines, was Sir Sidney single, and would I be putting on more productions. I replied that cutting the play had required some ingenuity, I had written the narrator's lines, Sir Sidney was very single and most eligible, and more productions depended on the family.

"And naturally we will be putting on more productions," said a familiar voice. The dowager had materialised next to me. "Given the success of this wonderful evening, I have high hopes of bringing more cultural events to the area." Then she said, "Amelia, my dear, Robert has just gone to perform a small errand for me, but he asked if you would meet him upstairs." She pointed to the balustraded patio, for want of a better word, that ran the length of the ballroom.

Thanking her for the message, I made my way back up one of the sets of stone steps. Maybe I could spot him from that vantage point. I walked right down to the end of the patio and leaned on the stone balustrade, squinting in the lamplight to see where he was. The problem with men's evening dress is all the men looked the same. My thoughts wandered idly to the here and now and the where-to from here. I hadn't discovered the would-be assassin so, in essence, my mission had failed. Had there even been an assassin? Or had it just been a poacher's arrow gone astray that had struck Robert and a bad mushroom that had felled the dowager? It all seemed to have been for nothing. Had I made an iota of difference? I couldn't stay any longer although I had utterly no idea of how to return to 2015. Did I want to? But I had to. Despite the heartbreak, I couldn't leave Amelia, either in limbo or in 2015 trying to negotiate the madhouse of life in the modern world. The question was how on earth was I going to get back?

As I looked closer at one group with what seemed to be a familiar face in it, I leaned further over. Below me was a patch of dense shrubbery with some large, thick bushes. Suddenly, someone pushed me hard from behind, a quick shove that propelled me over the balustrade in seconds. Shocked, I barely had time to register the fact of falling head over heels. My head whirling and my stomach churning, I flailed my arms desperately, grabbing at anything to stop myself falling but my gloves slipped on the stone ledge. As I clutched wildly, I gripped fabric that tore in my grasp, but it wasn't enough to stop my headlong flight and I crashed into the bushes with a thud. Ripping sounds indicated that my dress was torn but worse was to come. Although the breath had been knocked out of me, I fought to get up and get away, hampered by my finery. The dress skirt was too narrow, the stole caught in some branches, almost tying me down like an animal trapped in a snare. My heart was pounding frantically as I panted, but all I could think of was escaping because anyone bold enough to push me over the balustrade had sinister intentions. Try as I might, I couldn't even get to my knees with the thorny branches of a damned bush holding my dress fast. As a rustling sound came from behind me, I opened my mouth to scream. A large hand clamped a cloth over my nose and mouth, almost suffocating me. Total darkness descended.

When I woke up, I was still in darkness but now in a confined space. A very strange, confined space that smelled of pine, rosemary, and, oddly enough, decay. As I felt carefully around me, my groping hands touched a barrier on each side. Feeling above me, I touched the same. I was in a long, narrow box with soft padding all around and very little space to move. It was uncomfortable as well because I was lying on top of something lumpy. My gloved fingers gingerly explored the lumpy something that was covered in a thin cloth. Then I touched what felt like a hand and almost passed out again. Even through the gloves, there was no mistaking what I had touched. I was buried alive in a coffin with its original occupant!

The bitter taste of bile rose in my throat from sheer terror and a cold sweat broke out over my whole body. This was a terrible nightmare from which there was no escape. I was trapped in a coffin, possibly buried six feet under, with no hope of anyone finding me, no hope of escape. My chest tightened as I tried to breathe slowly and calmly.

Breathe in, breathe out, slowly, very slowly.

Thinking of all those crime and disaster movies I'd watched so avidly, preserving my oxygen was paramount. How long did I have left? That depended on how long I'd been out cold. Maybe I had a few hours left. Maybe only minutes. This was no accident. A cunning trap had been set and I'd walked right into it. What a fool I was to imagine I could flush out the villain of the piece when it was clear they had been playing me all along.

Forgetting the need to preserve oxygen, I screamed with rage, utter frustration, and desperation until my chest ached. My body spasmed as shrieks tore painfully at my throat. Then I wept at the futility of it all. Hot tears trickled down my temples and ran into my ears. I never imagined in a million years I would die like this. This was a nightmare of monumental proportions, almost unbelievable to imagine. How far was the churchyard from the house? I hadn't gone to church on Sunday, but the dowager had, and there's no way she would have walked. But carriages were for the wealthy. What about the household servants? They would have walked, so maybe it was close enough to reach on foot. It had to be for my abductor to have carried me from the house to the cemetery. In all the excitement of the after-party, no one had noticed me being pushed into a clump of dense bushes in a secluded corner of the garden. My second attacker must have dragged me away quickly out of sight. Surely, once I was missed, then people would start looking for me. But did I have enough air to last until then and would they even go in the right direction? No one looks for a lost person in a churchyard, let alone a grave. My thoughts churned wildly, fruitlessly, as terror squeezed my chest in a suffocating grip.

Flashes of the past few days popped into my mind and then suddenly I knew the identity of the architect of this complex, but carefully planned, crime. The irony was that, until this moment, although suspicious, I had never pinpointed that her hand was behind the botched assassination attempt, the fire in Robert's bedroom, and the failed poisoning. But she, clearly, thought I did know. My initial suspicions were right.

It all made perfect sense to me now. Of course, Robert must be eliminated so that the estate would pass on to the next heir. Rupert would come of age soon but, in the meantime, the dowager would control the management of the estate and the purse strings. Rupert, no longer the second son with few prospects, would inherit the title and be very worthy of Miss Eccles' affections.

No wonder the dowager hadn't blocked the romance between Rupert and Clementine. Rupert's social elevation would find favour with Clementine's social climbing mother who had her sights set on a duke for her daughter. The new bride's fortune from her grandmother would soon repair the ravaged estate and restore it to its former glory. It was all so neatly planned, but then Amelia came along, and Robert fell in love with his cousin and childhood playmate whom he had always cherished. The dowager had to get rid of Amelia to pick up where her foiled plans had left off. There would no doubt be another attempt on Robert's life, and this time it would succeed.

The dowager was fiendishly clever. She had lured me back up to the patio with a message from Robert that didn't exist. However, at least one of her accomplices had revealed themselves. The smell of mothballs was pungent. I felt around for the scrap of fabric I'd grabbed in my fall. So Milvers had pushed me over the balustrade, but someone else had semi-suffocated me, dragged, or carried me to the cemetery, and then buried me alive. No one would be out looking for me right away. Everyone would think I was somewhere else. Robert would think I'd gone to bed, possibly exhausted by the evening's entertainment. The cast would think I was with Robert. The only person who would know something was wrong was Maisie, so loyal and devoted, waiting up for me.

But who would listen to her? She was only a parlour maid briefly elevated to be my dresser.

I wriggled my toes. My shoes had fallen off, as had my stole. A flicker of hope rippled through me. Would someone spot these items if the household eventually started looking for me? But would they look for me right away? Perhaps they'd think I had decided to go home to Plymouth, although in 1815 this was not as simple as it would be in 2015. No, someone would ask questions and send out a search party eventually. But it would be too late. I clenched my fists in blind rage. And yet *how* could I die, given that Robert and Amelia had married and created a family of which Dad and I were twigs on a side branch. I couldn't die said my practical brain, given the fact that I even existed, but I was going to anyway, unless a miracle happened. My cynical side had serious doubts about miracles too.

It was pitch dark, a horrible claustrophobic blackness that pressed down on me. I'd never experienced total blackout before. Living in the city meant that ambient light filtered through even when the power and the streetlights were out. This was blacker than black. Despite trying to stay awake, I felt so sleepy. My eyelids were becoming heavier and heavier, and it was easier just to close my eyes and surrender to my fate. This light-headedness was clearly from lack of oxygen and dehydration. Was I dying now? Strangely, it wasn't as awful as I'd feared. It was like floating away on a cloud. It would be so easy to let go, to stop fighting to live. To just give up.

My breaths became shallower and shallower as I drifted deeper and deeper into what was no doubt a coma leading to death. My head throbbed, my throat was parched, and I longed for water as a fiery thirst consumed me. Visions of mountains of ice cubes, glaciers, icebergs, and sparkling waterfalls cascading into lakes filled my brain. Glasses of cold water, with droplets trickling down the sides, danced just in front of me. Azure pools that I could swallow in one gulp. More tears flowed, burning my already scratchy eyes. If only this torture would end.

John Keats's famous line came to mind: *"I have been half in love with easeful Death, Call'd him soft names in many a musèd rhyme, To take into the air my quiet breath."*

Yes, death would ease this pain. If only it would come quickly now.

"I'm sorry, Dad. I'm sorry, Amelia. I failed you both." Even just this hoarse whisper scraped agonisingly at my aching throat.

As I floated deeper into blissful oblivion, something tugged at my consciousness. The sound of a dog barking. Impossible, of course. No dog was here. Then came faint voices and the sound of digging. Again, impossible. I was six feet under, and they'd never find me in time. The soft dark wings of the angel of death caressed my face temptingly, then closed gently around me, and were welcome. With no hope of getting out alive anyway, I was ready to surrender. But the clang of metal above jolted me out of my lethargy. By now I could hardly breathe, my body was cold, my limbs heavy, and my lungs burned with every breath I tried to take. Then the coffin lid was flung off and radiant light burst brightly into my vision. Someone's arms reached for me, and it was not the embrace of death but the embrace of love. Robert lifted me up and held me against his chest, clutching me as if he would never let go. Wonderful lifegiving air flowed into my lungs as I breathed thankfully in huge gulps.

"My love," he whispered, his voice breaking with emotion. "You're alive! We got here just in time."

Cheers broke out above us. Holding lanterns, the entire cast lined the grave, with several footmen leaning on spades, all waving and calling to me. Russet danced along the edge, barking happily, his tail wagging. Rupert jumped down into the grave on the other side of the coffin.

"You brought Russet?" I croaked. Each word rasped in my dry throat like sandpaper.

Robert looked at me with tears rolling down his cheeks. He smiled. "Brought him? He's the one that found you. Between Russet and Maisie, you were saved."

My brain wasn't working very well. "Maisie?"

I glanced upwards again. There was Maisie, huddled in a blanket, sobbing pitifully. Parker stood next to her, with one arm protectively around her thin shoulders.

"Oh, miss," she cried. "I thought ye was gone forever."

I looked at Robert. "I don't understand."

Robert smoothed strands of hair off my face. "I thought you'd gone to bed after the excitement of the evening, as did most of the household. When you failed to return to your room, Maisie waited for an hour and then decided to raise the alarm. She woke Parker, who very sensibly alerted me. Clever Russet found your shoes, then your stole, and then he must have picked up your scent. He led the search party straight here."

Rupert interjected, "Come, Robert, we must get Amelia back to the house and into bed."

Robert and Rupert lifted me up and Johnson and Peters reached down to haul me to the surface. My knees were so wobbly that I could hardly stand.

"Water!" I whispered. "I'm so thirsty."

Robert held a flask to my lips and only allowed me to take tiny sips. The cool water soothed and yet it burned my raw throat. Then he swept me up and strode back to the house. If anything, just him holding me like this was wonderful. In 2015, I'm sure I would have insisted on walking by myself. But this was 1815 and I wanted to be in his embrace. I could feel his heart beating through his shirt and if his shoulder hurt, he never let on. His masculinity, his scent, his strength, enveloped me. All those corny things I'd read in romance novels were real to me now. But much as I wanted to simply sink into the pleasure of his embrace, I had to tell him it was the dowager. Maybe he didn't know yet? Since he hadn't said a word that he suspected the arrow incident to be an attempt on his life, he could be walking into yet another trap somewhere down the line. I had to tell him.

"I must speak to you," I mumbled. "I have something very important to tell you."

He looked down at me with the fire of love in his eyes. "As I have to tell you, my dearest, but not now. Tomorrow will be time enough."

Clearly, he thought I meant something else. If only it could be. This time the tears that trickled down my cheeks were for what I was about to lose as I clung desperately to the man I loved. Once in the safety of my own bedroom, Maisie and Mrs Barlow took over, wiping my face and hands clean, giving me another long drink of water, taking off my ruined and filthy ballgown, putting me into a nightdress, and tucking me into bed. Doctor Potts, still dressed as Friar Laurence, made up a laudanum mixture and this time I was grateful to take it and surrender to its soothing effects.

I reached out for Maisie's hand and squeezed it hard. "Maisie, thank you. I owe you my life."

Maisie burst into fresh sobbing. "Don't say that. I knew sumfink was wrong when ye did'na return. Who would listen to me I asked meself? I'm nobody, just a parlour maid. But I knew Mr Parker would listen and he did."

By then I was falling asleep. Mrs Barlow gently drew Maisie away and then blew out the candle. I slept and it was in the gentle arms of restful Morpheus, not Azrael.

Chapter Seventeen

Sunday, 7 May 1815

I woke up surprisingly refreshed and none the worse for wear after my life and death ordeal, accent more on the death side. My throat felt better, albeit a tad scratchy still. A glance in the mirror revealed slightly puffy eyes from all the crying. Maisie peered around the door and then tiptoed into the room with my breakfast on a tray.

"Ye look as good as new, miss," she said cheerfully. "Cook insisted ye have breakfast in the comfort of yer own bed, considerin' ye was just about murdered, being buried alive 'n' all!"

Would the excitement of my abduction and potential death, but mercifully an eleventh-hour dramatic rescue, possibly be the subject of many dinner table conversations for years to come?

She placed the tray on the bed, within my reach. "And when yer ready and washed and dressed, His Grace asks fer yer presence in the drawing room at eleven."

This would be the perfect opportunity to lay my suspicions before him. "What time is it?"

"It's after nine-thirty," Maisie said while busying herself

with laying out clothing and toiletries. "Plenty of time, don't worry."

"Whose grave was I buried in?" I asked, curiosity getting the better of me as I cracked a boiled egg.

Maisie stifled a snort of laughter. "That was Mr Polycarp's coffin. The old draper in the village. Mrs Polycarp heard this mornin' that the grave had been dug up, so she went straight to Reverend Wilby to lay a grievous complaint. She said it's a disgrace and a cryin' shame that there's grave robbers about when the poor man was only buried on Friday. Reverend Wilby had to check Mr Polycarp still had his watch and his weddin' ring on him."

She rolled her eyes expressively. "Obviously, no one had robbed the old man's body. They just wanted a space to hide yer body, beggin' yer pardon." She bit her bottom lip and went red.

Talk about gallows humour! But she looked so mortified that I said, "That's all right, Maisie. No harm done. But will the whole village know about what happened to me?"

She pursed her lips primly. "Of course not. His Grace spoke with the servants this morning and asked us not to say anythin' to preserve the honour of the family, and Mr Polycarp's dignity as well. And we all promised so no one will say nuffink. Mr Polycarp's been laid to rest again already with Reverend Wilby sayin' a few solemn words."

After this juicy bit of scandal, how could anyone resist gossiping about it? Someone buried alive, a coffin violated, sinister midnight graveyard shenanigans. This was the stuff of legend, both ancient and urban. I looked at her sceptically. "Really?"

She goggled at me, looking slightly affronted. "When His Grace asks fer a promise, ye don't break it. Where would we be without our jobs?"

"But word will get out somehow. What will people think happened to Mr Polycarp's coffin since the gravediggers had to rebury him."

Maisie gave me a smug look. "Vandals! That's what happened. Ruffians without godliness playin' pranks in the middle of the night. Nuffink t' do with Chelston Hall."

She held up a charming dress of eggshell blue muslin. "Shall I lay this one out?"

Such was the high esteem Robert enjoyed among his household staff that he could ask them to seal their lips on the most exciting event that had happened in Hadley for possibly the last hundred years, and they all said yes. It was incredible. Their loyalty spoke volumes about the man.

Once I had eaten, washed, and dressed, I made my way down to the drawing room. The door was closed and, surprisingly, Higgins stood sombre faced on guard. He opened it and ushered me inside, but I had the feeling entry was limited. Indeed, it was. Robert, looking sternly handsome in a superbly cut navy coat—even to my untutored eye—and fawn pantaloons tucked into gleaming Hessians, stood in front of the fireplace. He had the best view of the semi-circle of several chairs and a small sofa arranged around it. Rupert, in his usual casual country attire of breeches and top boots, was pacing behind the chairs, frowning. Sidney, pale and anxious, sat huddled in an armchair. This morning's gathering had affected his toilette because he was positively under-dressed, or that might just have been the lack of trinkets which he seemed to have eschewed after Clementine's advice. Doctor Potts sat ramrod straight in a chair, also with a serious expression.

The dowager sat regally upright, her expression defiant. Whatever her thoughts, she presented a brave face and was as elegantly attired and coiffured as always. Only her fingers plucking at a small lace-edged handkerchief betrayed her nervousness. I could barely look at her and her gaze did not meet mine. Seated on the small sofa was a village family of three dressed in their Sunday best; a harassed-looking woman, a care-worn man, and between them a young man who was most likely their son. Their homespun presence struck an incongruous note. What on earth could they have to do with my abduction; it was clear the gathering was about just that.

The last person in this coterie was Milvers, obviously unhappy at being here, wearing her usual black mothball-scented attire. She turned her face away as I looked at her. She knew that I knew she had pushed me over the balustrade. It was all very Poirot-esque; the crime now solved, and the culprits revealed in a showdown scene. When Robert began speaking, his voice was cold and his gaze incisive. Even I was a little intimidated and I was the victim! His next words told me he had worked everything out already for himself.

"Good morning, everyone. We are here to discuss matters that have transpired over the past few days. I won't go over the attempt on my life," he said. "Suffice it to say, this failed, I am still alive, and I've done the necessary investigation to get to the bottom of things."

He knew all this time and never said a word? Everyone, except Doctor Potts and Rupert, either looked away or looked down at their feet. The village woman gave a muffled squeak and then covered her mouth with one hand.

"Oh, Cousin Robert," Sidney bleated as he wrung his hands in despair. "Whatever happened, I'm sure I had nothing to do with it. I'm as ignorant as anyone here about the details. Everything has been a huge shock to me. My nerves are quite frayed." He then subsided into his chair.

Rupert came up behind him and patted his shoulder. Sidney looked up gratefully with a weak smile.

"I know you had nothing to do with it, Sidney," said Robert. "You are here this morning for a completely different reason."

Sidney gawked at him and then shrank back against the cushion, chewing one of his fingernails.

Robert continued, "I would like to introduce the Miller family." He gestured in their direction.

The family gave terrified grimaces that passed for smiles and the young man hung his head and gave a muffled sob.

"Mr Miller is one of the tenant farmers on the estate. Mrs Miller assists her husband and arranges the flowers for the church. Sam is their son, and he helps his father and does odd jobs for Reverend Wilby in the church and churchyard."

"Get on with it, Robert!" The dowager's voice was low and harsh. Everyone looked at her, astonished. "Whatever you have to say, say it. Why are these peasants here? What have they got to do with us?"

The Millers cowered together miserably, the parents each holding one of their son's hands.

Robert glared at her. "Mr and Mrs Miller are blameless in this fiasco, but Sam, unfortunately, has been drawn into what can only be described as a Machiavellian web of intrigue and deceit. They came to me very early this morning to make a clean breast of their son's involvement, once he had divulged all the details to them."

Sam burst into loud sobs, with his mother on one side trying to stop him crying, and his father on the other, patting his back and muttering that he should be a man and try to be brave. Robert went over to the hapless trio. The father jumped up to surrender his seat and Robert sat next to Sam, who soon subsided into sniffles.

Robert was calm as he spoke. "Tell me, Sam, why did you shoot that arrow in the woods?"

"T'was a contest, sir," Sam mumbled, hanging his head. "And the lady said I was t' have a whole shillin' if I hit my target and won. A nice bright, shiny, silver shillin' all t' myself."

"And you are such a good marksman," said Robert, "that you hit your target and won."

Sam's face was a picture of confusion. "But I did'na know t'was yerself, sir. I could'na see properly through the trees. T'was supposed to be an *archery* contest with a target. I'm good at archery. I win all the time. But I don't shoot people. I only shoot targets."

Robert nodded. "I know, Sam. Whoever told you it was a contest lied to you. They misled you."

"But she gave me the shillin'," Sam burst out, tears trickling down his ruddy cheeks. He ducked his head to wipe his face with one sleeve. "I told her I did'na want it no more because I saw I'd done ye harm, sir. But she made me take it and said now I was guilty, the shillin' was proof, and I could be transported for murder. Murder!" He buried his face in his hands and sobbed piteously, his body heaving.

Next to him, Sam's mother cried silently, huge tears rolling down her face. Her husband stood behind her, helpless, anguished, patting his wife's shoulders. Tears prickled behind my eyes as well. Sam's sobs were heartrending. The dowager tossed her head and looked away while Rupert paced even more.

"He's a good boy, Yer Grace!" the man said, his voice cracking. "He was'na always simple. When he was twelve, he had an accident on the farm and hit his head. Before that time, he was clever. Knows his letters and his sums still. He's good wiv his hands too. He can carve anything you like."

Robert looked up at the father and said quietly, "I know. He is a son to be proud of." Then he turned to Sam. "Tell me, Sam, of the ladies present, which one here gave you the shilling?"

Sam looked around, sniffed loudly, and pointed at Milvers. "That's the lady. The one sittin' over there."

Milvers blanched, her usually white face turning almost grey with shock and fear. This news was astounding. Milvers of all possible suspects was the architect of this assassination attempt? But how was it possible and why? After adding up all the evidence, I'd been convinced it was the dowager. Rupert and Sidney, united in their astonishment and disbelief, just stared open-mouthed.

The dowager pointed a shaking finger at Milvers. "Traitor!" she screeched. "After all I've done for you? And this is how you repay me?"

Milvers looked stunned at the outburst but shook it off. She sat up straighter and composed herself, her expression impassive.

Robert looked at her. "Would you care to explain yourself?" He held out the scrap of material I'd torn off her clothing in my tumble over the balustrade. Someone must have retrieved it from the coffin.

"This piece of fabric places you directly in the attack on Miss Carstairs after the play. An event which led to her near-death in a newly dug grave. Attempted murder is a serious matter indeed, Milvers, so think very carefully before you answer."

Milvers looked down for a moment, as if deciding which way to play her hand because it would be impossible to deny her involvement. Then she looked up at Robert. Her answer was surprising.

"Your Grace," she said humbly, "I deny nothing, and I will

tell you everything, the unvarnished truth. I'm also prepared to take my punishment."

She cast a malevolent glance at the dowager. It appeared that Milvers had a card or two up her sleeve.

The dowager almost exploded with rage. She half rose and then fell back into her seat. "Throw her out now! No, wait, call the magistrate, and have her locked up—"

Robert raised one hand, and that simple gesture silenced her. The dowager turned her face aside. In her agitation she began to tear her handkerchief into small pieces, shredding the delicate lace like confetti.

Milvers stood, clasped her hands in front of her, and began. "Your Grace, I apologise for my part in the incident with the arrow, and—" she glanced at me "—for pushing you into the bushes, Miss Carstairs." She took a breath as if to calm herself and when she spoke again, her voice shook.

"My history is not clean. When I was younger, I had a conviction for theft and was about to be imprisoned. Her Grace, who was yet unmarried, being still Miss Minerva Cole at the time, somehow managed to intervene and saved me from what would have been hell or a hanging. She offered me employment and I've been loyal to her ever since. I have obeyed every order she ever gave me, without question." She glanced briefly at the dowager. "Those orders included making the arrangements to pay the young man to shoot at His Grace when he was out riding last Tuesday morning."

A collective gasp of shock swept through the goggling captive audience, me included.

She looked at me. "I only went along with Her Grace's plan to get rid of you because I thought at first you were what she said you were, a viper in the bosom of the family."

I just stared at her, speechless, my temper boiling. The old bat of a dowager! My instincts were right. She hated Amelia enough to want to kill her.

Milvers continued, "I was reluctant to embark on what I knew were criminal activities, such as trying to murder His Grace, but since I owed everything to my employer, I had no option but to obey." She bowed her head. "I apologise, Your Grace. You've always treated me most kindly and with respect when others have not. I hope you can forgive me although nothing can undo what I have done."

Robert did not say a word. The Millers looked dazed, and Rupert and Sidney were still gob smacked, which was just as well. Rupert losing his temper would not have improved the situation. He and Sidney looked like Tweedledee and Tweedledum, wide-eyed and stunned.

"When the arrow attempt failed, Her Grace thought the young man might talk so she feigned a poisoning plot to throw suspicion that there was still someone trying to kill the duke, but in fact no one else was poisoned." Milvers' gaze darted briefly to the dowager. "Her Grace ate a dried poisonous mushroom to make herself sick. No one else was ever in any danger."

Given her matter-of-fact tone and the blunt presentation of the facts, Milvers seemed to be telling the truth. What did she have to lose anyway?

The dowager must have thought otherwise. She gave a disbelieving snort. "What a ridiculous pack of lies! I'm astounded you're willing to listen to this mendacity, Robert, spewed by a servant and a simpleton. How would I even get a dried poisonous mushroom to pretend to be poisoned to throw off suspicion?" She waved her hands in the air dismissively and shot a dagger look at Milvers.

"Interestingly, Doctor Potts has found such evidence," said

Robert. "You were not poisoned badly but you made yourself sick enough to be credible and to suggest to the household that someone had malicious intentions towards the family."

He gestured to Doctor Potts who rummaged in his medical bag and brought out something wrapped in a piece of cloth. He opened the cloth to show the riveted audience a dried piece of what certainly looked like a mushroom. We all leaned forward to see the small, blackened piece of fungus.

The dowager stared for a moment, speechless, and then blustered. "Humph! As if I even knew how to obtain such an item? As if I would even *swallow* such a thing? Prove it."

Milvers addressed Robert. "Your Grace, I procured the mushroom. I saw Her Grace eat it shortly before dinner that evening in time for the poison to work."

"More lies," the dowager said harshly. She thumped the arm of her chair. "I said prove it. This piece of mushroom could have come from anywhere. Maybe someone went digging in the woods for the express purpose of incriminating me in their wicked plan."

Doctor Potts spoke for the first time, standing up and addressing the riveted audience. "I can prove it, I'm sorry to say, Your Grace. I found this in the vomit you expelled after eating the soup. You did indeed poison yourself, but only enough to cause acute discomfort, not death." He looked so sad saying this. Once finished, he sat down and simply stared at the floor.

"Thank you, Doctor," said Robert. "And now to the utterly heinous crime of the attempted murder of Miss Carstairs."

A chill rippled down my spine. Would I ever get over being trapped in that coffin? Up until now, the dowager hadn't admitted her guilt or that she'd had any part in it.

"So now you're trying to saddle me with something I could

not possibly have done?" she cried. "How could I have put Amelia in that coffin when I was busy with our guests? Indeed, how could I even manage to pick her up at all?"

Robert looked grim. When he spoke, he sounded so formal, so much older.

"No, you did not sully your hands with any part of this diabolical plan. You simply ordered two people who were afraid of you and could be coerced to do your bidding. Milvers owed you her livelihood and to keep her dark past secret. Sam was terrified of being tried for attempted murder and either hanged or transported. Milvers pushed Amelia into the bushes once you'd managed to lure her away from the other guests. Sam then dragged her off to the churchyard where it was easy to uncover a freshly dug grave and stow her in Mr Polycarp's coffin. She would never have been found and would slowly have suffocated."

Next to him, Sam nodded frantically while his mother held his hand. Behind them, his father coughed nervously.

Robert stared at the dowager with a puzzled expression. "What I want to know is why. Your life here is very comfortable despite the economies we must practise. You have servants to do your bidding. You have friends who visit, and you visit them. You can go to town any time you like for shopping or entertainment. You have everything at your fingertips to be happy. You have a loving son, Rupert, and you have my respect as the wife of my late beloved father—"

Her screech of rage took us by complete surprise. She must have decided to fling all caution to the wind because she leaped out of her chair and pointed to Rupert, her face contorted with rage into an ugly mask. Instinctively, we shrank back in our seats, except Milvers who calmly sat down again. No doubt she'd experienced this side of the dowager before. One could only imagine what she'd seen in her long and loyal service to this Gorgon.

"My son?" she shrieked at Robert. "So many soldiers died in the Battle of Vitoria. Why weren't *you* among the dead? You weren't even wounded in all your years of military service! Why didn't *you* die in the war so *he* could inherit the title? Once the old man was gone, the path would have been clear for Rupert to inherit the title and the properties but for you hindering my ambitions for him. You were in the way. I had to take precautions to protect my position and that of my son until he attained his majority."

Rupert was stunned. "Mama!" he cried, taking a step towards her. "Is this all true?"

"Aunt Minerva?" Sidney whimpered. He sat up in alarm. "What have you done?"

She turned on them both like an avenging Valkyrie. "Done?" Her laughter was maniacal. "I only did what I had to do so you would get your birthright, Rupert, and to secure my family's future."

I thought Rupert would faint from the shock of his mother's words. He ran both hands through his hair. He was so stunned that it took him a few moments to even speak.

"You tried to kill my brother?" he said faintly. "For the title? For the estate? I don't even want the title and the estate."

"You don't know what you want," she said sneeringly. "I'm your mother and I know what's good for you and what you deserve. Once it was clear your *half-brother* had marital intentions, that golden opportunity would pass us by. We'd be pushed aside. Robert would get rid of us and my plans for you would collapse."

Marital intentions? With all eyes on me now, my cheeks burned. Robert still said nothing. Perhaps he was hoping she would confess by blurting everything out in her rage.

"Yes!" said the dowager, swinging in my direction with a malevolent glare. Two spots of red glowed on her cheeks from her agitation.

"Miss Mealy-Mouthed Amelia Carstairs. I thought I'd gotten rid of you years ago when I made the old duke send you and your father away. When I heard that Robert had invited you both on a visit, I knew what his plans were."

Then she looked at Rupert. "Why do you think I said yes to that encroaching Eccles woman pestering me to let Clementine come to stay on an extended visit?"

She laughed grimly. "All the time the woman was dangling after Robert to marry her daughter, but I had other plans to cement your position, my boy. Clementine is young, rich, and beautiful. You are young, titled, and handsome. A match made in heaven."

"I had no idea you planned all this," said Rupert, aghast. He looked at Robert. "I had no idea of any of this."

"Naturally I planned it," she said triumphantly. "Clementine will inherit a fortune from that common grandmother of hers. Once Robert was out the way, I knew you and Clementine would fall in love. It would all have worked out so well."

She turned back to me, her gaze hard with loathing. "Then you came along, and my plans started falling apart. But, ironically, you did me a favour. The idea of the play was perfect to throw Rupert and Clementine together."

The dowager was on a roll. Nothing could stop her now as the words continued to spill out in a torrent of poison, sealing her guilt. She threw her head back and laughed. "Oh, how fortunate it all was. Never mind that the village idiot failed to kill you, Robert. Once Amelia had disappeared for good, my chance would have arisen again to get rid of you. And that next time, I would *not* have failed."

She glared at him, her dark eyes smouldering with hatred. It was quite terrifying that one person could wreak such havoc in the name of naked ambition.

Robert stared at her, stony-faced. "I'm astounded that you actually waited for two years after my father's death, and you did not try sooner to have me murdered."

She laughed grimly. "It would have aroused suspicion coming so hard upon the heels of your father's death. I was prepared to bide my time until you invited Amelia here. Then I knew I had to strike."

Robert stood. "I think you've said enough, madam. You're guilty of attempted murder and blackmailing two people unfortunate enough to cross your path."

She tossed her head defiantly. "Ha! What can you do to me? What will you dare to do? Nothing! You'll never sully the reputation of this family."

Robert's voice was glacial, his expression hard. "No, I will never sully the reputation of this family, and neither will you do any more damage. You will retire to Scotland to stay with your older sister. She is widowed and alone and possibly will be glad of the company."

The dowager blanched and sat down heavily. "What? You mean stay with that mean-spirited, penny-pinching Augusta? In that cold, draughty, run-down place she has the gall to call a castle? Surrounded by barren hills and bawling sheep?"

He nodded. "The very person and the very place."

Now she looked terrified, gripping the arms of the chair, staring at him wild-eyed. "I will not go. You cannot force me to go. She hates me, and I hate her. There's nothing there for me."

"There's nothing here for you anymore," he replied. "You

certainly cannot stay in this house a moment longer than is necessary."

"What about money?" she demanded, narrowing her eyes at him. "You're going to cast me off penniless?"

Robert raised his eyebrows. "What? And have it said that the Dowager Duchess of Hadley was sent into exile without a penny to her name? Of course not. Your personal money is your own. I will also send Augusta a generous monthly allowance to cover your board and lodging, which I'm sure she will appreciate. You will want for nothing, and in return you will say nothing about what happened here, your part in it, or anyone else's part in it. Your silence will guarantee that you live out your remaining years comfortably.

"Let me live in London!" she cried. "Living on that bleak inhospitable crag of rock will be unbearable." She bowed her head, beaten. "Augusta keeps no company nor servants. Life with her is a prison sentence. It will kill me."

Robert glared at her with such intensity that it was a miracle how he managed to sound so calm. He must have had iron control over his emotions.

"Oddly enough, you had not a single thought for what might happen to the two people, the servant and the simpleton, as you describe them, whom you dragged into your dastardly plans. Nor did you think of the lives you might have taken, mine and Amelia's. You must live now with the consequences of your foul actions."

The dowager looked at Rupert. Her haggard face lit up. "Rupert, my darling boy. Come with me and we'll make a life together. You won't be happy without me. Robert will make your existence here a misery." She reached out her hand in a pleading gesture.

He recoiled instantly. "Mama, you planned to murder

two people, one of them my own brother. How could I spend another day in your company? When might you decide to get rid of me? When I'm no longer useful?"

Her shock was palpable, her face ashen. "What do you mean?"

Rupert's expression was a mixture of anger and sadness. "I was supposed to go with Robert that morning. You knew we'd planned to ride but you lured me back at the last minute on some flimsy pretext, leaving my brother to ride to his possible death."

The dowager grasped at this straw. "Yes, yes, I called you back to save you in case that idiotic fool hit you by accident. I left it to the last minute so as not to arouse suspicion." She glared at the Millers who flinched in horror. "I couldn't take that chance. I couldn't lose you, my only son."

He shook his head. "There's nothing more I can say to you, Mama. You have absolutely no idea of what you've done. You have no remorse either."

Confused, the dowager turned from Rupert to Sidney, wide-eyed and still cowering in his seat. "Sidney? You'll come with me and help me bear it. After all I've done for you when your parents passed away."

Sidney jumped up and went to stand next to Rupert. "And I'm very grateful, Aunt Minerva, but no. Murder?" He shuddered. "I still cannot believe you even stooped to this."

She glowered at him. "So expedient. Feathering your own nest already, eh?" She clasped both hands to her breasts, surely winning the Mrs Siddons Award for melodrama. "I have been nourishing a viper in my bosom."

The dowager seemed to like that expression.

"Expedient? Viper?" Sidney squawked in indignation. He was outraged. "Aunt, pardon my pointing this out but murder is murder, and it's a crime. Have you no thought for any repercussions?" He folded his arms and looked stubborn. "Well, I do."

The dowager gave a contemptuous snort. "Do you think you still have a home here?" she said sarcastically. "Think again. They'll throw you out the moment I'm gone. See if they don't, Sidney. Robert despises you."

Sidney looked crushed but Robert intervened. "Sidney is very welcome here, any time," he said. "This is still his home."

Rupert put one arm around Sidney's shoulder. "That's right, Sidney."

"As for you, madam," Robert continued. "Mrs Barlow will escort you to your room where one of the maids will start packing for you. You need only take what is necessary for the journey. You will leave tomorrow morning. Higgins and Mrs Barlow will supervise the packing of all your remaining belongings which will be sent on to you in Scotland."

The dowager said with a sneer, "Will you put me on the Mail Coach to travel in disgrace?"

He frowned. "Of course not. You'll travel in style in the family carriage, properly escorted, and make the journey comfortably in stages. What would people think if you travelled any other way?"

"What will people think when I've gone?" she retorted with some of her old fire. "What excuse will you make up to explain my absence?"

"They will think what they've been told," he replied. "That you've gone to tend to your widowed older sister who is ailing. In the meantime, life will go on here and I have no doubt there will be many more interesting events to capture the attention of the locals and gentry. If anyone asks, I'll inform them that your sister needs you, and the sisterly ties that bind you two are so strong you could not even consider abandoning Augusta in her hour of need."

Her expression was one of pure evil. If looks could kill, Robert would be stone dead. Robert ignored her, went over to the bell pull, and yanked it.

When Mrs Barlow arrived moments later, he said, "Thank you, Mrs Barlow. Her Grace needs help in preparing for an unexpected trip to Scotland."

Whatever Mrs Barlow felt or thought, she concealed it behind a wooden expression. "Very good, Your Grace."

The dowager swept to the door with her head held high. She turned and gave us all a final withering stare. Once she and the housekeeper had left, Milvers asked, "What about me, Your Grace? I'm not afraid any longer to get what I deserve. I cast myself upon your mercy."

Milvers had cunningly played the right hand from the cards Fate had dealt her. Confessing her role in this plot put the ball in Robert's court.

He looked at her with an enigmatic expression. "I'm not your judge and jury, Milvers, and I have no intention, as I said, of dragging this family through the mud of a scandal. You also have a sister, I believe."

She looked surprised. "Yes, yes, Your Grace, I do. My sister is in Brighton." Her expression had a glimmer of hope.

"Would she be willing to have you stay with her?"

"Oh yes, Your Grace," Milvers said eagerly. "She runs a small boarding house and she's always writing to me saying if I want to give up working here there's a place for me there because she needs the help."

Robert nodded. "Good. And there you shall go. I'll give you whatever is owed in wages, a small lump sum to help you get settled, and a monthly stipend or pension so you are not a burden on your family. The money will help you."

Milvers flushed bright red. "B-But why, Your Grace? I did a wicked thing. Things could have turned out very badly for you and for Miss Carstairs. Why are you being so kind to me when you could call the magistrate now and have me flung in prison?"

Robert shook his head. "I can only imagine what it's like to have a threat hanging like the sword of Damocles over one's head. I'm not being kind, Milvers. I'm being impartial and practical. Your side of the bargain is never to speak of this to anyone. If your family asks, you've decided to retire and you've been rewarded for your loyal years of service to Her Grace."

Milvers curtseyed. "I am very grateful, sir."

"Higgins will assist you with the ticket for the stagecoach and any traveling expenses. Furnish him with your destination address as well."

She curtseyed again. "Thank you." Then she turned to me. "I am sorry, Miss Carstairs. Truly sorry. I wish you very well."

Oddly enough, I believed her.

Once she had left the room, Rupert bounded up to Robert, his mouth already open to demand an explanation. But Robert's raised hand silenced him, as it had the dowager. Rupert flopped into a chair, muttering to himself. Sidney sidled over to Robert, his expression anxious.

"Cousin Robert, do you really mean I'm still welcome here?"

Robert smiled. "Of course, Sidney. Why on earth would I banish the one person who is perfect for the part of the narrator in next year's Shakespearean performance? If you're still willing to take part and will be available?"

Sidney went red with pleasure. "I say, that's very kind of

you," he tittered. "I'm overwhelmed. I'm gratified. I'm—"

Robert patted his shoulder. "I think you should share this good news with Sir Harold, given that he was instrumental in you discovering your hidden thespian talent."

"A capital idea. Thank you, Cousin," Sidney trilled as he pranced out the room, his spirits restored.

Doctor Potts quietly took his leave and then it was just me, Robert, Rupert, and the Miller family, who stared at us with ever-widening eyes and fearful faces.

"Am I t' be transported?" Sam burst out, before dissolving into more tears. He fumbled in his coat pocket for a large handkerchief and buried his face in it, honking as he blew his nose hard. "I'm very sorry I shot at ye, sir, and I'm also very sorry I put the young lady in Mr Polycarp's coffin."

Mrs Miller trembled as she embraced her son. Mr Miller put his arms around both from behind the sofa. Robert sat down next to Sam again.

"No, Sam," he said gently. "No one is being transported. You did the right thing to tell your parents what had happened."

Sam stopped sobbing and stared at Robert, while wiping his cheeks. "I did the right thing?"

"Yes, you certainly did. Your honesty is most commendable. You're an upright young man and I think you should be given the chance to help your parents."

Now interested, Sam blinked back his tears. "But how, sir? What can I do? People keep tellin' me I'm stupid and good for nothin' after my accident."

Robert smiled. "Your father tells me you're very good with your hands and can fix just about anything."

Sam gave a loud sniff and thrust his chest out proudly. "That's right, sir. I'm very good wi' carving and woodwork.

Anythin' like that, I'm yer man."

Robert continued, "And that's why you shall have gainful employment at the church with any repairs or woodwork that needs fixing. I'm sure Reverend Wilby will be pleased. There always seems to be something needing to be mended in the church. He's been complaining that he can't manage alone."

Sam stared, perplexed. "What's that mean, sir? Still helpin'?"

Robert laughed. "Yes, but this time you'll be paid a proper wage for your work. You can contribute to the family now."

Transformed, Sam flung his arms around his mother, who sat with tears trickling down her cheeks and a bewildered smile. "D'ye hear that, Ma? A proper wage! Me havin' a proper job and a proper wage."

Sam looked up at his father, his smile stretching from ear to ear, radiating pure happiness. "Pa! D'ye hear that? I'll be workin' properly, like ye. I can't believe it. A proper job. It's a miracle."

Mr Miller harrumphed and said, "A miracle indeed when we was expectin' somethin' else entirely. That's very kind of Yer Grace. Thank ye, sir." Then he patted Sam's shoulder. "Show His Grace what ye made fer him, Sam."

Sam reached down for a satchel next to his feet and carefully took something out. He handed it to Robert.

"This is fer ye, sir. It's Tempest, sir."

Robert looked stunned. The gift was a wooden carving, about ten inches high, of a horse but not just any horse. This was Tempest, Robert's horse, done in a pale wood to reflect the true colour of the animal. The features were beautifully and delicately worked. The silvery mane and tail seemed to float in an imaginary breeze as the creature flared its nostrils, sniffing the air, one hoof raised.

When Robert spoke, his voice was gruff, as if he was controlling his emotions. "Thank you, Sam. This is exquisite. I shall treasure it always." He went over to the mantelpiece and placed it in the centre, moving aside a Dresden shepherdess. "This is where it will stay."

Sam grinned. "I was hopin' ye'd like it, sir."

"And now why don't you go off to Reverend Wilby and discuss your working hours and tasks with him? I'm sure the morning service is over."

Sam looked hesitant, casting a glance at his mother and then back to Robert. "Me? Talk to Reverend Wilby? By meself? Without Ma and Pa?"

Robert nodded. "It's your job, Sam, so you should do the talking now."

Mr Miller scurried around the sofa to face Robert. "We're very grateful, Yer Grace. What can we do to thank ye?"

"Your silence and discretion on this matter will be enough," said Robert.

Mr Miller nodded. "Lips is sealed, sir. Lips is sealed."

After the Millers had bowed and bobbed their way out the room with profuse thanks, Rupert burst out, "Robert! You just let everyone go. The very people who tried to kill you. Why?"

Robert sighed and slumped into the nearest chair. He suddenly looked exhausted. "What would you have me do, Rupert? Lock them all up? One of them is your own mother. The other is a vulnerable young man who has been grossly misled and misused."

"But Milvers," Rupert exclaimed. "You could have said much more to frighten her, to show her what's in store for her if she puts a foot wrong or opens her mouth."

Robert stared at him. "Why must I frighten a woman who has lived in fear all her life, enduring the daily humiliation and slights that come with the position? She was your mother's puppet and forced to obey her every whim. Milvers would never have done any of this on her own. By treating her fairly and without prejudice, I have secured her silence."

He rubbed one temple. "As for your mother, there was no point in stooping to insults and veiled threats. I made the best decision to remove her as far as possible from this house. You're free to visit and write to her. She's still your mother, and it will be very hard on her if she feels you've abandoned her."

Rupert stalked over to the large window. "I don't know what to believe about Mama. How could she? She must have completely lost her senses. What was she thinking? I thought she loved me."

"She did this because she *does* love you. To her it was the only way to achieve her dreams for you. She was thinking of you and securing your future," said Robert.

"At the expense of yours," Rupert snapped. "What are we to do now? What am I to do now?"

He sounded like a small lost boy, a boy whose mother had left him bereft. A boy who no longer understood his mother and the world around him.

Robert straightened up. "Nothing. It's all arranged. Milvers and your mother will be on their way soon to their respective destinations. The Millers have had their son restored to them and given the dignity of employment. This will all blow over soon enough. Give it time."

He stood and came over to me. "My dear Amelia. I'm sorry you've had to endure the distress of last night, the embarrassment of the past hour, and the washing of dirty family linen in public. In the meantime, we still have Miss Eccles to consider—"

The sound of a commotion came from outside the drawing room door, which burst open seconds later. Higgins, bobbing up and down anxiously, was trying to bar two people from entering. A man and a woman, both well-dressed, both red-faced and puffing, both irate, elbowed their way into the drawing room.

"I'm sorry, Your Grace," Higgins said abjectly, looking a tad dishevelled behind them. "I tried my best to stop them."

"Where is my daughter?" demanded the woman in thrilling tones worthy of any melodrama. Another Mrs Siddons in the making.

Chapter Eighteen

The couple stared at us, the woman aggressively but the man looked rather embarrassed. Obviously, Clementine's parents. This is where the mystery murder ended, and the French farce began in true farcical fashion. We'd gone from Poirot to Feydeau within minutes.

Mrs Eccles glared at Robert; her eyes narrowed in suspicion. "I said, where is my daughter, Your Grace?" She took a determined step forward.

Her husband tried to pull her back. "Now, my dear, there's no need—"

She pushed him aside and came right up to Robert. Since he was a lot taller, she had to look up at him and this rather reduced the effect I suspect she was hoping to achieve. Robert looked down at her with what can only be described as a frosty ducal expression. It worked because she retreated a few steps.

"Miss Eccles is just behind you," said Robert.

The couple swung round to see their darling daughter, as usual arrayed in a very fetching outfit, advancing upon them with a positively martial light in her eyes.

"Mama! Papa! How dare you embarrass me with this unseemly behaviour? What are you even doing here?"

Her parents gasped in unison, and I got the distinct

impression that Clementine pre and post the Shakespearian production were two different people. Something had happened to her. After Maria Wilby's determined stand for female artistic liberty, another worm had turned.

Glaring at them, Clementine forged on. "You know exactly where I've been, Mama, since it was your idea to push me headlong into His Grace's arms. You put me into a most mortifying situation. How do you think I felt being here, all the while knowing that the only thing you had in mind was for me to marry a title and an estate? Now you demand to know where I am?"

She put her hands on her hips and scowled at them. "Well, *here* I am."

Mrs Eccles gaped at her daughter, gave a little screech, and affected dizziness. "Oh, oh, my nerves!" She put one hand feebly to her brow while looking around for something to fall into. "I feel quite overcome by your insensitive, ungracious, undaughterly behaviour."

Rupert came forward and obligingly shoved a chair into the right position behind her. She sank into it with a loud sigh. "Thank you, sir."

Robert gestured to Higgins who was still standing in the doorway, this time riveted, his mouth open. "Higgins, get ratafia for the ladies and something for the gentlemen. The Madeira will do." Higgins scuttled off.

He turned to Mr Eccles. "Now, sir, let's all sit down comfortably with a little refreshment."

Mr Eccles looked relieved and sank into a chair next to his wife. "Gladly!"

Mrs Eccles rummaged in her reticule for a bottle of smelling salts, took a huge sniff and, thus fortified, bounced back into the fray. "I cannot tell you how shattered my nerves have been upon discovering that my daughter has taken part in a *theatrical* piece."

She made it sound like a scene from an X-rated movie.

Clementine gave an exasperated huff and flounced over to the window. "Mama! What nonsense. I wrote to tell you of it myself. You didn't *discover* it at all. Stop being so dramatic. What will His Grace think of you?"

Robert looked as if he was enjoying himself hugely. "And a more beautiful Juliet there never was than Miss Eccles. She was the toast of the production. Moved the audience to tears in the death scene. She almost had me crying and looking for my handkerchief as well." He winked so wickedly at me that I nearly burst out laughing.

Mr Eccles gave a sheepish grin. "Thank you, Your Grace." Then he looked past Clementine, not daring to meet her gaze. "I think, my dear, that your mother means there was an ... er ... unfortunate moment ... er ... unseemly behaviour. Unbecoming of a ... er ... gently reared young female."

He went bright red and wriggled uncomfortably. Mr Eccles was as henpecked as Clementine had described him at our first meeting.

Clementine bristled. "I think you mean at the end where Juliet kisses Romeo and I kissed Rupert."

Her mother moaned and covered her eyes with one hand. "In front of the whole village. All those distinguished guests. What will people think? What will people say?"

"I don't think they'll say anything, ma'am," said Rupert with a sharp edge to his voice. He bowed in introduction as Robert smoothly said, "My brother, Lord Rupert."

Rupert continued, "I was fortunate enough to play Romeo opposite Miss Eccles' Juliet and if the audience reaction is to be believed, after the play all people could talk about was how beautiful Clem—I mean, Miss Eccles— looked and how affecting was her performance."

Mrs Eccles glowered at him. Her jaw clenched. "I know this is not the Middle Ages, but when I was a young woman, no self-respecting female would even *consider* kissing a young man in public."

Another explosion came from the window. "Mama, don't be so gothic. It was part of the play. I was performing as the character of Juliet."

Rupert opened his mouth to retort, but Robert intervened smoothly. "And here we have some refreshing ratafia for the ladies, and something a little stronger for the gentlemen."

Higgins had arrived with a large tray and set about arranging the glasses and the decanters before exiting and closing the door firmly behind him. Robert poured and took a glass over to Mrs Eccles who sat up and straightened her bonnet before accepting it.

"Very restorative," he murmured as she took a large gulp. "You'll feel much better shortly."

Mr Eccles must have decided that discretion was the better part of valour. He stayed huddled in his chair, nursing a large wineglass. The sun was definitely not over the yardarm, but who knew what social drinking rules were followed in 1815. It was six o'clock somewhere in the world.

Robert brought me a glass. "Drink," he said, smiling ruefully. "I think we'll need some fortifying for as long as they remain."

I took a cautious sip of the ratafia. It tasted of almonds, like those deceptively sweet cocktails that don't seem alcoholic until you try to stand up after downing a few. A blessed silence descended while Mr and Mrs Eccles sipped their drinks and ruminated, Rupert joined Clementine at the window and exchanged whispers, and Robert poured himself whatever Mr Eccles was drinking. Just as I was wondering where to next, there was another scuffle behind the drawing room door and a loud female voice said, "Unhand me, you rascal!" Then came a thunk sound and a yelp of pain.

Mr and Mrs Eccles looked up, appalled at the sound of that voice, their faces etched with "rabbits caught in the headlights" expressions. Clementine was ecstatic as she danced over to the door. It burst open with Higgins once again trying desperately to repel invaders by fielding blows from an elderly lady wielding a reticule twice the size of Mary Poppins' carpet bag.

"Grandmama!" she cried, overjoyed at the sight of the visitor.

"My love!" replied the old lady, enfolding Clementine in her arms.

"I tried my best, Your Grace," said Higgins miserably. "The lady would not take no for an answer. She became quite violent."

"Thank you, Higgins, that will be all," said Robert, trying to stifle his laughter as he closed the door.

This had to be Clementine's grandmother, the eccentric old lady who had loads of money and was an embarrassment to her daughter. Mrs Eccles was frozen in horror at the sight of her mother. This was no surprise since the sprightly old woman wore what even I could see was the fashion of yesteryear, with wide skirts in a hideous striped material of violent purple and gold. She wore a huge poke bonnet of unparalleled ugliness, also in purple and gold, with flowers, ribbons, and dyed feathers festooning the crown. It was easy to see why Mrs Eccles was ashamed of her mother. But the old lady's dark beady eyes twinkled naughtily, and her smile was infectious. She looked as if she could be more fun than a barrel of monkeys at a party. With her, age was definitely just a number.

"Humph!" she said to Robert, looking him up and down. "I suppose you're the famous duke everyone's talking about."

Unperturbed, Robert bowed. "I am he, madam, although I'm not sure everyone is talking about me or that I am even famous."

She stared at him for a moment. "Well, I don't care what my daughter Eliza says. You might be a handsome fellow but you're far too old for my Clemmie."

She nudged Clementine while Mrs Eccles gave a faint groan and gulped the rest of her drink. Mr Eccles closed his eyes and shook his head.

Robert suppressed a smile and tried to look solemn. "Yes, I am, madam, far too old for Miss Eccles. And that's why, fortunately, she has met a wonderful younger man, eminently more suited to be her husband. He's also good-looking and intelligent." He looked over at Rupert, still standing at the window with his mouth open in shock. "Come over here and meet Miss Eccles' grandmother, Rupert."

Good manners trump awkwardness and Rupert proved this admirably as he bowed and greeted the old lady. He and Clementine could not meet each other's gaze, looking past each other. Robert then introduced me as his dear cousin and the director of the now infamous theatrical production.

The old lady looked me up and down as well, pursed her lips, and said, "Hmm, I see which way the wind blows here."

Robert took her elbow and steered her to a comfy chair. "Allow me to offer you a seat and refreshment after your journey, Mrs...?"

"Mudge," she replied. "Clara Mudge. I might not be all

that my daughter would like me to be, but it's my money what's put the clothes on their backs and the roof over their heads." She glared at the Eccles duo, now both squirming with mortification. "And don't give me that namby-pamby watered-down stuff for ladies. I'll have what you're having, Duke."

Robert seated Mrs Mudge and poured her a drink. She tossed it off like a pro, and then stared at Rupert. "So, this is the young man you've bin kissing in front of the whole county, Clemmie?"

Clementine went scarlet while Rupert made a kind of gargling noise. Mrs Eccles moaned feebly and mouthed to her husband, "Do something." His reply was that timeless plea made by many a husband: "What do you want me to do? She's your mother."

"It's not like that, Grandmama," Clementine finally said. "It was part of the play. We were both caught up in being the characters."

The old lady let out a huge cackle of laughter and wagged one finger at her granddaughter. "Oh, yes, the play, blame the play. And what're his prospects? From what I hear, Clemmie's inheritance would've been very welcome here, a fair exchange for a title." She glanced at Robert. "Just to let you know, Duke, that I ain't tossing my money away on some penniless scamp with a handsome face. You know what they say. Handsome is as handsome does."

An indignant squeal came from the Eccles contingent. "Mama! Please don't be so common. What will His Grace think? Stop talking about money. You're embarrassing the family."

The old lady glared at her daughter. "Really? If money ain't so important to you both then why d'ye keep asking me for it? And as far as embarrassing the family goes, you're doing that all by yourself without any help from me."

She looked at Robert again. "I'm a plain-speaking woman, Duke, and I call a spade a spade. We all know why Eliza wangled an invitation for Clemmie to visit here. Just didn't turn out the way she thought, what with Clemmie falling in love with the wrong brother and upending her careful plans."

Rupert looked boiling mad but managed to control his temper. "Mrs Mudge, please don't think that an event on stage is necessarily a prelude to marriage. Miss Eccles is free to choose the man she wishes to marry. Money does not come into it at all."

"Oh ho," came her quick reply. "Stiff-rumped and proud, are we?" She fixed him with a gimlet gaze. "So, you don't want to marry Clemmie, is that it?"

"Of course, I do," Rupert burst out but then realised what he was saying. He gave an exasperated huff and went over to the window again. Clementine, looking very pale and agitated, joined him. They stood close together, with Rupert holding her hand.

Robert stepped in and poured tactful oil on troubled family waters. "Mrs Mudge, since you welcome plain speaking as I do, allow me to enlighten you on Rupert's prospects."

She raised an eyebrow. "I'm listening. Here, pour me some more of whatever I'm drinking." She held out her now empty wineglass.

Coming from 2015 and while not knowing that much about 1815 manners, even I could see how Mrs Mudge would be considered dreadfully common, *de trop*, and certainly not welcome in the most elegant of drawing rooms. Plus speaking so openly about money—shock, horror! But Robert took it all in his stride. He spoke to her the way he'd spoken to the Millers, with sincerity, grace, and charm. They must learn this diplomatic stuff from day one, how to handle people from all walks of life, how to defuse situations, how to deal with family murderers and the like.

"Rupert is my younger brother but is not without his own money and property," he said, handing the old lady her drink.

Mrs Eccles sat up and looked very interested. She nudged her husband and they both leaned forward.

"Obviously you want to see your granddaughter safely settled, but with someone she loves."

The old lady took a large slurp and nodded. "That's right. If I left it up to them two—" she jerked her head in the direction of the Eccles couple "—they'd sell Clemmie off to the highest bidder in the twinkling of an eye if there's a title involved. When I got Clemmie's letter and read about what them two was up to, I had to come down here myself to sort it out."

Mr Eccles made an explosive sound of denial, but his wife shushed him.

Robert continued smoothly, "And you want to be sure he's offering for her hand because he loves her, and not from nefarious intentions. You don't want her to fall into the clutches of a greedy and unscrupulous fortune-hunter."

Another slurp and more nodding. "That's right! No scoundrels with nerafioush intentions, thank you! So, tell me about his money and properties," she demanded, waving her glass in Rupert's direction.

Robert smiled. "Rupert has a portion our father left him that was unencumbered by any foolish speculating on the previous duke's part, given as he was to taking the wrong financial advice."

An expression flitted across his face as he spoke. Was it pain, bitterness, or sadness? I couldn't tell. He was good at hiding his feelings, or at least cloaking them.

"The Hadley family estate owns several smallish but charming country houses with land that the couple might choose from to be their out-of-town abode, and there are also two delightful townhouses to consider as a London address. None of these is as sumptuous as Chelston Hall, of course. Quite compact, but still very desirable for a newly married couple starting out life together."

The old lady was impressed. "I thought you said the younger one was a penniless nobody," she said to Mrs Eccles, who blushed and looked away.

Robert laughed. "Not at all. I can assure you, madam, that Rupert's prospects are both assured and solid. But first, as his older brother and guardian, and I'm sure you'll appreciate this considering Miss Eccles' youth, I've been thinking that Rupert should travel for a year to get some experience of the world. Perhaps he'd like to visit our estate in Australia." He nodded to Mr Eccles. "Cattle farming."

Rupert was transformed. "Really? A year of travelling?" He bounded over to grab his brother's hand and pumped it. "It's what I've always wanted—to see the world. Thank you, Robert!"

"If you can tear yourself away from Miss Eccles," Robert said, "who I believe would also like to travel and perhaps should visit Europe and see all the cultural sights. After a year apart, if they still feel the same way about each other, then Mr and Mrs Eccles can consider a formal engagement for their daughter."

Clementine squealed and went over to her grandmother. "Oh, Grandmama, say yes. Say yes. Please. It would be so wonderful."

She gazed at Rupert, with adoration clear in her eyes. "We can write to each other and get to know each other more and then no one can say we didn't make the effort and that we're rushing into things."

Robert, ever suave and in control, went over to Mrs Eccles and gave her his hand, helping her out of her seat. "Perhaps, madam, you and Mrs Mudge and Miss Eccles would like to visit the rose garden and discuss Clementine's future plans and forthcoming engagement."

"Yes, Mama," said Clementine, helping her grandmother to her feet. "I have so many places I want to see. So many sights to visit."

Mrs Mudge wasn't finished with Robert. "I can see you're doubtful about Clemmie's parents, given my daughter's behaviour, throwing Clemmie at your head, so to speak." She shook her head and the hideous bonnet waggled alarmingly. "But you won't find a lovelier girl in London than my granddaughter, nor one with prettier manners."

She gave her daughter and son-in-law a searing glance. "You wouldn't say so now of course but I was an Accredited Beauty in my heyday. Mr Mudge took one look at me and fell head over heels in love." She winked at Rupert. "I don't blame your young Lord Rupert here for losing his heart to her."

Robert, always tactful, said smoothly, "The family likeness is very evident, ma'am. One couldn't miss it."

The old lady gave a hoot of laughter and poked him in the chest. "Such flannel! But I like you already, Duke."

"We shall endeavour to entertain you adequately at Chelston Hall and then perhaps the Eccles family and you, Mrs Mudge, will dine with us this evening? We keep country hours, and it will be simple home-grown fare but well prepared and delicious, I can promise."

Mrs Eccles blushed and flapped her hands in meaningless pretend protest while her husband, who seemed to have had his backbone restored with the wine, said, "Thank you, Your Grace. We'd be delighted."

Robert then turned to Rupert. "I think this would be a good time to take Mr Eccles on a small tour of the grounds, maybe discuss your future plans and get his advice, have a ... er ... man to man discussion?"

He widened his eyes at Rupert who stammered, "Y-Yes. Good idea."

In no time at all, they disappeared, leaving me alone with Robert. This was the moment I had been dreading.

Chapter Nineteen

Robert took my hand. "Thank God, we're rid of them for a little while at least. Come with me."

He led me to the library where Russet lay sprawled on the hearth rug. Drawing me closer, Robert looked deep into my eyes. The way he looked at me made my knees turn weak, but his next words took my breath away. His voice thrilled me to the bottom of my heart.

"You must know, my dearest Amelia, how much I've been longing to speak with you about a very important matter, something of pressing urgency."

This was intense passion in Regency speak, I guessed. Oh my gosh, this was the Mr Darcy moment I had ached for, and one that millions of women worldwide would have torn me limb from limb to revel in themselves, but I had to stop him. The yearning to simply fall into his arms and say, "Yes, yes, I'll marry you!" almost overwhelmed me but I steeled myself. It was torture. Smiling down at me, he was so close that I could feel the warmth of his skin and smell his cologne. All I had to do was reach up and kiss those firm chiselled lips and he would be mine. One kiss would seal our fates. And Amelia's. The thought of her instantly brought me back to a cold, harsh reality with a mental thud.

"No, Robert, please stop," I said quickly. He released me and I stepped back. His expression was hurt for a moment and then he smiled.

"Of course, how stupid of me. I am too hasty, too precipitate in my courtship. When I thought I'd lost you last night, it changed everything. Forgive my bad manners, Amelia. I seem to have forgotten how to behave towards a lady."

I took his hand and led him to the sofa, one of those big leather ones found in posh gentlemen's clubs and expensive shops. I sat and gently pulled him down next to me. It was now or never, and I had to handle this with kid gloves. Robert and Amelia must marry and continue the line.

Choosing my words carefully, I said, "I'm not who you think I am, Robert."

He stared at me, bewildered at first. Then his expression cleared, and he laughed. "And neither am I. Ten years have passed, and you're no longer a naïve young girl of fourteen and I a callow youth of twenty. You're now a lovely, confident young woman of twenty-four and I am a battle-hardened old soldier of thirty."

He raised my hand to his lips and held it there briefly. "Given our letters, few and far between as they were, and taking into consideration that you did become engaged to another man who sadly passed away, I had hoped that you still had feelings for me." He gently squeezed my fingers. "Not the platonic feelings of childhood, but deeper and more mature feelings that can grow and strengthen. Don't you think we should simply say what we both feel and start a new life together?"

That was as bold a formal proposal as ever I've read in a Regency novel but, alas, it was not mine to accept. Taking a deep breath, I forged on, praying that whatever I said would come out as rational and not the demented babblings of a madwoman.

"I mean that I'm not the Amelia Jane Carstairs you think I am."

He dropped my hand like a hot potato. "I am utterly bewildered. I pour out my heart to you, declare my love, and you rebuff me with this fantasy? How can you not be you?"

This was not going well but hardly surprising, given that the concept of time travel took some swallowing. But I pressed on undaunted.

Slowly and carefully, I said, "I am Jane Amelia Carstairs and I come from 2015, not 1815. I am a descendant of Amelia, whom you will marry to continue the family line."

Stunned, he just stared in utter disbelief for a few moments. He jumped up and went over to the fireplace, leaning on the mantelpiece with both hands. Then he turned to look at me. "Who are you then? An imposter? What do you want? Where is Amelia? What have you done with her?"

Now I was beginning to get annoyed although, to be honest, he had every right to call me an imposter. That's exactly how I'd felt since I arrived.

"I've not done anything with her," I said calmly. "Let me explain. I am not an imposter. I'm from a different era, but I'm a direct descendant of the Amelia you know. I'm just a different version of her, if you like."

That was an exaggeration since I hadn't done any research yet. I hadn't had time. A malevolent Fate had whisked me away before I could even open the first folder in the pile the secretary had put on the desk in 2015.

He shook his head. "You're the living image of Amelia.

The likeness is so exact, but I feel as if I now doubt my own eyes. You speak with her voice. I see her mannerisms. I want to believe you but how can you be another version of Amelia? Why should I believe you?"

Thank heavens, he didn't sound angry or offended, just puzzled. This was my chance to win him over. For Amelia's sake, I had to explain it logically and coherently because, evidently, I had been too blunt and sounded crazy. I patted the sofa seat. Hopefully, my smile concealed just how nervous I was. I couldn't blow Amelia's chances; not after I'd just turned him down as Jane. I also couldn't risk him summoning a couple of hefty footmen to throw me out the front door.

"I have not been drinking. I have not secretly indulged in Doctor Potts's laudanum. I can explain. I just hope you can understand."

He sat down next to me, still puzzled but with a guarded smile. "You're from two hundred years in the future? How is such a thing possible? Can one even comprehend such a leap in time? Tell me why I should take such a concept seriously? Please tell me you're joking or convince me that you're telling the truth."

Since I wasn't joking, I had to be convincing. As basically as I could, even though I still had no clear idea how time travel worked, I told him about the time slip. I included the Moberly-Jourdain incident, which would hopefully make sense, given that it involved the familiar historical figure of Marie-Antoinette, and why I had even been at Chelston Hall in the first place.

He frowned. "A time slip? Somehow timelines have become blurred, and you 'slipped' through. Is it possible? I had thought the various academic and romantic writings on the topic of time travel were just fantastical imaginings. But now your assertion has stirred my memory."

He walked over to one of the bookshelves and ran his hand along the gold lettered spines of books.

"Here's something a friend of mine sent me. Most of the books were destroyed shortly after publication but a few copies survived, and fortunately I have one."

He pulled out a book. *"The Memoirs of the Twentieth Century*, published in 1733 by Samuel Madden, an English minister. I glanced at it but thought it was merely idle speculation. Imagine the story of an angel that travels to the years 1997 and 1998 and then returns, bringing letters." Flipping the pages, he continued, "In his preface the author talks of scientific discoveries, steam power, and weapons of war 'joining fire with the sword.' And that was in relation to what had already been accomplished. How much more could mankind achieve in the future?"

He put the book back and returned to the sofa. "Having seen the terrible ravages of war, I'd hoped that war would somehow be abolished in the future and that nations would come together to make sure this kind of atrocity never happened again."

He looked at me. "Is my hope in vain? Is one right in thinking that, given the progress of inventions, weapons of war will be even more deadly?"

Curiosity and his natural enquiring mind had got the better of him in my favour. He seemed to be open to believing my time travel explanation but how could I then tell him that the devastation he and his comrades in arms had endured was nothing compared to the horrors of modern warfare? That death tolls would rocket, and the atomic bomb, modern weapons, and the threat of a global nuclear wasteland would change the face of war forever. That PTSD would be recognised as an after-effect of war and would continue to wreck the lives of returning combatants. That weapons manufacturing was big business and very lucrative and the world leaders were in an arms race "just in case of an attack" to justify their weapons' proliferation. How could I dash his hopes? But I had to be honest. I nodded.

He took my hand almost absently, turning it over in his. "I suppose that war and death are inevitable in the world when one nation seeks to exert power over its neighbours. And advanced scientific discoveries and flying machines? Do they exist?"

"Yes, there are more scientific discoveries than you can ever imagine. People travel from one country to another in flying machines." I didn't say that bombs, those weapons of death and destruction, were also dropped from planes onto other countries, killing innocent civilians as well as combatants.

He shook his head. "Incredible to even think of it, and yet Leonardo da Vinci drew images of what appeared to be a flying machine. But tell me something. If you were at Chelston Hall compiling the family tree, this must mean the line has survived."

This was the hook; his love for his family and the continuation of his heritage. I cudgelled my brain to remember the extent of the property.

"Chelston Hall is a flourishing estate. There are farmlands, the great park is filled with deer and other wildlife, and there are now chalets for tourists to stay for fishing and birdwatching. Artists' retreats, all sorts of things."

He looked astonished. "I'd hoped to build something for the future with the estate and now you say I've achieved my goal?"

I gave him my brightest, most reassuring smile. "Very much so. I can assure you that since Chelston Hall is thriving in 2015 and your descendants, the current duke and duchess, wrote to my father to ask him to do the genealogical research, all is well. The present family has worked hard to create a gem of an estate. I think they even have Regency reenactments."

This was a bit of a stretch, but I remembered the mention of an annual Regency ball.

He stared at me, bewildered. "Regency enactments? What's that? Enactments of the Regency era, of this era? How? And why?"

Honestly, it sounded so silly describing this to someone actually living in the Regency era. "These are very popular on some of the big estates. Balls and dances where people dress up in the style of clothes we're wearing now and enjoy themselves."

He burst out laughing. "They dress up in clothes of a bygone era, have balls and dances, I assume also from the era, and that's considered entertainment?"

Clearly no one in Regency England had thought of doing a Renaissance Faire yet. I had to laugh as well. "Miss Jane Austen's books are very popular, and people have taken a shine to her stories and how society lived, I mean lives. *Pride and Prejudice* is the most popular."

He nodded. "I know of Miss Austen's work although I haven't read any of her books." He cocked his head at me and smiled. "Should I? Will I learn anything about relationships between men and women?"

"Absolutely. She's a master at knowing how people think. Read them. You'll be amazed. Jane Austen is a celebrated household name worldwide."

He put my hand against his heart and held it there. "This all sounds so fanciful. I'm not sure if we're just talking nonsense now because you cannot find an excuse to refuse my suit, or you really are from 2015."

He gazed at me with such a loving expression that my heart didn't go *pitter-patter*. It went *boom-di-di-boom* like a big kettle drum. He reached out and tucked a stray wisp of hair behind my ear. That simple gesture was so loving and intimate, his expression so warm and inviting, almost weakening my resolve. For two pins I could have flung myself into his arms and kissed him forever, drowning in his ardent love. The agony of having to leave him tore me apart inside. The pain was terrible; like a knife twisting in my chest. A river of tears was ready to flow, if only I would let it. But I could not stay; I had to leave. I had to let history unfold. I had to return for everyone's sake, not just my own. Ruthlessly crushing my grief, I smiled back at him.

With a composure I certainly didn't feel, I gently withdrew my hand from his grasp. "I can tell you something to prove that I'm speaking the truth."

He looked at me half-disbelieving. "How? What can you tell me?"

"I'm a history research assistant, and my field is military history."

His eyebrows raised. "Military history? Now I am intrigued."

Talking about history helped to suppress my emotions although my voice sounded a bit wobbly to me. "Today is Sunday, 7 May 1815."

He nodded. "That's right. So can you tell me something that will happen in the future?"

His tone was still teasing, as if he still didn't quite believe me but was just humouring me.

"Yes. Something important that will affect the nation."

He stiffened and his smile disappeared. "What? Is this to do with Napoleon?"

Now I had his attention. "By the Treaty of Chaumont of March 1814, Austria, Russia, Prussia, and Great Britain bound themselves together for twenty years, undertook not to negotiate separately, and promised to continue the struggle until Napoleon was overthrown."

Robert was astounded. "How would you, a woman unversed in military matters, know about these political dealings?" He stared hard at me. "Unless, of course, you're not making this up. You *are* from the future and you're telling me today what will be so in the future."

I was right; he had been humouring me just a little.

"I am, and I can," I said. "Napoleon escaped from Elba on 26 February this year and landed at Golfe-Juan, Antibes on 1 March with a small contingent of around a thousand loyal soldiers. On 20 March he entered Paris. From that date until his final defeat will be known as The Hundred Days. He has succeeded in rallying supporters to his banner. As you probably already know, even Marshal Ney, sent to arrest him, joined Napoleon, and brought six thousand men."

"I cannot believe you know all this," said Robert, looking amazed. "What will happen?"

"He will defeat the Prussians at Ligny on 16 June, but he'll be defeated at the Battle of Waterloo on 18 June by the British under Wellington. Napoleon will nearly win, in fact, but Wellington's Prussian ally, General Gebhard Blücher, will arrive in time to reinforce the British. Napoleon will abdicate in favour of his son and in October he will be exiled to Saint Helena in the South Atlantic Ocean. He will die on 5 May 1821."

Robert's eyes were like saucers as I glibly rattled off these facts.

"Incredible. How could you even know this amount of detail?"

Chapter Twenty

S omething strange happened as I glanced past him at the bookshelves. The shelves shimmered in the way bad television reception makes a picture jump. Russet looked up and barked. This was it; my time was nearly up. I had to hurry but then again, how did I even know what to do? Last time the time slip had happened without my knowledge, and I'd simply been catapulted into the past. Hopefully, I'd be flung forward to 2015 and not back into an ancient war or the outbreak of the Black Death.

"It's my favourite period in history," I said. "And Waterloo is an iconic battle embedded in the nation's heart. It'll be studied in schools and universities, written about in books, and artists will paint many renditions. Wellington will be a national hero. Many statues and monuments will be erected in his honour. Even his horse Copenhagen will have a monument over his grave in Hampshire. This battle will never be forgotten."

He looked so stunned that I pressed on with this familiar military hero. "You'll see, a statue will be erected in his honour called the Wellington Monument. After Waterloo, a patriotic group known as the Ladies of England will commission a statue of Wellington on behalf of the nation's women. The sculptor will be the famous Richard Westmacott. He'll cast the statue out of thirty-three tons of bronze from enemy cannons captured in the Battles of Salamanca in 1812, Vitoria in 1813, Toulouse in 1814, and Waterloo, which is still to come."

If that didn't convince him, I didn't know what would. He looked thoughtful for a few moments, as if something was bothering him. That was not unexpected. I'm not sure I would have believed someone popping back from the future telling me things that hadn't happened yet. But surprisingly, he seemed to have accepted the concept.

"I have another question," he said. "Where is Amelia if you are Jane and you are here? Is she safe?"

I had to be honest. "I don't know but nature hates a vacuum, so I think she is in 2015, in my life."

He shook his head. "In a world so different from the one she knows. How will she cope?"

He sounded so pompous that, against my better judgement, I snapped at him. "Please give her some credit for being a sensible, educated, and perceptive woman. She's not a child. I think she'll react the way I did and that was to adapt, watch, learn."

His expression hardened. "But you have the benefit of hindsight. You already know from your study of history how things work in 1815. What would Amelia know of the workings of a strange and modern world?"

My temper flared. "Don't blame me. I didn't ask to come here. I was just swept away and dumped here. I don't even think I was any use at all. Matters unfolded, the dowager revealed herself, and everything was resolved. And besides, if I exist in 2015 and we're related, somewhat tenuously but related anyway, it means she survives and is returned to 1815."

He frowned. "Of course, you're right and I'm not blaming

you. I'm just deeply concerned for her." His expression softened. "I think I can answer the question as to why you were sent here."

The burning question because all I could see was a big upheaval and nothing had changed by my being here instead of Amelia.

He smiled. "Consider this theory. You are here right now, at this very moment. Forget the future. The future hasn't happened yet even though in the future you exist, and the line is secure because, as you say, Amelia and I marry and perpetuate the line."

I stared at him. "What are you saying?"

"I'm saying that without you coming through the time slip, upending life here at Chelston Hall, and putting on the play, the dowager might not have revealed herself. She might well have tried again to kill me and succeeded. Because of you, in the space of the past week she was forced to overplay her hand. Without you—" he shrugged "—who knows what might have happened?"

"But Sam missed," I said. "He's supposed to be a champion archer, but it was just a flesh wound in the shoulder."

He shook his head mournfully. "You're mistaken. I am only alive *because* he is a champion archer and at the last second jerked his bow up to miss my heart. His father was distraught, as he took great pains to explain to me, that this was the case and that I should be dead. Sam was incoherent, which is understandable."

"But why me of all people?"

"I think I can even answer that one with a stretch of my imagination," he said. "Perhaps you are the only descendant who looks exactly like Amelia. If someone else, let's say your father, had come through, things would not have worked out in exactly the way they did."

That was certain. "If my father had arrived in my stead, I'm sure he would have just loved being here, but he would have blown his cover in five minutes."

Robert looked astounded. "Blown his what?"

"I meant revealed himself. He already knows a lot about the family, in fact much more than I do, but he wouldn't have the faintest idea about pretending to be Amelia's father and I'm sure he would've been carted off to the nearest lunatic asylum."

Besides, the wheels had been set in motion with Amelia's father having to stay behind. It was already written in her diary. No, it was clear that Fate had chosen me. Robert's explanation didn't really answer the question because although he'd said ignore the future, I could not. I was from the future. In two hundred years' time I would be at Chelston Hall and would be the descendant of the woman who had saved Robert. But here I was doing the saving, being that woman. My brain struggled to process the ramifications, no matter which way one put it.

He took my hand again. "I'm very glad it was you, although your father is no doubt a most worthy gentleman."

It was wonderful to sit next to him and have him hold my hand in such a chaste but loving manner. This was courtship *à la* Jane Austen and I agreed wholeheartedly with it.

"There is another reason as well, which I think is valid."

What other reason could there be?

He continued, "Being stuffed into that airless coffin for hours would be too much even for a strapping man to endure. Just trying to imagine it, well, I'm not sure even I would emerge unscathed. As a modern woman and having been exposed to a very different world, one in which women appear to be stronger and more resilient, you survived. Perhaps Amelia wouldn't have survived the shock and horror of being buried alive. Not knowing if anyone would miss her presence, if anyone would look for her, and if anyone would even think of where to look for her before the air ran out."

He had a point. The ordeal had almost been too much for me. I'd given up and was on the point of surrender, okay, death, when the rescue party arrived.

"The estate is enormous, and Sam could have hidden her anywhere. Imagine if we'd wasted time looking in the stables, outhouses, and various buildings, she might have suffocated and thus not have survived to have any descendants."

It was a thought. It made me feel slightly better to think that there had been a purpose to my coming here after all, even though I was sure Amelia herself could have handled things successfully. Maybe she wouldn't have thought of the play, but she would have sussed out what was going on with the wicked dowager. Her diary entries had already indicated that.

"Russet played his part as well and it's lucky he has what one would call 'a nose.' Finding your shoes and your stole led him right to the grave. I think you dealt very well with the situation on the whole, considering you came here knowing nothing about my stepmother's plans."

I shook my head. "No, that's not true. I didn't know she was the one behind the attempt, but I already knew someone had tried to kill you twice."

His shocked expression was almost comical except that it wasn't funny to learn there had been a second attempt on one's life.

"What do you mean you already knew?"

I had to be tactful here given that Robert had sworn the

staff to secrecy. "My father unearthed a little snippet in the surviving family papers mentioning several attempts on your life but that these hadn't succeeded. And, of course, they hadn't since the family is alive and well in 2015."

He looked so aghast that I quickly added, "Nothing official, of course, a brief mention in some letter, and no names, just a vague statement. I don't think any of the staff had broken their promise to say nothing. My father said this was in personal correspondence."

"And what was the second attempt?"

"I wouldn't say I was prepared, but I wasn't surprised when a fire broke out in your bedroom, on the same night of the arrow attack."

He was incredulous. "A fire? In my bedroom? And who discovered it and put it out?"

"Russet discovered it and came to fetch me in the library." Russet thumped his tail on the floor when he heard his name. "I was looking at newspapers and trying to work out if I'd really gone back in time or if it was all an elaborate hoax. Parker and I put the fire out. Luckily it hadn't spread very far, just to the bed curtains, and we dragged you into the adjoining dressing room to keep you safe while we did so."

Robert jumped up and paced in front of me. "I can't believe it. Parker never said a word."

"He didn't want to worry you, but he was also suspicious of events. Remember he told you that while you were convalescing, he and Cook prepared your food separately from the rest of the family just to be safe."

He frowned. "Parker should have told me. I was uneasy about the arrow incident because we have excellent relations with everyone in the village, my tenant farmers, and even the travellers passing through. There's no poaching because I allow an acceptable level of hunting for the pot."

He sat down next to me. "*You* never said a word."

"I didn't want to worry you. And you never noticed the new bed curtains, so I thought it best to say nothing."

He began to laugh. "We've been going round in circles. I never said anything because I didn't want to worry you as well. No, I didn't even notice the change in bed curtains. It just shows how inobservant I am."

"Neither Milvers nor the dowager confessed to their part in setting the fire," I said. "I don't think Sam was involved. He was so afraid just being in the same room as you."

Robert looked thoughtful. "My guess is both had no idea how much was going to come out, when the truth started to come out, and since no one said anything but I miraculously survived, they must have decided that discretion was the better part of valour in this case."

"I'm amazed that you fitted in so well," he continued. "Coming from a very different era but you already knew the language and manners of this one. How?"

I smiled. "That's easy. I majored in history at university, and I also love Jane Austen's novels. Miss Austen explains a lot about living in the Regency era."

Then he asked the question I'd been dreading. "How did you know about the things we discussed? You seemed to know a lot about Amelia and her relationship with me." He added, "And ... er ... others."

Burning with shame, I had to confess. "I read her diary."

His expression said it all. I felt lower than the lowest scum of the earth. An invasion of privacy is not acceptable, even in the twenty-first century where it seems that anything goes, people troll each other online, and do and say the most terrible things to other people they don't even know.

Two hundred years ago, reading a private diary would be utterly unthinkable.

"You read her diary?"

Grasping at an analogy that he would appreciate, I said, "Yes, I had to. Think of it as a military manoeuvre. Imagine if you found the diary of your enemy. Let's say Napoleon. You'd read it to find out how he thought, how his mind worked, what he might do next. Being stuck here, so to speak, I had to make the best of the situation and not create any doubt in anyone's mind that I was Amelia. What would people think or do if I ran around saying I was from the future and I wasn't Amelia. I would be locked up in an institution."

Madhouse was possibly the operative word, but I was trying to be tactful. He looked pensive but it was clear he was considering my words.

"You know how the dowager hated Amelia because she was a hindrance to her ... er ... plans. If I, as Amelia, gave any indication that I was not of sound mind, then who knows what the dowager would have done?"

He nodded slowly.

"I also had to make sure Amelia could come back and be able to pick up what had happened while she was gone by writing in her diary every night to tell her about the play—" I stopped because of what I'd written about my feelings as her, or were these her feelings, as me, about him. "And other stuff," I said weakly.

His expression was enigmatic. "I see," he said. "That was very sensible and thoughtful. Thank you."

"I hoped that when she came back, she might just think it was all a strange dream and that the things she read in the diary had actually happened with her participation. I only got up to describing the dress rehearsal so you can fill in the details about the success of the play and perhaps just leave out the harrowing experience of being in the coffin and the dowager's confession."

Hopefully that would work because the servants' lips were sealed, and Rupert and Clementine would be off on their various world travels soon. I'd just dumped it all on Robert to explain everything and allay her fears. He might tell her everything, or he might give her the censored version. My time was up though, and he would just have to manage. He seemed satisfied but I still felt ashamed.

"I wish you hadn't deceived me," he said suddenly. "You could have taken me into your confidence from the outset."

I glared at him, outrage threatening to undo all the convincing I had just achieved for Amelia's sake. The ingrate! After all I had gone through for him.

"Deceived you? I *saved* you! And you wouldn't have believed me if I'd told you right away I was from the future."

He shook his head and folded his arms. "No, you didn't save me. Russet saved me. And since I accept your time slip explanation now, I'm sure I would have accepted it from the start."

Hearing his name yet again, Russet looked up at us, tail wagging, hopeful of pats or treats.

"I beg your pardon," I practically snarled. "Without me being transported ignominiously against my will two hundred years into the past and just so happening to arrive in the woods, you could have bled to death. Russet had no way of staunching the wound."

"And you had no way of making your way alone, through the woods and back to the house to get help since, as you told me, you'd only ever been there once in 2015. He went back to the house to alert everyone."

His gaze locked with mine in a death stare. Only the loud ticking from the mantel clock broke the silence.

"Besides," he remarked, "if you remember, I saved you from certain death by suffocation in Mr Polycarp's coffin." His lips twitched as he tried unsuccessfully to suppress a smile.

The memory of how wonderful I'd felt being cradled in his arms surged into my mind and was as quickly repressed. There was no time for fond memories and, in fact, the sooner I dispensed with them, the better.

"Aha!" I wagged one finger under his nose. "Russet saved me, not you. You just said so. Without his nose, no one would have tracked me to the cemetery and the grave. And I'm still positive you wouldn't have believed me had I told you the truth from the start."

He burst out laughing. "You're right. I think it's only the dowager's outrageous attempts to kill me that lead me to believe your time slip story. Perhaps I would have thought that Amelia was—" He stopped. "It no longer matters. Events have unfolded to bring us to what I hope is supposed to happen. But I shall miss sparring with you, Jane Amelia Carstairs."

Then the whole room shimmered. Russet got up and barked again loudly. Animals always know when the universe is out of kilter. Was I going to leave in a clap of thunder and a flash of lightning? Robert must have felt something too because he looked around. The way he gazed at me then almost made my rapidly dwindling resolve finally crumble. His voice was so gentle and loving. All I could think was please, God, let me find a man like him on the other side of wherever I'm going.

"My dearest Jane, whoever you are, and why you came is not important. I must tell you that I l—"

Although it broke me inside, I put my fingers against his lips, silencing him. I couldn't let him speak the words I longed to hear. I couldn't allow myself or him to indulge in anything that would hinder his relationship with Amelia.

"Please, hush. Don't say it, don't say anything. I'm not the one you must say this to." I glanced at the library window overlooking the park. Was that a shadow or was it the silhouette of a woman walking through the trees? I jumped up and Russet barked again. "She's here!"

Robert stood and held me tightly, bending to rest his cheek against my hair. "My world is upside-down, but I don't want to let you go," he whispered.

I looked up at his face when he released me. His distraught expression crushed me inside.

"You will love her." My voice cracked as I spoke the words I wanted to hear for myself. "She is your soul mate, your heart, the love of your life. Trust me. I promise that all will be well, and you will both be so happy."

He didn't speak but tears ran down his face. As I stepped away from him, he reached out one hand as if to touch me for the last time. Then everything went black.

Epilogue

T he sound of a dog barking woke me ... again! I opened my eyes, blinked, and looked down at the most gorgeous russet-coloured retriever. For a heart-stopping few seconds I wondered if I was back in 1815. Had it all gone wrong? I was back in the library at Chelston Hall, sitting at the desk, but dressed in my usual jeans and T-shirt, so I was in 2015. My cheeks were wet, so I'd been crying. Everything looked exactly as I had left it, so it seemed that Amelia had not been catapulted into the library; hopefully she had been plonked into my flat where she would have been confused but safe. My laptop was open on the desk, and next to it my mobile phone, along with a pile of what I assumed were the family papers to work through. A flip over desk calendar displayed the date. Today's date. I'd been gone a few hours in 2015 but in 1815 I'd spent thirteen days living another life. Did I even want to be back here? I looked at the dog. He cocked his head at me, wagging his tail. He was the spitting image of Russet.

"Russet?"

The dog put one paw on my knee and gave me a doggy grin. I smiled back at him.

This felt like old times all over again. There were the same books as before but with new shelves and newer looking editions. The candelabra of old, the mantel clock ticking away, the sounds of birds twittering outside the window, sunlight filtering through the mullioned glass windows where I'd last seen the person I thought was Amelia—

"Hello."

A man's voice from behind me broke into my reverie. His voice! Startled, I swung round in the swivel chair and there was Robert standing in the doorway. It was impossible. I'd just left him behind but here he was in the flesh. My heart leaped and I could hardly speak for a moment before noticing he was wearing jeans, sneakers, and a sweatshirt.

"Robert?"

He came towards me. "That's me," he said, reaching down to ruffle the dog's ears. "How do you know his name?"

"Lucky guess, I suppose," I said.

"It's a family name for the dogs over the years. Somehow, we always end up owning a retriever called Russet. You must be Jane Carstairs. You're assisting your dad in updating the family tree while he's sick."

"That's right," I said, glad to grasp any topic to still my stupidly pounding heart. "That's me."

"Your coffee and sandwich don't look very appealing."

Someone had put my lunch on the desk. The sandwich edges were curling upwards, and the coffee had a skin on top. Not at all appetising.

"How about a spot of lunch at the local pub? Then you can tell me how you're getting along with the family papers."

I still felt dazed. This wasn't my Robert of 1815, of course. This was the Robert of 2015. The marquis that I thought had been murdered but who hadn't, thankfully. It felt very weird speaking to him in modern parlance in modern times. Even his voice and way of speaking were the same. He fitted into those jeans so nicely too.

"Sounds good to me." Anything would be better than the limp sarnie in front of me.

"The pub doesn't do anything fancy but there's a decent ploughman's lunch, as long as you don't ask for anything more sophisticated than Cheddar or Gouda, and like pickles."

"I love a good ploughman's," I said. "And I love pickles."

"It's called *The Rude Mechanical*, with quite a story behind the name."

"Oh, yes?" I said, patting Russet, although I already had a good idea of how it came about.

"I'll tell you once we're there." He held out his hand as if it were the most natural thing in the world. "Shall we?"

And I took his hand as if it were the most natural thing in the world.

He stared at me for a moment, his gaze searching my face. "Haven't we met before? I know we're somehow related from way back when, but haven't we bumped into each other at a function or something?"

"No, we haven't met before now," I said. "Most definitely not. I'd remember. I'm good with faces."

"Hmm," he said, leading the way. "I just feel as if we've met somewhere. You seem so familiar." He glanced back at me with a smile. "Maybe in another lifetime?"

"It's a thought," I said, my heart melting in the warmth of that smile.

The End

COMING NEXT

To Marry a Marquis

A Regency Time Slip Mystery

BOOK TWO

Back in 2015, Jane is involved in helping with the Chelston Hall annual Shakespearean performance. To her dismay, her ex-fiancé Allan has been invited to direct and this year's choice is A *Midsummer Night's Dream*. Jane is cast as Puck, the narrator, while Allan's latest squeeze Tawnee is cast as the fairy queen Titiania. All is going swimmingly, both Jane's romance with Robert and the production. However, there is another murder attempt, but this time Allan is the victim and Jane is arrested! The police say she has a motive. What happened in 2015 while Jane was trapped in 1815?

FROM THE AUTHOR

Many thanks to my editorial and design team of Nancy Bell, Amanda Matthews, and Sonia Killik. Where would I be without their expertise? Thanks go to my beta readers who provided wonderful reviews and reminded me where I had slipped up or forgotten things. Praise must also go to my distributor Bublish, that does a sterling job, and especially to CEO Kathy Meis who is never too busy to answer any questions. Thanks to historical murder mystery author K.T. McGivens, creator of the Katie Porter Mysteries Series, for her valuable input.

For readers who are wondering why I used the term 'marquis' and not 'marquess' in a Regency romance set in England, very simply, it fitted and looked better on the cover, and I prefer 'marquis.' For readers curious about the mention of time travel in relation to Samuel Madden, this historical writer helped to spark my foray into the tricky genre of time travel. Samuel Madden (1686—1785) was an Irish author. Wikipedia says this about his work of speculative fiction, *Memoirs of the Twentieth Century*, written in 1733: "The book is notable as an early work to feature time travel. In his 1987 work *Origins of Futuristic Fiction*, Paul Alkon describes the book as the earliest in English literature to feature time travel, but notes that it does not explain how it was performed. In the 2008 book *Physics of the Impossible*, Michio Kaku calls the work arguably the first account of time travel in fiction."

This Regency novel is my first time travel mystery with a dash of murder. I love murder mysteries but never thought

I could write one, let alone a time travel adventure. It was such an exhilarating experience that no sooner had Jane been deposited safely back in 2015 than I started on the next book. I hope time travel experts will be tolerant of any deficiencies in my knowledge of how the concept works, although the Moberly-Jourdain incident did rather convince me that the time slip is a real phenomenon.

ABOUT THE AUTHOR

From Jane Austen to Georgette Heyer, Arabella finds both enjoyment and inspiration in sparkling, witty Regency novels. She also loves history and generally finds the past more fascinating than the future. Arabella wrote her first Regency romance to entertain her mom who loved the genre. Arabella is honoured to share the adventures of her heroes and heroines with readers. Please visit her website for updates on her forthcoming novels and to follow her on social media.

Arabella's website: www.arabellasheratonbooks.com

BOOKS BY ARABELLA SHERATON

The Dangerous Duke

The Reluctant Bridegroom

Married at Midnight

The Wayward Miss Wainwright

Lord Blackwood's Valentine Ball
(Lord Blackwood Book One)

The Lady's Revenge
(Lord Blackwood Book Two)

Miss Dashwood's Dilemma

The Secret of Love *(non-fiction/self-help)*

www.ingramcontent.com/pod-product-compliance
Lightning Source LLC
Chambersburg PA
CBHW021500110726
47899CB00001BA/236